WHAT MOST WOMEN HEAR DURING THE HOLIDAY SEASON:

From son: "Mom, I want a motorcycle for Christmas!"

From salesclerk: "The sale ended yesterday."

From toddler: "I feel sick, Mommy."

From husband: "I thought you *wanted* a new vacuum cleaner!"

From teenage daughter: "You're wearing *that?*"

From crowd: "Pardon me." "Sorry!" "Ouch!" "I was next!"

From mother-in-law: "In *my* day, we baked from scratch."

WHAT THESE HEROINES HEAR DURING THE HOLIDAY SEASON:

Wedding Bells! Wedding Bells! Wedding Bells!

So snuggle up as quietly as possible with JINGLE BELLS, WEDDING BELLS—four romantic, heartwarming love stories by *New York Times* bestselling author Nora Roberts, Barbara Boswell, Myrna Temte and Elizabeth August. And let Silhouette Books take you away from it all—our way of saying Happy Holidays!

D0957224

ALL I WANT FOR CHRISTMAS
by Nora Roberts

They were precocious, identical six-year-old twins, and they knew what they wanted for Christmas: a mom. Fortunately, their new music teacher fit all the requirements...but *un*fortunately, their dad didn't agree. Clearly it was up to the twins to make Christmas magic—and they were definitely up to the challenge.

A VERY MERRY STEP-CHRISTMAS
by Barbara Boswell

Christmas? Bah, humbug! Claudia Nolan had no time for the holidays. Her kids were in rebellion, her job was driving her crazy, and all she wanted was to get through New Year's Eve—dateless. Then Zack Ritter came along. He was the wrong man in every way, but suddenly Claudia had thoughts of getting stuck under the mistletoe....

JACK'S ORNAMENT
by Myrna Temte

For lonely rancher Jack Zorn, work always came first—until he met wealthy Elizabeth Davies-Smythe. Although the lady was lovely, Jack believed cowboys and socialites didn't mix. Would Christmas in cowboy country help lasso lasting joy?

THE FOREVER GIFT
by Elizabeth August

The holidays were hard for Abigail Jones. She could never have a real home or a man to call her own—not when her past kept her on the run. But when she met Kane Courtland, leaving was all the more difficult. And loving him made it all the more necessary....

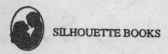

SILHOUETTE BOOKS

JINGLE BELLS, WEDDING BELLS

Copyright © 1994 by Harlequin Enterprises B.V.

ISBN 0-373-48331-7

The publisher acknowledges the copyright holders of the individual works as follows:

ALL I WANT FOR CHRISTMAS
Copyright © 1994 by Nora Roberts
A VERY MERRY STEP-CHRISTMAS
Copyright © 1994 by Barbara Boswell
JACK'S ORNAMENT
Copyright © 1994 by Myrna Temte
THE FOREVER GIFT
Copyright © 1994 by Elizabeth August

Jingle
BELLS,
Wedding
BELLS

NORA ROBERTS
BARBARA BOSWELL
MYRNA TEMTE
ELIZABETH AUGUST

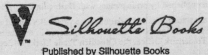

Published by Silhouette Books
America's Publisher of Contemporary Romance

CONTENTS

All I Want For Christmas

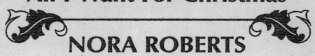

NORA ROBERTS

A Note from Nora Roberts

Dear Reader,

It's that time of year again. Time for secrets and wishes and sleigh bells. It's time for magic. In our house, Christmas isn't just one frantic morning with wrapping paper being ripped and tossed and stockings emptied on the rug—though that's certainly part of it. For my family, Christmas is an event that spreads over weeks.

We live in the country, well back on a wooded hill. Around the first of December, my hero risks life and limb to wire a lighted star to the roof. It shines through the woods and can be seen from the road half a mile away. There are cookies to bake, presents to wrap. Presents to hide. Conspiracies abound. We buy and decorate our tree early, and though our boys are men now, we hang the stockings from the mantel.

No matter how early I start or how well I prepare, there are always a dozen last-minute details to rush through as the big day approaches. You know how it is. Magic takes a lot of effort.

There are friends and family to visit, friends and family to entertain. More baking to do as my men gobble down my cookies. Okay, I eat them, too. I always consider it a minor miracle that everything gets done in time. But then, it's the season for miracles. The season for wishes.

So, as this magic season approaches, I'd like to wish you all the magic and the wonder and the music of sleigh bells. I hope each and every one of you finds all you want for Christmas.

Nora Roberts

Prologue

Zeke and Zack huddled in the tree house. Important business, any plots or plans, and all punishments for infractions of the rules, were discussed in the sturdy wooden hideaway tucked in the branches of the dignified old sycamore.

Today, a light rain tapped on the tin roof and dampened the dark green leaves. It was still warm enough in the first days of September that the boys wore T-shirts. Red for Zeke, blue for Zack.

They were twins, as identical as the sides of a two-headed coin. Their father had used the color code since their birth to avoid confusion.

When they switched colors—as they often did—they could fool anyone in Taylor's Grove. Except their father.

He was on their minds at the moment. They had already discussed, at length, the anticipated delights and terrors of their first day in real school. The first day in first grade.

They would ride the bus, as they had done the year before, in kindergarten. But this time they would stay in Taylor's Grove Elementary for a full day, just like the big kids. Their cousin Kim had told them that *real* school wasn't a playground.

Zack, the more introspective of the two, had thought over, worried about and dissected this problem for weeks. There were terrible, daunting terms like *homework* and *class participation,* that Kim tossed around. They knew that she, a sophomore in high school, was often loaded down with books. Big, thick books with no pictures.

And sometimes, when she was baby-sitting for them, she had her nose stuck in them for hours. For as long a time as she would have the telephone stuck to her ear, and that was long.

It was pretty scary stuff for Zack, the champion worrier.

Their father would help them, of course. This was something Zeke, the eternal optimist, had pointed out. Didn't they both know how to read stuff like *Green Eggs and Ham* and *The Cat in the Hat* because their dad helped them sound out the words? And they both knew how to write the whole alphabet, and their names and short things, because he showed them.

The trouble was, he had to work and take care of the house and them, as well as Commander Zark, the big yellow dog they'd saved from the animal shelter two years before. Their dad had, as Zack pointed out, an awful lot to do. And now that they were going to go to school, and have assignments and projects and real report cards, he was going to need help.

"He's got Mrs. Hollis to come in once a week and do stuff." Zeke ran his miniature Corvette around the imaginary racetrack on the tree-house floor.

"It's not enough." A frown puckered Zack's forehead and clouded his lake blue eyes. He exhaled with a long-suffering sigh, ruffling the dark hair that fell over his forehead. "He needs the companionship of a good woman, and we need a mother's love. I heard Mrs. Hollis say so to Mr. Perkins at the post office."

"He hangs around with Aunt Mira sometimes. She's a good woman."

"But she doesn't live with us. And she doesn't have time to help us with science projects." Science projects were a particular terror for Zack. "We need to find a mom." When Zeke only snorted, Zack narrowed his eyes. "We're going to have to spell in first grade."

Zeke caught his lower lip between his teeth. Spelling was his personal nightmare. "How're we going to find one?"

Now Zack smiled. He had, in his slow, careful way, figured it all out. "We're going to ask Santa Claus."

"He doesn't bring moms," Zeke said with the deep disdain that can only be felt by one sibling for another. "He brings toys and stuff. And it's forever until Christmas, anyway."

"No, it's not. Mrs. Hollis was bragging to Mr. Perkins how she already had half her Christmas shopping done. She said how looking ahead meant you could enjoy the holiday."

"Everybody enjoys Christmas. It's the best."

"Uh-uh. Lots of people get mad. Remember how we went to the mall last year with Aunt Mira and she complained and complained about the crowds and the prices and how they weren't any parking spaces?"

Zeke merely shrugged. He didn't look back as often, or as clearly, as his twin, but he took Zack at his word. "I guess."

"So, if we ask now, Santa'll have plenty of time to find the right mom."

"I still say he doesn't bring moms."

"Why not? If we really need one, and we don't ask for too much else?"

"We were going to ask for two-wheelers," Zeke reminded him.

"We could still ask for them," Zack decided. "But not a bunch of other things. Just a mom and the bikes."

It was Zeke's turn to sigh. He didn't care for the idea of giving up his big, long list. But the idea of a mother was beginning to appeal. They'd never had one, and the mystery of it attracted. "So what kind do we ask for?"

"We got to write it down."

Zack took a notebook and a stubby pencil from the table pushed against the wall. They sat on the floor and, with much argument and discussion, composed.

Dear Santa,
We have been good.

Zeke wanted to put in very good, but Zack, the conscience, rejected the idea.

We feed Zark and help Dad. We want a mom for Crissmas. A nice one who smells good and is not meen. She can smile a lot and have yello hair. She has to like little boys and big dogs. She wont mind dirt and bakes cookys. We want a pretty one who is smart and helps us with homework. We will take good care of her. We want biks a red one and a bloo one. You have lots of time to find the mom and make the biks so you can enjoi the hollidays. Thank you. Love, Zeke and Zack.

Chapter One

Taylor's Grove, population two thousand three hundred and forty. No, forty-one, Nell thought smugly, as she strolled into the high school auditorium. She'd only been in town for two months, but already she was feeling territorial. She loved the slow pace, the tidy yards and little shops. She loved the easy gossip of neighbors, the front-porch swings, the frost-heaved sidewalks.

If anyone had told her, even a year before, that she would be trading in Manhattan for a dot on the map in western Maryland, she would have thought them mad. But here she was, Taylor's Grove High's new music teacher, as snug and settled in as an old hound in front of a fire.

She'd needed the change, that was certain. In the past year she'd lost her roommate to marriage and inherited a staggering rent she simply wasn't able to manage on her own. The replacement roommate, whom Nell had carefully interviewed, had moved out, as well. Taking everything of value out of the apartment. That nasty little adventure had led to the final, even nastier showdown with her almost-fiancé. When Bob berated her, called her stupid, naive and careless, Nell had decided it was time to cut her losses.

She'd hardly given Bob his walking papers when she received her own. The school where she had taught for three years was downsizing, as they had euphemistically put it. The position of music teacher had been eliminated, and so had Nell.

An apartment she could no longer afford, all but empty, a fiancé who had considered her optimistic nature a liability and the prospect of the unemployment line had taken the sheen off New York.

Once Nell decided to move, she'd decided to move big. The idea of teaching in a small town had sprung up fully rooted. An inspiration, she thought now, for she already felt as if she'd lived here for years.

Her rent was low enough that she could live alone and like it. Her apartment, the entire top floor of a remodeled old house, was a short, enjoyable walk from a campus that included elementary, middle and high schools.

Only two weeks after that first nervous day of school, she was feeling proprietary about her students and was looking forward to her first after-school session with her chorus.

She was determined to create a holiday program that would knock the town's socks off.

The battered piano was center stage. She walked to it and sat. Her students would be filing in shortly, but she had a moment.

She limbered up her mind and her fingers with the blues, an old Muddy Waters tune. Old, scarred pianos were meant to play the blues, she thought, and enjoyed herself.

"Man, she's so cool," Holly Linstrom murmured to Kim as they slipped into the rear of the auditorium.

"Yeah." Kim had a hand on the shoulder of each of her twin cousins, a firm grip that ordered quiet and promised reprisals. "Old Mr. Striker never played anything like that."

"And her clothes are so, like, now." Admiration and envy mixed as Holly scanned the pipe-stem pants, long overshirt and short striped vest Nell wore. "I don't know why anybody from New York would come here. Did you see her earrings today? I bet she got them at some hot place on Fifth Avenue."

Nell's jewelry had already become legendary among the female students. She wore the unique and the unusual. Her taste in clothes, her dark gold hair, which fell just short of her shoulders and always seemed miraculously and expertly tousled, her quick, throaty laugh and her lack of formality had already gone a long way toward endearing her to her students.

"She's got style, all right." But, just then, Kim was more intrigued by the music than by the musician's wardrobe. "Man, I wish I could play like that."

"Man, I wish I could look like that," Holly returned, and giggled.

Sensing an audience, Nell glanced back and grinned. "Come on in, girls. Free concert."

"It sounds great, Miss Davis." With her grip firm on her two charges, Kim started down the sloping aisle toward the stage. "What is it?"

"Muddy Waters. We'll have to shoehorn a little blues education into the curriculum." Sitting back, she studied the two sweet-faced boys on either side of Kim. There was a quick, odd surge of recognition that she didn't understand. "Well, hi, guys."

When they smiled back, identical dimples popped out on the left side of their mouths. "Can you play 'Chopsticks'?" Zeke wanted to know.

Before Kim could express her humiliation at the question, Nell spun into a rousing rendition.

"How's that?" she asked when she'd finished.

"That's neat."

"I'm sorry, Miss Davis. I'm kind of stuck with them for an hour. They're my cousins. Zeke and Zack Taylor."

"The Taylors of Taylor's Grove." Nell swiveled away from the piano. "I bet you're brothers. I see a slight family resemblance."

Both boys grinned and giggled. "We're twins," Zack informed her.

"Really? Now I bet I'm supposed to guess who's who." She came to the edge of the stage, sat and eyed the boys narrowly. They grinned back. Each had recently lost a left front tooth. "Zeke," she said, pointing a finger. "And Zack."

Pleased and impressed, they nodded. "How'd you know?"

It was pointless, and hardly fun, to mention that she'd had a fifty-fifty shot. "Magic. Do you guys like to sing?"

"Sort of. A little."

"Well, today you can listen. You can sit right in the front row and be our test audience."

"Thanks, Miss Davis," Kim murmured, and gave the boys a friendly shove toward the seats. "They're pretty good most of the time. Stay," she ordered, with an older cousin's absolute authority.

Nell winked at the boys as she stood, then gestured to the other students filing in. "Come on up. Let's get started."

A lot of the business onstage seemed boring to the twins. There was just talking at first, and confusion as sheet music was passed out and boys and girls were assigned positions.

But Zack was watching Nell. She had pretty hair and nice big brown eyes. Like Zark's, he thought with deep affection. Her voice was kind of funny, sort of scratchy and deep, but nice. Now and again she looked back toward him and smiled. When she did, his heart acted strange, kind of beating hard, like he'd been running.

She turned to a group of girls and sang. It was a Christmas song, which made Zack's eyes widen. He wasn't sure of the name, something about a midnight clear, but he recognized it from the records his dad played around the holiday.

A Christmas song. A Christmas wish.

"It's her." He hissed it to his brother, rapping Zeke hard in the ribs.

"Who?"

"It's the mom."

Zeke stopped playing with the action figure he'd had stuck in his pocket and looked up onstage, where Nell was now directing the alto section. "Kim's teacher is the mom?"

"She has to be." Deadly excited, Zeke kept his voice in a conspiratorial whisper. "Santa's had enough time to get the letter. She was singing a Christmas song, and she's got yellow hair and a nice smile. She likes little boys, too. I can tell."

"Maybe." Not quite convinced, Zeke studied Nell. She was pretty, he thought. And she laughed a lot, even when some of the big kids made mistakes. But that didn't mean she liked dogs or baked cookies. "We can't know for sure yet."

Zack huffed out an impatient breath. "She knew us. She knew which was which. Magic." His eyes were solemn as he looked at his brother. "It's the mom."

"Magic," Zeke repeated, and stared, goggle-eyed, at Nell. "Do we have to wait till Christmas to get her?"

"I guess so. Probably." That was a puzzle Zack would have to work on.

When Mac Taylor pulled his pickup truck in front of the high school, his mind was on a dozen varied problems. What to fix the kids for dinner. How to deal with the flooring on his Meadow Street project. When to find a couple hours to drive to the mall and pick up new underwear for the boys. The last time he folded laundry, he'd noticed that most of what they had was doomed for the rag pile. He had to deal with a lumber delivery first thing in the morning and a pile of paperwork that night.

And Zeke was nervous about his first spelling test, which was coming up in a few days.

Pocketing his keys, Mac rolled his shoulders. He'd been swinging a hammer for the better part of eight hours. He didn't mind the aches. It was a good kind of fatigue, a kind that meant he'd accomplished something. His renovation of the house on Meadow Street was on schedule and on budget. Once it was done, he would have to decide whether to put it on the market or rent it.

His accountant would try to decide for him, but Mac knew the final choice would remain in his own hands. That was the way he preferred it.

As he strode from the parking lot to the high school, he looked around. His great-great-grandfather had founded the town—hardly more than a village back then, settled along Taylor's Creek and stretching over the rolling hills to Taylor's Meadow.

There'd been no lack of ego in old Macauley Taylor.

But Mac had lived in DC for more than twelve years. It had been six years since he returned to Taylor's Grove, but he hadn't lost his pleasure or his pride in it, the simple appreciation for the hills and the trees and the shadows of mountains in the distance.

He didn't think he ever would.

There was the faintest of chills in the air now, and a good strong breeze from the west. But they had yet to have a frost, and the leaves were still a deep summer green. The good weather made his life easier on a couple of levels. As long as it held, he'd be able to finish the outside work on his project in comfort. And the boys could enjoy the afternoons and evenings in the yard.

There was a quick twinge of guilt as he pulled open the heavy doors and stepped into the school. His work had kept them stuck inside this afternoon. The coming of fall meant that his sister was diving headfirst into several of her community projects. He couldn't impose on her by asking her to watch the twins. Kim's after-school schedule was filling up, and he simply couldn't accept the idea of having his children becoming latchkey kids.

Still, the solution had suited everyone. Kim would take the kids to her rehearsals, and he would save his sister a trip to school by picking them all up and driving them home.

Kim would have a driver's license in a few more months. A fact she was reminding everyone about constantly. But he doubted he'd plunk his boys down in the car with his sixteen-year-old niece at the wheel, no matter how much he loved and trusted her.

You coddle them. Mac rolled his eyes as his sister's voice played in his head. *You can't always be mother and father to them, Mac. If you're not interested in finding a wife, then you'll have to learn to let go a little.*

Like hell he would, Mac thought.

As he neared the auditorium, he heard the sound of young voices raised in song. Subtle harmony. A good, emotional sound that made him smile even before he recognized the tune. A Christmas hymn. It was odd to hear it now, with the sweat from his day just drying on his back.

He pulled open the auditorium doors, and was flooded with it. Charmed, he stood at the back and looked out on the singers. One of the students played the piano. A pretty little thing, Mac mused, who looked up now and then, gesturing, as if to urge her classmates to give more.

He wondered where the music teacher was, then spotted his boys sitting in the front row. He walked quietly down the aisle, raising a hand when he saw Kim's eyes shift to his. He settled behind the boys and leaned forward.

"Pretty good show, huh?"

"Dad!" Zack nearly squealed, then remembered just in time to speak in a hissing whisper. "It's Christmas."

"Sure sounds like it. How's Kim doing?"

"She's real good." Zeke now considered himself an expert on choral arrangements. "She's going to have a solo."

"No kidding?"

"She got red in the face when Miss Davis asked her to sing by herself, but she did okay." Zeke was much more interested in Nell right then. "She's pretty, isn't she?"

A little amazed at this announcement—the twins were fond of Kim, but rarely complimentary—he nodded. "Yeah. The prettiest girl in school."

"We could have her over for dinner sometime," Zack said slyly. "Couldn't we?"

Baffled now, Mac ruffled his son's hair. "You know Kim can come over whenever she wants."

"Not her." In a gesture that mimicked his father, Zack rolled his eyes. "Jeez, Dad. Miss Davis."

"Who's Miss Davis?"

"The m—" Zeke's announcement was cut off by his twin's elbow.

"The teacher," Zack finished with a snarling look at his brother. "The pretty one." He pointed, and his father followed the direction to the piano.

"She's the teacher?" Before Mac could reevaluate, the music flowed to a stop and Nell rose.

"That was great, really. A very solid first run-through." She pushed her tousled hair back. "But we need a lot of work. I'd like to schedule the next rehearsal for Monday after school. Three forty-five."

There was already a great deal of movement and mumbling, so Nell pitched her voice to carry the rest of her instructions over the noise. Satisfied, she turned to smile at the twins and found herself grinning at an older, and much more disturbing version, of the Taylor twins.

No doubt he was the father, Nell thought. The same thick dark hair curled down over the collar of a grimy T-shirt. The same lake-water eyes framed in long, dark lashes stared back at her. His face might lack the soft, slightly rounded appeal of his sons', but the more rugged version was just as attractive. He was long, rangy, with the kind of arms that looked tough without being obviously muscled. He was tanned and more than a little dirty. She wondered if he had a dimple at the left corner of his mouth when he smiled.

"Mr. Taylor." Rather than bother with the stairs, she hopped off the stage, as agile as any of her students. She held out a hand decorated with rings.

"Miss Davis." He covered her hand with his callused one, remembering too late that it was far from clean. "I appreciate you letting the kids hang out while Kim rehearsed."

"No problem. I work better with an audience." Tilting her head, she looked down at the twins. "Well, guys, how'd we do?"

"It was really neat." This from Zeke. "We like Christmas songs the best."

"Me too."

Still flustered and flattered by the idea of having a solo, Kim joined them. "Hi, Uncle Mac. I guess you met Miss Davis."

"Yeah." There wasn't much more to say. He still thought she looked too young to be a teacher. Not the teenager he'd taken her for, he realized. But that creamy, flawless skin and that tidy little frame were deceiving. And very attractive.

"Your niece is very talented." In a natural movement, Nell wrapped an arm around Kim's shoulders. "She has a wonderful voice and a quick understanding of what the music means. I'm delighted to have her."

"We like her, too," Mac said as Kim flushed.

Zack shifted from foot to foot. They weren't supposed to be talking about dumb old Kim. "Maybe you could come visit us sometime, Miss Davis," he piped up. "We live in the big brown house out on Mountain View Road."

"That'd be nice." But Nell noted that Zack's father didn't second the invitation, or look particularly pleased by it. "And you guys are welcome to be our audience anytime. You work on that solo, Kim."

"I will, Miss Davis. Thanks."

"Nice to have met you, Mr. Taylor." As he mumbled a response, Nell hopped back onstage to gather her sheet music.

It was too bad, she thought, that the father lacked the outgoing charm and friendliness of his sons.

Chapter Two

It didn't get much better than a drive in the country on a balmy fall afternoon. Nell remembered how she used to spend a free Saturday in New York. A little shopping—she supposed if she missed anything about Manhattan, it was the shopping—maybe a walk in the park. Never a jog. Nell didn't believe in running if walking would get you to the same place.

And driving, well, that was even better. She hadn't realized what a pleasure it was to not only own a car but be able to zip it along winding country roads with the windows open and the radio blaring.

The leaves were beginning to turn now as September hit its stride. Blushes of color competed with the green. On one particular road that she turned down out of impulse, the big trees arched over the asphalt, a spectacular canopy that let light flicker and flit through as the road followed the snaking trail of a rushing creek.

It wasn't until she glanced up at a road sign that she realized she was on Mountain View.

The big brown house, Zack had said, she remembered. There weren't a lot of houses here, two miles outside of town, but she caught glimpses of some through the shading trees. Brown ones, white ones, blue ones—some close to the creek bed, others high atop narrow, pitted lanes that served as driveways.

A lovely place to live, she thought. And to raise children. However taciturn and stiff Mac Taylor might have been, he'd done a wonderful job with his sons.

She already knew he'd done the job alone. It hadn't taken long for Nell to understand the rhythm of small towns. A comment here, a casual question there, and she'd had what amounted to a full biography of the Taylor men.

Mac had lived in Washington, DC, since his family moved out of town when he was a young teenager. Six years ago, twin infants in tow, he'd moved back. His older sister had gone to a local college and married a town boy and settled in Taylor's Grove years before. It was she, the consensus was, who had urged him to come back and raise his children there when his wife took off.

Left the poor little infants high and dry, Mrs. Hollis had told Nell over the bread rack at the general store. Run off with barely a word, and hadn't said a peep since. And young Macauley Taylor had been mother and father both to his twins ever since.

Maybe, Nell thought cynically, just maybe, if he'd actually talked to his wife now and again, she'd have stayed with him.

Not fair, she thought. There was no decent excuse she could think of for a mother deserting her infant children, then not contacting them for six years. Whatever kind of husband Mac Taylor had been, the children deserved better.

She thought of them now, those impish mirror images. She'd always been fond of children, and the Taylor twins were a double dose of enjoyment. She'd gotten quite a kick out of having them in the audience once or twice a week during rehearsals. Zeke had even shown her his very first spelling test—with its big silver star. If he hadn't missed just one word, he'd told her, he'd have gotten a gold one.

Nor had she missed the shy looks Zack sent her, or the quick smiles before he flushed and lowered his eyes. It was very sweet to be responsible for his first case of puppy love.

She sighed with pleasure as the car burst out from under the canopy of trees and into the light. Here were the mountains that gave the road its name, streaking suddenly into the vivid blue sky. The road curved and snaked, but they were always there, dark, distant and dramatic.

The land rose on either side of the road, in rolling hills and rocky outcroppings. She slowed when she spotted a house on the crest of a hill. Brown. Probably cedar, she thought, with a stone foundation and what seemed like acres of sparkling glass. There was a deck stretched across the second story, and there were trees that shaded and sheltered. A tire swing hung from one.

She wondered if this was indeed the Taylor house. She hoped her new little friends lived in such a solid, well-planned home. Then she passed the mailbox planted at the side of the road just at the edge of the long lane.

M. Taylor and sons.

It made her smile. Pleased, she punched the gas pedal and was baffled when the car bucked and stuttered.

"What's the problem here?" she muttered, easing off on the pedal and punching it again. This time the car shuddered and stopped dead. "For heaven's sake." Only mildly annoyed, she started to turn the key to start it again, and glanced at the dash. The little gas pump beside the gauge was brightly lit.

"Stupid," she said aloud, berating herself. "Stupid, stupid. Weren't you supposed to get gas *before* you left town?" She sat back, sighed. She'd meant to, really. Just as she'd meant to stop and fill up the day before, right after class.

Now she was two miles out of town without even fumes to ride on. Blowing the hair out of her eyes, she looked out at the home of M. Taylor and sons. A quarter-mile hike, she estimated. Which made it a lot better than two miles. And she had, more or less, been invited.

She grabbed her keys and started up the lane.

She was no more than halfway when the boys spotted her. They came racing down the rocky, pitted lane at a speed that stopped her heart. Surefooted as young goats, they streaked toward her. Coming up behind was a huge yellow dog.

"Miss Davis! Hi, Miss Davis! Did you come to see us?"

"Sort of." Laughing, she crouched down to give them both a hug and caught the faint scent of chocolate. Before she could comment, the dog decided he wanted in on the action. He was restrained enough to plant his huge paws on her thighs, rather than her shoulders.

Zack held his breath, then let it out when she chuckled and bent down to rub Zark on head and shoulders. "You're a big one, aren't you? A big beauty."

Zark lapped her hand in perfect agreement. Nell caught a look exchanged quickly between the twins. One that seemed both smug and excited.

"You like dogs?" Zeke asked.

"Sure I do. Maybe I'll get one now. I never had the heart to lock one up in a New York apartment." She only laughed again when Zark sat and politely lifted a paw. "Too late for formalities now, buddy," she told him, but shook it anyway. "I was out driving, and I ran out of gas right smack at the bottom of your lane. Isn't that funny?"

Zack's grin nearly split his face. She liked dogs. She'd stopped right at their house. It was more magic, he was sure of it. "Dad'll fix it. He can fix anything." Confident now that he had her on his own ground, Zack took her hand. Not to be outdone, Zeke clasped the other.

"Dad's out back in the shop, building a 'rondak chair."

"A rocking chair?" Nell suggested.

"Nuh-uh. A 'rondak chair. Come see."

They hauled her around the house, passed a curving sun room that caught the southern light. There was another deck in the back, with steps leading down to a flagstone patio. The shop in the backyard—the same cedar as the house—looked big enough to hold a family of four. Nell heard the thwack of a hammer on wood.

Bursting with excitement, Zeke raced through the shop door. "Dad! Dad! Guess what?"

"I guess you've taken another five years off my life."

Nell heard Mac's voice, deep and amused and tolerant, and found herself hesitating. "I hate to bother him when he's busy," she said to Zeke. "Maybe I can just call the station in town."

"It's okay, come on." Zack dragged her a few more feet into the doorway.

"See?" Zeke said importantly. "She came!"

"Yeah, I see." Caught off-balance by the unexpected visit, Mac set his hammer down on his workbench. He pushed up the brim of his cap and frowned without really meaning to. "Miss Davis."

"I'm sorry to bother you, Mr. Taylor," she began, then saw the project he was working on. "An Adirondack chair," she murmured, and grinned. "A 'rondak chair. It's nice."

"Will be." Was he supposed to offer her coffee? he wondered. A tour of the house? What? She shouldn't be pretty, he thought irrelevantly. There was nothing particularly striking about her. Well, maybe the eyes. They were so big and brown. But the rest really was ordinary. It must be the way it was put together, he decided, that made it extraordinary.

Not certain whether she was amused or uncomfortable at the way he was staring at her, Nell launched into her explanation. "I was out driving. Partly for the pleasure of it, and partly to try to familiarize myself with the area. I've only lived here a couple months."

"Is that right?"

"Miss Davis is from New York City, Dad," Zack reminded him. "Kim told you."

"Yeah, she did." He picked up his hammer again, set it down. "Nice day for a drive."

"I thought so. So nice I forgot to get gas before I left town. I ran out at the bottom of your lane."

A flicker of suspicion darkened his eyes. "That's handy."

"Not especially." Her voice, though still friendly, had cooled. "If I could use your phone to call the station in town, I'd appreciate it."

"I've got gas," he muttered.

"See, I told you Dad could fix it," Zack said proudly. "We've got brownies," he added, struggling madly for a way to get her to stay longer. "Dad made them. You can have one."

"I thought I smelled chocolate." She scooped Zack up and sniffed at his face. "I've got a real nose for it."

Moving on instinct, Mac plucked Zack out of her arms. "You guys go get some brownies. We'll get the gas."

"Okay!" They raced off together.

"I wasn't going to abduct him, Mr. Taylor."

"Didn't say you were." He walked to the doorway, glanced back. "The gas is in the shed."

Lips pursed, she followed him out. "Were you traumatized by a teacher at an impressionable age, Mr. Taylor?"

"Mac. Just Mac. No, why?"

"I wondered if we have a personal or a professional problem here."

"I don't have a problem." He stopped at the small shed where he kept his lawn mower and garden tools, then said, "Funny how the kids told you where we lived, and you ran out of gas right here."

She took a long breath, studying him as he bent over to pick up a can, straighten and turn. "Look, I'm no happier about it than you, and after this reception, probably a lot less happy. It happens that this is the first car I've ever owned, and I'm still a little rough on the finer points. I ran out of gas last month in front of the general store. You're welcome to check."

He shrugged, feeling stupid and unnecessarily prickly. "Sorry."

"Forget it. If you'll give me the can, I'll use what I need to get back to town, then I'll have it filled and returned."

"I'll take care of it," he muttered.

"I don't want to put you out." She reached for the can and that started a quick tug-of-war. After a moment, the dimple at the corner of his mouth winked.

"I'm bigger than you."

She stepped back and blew the hair out of her eyes. "Fine. Go be a man, then." Scowling, she followed him around the house, then tried to fight off her foul mood as the twins came racing up. They each held a paper towel loaded with brownies.

"Dad makes the best brownies in the whole world," Zack told her, holding up his offering.

Nell took one and bit in. "You may be right," she was forced to admit, her mouth full. "And I know my brownies."

"Can you make cookies?" Zeke wanted to know.

"I happened to be known far and wide for my chocolate-chip." Her smile became puzzled as the boys eyed each other and nodded. "You come visit me sometime, and we'll whip some up."

"Where do you live?" Since his father wasn't paying close attention, Zeke stuffed an entire brownie in his mouth.

"On Market Street, right off the square. The old brick house with the three porches. I rent the top floor."

"Dad owns that," Zack told her. "He bought it and fixed it all up and now he rents it out. We're in real estate."

"Oh." She let out a long breath. "Really." Her rent checks were mailed to Taylor Management . . . on Mountain View Road.

"So you live in our house," Zack finished up.

"In a manner of speaking."

"The place okay with you?" Mac asked.

"Yes, it's fine. I'm very comfortable there. It's convenient to school."

"Dad buys houses and fixes them up all the time." Zeke wondered if he could get away with another brownie. "He likes to fix stuff."

It was obvious from the tidy and thoughtful renovation of the old house she now lived in that their father fixed them very well. "You're a carpenter, then?" she asked, reluctantly addressing Mac.

"Sometimes." They'd reached her car. Mac merely jerked his thumb to signal the boys and dog to keep off the road. He unscrewed the gas cap and spoke without looking around. "If you eat another one of those, Zeke, I'm going to have to have your stomach pumped."

Sheepishly Zeke replaced the brownie on the paper towel.

"Excellent radar," Nell commented, leaning on the car as Mac added the gas.

"Goes with the territory." He looked at her then. Her hair was windblown and gilded by the sun. Her face was rosy from the walk and the breeze. He didn't like what looking at her did to his pulse rate. "Why Taylor's Grove? It's a long way from New York."

"That's why. I wanted a change." She breathed deep as she looked around, at rock and tree and hill. "I got one."

"Pretty slow, compared to what you'd be used to."

"Slow's something I do very well."

He only shrugged. He suspected she'd be bored senseless in six months and heading out. "Kim's pretty excited about your class. She talks about it almost as much as she does getting her driver's license."

"That's quite a compliment. It's a good school. Not all of my students are as cooperative as Kim, but I like a challenge. I'm going to recommend her for all-state."

Mac tipped the can farther up. "She's really that good?"

"You sound surprised."

He shrugged again. "She always sounded good to me, but the old music teacher never singled her out."

"Rumor is he never took much interest in any of his students individually, or in extra work."

"You got that right. Striker was an old—" He caught himself, glanced back at his kids, who were standing close by, all ears. "He was old," Mac repeated. "And set in his ways. Always the same Christmas program, the same spring program."

"Yes, I've looked over his class notes. I'd say everyone should be in for a surprise this year. I'm told no student from Taylor's Grove ever went to all-state."

"Not that I heard."

"Well, we're going to change that." Satisfied now that they had managed a reasonable conversation, she tossed back her hair. "Do you sing?"

"In the shower." His dimple flickered again as his sons giggled. "No comments from the brats."

"He sings really, really loud," Zeke said, without fear of reprisal. "And he gets Zark howling."

"I'm sure that would be quite a show." Nell scratched the grinning dog between the ears. He thumped his tail, and then some internal clock struck and had him pivoting and racing up the hill.

"Here you go, Miss Davis. Here." Both boys stuffed the loaded paper towels into her hands and barreled off after the dog.

"I guess they don't keep still very long," she murmured, watching them chase the dog up the rise.

"That was nearly a record. They like you."

"I'm a likable person." She smiled, glancing back at him, only to find him staring at her again with that not-quite-pleased look in his eyes. "At least in most cases. If you'd just put that on the back seat, I'll have it filled up for you."

"It's not a problem." Mac replaced her gas cap and kept the empty can. "We're friendly in Taylor's Grove. In most cases."

"Let me know when I'm off probation." She leaned into her car to set the brownies on the passenger seat. Mac had a tantalizing and uncomfortable view of her jean-clad bottom. He could smell her, too, something light and spicy that spun in his head a lot more potently than the gas fumes.

"I didn't mean it like that."

Her head popped back out of the car. She licked a smear of brownie from her finger as she straightened. "Maybe not.

In any case, I appreciate the help.'' Her grin flashed as she opened the car door. ''And the chocolate.''

''Anytime,'' he heard himself say, and wanted to regret it.

She settled behind the steering wheel, tossed him a quick, saucy smile. ''Like hell.'' Then she laughed and turned the ignition, revving the engine in a way that made Mac wince. ''You should drop in on rehearsals now and again, Mac, instead of waiting out in the parking lot. You might learn something.''

He wasn't certain he wanted to. ''Put on your seat belt,'' he ordered.

''Oh, yeah.'' Obligingly, she buckled up. ''Just not used to it yet. Say bye to the twins.'' She zoomed off at a speed just this side of reckless, waving a careless and glittering hand out the window.

Mac watched her until she rounded the bend, then slowly rubbed his stomach where the muscles were knotted. Something about that woman, he thought. Something about the way she was put together made him feel like he was defrosting after a very long freeze.

Chapter Three

Another half hour, Mac figured, and he could finish taping the drywall in the master bedroom. Maybe get the first coat of mud on. He glanced at his watch, calculated that the kids were home from school. But it was Mrs. Hollis's day, and she'd stay until five. That would give him plenty of time to hit the drywall, clean up and get home.

Maybe he'd give himself and the kids a treat and pick up pizza.

He'd learned not to mind cooking, but he still resented the time it took—the thinking, the preparation, the cleaning up afterward. Six years as a single parent had given him a whole new perspective on how hard his mother—that rare and old-fashioned homemaker—had worked.

Pausing a moment, he took a look around the master suite. He'd taken walls out, built others, replaced the old single-pane windows with double glazed. Twin skylights let in the fading sunlight of early October.

Now there were three spacious bedrooms on the second floor of the old house, rather than the four choppy rooms and oversize hallway he'd started with. The master suite would boast a bathroom large enough for tub and separate shower stall. He was toying with using glass block for that. He'd been wanting to work with it for some time.

If he stayed on schedule, the place would be put together by Christmas, and on the sale or rental market by the first of the year.

He really should sell it, Mac thought, running a hand over the drywall he'd nailed up that afternoon. He had to get over this sense of possession whenever he worked on a house.

In the blood, he supposed. His father had made a good living buying up damaged or depressed property, rehabing and renting. Mac had discovered just how satisfying it was to own something you'd made fine with your own hands.

Like the old brick house Nell lived in now. He wondered if she knew it was more than a hundred and fifty years old, that she was living in a piece of history.

He wondered if she'd run out of gas again.

He wondered quite a bit about Nell Davis.

And he shouldn't, Mac reminded himself, and turned away for his tools and tape. Women were trouble. One way or the other, they were trouble. One look at Nell and a smart man could see she was no exception.

He hadn't taken her up on her suggestion that he drop by the auditorium and catch part of a rehearsal. He'd started to a couple of times, but good sense had stopped him. She was the first woman in a very, very long time who had stirred him up. He didn't want to be stirred up, Mac thought with a scowl as he taped a seam. Couldn't afford to be, he reminded himself. He had too many obligations, too little free time, and, most important, two sons who were the focus of his life.

Daydreaming about a woman was bad enough. It made a man sloppy in his work, forgetful and . . . itchy. But doing something about it was worse. Doing something meant you had to find conversation and ways to entertain. A woman expected to be taken places, and pampered. And once you started to fall for her—really fall for her—she had the power to cut out your heart.

Mac wasn't willing to risk his heart again, and he certainly wasn't willing to risk his sons.

He didn't subscribe to that nonsense about children needing a woman's touch, a mother's love. The twins' mother had felt less connection with the children she'd borne than a cat felt toward a litter of kittens. Being female didn't give you a leg up on maternal feelings. It meant you were physically able to carry a child inside you, but it didn't mean that you'd care once that child was in your arms.

Mac stopped taping and swore. He hadn't thought about Angie in years. Not deeply. When he did, he realized the spot was still sore, like an old wound that had healed poorly. That was what he got, he supposed, for letting some little blonde stir him up.

Annoyed with himself, he stripped the last piece of tape off the roll. He needed to concentrate on his work, not on a woman. Determined to finish what he'd started, he marched down the stairs. He had more drywall tape in his truck.

The light outside was softening with the approach of dusk. Shorter days, he thought. Less time.

He was down the steps and onto the walk before he saw her. She was standing just at the edge of the yard, looking up at the house, smiling a little. She wore a suede jacket in a deep burnished orange over faded jeans. Some glittery stones dangled from her ears. Over her shoulder hung a soft-sided briefcase that looked well used.

"Oh. Hi." Surprise lit her eyes when she glanced over, and that immediately made him suspicious. "Is this one of your places?"

"That's right." He moved past her toward the truck and wished he'd held his breath. That scent she wore was subtle and sneaky.

"I was just admiring it. Beautiful stonework. It looks so sturdy and safe, tucked in with all the trees." She took a deep breath. There was the slap of fall in the air. "It's going to be a beautiful night."

"I guess." He found his tape, then stood, running the roll around in his hands. "Did you run out of gas again?"

"No." She laughed, obviously amused at herself. "I like walking around town this time of day. As a matter of fact, I was heading down to your sister's. She's a few doors down, right?"

His eyes narrowed. He didn't like the idea of the woman he was spending too much time thinking about hanging out with his sister. "Yeah, that's right. Why?"

"Why?" Her attention had been focused on his hands. There was something about them. Hard, callused. Big. She felt a quick and very pleasant flutter in the pit of her stomach. "Why what?"

"Why are you going to Mira's?"

"Oh. I have some sheet music I thought Kim would like."

"Is that right?" He leaned on the truck, measuring her. Her smile was entirely too friendly, he decided. Entirely too attractive. "Is it part of your job description to make house calls with sheet music?"

"It's part of the fun." Her hair ruffled in the light breeze. She scooped it back. "No job's worth the effort or the headaches if you don't have some fun." She looked back at the house. "You have fun, don't you? Taking something and making it yours?"

He started to say something snide, then realized she'd put her finger right on the heart of it. "Yeah. It doesn't always seem like fun when you're tearing out ceilings and having insulation raining down on your head." He smiled a little. "But it is."

"Are you going to let me see?" She tilted her head. "Or are you like a temperamental artist, not willing to show his work until the final brush stroke?"

"There's not much to see." Then he shrugged. "Sure, you can come in if you want."

"Thanks." She started up the walk, glanced over her shoulder when he stayed by the truck. "Aren't you going to give me a tour?"

He moved his shoulders again, and joined her.

"Did you do the trim on my apartment?"

"Yeah."

"It's beautiful work. Looks like cherry."

He frowned, surprised. "It is cherry."

"I like the rounded edges. They soften everything. Do you get a decorator in for the colors or pick them out yourself?"

"I pick them." He opened the door for her. "Is there a problem?"

"No. I really love the color scheme in the kitchen, the slate blue counters, the mauve floor. Oh, what fabulous stairs." She hurried across the unfinished living area to the staircase.

Mac had worked hard and long on it, tearing out the old and replacing it with dark chestnut, curving and widening the landing at the bottom so that it flowed out into the living space.

It was, undeniably, his current pride and joy.

"Did you build these?" she murmured, running a hand over the curve of the railing.

"The old ones were broken, dry-rotted. Had to go."

"I have to try them." She dashed up, turning back at the top to grin at him. "No creaks. Good workmanship, but not very sentimental."

"Sentimental?"

"You know, the way you look back on home, how you snuck downstairs as a kid and knew just which steps to avoid because they'd creak and wake up Mom."

All at once he was having trouble with his breathing. "They're chestnut," he said, because he could think of nothing else.

"Whatever, they're beautiful. Whoever lives here has to have kids."

His mouth was dry, unbearably. "Why?"

"Because." On impulse, she planted her butt on the railing and pushed off. Mac's arms came out of their own volition to catch her as she flew off the end. "It was made for sliding," she said breathlessly. She was laughing as she tilted her head up to his.

Something clicked inside her when their eyes met. And the fluttering, not so pleasant this time, came again. Disconcerted, she cleared her throat and searched for something to say.

"You keep popping up," Mac muttered. He had yet to release her, couldn't seem to make his hands obey his head.

"It's a small town."

He only shook his head. His hands were at her waist now, and they seemed determined to slide around and stroke up her back. He thought he felt her tremble—but it might have been him.

"I don't have time for women," he told her, trying to convince himself.

"Well." She tried to swallow, but there was something hard and hot lodged in her throat. "I'm pretty busy myself." She let out a slow breath. Those hands stroking up and down her back were making her weak. "And I'm not really interested. I had a really bad year, as far as relationships go. I think..."

It was very hard to think. His eyes were such a beautiful shade of blue, and so intensely focused on hers. She wasn't sure what he saw, or what he was looking for, but she knew her knees were about to give out.

"I think," she began again, "we'd both be better off if you decide fairly quickly if you're going to kiss me or not. I can't handle this much longer."

Neither could he. Still, he took his time. He was, in all things, a thorough and thoughtful man. His eyes were open and on hers as he lowered his head, as his mouth hovered a breath from hers, as a small, whimpering moan sounded in her throat.

Her vision dimmed as his lips brushed hers. His were soft, firm, terrifyingly patient. The whisper of contact slammed a punch into her stomach. He lingered over her like a gourmet sampling delicacies, deepening the kiss degree by staggering degree until she was clinging to him.

No one had ever kissed her like this. She hadn't known anyone could. Slow and deep and dreamy. The floor seemed to tilt under her feet as he gently sucked her lower lip into his mouth.

She shuddered, groaned, and let herself drown.

She was very potent. The scent and feel and taste of her was overwhelming. He knew he could lose himself here, for a moment, for a lifetime. Her small, tight body was all but plastered to his. Her hands clutched his hair. In contrast to that aggressive gesture, her head fell limply back in a kind of sighing surrender that had his blood bubbling.

He wanted to touch her. His hands were aching with the need to peel off layer after layer and find the pale, smooth skin beneath. To test himself, and her, he slipped his fingers under her sweater, along the soft, hot flesh of her back, while his mouth continued its long, lazy assault on hers.

He imagined laying her down on the floor, on a tarp, on the grass. He imagined watching her face as he pleasured them both, of feeling her arch toward him, open, accepting.

It had been too long, he told himself as his muscles began to coil and his lungs to labor. It had just been too long.

But he didn't believe it. And it frightened him.

Unsteady, he lifted his head, drew back. Even as he began the retreat, she leaned against him, letting her head fall onto his chest. Unable to resist, he combed his fingers through her hair and cradled her there.

"My head's spinning," she murmured. "What was that?"

"It was a kiss, that's all." He needed to believe that. It would help to ease the tightness around his heart and his loins.

"I think I saw stars." Still staggered, she shifted so that she could look up at him. Her lips curved, but her eyes didn't echo the smile. "That's a first for me."

If he didn't do something fast, he was going to kiss her again. He set her firmly on her feet. "It doesn't change anything."

"Was there something to change?"

The light was nearly gone now. It helped that he couldn't see her clearly in the gloom. "I don't have time for women. And I'm just not interested in starting anything."

"Oh." Where had that pain come from? she wondered, and had to fight to keep from rubbing a hand over her heart. "That was quite a kiss, for a disinterested man." Reaching down, she scooped up the briefcase she'd dropped before she'd run up the stairs. "I'll get out of your way. I wouldn't want to waste any more of your valuable time."

"You don't have to get huffy about it."

"Huffy." Her teeth snapped together. She jabbed a finger into his chest. "I'm well beyond huffy, pal, and working my way past steamed. You've got some ego, Mac. What, do you think I came around here to seduce you?"

"I don't know why you came around."

"Well, I won't be around again." She settled her briefcase on her shoulder, jerked her chin up. "Nobody twisted your arm."

He was dealing with an uncomfortable combination of desire and guilt. "Yours, either."

"I'm not the one making excuses. You know, I can't figure out how such an insensitive clod could raise two charming and adorable kids."

"Leave my boys out of this."

The edge to the order had her eyes narrowing to slits. "Oh, so I have designs on them now, too? You idiot!" She stormed for the door, whirling at the last moment for a parting shot. "I hope they don't inherit your warped view of the female species!"

She slammed the door hard enough to have the bad-tempered sound echoing through the house. Mac scowled and jammed his hands in his pockets. He didn't have a warped view, damn it. And his kids were his business.

Chapter Four

Nell stood center stage and lifted her hands. She waited until she was sure every student's eyes were on her, then let it rip.

There was very little that delighted her more than the sound of young voices raised in song. She let the sound fill her, keeping her ears and eyes sharp as she moved around the stage directing. She couldn't hold back the grin. The kids were into this one. Doing Bruce Springsteen and the E Street Band's version of "Santa Claus Is Coming to Town" was a departure from the standard carols and hymns their former choral director had arranged year after year.

She could see their eyes light up as they got into the rhythm. Now punch it, she thought, pulling more from the bass section as they hit the chorus. Have fun with it. Now the soprano section, high and bright... And the altos... Tenors... Bass...

She flashed a smile to signal her approval as the chorus flowered again.

"Good job," she announced. "Tenors, a little more next time. You guys don't want the bass section drowning you out. Holly, you're dropping your chin again. Now we have time for one more run-through of 'I'll Be Home for Christmas.' Kim?"

Kim tried to ignore the little flutter around her heart and the elbow nudge from Holly. She stepped down from her position in the second row and stood in front of the solo mike as though she were facing a firing squad.

"It's okay to smile, you know," Nell told her gently. "And remember your breathing. Sing to the last row, and don't forget to feel the words. Tracy.'' She held out a finger toward the pianist she'd dragooned from her second-period music class.

The intro started quietly. Using her hands, her face, her eyes, Nell signaled the beginning of the soft, harmonious, background humming. Then Kim began to sing. Too tentatively at first. Nell knew they would have to work on those initial nerves.

But the girl had talent, and emotion. Three bars in, Kim was too caught up in the song to be nervous. She was pacing it well, Nell thought, pleased. Kim had learned quite a bit in the past few weeks about style. The sentimental song suited her, her range, her looks.

Nell brought the chorus in, holding them back. They were background now for Kim's rich, romantic voice. Feeling her own eyes stinging, Nell thought that if they did it this well on the night of the concert, there wouldn't be a dry eye in the house.

''Lovely,'' Nell said when the last notes had died away. ''Really lovely. You guys have come a long way in a very short time. I'm awfully proud of you. Now scram, and have a great weekend.''

While Nell moved to the piano to gather up music, the chatter began behind her.

''You sounded really good,'' Holly told Kim.

''Honest?''

''Honest. Brad thought so, too.'' Holly shifted her eyes cagily to the school heartthrob, who was shrugging into his school jacket.

''He doesn't even know I'm alive.''

''He does now. He was watching you the whole time. I know, because I was watching him.'' Holly sighed. ''If I looked like Miss Davis, *he'd* be watching *me.*''

Kim laughed, but shot a quick glance toward Brad under her lashes. ''She's really fabulous. Just the way she talks to us and stuff. Mr. Striker always crabbed.''

''Mr. Striker *was* a crab. See you later, huh?''

"Yeah." It was all Kim could manage, because it looked, it really looked, as though Brad were coming toward her. And he *was* looking at her.

"Hi." He flashed a grin, all white teeth, with a crooked incisor that made her heart flop around in her chest. "You did real good."

"Thanks." Her tongue tied itself into knots. This was Brad, she kept thinking. A senior. Captain of the football team. Student council president. All blond hair and green eyes.

"Miss Davis sure is cool, isn't she?"

"Yeah." Say something, she ordered herself. "She's coming to a party at my house tonight. My mom's having some people over."

"Adults only, huh?"

"No, Holly's coming by and a couple other people." Her heart thundered in her ears as she screwed up her courage. "You could drop by if you wanted."

"That'd be cool. What time?"

She managed to close her mouth and swallow. "Oh, about eight," she said, struggling for the casual touch. "I live on—"

"I know where you live." He grinned at her again, and all but stopped her thundering heart. "Hey, you're not going with Chuck anymore, are you?"

"Chuck?" Who was Chuck? "Oh, no. We hung out for a while, but we sort of broke up over the summer."

"Great. See you later."

He strolled off to join a group of boys who were trooping offstage.

"That's a very cute guy," Nell commented from behind Kim.

"Yeah." The word was a sigh. Kim had stars in her eyes.

"Kimmy has a boyfriend," Zeke sang, in the high-pitched, annoying voice that was reserved for addressing younger siblings—or female cousins.

"Shut up, brat."

He only giggled and began to dance around the stage, singsonging the refrain. Nell saw murder shoot into Kim's eyes and created a diversion.

"Well, I guess you guys don't want to practice 'Jingle Bells' today."

"Yes, we do." Zack stopped twirling around the stage with his brother and dashed to the piano. "I know which one it is," he said, attacking Nell's neat pile of sheet music. "I can find it."

"I'll find it," Zeke said, but his brother was already holding the music up triumphantly.

"Good going." Nell settled on the bench with a boy on either side of her. She played a dramatic opening chord that made them both giggle. "Please, music is a serious business. And one, and two, and..."

They actually sang it now, instead of screaming it, as they had the first time she invited them to try. What they lacked in style, they made up for in enthusiasm. In spades.

Even Kim was grinning by the time they'd finished.

"Now you do one, Miss Davis." Zack gave her his soulful look. "Please."

"Your dad's probably waiting."

"Just one."

"Just one," Zeke echoed.

In a few short weeks, it had become impossible for her to resist them. "Just one," Nell agreed, and reached into the now-messy pile of music. "I picked up something you might like at the mall. I bet you've seen *The Little Mermaid*."

"Lots of times," Zeke boasted. "We've got the tape and everything."

"Then you'll recognize this." She played the opening of "Part of Your World."

Mac hunched his shoulders against the wind as he headed into the school. He was damn sick and tired of waiting out in the parking lot. He'd seen the other kids filing out more than ten minutes before.

He had things to do, damn it. Especially since he was stuck going over to Mira's for a party.

He hated parties.

He stomped down the hall. And he heard her. Not the words. He couldn't make out the words, because they were muffled by the auditorium doors. But the sound of her voice, rich and deep. A Scotch-and-soda voice, he'd thought more than once. Sensual, seductive. Sexy.

He opened the door. He had to. And the lush flow of it rolled over him.

A kid's song. He recognized it now from the mermaid movie the boys were still crazy about. He told himself no sane man would get tied up in knots when a woman sang a kid's song.

But he wasn't feeling very sane. Hadn't been since he made the enormous mistake of kissing her.

And he knew that if she'd been alone he would have marched right over to the piano and kissed her again.

But she wasn't alone. Kim was standing behind her, and his children flanked her. Now and again she glanced down at them as she sang, and smiled. Zack was leaning toward her, his head tilting in the way it did just before he climbed into your lap.

Something shifted inside him as he watched. Something painful and frightening. And very, very sweet.

Shaken, Mac stuffed his hands into his pockets, curled those hands into fists. It had to stop. Whatever was happening to him had to stop.

He took a long breath when the music ended. He thought—foolishly, he was sure—that there was something magical humming in the instant of silence that followed.

"We're running late," he called out, determined to break the spell.

Four heads turned his way. The twins began to bounce on the bench.

"Dad! Hey, Dad! We can sing 'Jingle Bells' really good! Want to hear us?"

"I can't." He tried to smile, softening the blow, when Zack's lip poked out. "I'm really running late, kids."

"Sorry, Uncle Mac." Kim scooped up her coat. "We kind of lost track."

While Mac shifted uncomfortably, Nell leaned over and murmured something to his sons. Something, Mac noted, that put a smile back on Zack's face and took the mutinous look off Zeke's. Then both of them threw arms around her and kissed her before they raced offstage for their coats.

"Bye, Miss Davis! Bye!"

"Thanks, Miss Davis," Kim added. "See you later."

Nell made a humming sound and rose to straighten her music.

Mac felt the punch of her cold shoulder all the way in the back of the auditorium. "Ah, thanks for entertaining them," he called out.

Nell lifted her head. He could see her clearly in the stage lights. Clearly enough that he caught the lift of her brow, the coolness of her unsmiling mouth, before she lowered her head again.

Fine, he told himself as he caught both boys on the fly. He didn't want to talk to her anyway.

Chapter Five

She didn't have to ignore him so completely. Mac sipped the cup of hard cider his brother-in-law had pressed on him and resentfully studied Nell's back.

She'd had it turned in his direction for an hour.

A hell of a back, too, he thought, half listening as the mayor rattled on in his ear. Smooth and straight, topped off by the fluid curve of her shoulders. It looked very seductive in the thin plum-colored jacket she wore over a short matching dress.

She had terrific legs. He didn't think he'd ever actually seen them before. He would have remembered. Every other time he'd run into her she'd had them covered up.

She'd probably worn a dress tonight to torment him.

Mac cut the mayor off in midstream and strode over to her. "Look, this is stupid."

Nell glanced up. She'd been having a pleasant conversation with a group of Mira's friends—and thoroughly enjoying the simple act of ignoring Mira's brother.

"Excuse me?"

"It's just stupid," he repeated.

"The need to raise more money for the arts in public school is stupid?" she asked, well aware he wasn't referring to the topic she'd been discussing.

"What? No. Damn it, you know what I mean."

"I'm sorry." She started to turn back to the circle of very interested faces, but he took her arm and pulled her aside. "Do you want me to cause a scene in your sister's house?" Nell said between her teeth.

"No." He weaved his way through the minglers, around the dining room table and through the kitchen door. His sister was busy replenishing a tray of canapés. "Give us a minute," he ordered Mira.

"Mac, I'm busy here." Distracted, Mira smoothed a hand over her short brunette hair. "Would you find Dave and tell him we're running low on cider?" She sent Nell a frazzled smile. "I thought I was organized."

"Give us a minute," Mac repeated.

Mira let out an impatient breath, but then her eyebrows shot up, drew in. "Well, well," she murmured, amused and clearly delighted. "I'll just get out of your way. I want a closer look at that boy Kim's so excited about." She picked up the tray of finger food and swung through the kitchen door.

Silence fell like a hammer.

"So." Casually, Nell plucked a carrot stick from a bowl. "Something on your mind, Macauley?"

"I don't see why you have to be so..."

"So?" She crunched into the carrot. "What?"

"You're making a point of not talking to me."

She smiled. "Yes, I am."

"It's stupid."

She located an open bottle of white wine, poured some into a glass. After a sip, she smiled again. "I don't think so. It seems to me that, for no discernible reason, I annoy you. Since I'm quite fond of your family, it seems logical and courteous to stay as far out of your way as I possibly can." She sipped again. "Now, is that all? I've been enjoying myself so far this evening."

"You don't annoy me. Exactly." He couldn't find anything to do with his hands, so he settled on taking a carrot stick and breaking it in half. "I'm sorry...for before."

"You're sorry for kissing me, or for behaving like a jerk afterward?"

He tossed the pieces of carrot down. "You're a hard one, Nell."

"Wait." Eyes wide, she pressed a hand to her ear. "I think something's wrong with my hearing. I thought, for just a minute, you actually said my name."

"Cut it out," he said. Then, deliberately: "Nell."

"This is a moment," she declared, and toasted him. "Macauley Taylor has actually initiated a conversation with me, *and* used my name. I'm all aflutter."

"Look." Temper had him rounding the counter. He'd nearly grabbed her before he pushed his anger back. "I just want to clear the air."

Fascinated, she studied his now-impassive face. "That's quite a control button you've got there, Mac. It's admirable. Still, I wonder what would happen if you didn't push it so often."

"A man raising two kids on his own needs control."

"I suppose," she murmured. "Now, if that's all—"

"I'm sorry," he said again.

This time she softened. She was simply no good at holding a grudge. "Okay. Let's just forget it. Friends," she offered, and held out a hand.

He took it. It was so soft, so small, he couldn't make himself give it up again. Her eyes were soft, too, just now. Big, liquid eyes you'd have expected to see on a fawn. "You . . . look nice."

"Thanks. You too."

"You like the party?"

"I like the people." Her pulse was starting to jump. Damn him. "Your sister's wonderful. So full of energy and ideas."

"You have to watch her." His lips curved slowly. "She'll rope you into one of her projects."

"Too late. She's got me on the arts committee already. And I've been volunteered to help with the recycling campaign."

"The trick is to duck."

"I don't mind, really. I think I'm going to enjoy it." His thumb was brushing over her wrist now, lightly. "Mac, don't start something you don't intend to finish."

Brow creased, he looked down at their joined hands. "I think about you. I don't have time to think about you. I don't want to have time."

It was happening again. The flutters and quivers she seemed to have no control over. "What do you want?"

His gaze lifted, locked with hers. "I'm having some trouble with that."

The kitchen door burst open, and a horde of teenagers piled in, only to be brought up short as Kim, in the lead, stopped on a dime.

Her eyes widened as she watched her uncle drop her teacher's hand, and the two of them jumped apart like a couple of teenagers caught necking on the living room sofa.

"Sorry. Ah, sorry," she repeated, goggling. "We were just..." She turned on her heel and shoved back at her friends. They scooted out, chuckling.

"That ought to add some juice to the grapevine," Nell said wryly. She'd been in town long enough to know that everyone would be speculating about Mac Taylor and Nell Davis by morning. Steadier now, she turned back to him. "Listen, why don't we try this in nice easy stages? You want to go out to dinner tomorrow? See a movie or something?"

Now it was his turn to stare. "A date? Are you asking me out on a date?"

Impatience flickered back. "Yes, a date. It doesn't mean I'm asking to bear you more children. On second thought, let's just quit while we're ahead."

"I want to get my hands on you." Mac heard himself say the words, knew it was too late to take them back.

Nell reached for her wine in self-defense. "Well, that's simple."

"No, it's not."

She braced herself and looked up at him again. "No," she agreed quietly. Just how many times, she wondered, had his face popped into her mind in the past few weeks? She couldn't count them. "It's not simple."

But something had to be done, he decided. A move forward, a move back. Take a step, he ordered himself. See what happens. "I haven't been to a movie without the kids... I can't remember. I could probably line up a sitter."

"All right." She was watching him now almost as carefully as he watched her. "Give me a call if it works out. I'll be home most of tomorrow, correcting papers."

It wasn't the easiest thing, stepping back into the dating pool—however small the pool and however warm the water. It irritated him that he was nervous, almost as much as his niece's grins and questions had irritated when she agreed to baby-sit.

Now, as he climbed the sturdy outside steps to Nell's third-floor apartment, Mac wondered if it would be better all around if they forgot the whole thing.

As he stepped onto her deck, he noted that she'd flanked the door with pots of mums. It was a nice touch, he thought. He always appreciated it when someone who rented one of his homes cared enough to bother with those nice touches.

It was just a movie, he reminded himself, and rapped on the door. When she opened it, he was relieved that she'd dressed casually—a hip-grazing sweater over a pair of those snug leggings Kim liked so much.

Then she smiled and had his mouth going dry.

"Hi. You're right on time. Do you want to come in and see what I've done to your place?"

"It's your place—as long as you pay the rent," he told her, but she was reaching out, taking his hand, drawing him in.

Mac had dispensed with the walls that had made stingy little rooms and had created one flowing space of living, dining and kitchen area. And she'd known what to do with it.

There was a huge L-shaped couch in a bold floral print that should have been shocking, but was, instead, perfect.

A small table under the window held a pot of dried autumn leaves. Shelves along one wall held books, a stereo and a small TV, and the sort of knickknacks he knew women liked.

She'd turned the dining area into a combination music room and office, with her desk and a small spinet. A flute lay on a music stand.

"I didn't bring a lot with me from New York," she said as she shrugged into her jacket. "Only what I really cared about. I'm filling in with things from antique shops and flea markets.

"We got a million of them," he murmured. "It looks good." And it did—the old, faded rug on the floor, the fussy priscillas at the windows. "Comfortable."

"Comfortable's very important to me. Ready?"

"Sure."

And it wasn't so hard after all.

He'd asked her to pick the movie, and she'd gone for comedy. It was surprisingly relaxing to sit in the darkened theater and share popcorn and laughter.

He only thought about her as a woman, a very attractive woman, a couple of dozen times.

Going for pizza afterward seemed such a natural progression, he suggested it himself. They competed for a table in the crowded pizzeria with teenagers out on date night.

"So..." Nell stretched out in the booth. "How's Zeke's career in spelling coming along?"

"It's a struggle. He really works at it. It's funny, Zack can spell almost anything you toss at him first time around, but Zeke has to study the word like a scholar with the Dead Sea Scrolls."

"He's good at his arithmetic."

"Yeah." Mac wasn't sure how he felt about her knowing so much about his kids. "They're both taken with you."

"It's mutual." She skimmed a hand through her hair. "It's going to sound odd, but..." She hesitated, not quite sure how to word it. "But that first day at rehearsal, when

I looked around and saw them? I had this feeling, this— I don't know, it was like, 'Oh, there you are. I was wondering when you'd show up.' It sounds strange, but it was as if I was expecting them. Now, when Kim comes without them, I feel let down."

"I guess they kind of grow on you."

It was more than that, but she didn't know how to explain. And she wasn't entirely sure Mac would accept the fact that she'd very simply fallen for them. "I get a kick out of them telling me about their school day, showing me their papers."

"First report cards are almost here." His grin flashed. "I'm more nervous than they are."

"People put too much emphasis on grades."

His brows shot up at the comment. "This from a teacher?"

"Individual ability, application, effort, retention. Those things are a lot more important than *A*, *B* or *C*. But I can tell you, in confidence, that Kim's aceing advanced chorus and music history."

"No kidding?" He felt a quick surge of pride. "She never did that well before. *B*s mostly."

"Mr. Striker and I have markedly different approaches."

"You're telling me. Word around town is that the chorus is dynamite this year. How'd you pull it off?"

"The kids pull it off," she told him, sitting up when their pizza was served. "My job is to make them think and sing like a team. Not to slam Mr. Striker," she added, taking a generous bite. "But I get the impression he was just putting in time, counting the days until he could retire. If you're going to teach kids, you have to like them, and respect them. There's a lot of talent there, some of it extremely rough." When she laughed, the roses in her cheek bloomed deeper. "And some of those kids will do nothing more than sing in the shower for the rest of their lives—for which the world can be grateful."

"Got some clinkers, huh?"

"Well . . ." She laughed again. "Yes, I have a few. But they're enjoying themselves. That's what counts. And there are a few, like Kim, who are really something special. I'm sending her and two others for auditions to all-state next week. And after the holiday concert I'm going to hold auditions for the spring musical."

"We haven't had a musical at the high school in three years."

"We're going to have one this year, Buster. And it's going to be terrific."

"It's a lot of work for you."

"I like it. And it's what I'm paid for."

Mac toyed with a second slice. "You really do like it, don't you? The school, the town, the whole bit?"

"Why shouldn't I? It's a fine school, a fine town."

"It ain't Manhattan."

"Exactly."

"Why'd you leave?" He winced. "Sorry, none of my business."

"It's all right. I had a bad year. I guess I was getting restless before that, but the last year was just the pits. They eliminated my job at the school. Economic cutbacks. Downsizing. The arts are always the first to suffer." She shrugged. "Anyway, my roommate got married. I couldn't afford the rent on my own—not if I wanted to eat with any regularity—so I advertised for another one. Took references, gauged personalities." With a sigh, she propped her chin on her elbow. "I thought I was careful. But about three weeks after she moved in, I came home and found that she'd cleaned me out."

Mac stopped eating. "She robbed you?"

"She skinned me. TV, stereo, whatever good jewelry I had, cash, the collection of Limoges boxes I'd started in college. I was really steamed, and then I was shaken. I just wasn't comfortable living there after it happened. Then the guy I'd been seeing for about a year started giving me lectures on my stupidity, my naiveté. As far as he was concerned, I'd gotten exactly what I'd deserved.''

"Nice guy," Mac muttered. "Very supportive."

"You bet. In any case, I took a good look at him and our relationship and figured he was right on one level. As long as I was in that rut, with him, I was getting what I deserved. So I decided to climb out of the rut, and leave him in it.''

"Good choice."

"I thought so." And so was he, she thought, studying Mac's face. A very good choice. "Why don't you tell me what your plans are with the house you're renovating."

"I don't guess you'd know a lot about plumbing."

She only smiled. "I'm a quick learner."

It was nearly midnight when he pulled up in front of her apartment. He hadn't intended to stay out so late. He certainly hadn't expected to spend more than an hour talking to her about wiring and plumbing and load-bearing walls. Or drawing little blueprints on napkins.

But somehow he'd manage to get through the evening without feeling foolish, or pinned down or out of step. Only one thing worried him. He wanted to see her again.

"I think this was a good first step." She laid a hand over his, kissed his cheek. "Thanks."

"I'll walk you up."

Her hand was already on the door handle. Safer, she'd decided for both of them, if she just hurried along. "You don't have to. I know the way."

"I'll walk you up," he repeated. He stepped out, rounded the hood. They started up the stairs together. The tenant on the first floor was still awake. The mutter of a television, and its ghost gray light, filtered through the window.

Since the breeze had died, it was the only sound. And overhead countless stars wheeled in a clear black sky.

''If we do this again,'' Mac began, ''people in town are going to start talking about us, making out that we're...'' He wasn't quite sure of the right phrase.

''An item?'' Nell supplied. ''That bothers you.''

''I don't want the kids to get any ideas, or worry, or...whatever.'' As they reached the landing, he looked down at her and was caught again. ''It must be the way you look,'' he murmured.

''What must?''

''That makes me think about you.'' It was a reasonable explanation, he decided. Physical attraction. After all, he wasn't a dead man. He was just a careful one. ''That makes me think about doing this.''

He cupped her face in his hands—a gesture so sweet, so tender, it had every muscle in her body going lax. It was just as slow, as stunning, as sumptuous, as the first time. The touch of his mouth on hers, the shuddering patience, the simple wonder of it.

Could it be this? she wondered. Could it be this that she'd been waiting for? Could it be him?

He heard her soft, breathy sigh as he eased his mouth from hers. Lingering, he knew, would be a mistake, and he let his hands fall away before they could reach for more.

As if to capture one final taste, Nell ran her tongue over her lips. ''You're awfully good at that, Macauley. Awfully good.''

''You could say I've been saving up.'' But he didn't think it was that at all. He was very much worried it wasn't that. ''I'll see you.''

She nodded weakly as he headed down the steps. She was still leaning dreamily against the door when she heard his car start and drive away.

For a moment, she would have sworn the air rang with the distant music of sleigh bells.

Chapter Six

The end of October meant parent-teacher conferences, and a much-anticipated holiday for students. It also meant a headache for Mac. He had to juggle the twins from his sister to Kim to Mrs. Hollis, fitting in a trip to order materials and an electrical inspection.

When he turned his truck into the educational complex, he was jumpy with nerves. Lord knew what he was about to be told about his children, how they behaved when they were out of his sight and his control. He worried that he hadn't made enough time to help them with their schoolwork and somehow missed a parental step in preparing them for the social, educational and emotional demands of first grade.

Because of his failure, his boys would become antisocial, illiterate neurotics.

He knew he was being ridiculous, but he couldn't stop his fears from playing over and over like an endless loop in his brain.

"Mac!" The car horn and the sound of his name had him turning and focusing, finally, on his sister's car. She leaned out the window, shaking her head at him. "Where were you? I called you three times."

"Bailing my kids out of jail," he muttered, and changed course to walk to her car. "I've got a conference in a minute."

"I know. I've just come from a meeting at the high school. Remember, we compared schedules."

"Right. I shouldn't be late."

"You don't get demerits. My meeting was about raising funds for new chorus uniforms. Those kids have been wearing the same old choir robes for twelve years. We're hoping to raise enough to put them in something a little snazzier."

"Fine, I'll give you a donation, but I shouldn't be late." Already he was imagining the young, fresh-faced first grade teacher marking him tardy, just another item on a growing list of negatives about Taylor males.

"I just wanted to say that Neil seemed upset about something."

"What?"

"Upset," Mira repeated, pleased that she finally had his full attention. "She came up with a couple of nice ideas for fund-raisers, but she was obviously distracted." Mira lifted a brow, eyeing her brother slyly. "You haven't done anything to annoy her, have you?"

"No." Mac caught himself before he shifted guiltily from foot to foot. "Why should I?"

"Couldn't say. But since you've been seeing her—"

"We went to the movies."

"And for pizza," Mira added. "A couple of Kim's friends spotted you."

The curse of small towns, Mac thought, and stuffed his hands in his pockets. "So?"

"So nothing. Good for you. I like her a lot. Kim's crazy about her. I suppose I'm feeling a bit protective. She was definitely upset, Mac, and trying not to show it. Maybe she'd talk to you about it."

"I'm not going to go poking around in her personal life."

"The way I see it, you're part of her personal life. See you later." She pulled off without giving him a chance for a parting shot.

Muttering to himself, Mac marched up to the elementary school. When he marched out twenty minutes later, he was in a much lighter mood. His children had not been declared social misfits with homicidal tendencies after all. In fact, their teacher had praised them.

Of course, he'd known all along.

Maybe Zeke forgot the rules now and then and talked to his neighbor. And maybe Zack was a little shy about raising his hand when he knew an answer. But they were settling in.

With the weight of first grade off his shoulders, Mac headed out. Impulse had him swinging toward the high school. He knew his conference had been one of the last of the day. He wasn't sure how teachers' meetings worked at the high school, but the lot was nearly empty. He spotted Nell's car, however, and decided it wouldn't hurt just to drop in.

It wasn't until he was inside that he realized he didn't have a clue as to where to find her.

Mac poked his head into the auditorium, but it was empty. Since he'd come that far, he backtracked to the main office and caught one of the secretaries as she was leaving for the day. Following her directions, he turned down a corridor, headed up a ramp and turned right.

Nell's classroom door was open. Not like any classroom he'd done time in, he thought. This one had a piano, music stands, instruments, a tape recorder. There was the usual blackboard, wiped clean, and a desk where Nell was currently working.

He watched her for a long moment, the way her hair fell, the way her fingers held the pen, the way her sweater draped at the neck. It occurred to him that if he'd ever had a teacher who looked like that, he would have been a great deal more interested in music.

"Hi."

Her head snapped up. There was a martial light in her eyes that surprised him, a stubborn set to her jaw. Even as he watched, she took a long breath and worked up a smile.

"Hello, Mac. Welcome to bedlam."

"Looks like a lot of work." He stepped inside, up to the desk. It was covered with papers, books, computer printouts and sheet music, all in what appeared to be ordered piles.

"Finishing up the first marking period, grades, class planning, fund-raising strategy, fine-tuning the holiday concert—and trying to make the budget stretch to producing the spring musical." Trying to keep her foul mood to herself, she sat back. "So, how was your day?"

"Pretty good. I just had a conference with the twins' teacher. They're doing fine. I can stop sweating report cards."

"They're great kids. You've got nothing to worry about."

"Worry comes with the territory. What are you worried about?" he asked before he could remind himself he wasn't going to pry.

"How much time have you got?" she shot back.

"Enough." Curious, he eased a hip onto the edge of her desk. He wanted to soothe, he discovered, to stroke away that faint line between her brows. "Rough day?"

She jerked her shoulders, then pushed away from her desk. Temper always forced her to move. "I've had better. Do you know how much school and community support the football team gets? All the sports teams." She began to slap cassette tapes into a box—anything to keep her hands busy. "Even the band. But the chorus, we have to go begging for every dollar."

"You're ticked off about the budget?"

"Why shouldn't I be?" She whirled back, eyes hot. "No problem getting equipment for the football team so a bunch of boys can go out on the field and tackle each other, but I have to spend an hour on my knees if I want eighty bucks to get a piano tuned." She caught herself, sighed. "I don't have anything against football. I like it. High school sports are important."

"I know a guy who tunes pianos," Mac said. "He'd probably donate his time."

Nell rubbed a hand over her face, slid it around to soothe the tension at the back of her neck. Dad can fix anything, she thought, just as the twins had claimed. Have a problem? Call Mac.

"That would be great," she said, and managed a real smile. "If I can beat my way through the paperwork and get approval. You can't even take freebies without going through the board." It irritated her, as always. "One of the worst aspects of teaching is the bureaucracy. Maybe I should have stuck with performing in clubs."

"You performed in clubs?"

"In another life," she muttered, waving it away. "A little singing to pay my way through college. It was better than waiting tables. Anyway, it's not the budget, not really. Or even the lack of interest from the community. I'm used to that."

"Do you want to tell me what it is, or do you want to stew about it?"

"I was having a pretty good time stewing about it." She sighed again, and looked up at him. He seemed so solid, so dependable. "Maybe I'm too much of an urbanite after all. I've had my first run-in with old-fashioned rural attitude, and I'm stumped. Do you know Hank Rohrer?"

"Sure. He has a dairy farm out on Old Oak Road. I think his oldest kid is in the same class as Kim."

"Hank, Jr. Yes. Junior's one of my students—a very strong baritone. He has a real interest in music. He even writes it."

"No kidding? That's great."

"You'd think so, wouldn't you?" Nell tossed her hair back and went to her desk again to tidy her already tidy papers. "Well, I asked Mr. and Mrs. Rohrer to come in this morning because Junior backed out of going to all-state auditions this weekend. I knew he had a very good chance of making it, and I wanted to discuss the possibility with his parents of a music scholarship. When I told them how talented Junior was and how I hoped they'd encourage him to change his mind about the auditions, Hank Senior acted as though I'd just insulted him. He was appalled." There was bitterness in her voice now, as well as anger. "'No son of his was going to waste his time on singing and writing music like some...'"

She trailed off, too furious to repeat the man's opinion of musicians. "They didn't even know Junior was in my class. Thought he was taking shop as his elective this year. I tried to smooth it over, said that Junior needed a fine-art credit to graduate. I didn't do much good. Mr. Rohrer could barely swallow the idea of Junior staying in my class. He went on about how Junior didn't need singing lessons to run a farm. And he certainly wasn't going to allow him to take a Saturday and go audition when the boy had chores. And I'm to stop putting any fancy ideas about college in the boy's head."

"They've got four kids," Mac said slowly. "Tuition might be a problem."

"If that were the only obstacle, they should be grateful for the possibility of scholarship." She slapped her grade book closed. "What we have is a bright, talented boy who has dreams, dreams he'll never be able to explore because his parents won't permit it. Or his father won't," she added. "His mother didn't say two words the entire time they were here."

"Could be she'll work on Hank once she has him alone."

"Could be he'll take out his annoyance with me on both of them."

"Hank's not like that. He's set in his ways and thinks he knows all the answers, but he isn't mean."

"It's a little tough for me to see his virtues after he called me—" she had to take a deep breath "—a slick-handed flatlander who's wasting his hard-earned tax dollars. I could have made a difference with that boy," Nell murmured as she sat again. "I know it."

"So maybe you won't be able to make a difference with Junior. You'll make a difference with someone else. You've already made one with Kim."

"Thanks." Nell's smile was brief. "That helps a little."

"I mean it." He hated to see her this way, all that brilliant energy and optimism dimmed. "She's gained a lot of confidence in herself. She's always been shy about her singing, about a lot of things. Now she's really opening up."

It did help to hear it. This time Nell's smile came easier. "So I should stop brooding."

"It doesn't suit you." He surprised himself, and her, by reaching down to run his knuckles over her cheek. "Smiling does."

"I've never been able to hold on to temperament for long. Bob used to say it was because I was shallow."

"Who the hell's Bob?"

"The one who's still in the rut."

"Clearly where he belongs."

She laughed. "I'm glad you dropped by. I'd have probably sat here for another hour clenching my jaw."

"It's a pretty jaw," Mac murmured, then shifted away. "I've got to get going. I've got Halloween costumes to put together."

"Need any help?"

"I . . ." It was tempting, too tempting, and far too dangerous, he thought, to start sharing family traditions with her. "No, I've got it covered."

Nell accepted the disappointment, nearly masked it. "You'll bring them by Saturday night, won't you? To trick-or-treat?"

"Sure. I'll see you." He started out but stopped at the doorway and turned back. "Nell?"

"Yes?"

"Some things take a while to change. Change makes some people nervous."

She tilted her head. "Are you talking about the Rohrers, Mac?"

"Among others. I'll see you Saturday night."

Nell studied the empty doorway as his footsteps echoed away. Did he think she was trying to change him? Was she?

She sat back, pushing away from the paperwork. She'd never be able to concentrate on it now.

Whenever she was around Macauley Taylor, it was hard to concentrate. When had she become so susceptible to the slow, thorough, quiet type? From the moment he'd walked into the auditorium to pick up Kim and the twins, she admitted.

Love at first sight? Surely she was too sophisticated, too smart, to believe in such a thing. And surely, she added, she was too smart to put herself in the vulnerable position of falling in love with a man who didn't return her feelings.

Or didn't want to, she thought. And that was even worse.

It couldn't matter that he was sweet and kind and devoted to his children. It shouldn't matter that he was handsome and strong and sexy. She wouldn't let it matter that being with him, thinking of him, had her longing for things. For home, for family, for laughter in the kitchen and passion in bed.

She let out a long breath, because it did matter. It mattered very much when a woman was teetering right on the edge of falling in love.

Chapter Seven

Mid-November had stripped the leaves from the trees. There was a beauty even in this, Nell had decided. Beauty in the dark, denuded branches, in the papery rustle of dried leaves along the curbs, in the frost that shimmered like diamond dust on the grass in the mornings.

She caught herself staring out of the window too often, wishing for snow like a child hoping for a school holiday.

It felt wonderful. Wonderful to anticipate the winter, to remember the fall. She often thought about Halloween night, and all the children who had come knocking on her door dressed as pirates and princesses. She remembered the way Zeke and Zack had giggled when she pretended not to recognize them in the elaborate astronaut costumes Mac had fashioned for them.

She found herself reminiscing about the bluegrass concert Mac had taken her to. Or the fun they'd had when she ran into him and the boys at the mall just last week, all of them on a mission to complete their Christmas lists early.

Now, strolling past the house Mac was remodeling, she thought of him again. It had been so sweet, the way he'd struggled over chosing just the right outfit for Kim's present. No thoughtless gifts from Macauley Taylor for those he cared about. It had to be the right color, the right style.

She'd come to believe everything about him was right.

She passed the house, drawing in the chilly air of evening, her mood buoyant. That afternoon she'd been proud to announce that two of her students would participate in all-state chorus.

She had made a difference, Nell thought, shutting her eyes on the pleasure of it. Not just the prestige, certainly not simply the delight of having the principal congratulate her. The difference, the important one, had been the look on her students' faces. The pride, not just on Kim's face and that of the tenor who would go to all-state with her. But on the faces of the entire chorus. They all shared in the triumph, because over the past few weeks they had become a team.

Her team. Her kids.

"It's cold for walking."

Nell jolted, tensed, then laughed at herself when she saw Mac step away from the shadow of a tree in his sister's yard. "Lord, you gave me a start. I nearly went into my repel-the-mugger stance."

"Taylor's Grove's a little sparse when it comes to muggers. Are you going to see Mira?"

"No, actually, I was just out walking. Too much energy to stay in." The smile lit her face. "You've heard the good news?"

"Congratulations."

"It's not me—"

"Yeah, it is. A lot of it." It was the only way he knew to tell her how proud he was of what she'd done. He glanced back toward the house, where lights gleamed. "Mira and Kim are in there crying."

"Crying? But—"

"Not that kind of crying." Female tears always embarrassed him. He shrugged. "You know, the other kind."

"Oh." In response, Nell felt her own eyes sting. "That's nice."

"Dave's going around with a big fat grin on his face. He was talking to his parents when I ducked out. Mira's already called ours, as well as every other friend and relative in the country."

"Well, it's a big deal."

"I know it is." His teeth flashed. "I've made a few calls myself. You must be feeling pretty pleased with yourself."

"You bet I am. Seeing the kids today when I made the announcement . . . well, it was the best. And it's a hell of a kickoff for our fund-raiser." She shivered as the wind shuddered through the trees.

"You're getting cold. I'll drive you home."

"That'd be nice. I keep waiting for snow."

In the way of every countryman since Adam, he sniffed the air, checked out the sky. "You won't have to wait much longer." He opened the truck door for her. "The kids have already gotten their sleds out."

"I might buy one for myself." She settled back, relaxed. "Where are the boys?"

"There's a sleepover at one of their friends'." He gestured toward the house across the street from Mira's. "I just dropped them off."

"They must be thinking a lot about Christmas now, with snow in the air."

"It's funny. Usually right after Halloween they start barraging me with lists and pictures of toys from catalogs, stuff they see on TV." He turned the truck and headed for the square. "This year they told me Santa's taking care of it. I know they want bikes." His brow creased. "That's all I've heard. They've been whispering together about something else, but they clam up when I come around."

"That's Christmas," Nell said easily. "It's the best time for whispers and secrets. What about you?" She turned to smile at him. "What do you want for Christmas?"

"More than the two hours' sleep I usually get."

"You can do better than that."

"When the kids come downstairs in the morning, and their faces light up, I've got all I want." He stopped in front of her apartment. "Are you going back to New York for the holiday?"

"No, there's nothing there."

"Your family?"

"I'm an only child. My parents usually spend the holiday in the Caribbean. Do you want to come in, have some coffee?"

It was a much more appealing idea than going home to an empty house. "Yeah, thanks." When they started up the stairs, he tried to swing tactfully back to the holidays and her family. "Is that where you spent Christmas as a kid? In the Caribbean?"

"No. We had a fairly traditional setting in Philadelphia. Then I went to school in New York, and they moved to Florida." She opened the door and took off her coat. "We aren't very close, really. They weren't terribly happy with my decision to study music."

"Oh." He tossed his jacket over hers while she moved into the kitchen to put on the coffee. "I guess that's why you got so steamed about Junior."

"Maybe. They didn't really disapprove so much as they were baffled. We get along much better long-distance." She glanced over her shoulder. "I think that's why I admire you."

He stopped studying the rosewood music box on a table and stared at her. "Me?"

"Your interest and involvement with your children, your whole family. It's so solid, so natural." Tossing back her hair, she reached into the cookie jar and began to spread cookies on a plate. "Not everyone is as willing, or as able, to put in so much time and attention. Not everyone loves as well, or as thoroughly." She smiled. "Now I've embarrassed you."

"No. Yes," he admitted, and took one of the cookies. "You haven't asked about their mother." When she said nothing, Mac found himself talking. "I was just out of college when I met her. She was a secretary in my father's real estate office. She was beautiful. I mean eye-popping beautiful, the kind that bowls you over. We went out a couple of times, we went to bed, she got pregnant."

The flat-voiced recitation had Nell looking up. Mac bit into the cookie, tasting bitterness. "I know that sounds like she did it on her own. I was young, but I was old enough to know what I was doing, old enough to be responsible."

He had always taken his responsibilities seriously, Nell thought, and he always would. You only had to look at him to see the dependability.

"You didn't say anything about love."

"No, I didn't." It was something he didn't take lightly. "I was attracted, so was she. Or I thought she was. What I didn't know was that she'd lied about using birth control. It wasn't until after I'd married her that I found out she'd set out to 'snag the boss's son.' Her words," he added. "Angie saw an opportunity to improve her standard of living."

It surprised him that even now, after all this time, it hurt both pride and heart to know he'd been so carelessly used.

"To make a long story short," he continued, in that same expressionless tone, "she hadn't counted on twins, or the hassle of motherhood. So, about a month after the boys were born, she cleaned out my bank account and split."

"I'm so sorry, Mac," Nell murmured. She wished she knew the words, the gesture, that would erase that cool dispassion from his eyes. "It must have been horrible for you."

"It could have been worse." His eyes met Nell's briefly before he shrugged it off. "I could have loved her. She contacted me once, telling me she wanted me to foot the bill for the divorce. In exchange for that, I could have the kids free and clear. Free and clear," he repeated. "As if they were stocks and bonds instead of children. I took her up on it. End of story."

"Is it?" Nell moved to him, took his hands in hers. "Even if you didn't love her, she hurt you."

She rose on her toes to kiss his cheek, to soothe, to comfort. She saw the change in his eyes—and, yes, the hurt in them. It explained a great deal, she thought, to hear him tell the story. To see his face as he did. He'd been disillusioned, devastated. Instead of giving in to it, or leaning on his parents for help with the burden, he'd taken his sons and started a life with them. A life for them.

"She didn't deserve you, or the boys."

"It wasn't a hardship." He couldn't take his eyes off hers now. It wasn't the sympathy so much as the simple, unquestioning understanding that pulled at him. "They're the best part of me. I didn't mean it to sound like it was a sacrifice."

"You didn't. You don't." Her heart melted as she slid her arms around him. She'd meant that, too, as a comfort. But something more, something deeper, was stirring inside her. "You made it sound as if you love them. It's very appealing to hear a man say that he thinks of his children as a gift. And to know he means it."

He was holding her, and he wasn't quite sure how it had happened. It seemed so easy, so natural, to have her settled in his arms. "When you're given a gift, an important one, you have to be careful with it." His voice thickened with a mix of emotions. His children. Her. Something about the way she was looking up at him, the way her lips curved. He lifted a hand to stroke her hair, lingered over it a moment before he remembered to back away. "I should go."

"Stay." It was so easy, she discovered, to ask him. So easy, after all, to need him. "You know I want you to stay. You know I want you."

He couldn't take his eyes off her face, and the need was so much bigger, so much sweeter, than he'd ever imagined. "It could complicate things, Nell. I've got a lot of baggage. Most of it's in storage, but—"

"I don't care." Her breath trembled out. "I don't even have any pride at the moment. Make love with me, Mac." On a sigh, she pulled his head down and pressed her lips to his. "Just love me tonight."

He couldn't resist. It was a fantasy that had begun to wind through him, body and mind, the moment he first met her. She was all softness, all warmth. He'd done without both of those miraculous female gifts for so long.

Now, with her mouth on his and her arms twined around him, she was all he could want.

He'd never considered himself romantic. He wondered if a woman like Nell would prefer candlelight, soft music, perfumed air. But the scene was already set. He could do nothing more than lift her into his arms and carry her to the bedroom.

He turned on a lamp, surprised at how suddenly his nerves vanished when he saw hers reflected in her eyes.

"I've thought about this a long time," he told her. "I want to see you, every minute I'm touching you. I want to see you."

"Good." She looked up at him and his smile soothed away some of her tension. "I want to see you."

He carried her to the bed and lay down beside her, stroking a hand through her hair, over her shoulders. Then he dipped his head to kiss her.

It was so easy, as if they had shared nights and intimacy for years. It was so thrilling, as if each of them had come to the bed as innocent as a babe.

A touch, a taste, patient and lingering. A murmur, a sigh, soft and quiet. His hands never rushed, only pleasured, stroking over her, unfastening buttons, pausing to explore.

Her skin quivered under his caress even as it heated. A hundred pulse points thrummed, speeding at the brush of a fingertip, the flick of a tongue. Her own hands trembled, pulling a laughing groan from her that ended on a broken whimper when she at last found flesh.

Making love. The phrase had never been truer to her. For here was an exquisite tenderness mixed with a lustful curiosity that overpowered the senses, tangled in the system like silken knots. Each time his mouth returned to hers, it went deeper, wider, higher, so that he was all that existed for her. All that needed to.

She gave with a depthless generosity that staggered him. She fit, body to body, with him, with a perfection that thrilled. Each time he thought his control would slip, he found himself sliding easily back into the rhythm they set.

Slow, subtle, savoring.

She was small, delicately built. The fragility he sensed made his hands all the more tender. Even as she arched and cried out the first time, he didn't hurry. It was gloriously arousing for him simply to watch her face, that incredibly expressive face, as every emotion played over it.

He fought back the need to bury himself inside her, clung to control long enough to protect them both. Their eyes locked when at last he slipped into her. Her breath caught and released, and then her lips curved.

Outside, the wind played against the windows, making a music like sleigh bells. And the first snow of the season began to fall as quietly as a wish.

Chapter Eight

He couldn't get enough of her. Mac figured at worst it was a kind of insanity, at best a temporary obsession. No matter how many demands there were on his time, his brain, his emotions, he still found odd moments, day and night, to think about Nell.

Though he knew it was cynical, he wished it could have been just sex. If it was only sex, he could put it down to hormones and get back to business. But he didn't just imagine her in bed, or fantasize about finding an hour to lose himself in that trim little body.

Sometimes, when she slipped into his head, she was standing in front of a group of children, directing their voices with her hands, her arms, her whole self. Or she'd be seated at the piano, with his boys on either side of her, laughing with them. Or she'd just be walking through town, with her hands in her pockets and her face lifted toward the sky.

She scared him right down to the bone.

And she, he thought as he measured his baseboard trim, she was so easy about the whole thing. That was a woman for you, he decided. They didn't have to worry about making the right moves, saying the right thing. They just had to... to be, he thought. That was enough to drive a man crazy.

He couldn't afford to be crazy. He had kids to raise, a business to run. Hell, he had laundry to do if he ever got home. And damn it, he'd forgotten to take the chicken out of the freezer again.

They'd catch burgers on the way to the concert, he told himself. He had enough on his mind without having to fix dinner. Christmas was barreling toward him, and the kids were acting strange.

Just the bikes, Dad, they told him. Santa's making them, and he's taking care of the big present.

What big present? Mac wondered. No interrogation, no tricks, had pulled out that particular answer. For once his kids were closed up tight. That was an idea that disturbed him. He knew that in another year, two if he was lucky, they'd begin to question and doubt the existence of Santa and magic. The end of innocence. Whatever it was they were counting on for Christmas morning, he wanted to see that they found it under the tree.

But they just grinned at him when he prodded and told him it was a surprise for all three of them.

He'd have to work on it. Mac hammered the trim into place. At least they'd gotten the tree up and baked some cookies, strung the popcorn. He felt a little twinge of guilt over the fact that he'd evaded Nell's offer to help with the decorating. And ignored the kids when they asked if she could come over and trim the tree with them.

Was he the only one who could see what a mistake it would be to have his children become too attached? She'd only been in town for a few months. She could leave at any time. Nell might find them cute, attractive kids, but she didn't have any investment in them.

Damn it, now *he* was making them sound like stocks and bonds.

It wasn't what he meant, Mac assured himself. He simply wasn't going to allow anyone to walk out on his sons again.

He wouldn't risk it, not for anything in heaven or on earth.

After nailing the last piece of baseboard in place, he nodded in approval. The house was coming together just fine. He knew what he was doing there. Just as he knew what he was doing with the boys.

He only wished he had a better idea of what to do with Nell.

"Maybe it'll happen tonight." Zeke watched his breath puff out like smoke as he and his twin sat in the tree house, wrapped against the December chill in coats and scarves.

"It's not Christmas yet."

"But it's the Christmas concert," Zeke said stubbornly. He was tired of waiting for the mom. "That's where we saw her first. And they'll have the music and the tree and stuff, so it'll be like Christmas."

"I don't know." Zack liked the idea, a lot, but was more cautious. "Maybe, but we don't get any presents until Christmas."

"We do, too. When Mr. Perkins pretends to be Santa at the party at the firehouse. That's whole weeks before Christmas, and he gives all the kids presents."

"Not *real* presents. Not stuff you ask for." But Zack set his mind to it. "Maybe if we wish real hard. Dad likes her a lot. Aunt Mira was telling Uncle Dave that Dad's found the right woman even if he doesn't know it." Zack's brow creased. "How could he not know it if he found her?"

"Aunt Mira's always saying stuff that doesn't make sense," Zeke said, with the easy disdain of the young. "Dad's going to marry her, and she's going to come live with us and be the mom. She has to be. We've been good, haven't we?"

"Uh-huh." Zack played with the toe of his boot. "Do you think she'll love us and all that?"

"Probably." Zeke shot his twin a look. "I love her already."

"Me too." Zack smiled in relief. Everything was going to be okay after all.

* * *

"All right, people." Nell pitched her voice above the din in the chorus room. It doubled as backstage on concert nights, and students were swarming around, checking clothes, makeup and hair and working off preperformance jitters by talking at the top of their lungs. "Settle down."

One of her students had his head between his knees, fighting off acute stage fright. Nell sent him a sympathetic smile as her group began to quiet.

"You've all worked really hard for tonight. I know a lot of you are jumpy because you have friends and family out in the audience. Use the nerves to sharpen your performance. Please try to remember to go out onstage in the organized, dignified manner we've practiced."

There were some snickers at that. Nell merely lifted a brow. "I should have said remember to be more dignified and more orderly than you've managed at practice. Diaphragms," she said. "Projection. Posture. Smiles." She paused, lifted a hand. "And above all, I expect you to remember the most vital ingredient in tonight's performance. Enjoy it," she said, and grinned. "It's Christmas. Now let's go knock 'em dead."

Her heart was doing some pretty fancy pumping of its own as she directed the children onstage, watched them take their positions on the risers as the murmurs from the audience rose and ebbed. For many, Nell knew, this concert would be her first test. Decisions from the community would be made tonight as to whether the school board had made a good or a bad choice in their new music teacher.

She took a deep breath, tugged at the hem of her velvet jacket and stepped onstage.

There was polite applause as she approached the solo mike.

"Welcome to Taylor's Grove High School's holiday concert," she began.

"Gosh, Dad, doesn't Miss Davis look pretty?"

"Yeah, Zack, she does." *Lovely* was more the word, he thought, in that soft-looking deep forest green suit, with holly berries in her hair and a quick, nervous smile on her face.

She looked terrific in the spotlight. He wondered if she knew it.

At the moment, all Nell knew was nerves. She wished she could see faces clearly. She'd always preferred seeing her audience when she was performing. It made it more intimate, more fun. After her announcement, she turned, saw every student's eyes on hers, then smiled in reassurance.

"Okay, kids," she murmured, in an undertone only they could hear. "Let's rock."

She started them off with a bang, the Springsteen number, and it had eyes popping wide in the audience. This was not the usual yawn-inspiring program most had been expecting.

When the applause hit, Nell felt the tension dissolve. They'd crossed the first hurdle. She segued from the fun to the traditional, thrilled when the auditorium filled with the harmony on "Cantate Domine," delighted when her sopranos soared on "Adeste Fideles," grinning when they bounced into "Jingle Bell Rock," complete with the little stage business of swaying and hand clapping they'd worked on.

And her heart swelled when Kim approached the mike and the first pure notes of her solo flowed into the air.

"Oh, Dave." Sniffling, Mira clutched her husband's hand, then Mac's. "Our baby."

Nell's prediction had been on target. When Kim stepped back in position, there were damp eyes in every row. They closed the concert with "Silent Night," only voices, no piano. The way it was meant to be sung, Nell had told her students. The way it was written to be sung.

When the last note died and she turned to gesture to her chorus, the audience was already on its feet. The kick of it jolted through her as she turned her head, saw the slack jaws, wide eyes and foolish grins of her students.

Nell swallowed tears, waiting until the noise abated slightly before crossing to the mike again. She knew how to play it.

"They were terrific, weren't they?"

As she'd hoped, that started the cheers and applause all over again. She waited it out.

"I'd like to thank you all for coming, for supporting the chorus. I owe a special thanks to the parents of the singers onstage tonight for their patience, their understanding, and their willingness to let me share their children for a few hours every day. Every student onstage has worked tremendously hard for tonight, and I'm delighted that you appreciate their talent, and their effort. I'd like to add that the poinsettias you see onstage were donated by Hill Florists and are for sale at three dollars a pot. Proceeds to go to the fund for new choir uniforms. Merry Christmas, and come back."

Before she could step away from the mike, Kim and Brad were standing on either side of her.

"There's just one more thing." Brad cleared his throat until the rustling in the audience died down. "The chorus would like to present a token of appreciation to Miss Davis for all her work and encouragement. Ah..." Kim had written the speech out, but Brad had been designated to say it. He fumbled a little, grinned self-consciously at Kim. "This is Miss Davis's first concert at Taylor High. Ah..." He just couldn't remember all the nice words Kim had written, so he said what he felt. "She's the best. Thanks, Miss Davis."

"We hope you like it," Kim murmured under the applause as she handed Nell a brightly wrapped box. "All the kids chipped in."

"I'm..." She didn't know what to say, was afraid to try. When she opened the box, she stared, misty-eyed, down at a pin shaped like a treble clef.

"We know you like jewelry," Kim began. "So we thought—"

"It's beautiful. It's perfect." Taking a steadying breath, she turned to the chorus. "Thanks. It means almost as much to me as you do. Merry Christmas."

"She got a present," Zack pointed out. They were waiting in the crowded corridor outside the auditorium to congratulate Kim. "That means we could get one tonight. We could get her."

"Not if she goes home right after." Zack had already worked this out. He was waiting for his moment. When he saw her, he pounced. "Miss Davis! Over here, Miss Davis!"

Mac didn't move. Couldn't. Something had happened while he sat three rows back, watching her on the stage. Seeing her smile, seeing tears in her eyes. Just seeing her.

He was in love with her. It was nothing he'd ever experienced. Nothing he knew how to handle. Running seemed the smartest solution, but he didn't think he could move.

"Hi!" She crouched down for hugs, squeezing the boys tight, kissing each cheek. "Did you like the concert?"

"It was real good. Kim was the best."

Nell leaned close to Zeke's ear. "I think so, too, but it has to be a secret."

"We're good at keeping secrets." He smiled smugly at his brother. "We've had one for weeks and weeks."

"Can you come to our house now, Miss Davis?" Zack clung to her hand and put all his charm into his eyes. "Please? Come see our tree and the lights. We put lights everywhere so you can see them from all the way down on the road."

"I'd like that." Testing the water, she glanced up at Mac. "But your dad might be tired."

He wasn't tired, he was flattened. Her lashes were still damp, and the little pin the kids had given her glinted against her velvet jacket. "You're welcome to come out, if you don't mind the drive."

"I'd like it. I'm still wired up." She straightened, searching for some sign of welcome or rebuff in Mac's face. "If you're sure it isn't a bad time."

"No." His tongue was thick, he realized. As if he'd been drinking. "I want to talk to you."

"I'll head out as soon as I'm finished here, then." She winked at the boys and melted back into the crowd.

"She's done wonders with those kids." Mrs. Hollis nodded to Mac. "It'll be a shame to lose her."

"Lose her?" Mac glanced down at his boys, but they were already in a huddle, exchanging whispers. "What do you mean?"

"I heard from Mr. Perkins, who got it from Addie McVie at the high school office, that Nell Davis was offered her old position back at that New York school starting next fall. Nell and the principal had themselves a conference just this morning." Mrs. Hollis babbled on as Mac stared blankly over her head. "Hate to think about her leaving us. Made a difference with these kids." She spied one of her gossip buddies and elbowed her way through the crowd.

Chapter Nine

Control came easily to Mac—or at least it had for the past seven years. He used all the control at his disposal to keep his foul mood and bubbling temper from the boys.

They were so excited about her coming, he thought bitterly. Wanted to make certain all the lights were lit, the cookies were out, the decorative bell was hung on Zark's collar.

They were in love with her, too, he realized. And that made it a hell of a mess.

He should have known better. He *had* known better. Somehow he'd let it happen anyway. Let himself slip, let himself fall. And he'd dragged his kids along with him.

Well, he'd have to fix it, wouldn't he? Mac got himself a beer, tipped the bottle back. He was good at fixing things.

"Ladies like wine," Zack informed him. "Like Aunt Mira does."

He remembered Nell had sipped white wine at Mira's party. "I don't have any," he muttered.

Because his father looked unhappy, Zack hugged Mac's leg. "You can buy some before she comes over next time."

Reaching down, Mac cupped his son's upturned face. The love was so strong, so vital, Mac could all but feel it grip him by the throat. "Always got an answer, don't you, pal?"

"You like her, don't you, Dad?"

"Yeah, she's nice."

"And she likes us, too, right?"

"Hey, who wouldn't like the Taylor guys?" He sat at the kitchen table, pulled Zack into his lap. He'd discovered when his sons were infants that there was nothing more magical than holding your own child. "Most of the time *I* even like you."

That made Zack giggle and cuddle closer. "She has to live all by herself, though." Zack began to play with the buttons of his father's shirt. A sure sign, Mac knew, that he was leading up to something.

"Lots of people live alone."

"We've got a big house, and two whole rooms nobody sleeps in except when Grandma and Pop come to visit."

His radar was humming. Mac tugged on his son's ear. "Zack, what are you getting at?"

"Nothing." Lip poked out, Zack toyed with another button. "I was just wondering what it would be like if she came and lived here." He peeked up under his lashes. "So she wouldn't be lonely."

"Nobody said she was lonely," Mac pointed out. "And I think you should—"

The doorbell rang, sending the dog into a fit of excited barking and jingling. Zeke flew into the kitchen, dancing from foot to foot. "She's here! She's here!"

"I got the picture." Mac ruffled Zack's hair, set him on his feet. "Well, let her in. It's cold out."

"I'll do it!"

"*I'll* do it!"

The twins had a fierce race through the house to the front door. They hit it together, fought over the knob, then all but dragged Nell over the threshold once they'd yanked the door open.

"You took so long," Zeke complained. "We've been waiting forever. I put on Christmas music. Hear? And we've got the tree lit and everything."

"So I see." It was a lovely room, one she tried not to resent having only now been invited into.

She knew Mac had built most of the house himself. He'd told her that much. He'd created an open, homey space, with lots of wood, a glass-fronted fireplace where stockings were already hung. The tree, a six-foot blue spruce, was wildly decorated and placed with pride in front of the wide front window.

"It's terrific." Letting the boys pull her along, Nell crossed over to give the tree a closer look. "Really wonderful. It makes the little one in my apartment look scrawny."

"You can share ours." Zack looked up at her, his heart in his eyes. "We can get you a stocking and everything, and have your name put on it."

"They do it at the mall," Zeke told her. "We'll get you a big one."

Now they were pulling at her heart, as well as her hands. Filled with the emotion of the moment, she crouched down to hug them to her. "You guys are the best." She laughed as Zark pushed in for attention. "You too." Her arms full of kids and dog, she looked up to smile at Mac as he stepped in from the kitchen. "Hi. Sorry I took so long. Some of the kids hung around, wanting to go over every mistake and triumph of the concert."

She shouldn't look so right, so perfect, snuggling his boys under the tree. "I didn't hear any mistakes."

"They were there. But we'll work on them."

She scooted back, sitting on a hassock and taking both boys with her. As if, Mac thought, she meant to keep them.

"We don't have any wine," Zack informed her solemnly. "But we have milk and juice and sodas and beer. Lots of other things. Or..." He cast a crafty look in his father's direction. "Somebody could make hot cocoa."

"One of my specialties." Nell stood to shrug out of her coat. "Where's the kitchen?"

"I'll make it," Mac muttered.

"I'll help." Baffled by his sudden distance, she walked to him. "Or don't you like women in your kitchen?"

"We don't get many around here. You looked good up onstage."

"Thanks. It felt good being there."

He looked past her, into the wide, anticipation-filled eyes of his children. "Why don't you two go change into your pajamas? The cocoa'll be finished by the time you are."

"We'll be faster," Zeke vowed, and shot toward the stairs.

"Only if you throw your clothes on the floor. And don't." He turned back into the kitchen.

"Will they hang them up, or push them under the bed?" Nell asked.

"Zack'll hang them up and they'll fall on the floor. Zeke'll push them under the bed."

She laughed, watching him get out milk and cocoa. "I meant to tell you, a few days ago they came in with Kim to rehearsal. They'd switched sweaters—you know, the color code. I really impressed them when I knew who was who anyway."

He paused in the act of measuring cocoa into a pan. "How did you?"

"I guess I didn't think about it. They're each their own person. Facial expressions. You know how Zeke's eyes narrow and Zack looks under his lashes when they're pleased about something. Inflections in the voice." She opened a cupboard at random, looking for mugs. "Posture. There are all sorts of little clues if you pay attention and look closely enough. Ah, found them." Pleased with herself, she took out four mugs and set them on the counter. She tilted her head when she saw him studying her. Analytically, she thought. As if she were something to be measured and fit into place. "Is something wrong?"

"I wanted to talk to you." He busied himself with heating the cocoa.

"So you said." She found she needed to steady herself with a hand on the counter. "Mac, am I misreading something, or are you pulling back?"

"I don't know that I'd call it that."

Something was going to hurt. Nell braced for it. "What would you call it?" she said, as calmly as she could.

"I'm a little concerned about the boys. About the fallout when you move on. They're getting too involved." Why did that sound so stupid? he wondered. Why did he feel so stupid?

"*They* are?"

"I think we've been sending the wrong signals, and it would be best for them if we backed off." He concentrated on the cocoa as if it were a nuclear experiment. "We've gone out a few times, and we've..."

"Slept together," she finished, cool now. It was the last defense.

He looked around, sharply. But he could still hear the stomping of little feet in the room overhead. "Yeah. We've slept together, and it was great. The thing is, kids pick up on more things than most people think. And they get ideas. They get attached."

"And you don't want them to get attached to me." Yes, she realized. It was going to hurt. "You don't want to get attached."

"I just think it would be a mistake to take it any further."

"Clear enough. The No Trespassing signs are back up, and I'm out."

"It's not like that, Nell." He set the spoon down, took a step toward her. But there was a line he couldn't quite cross. A line he'd created himself. If he didn't make certain they both stayed on their own sides of it, the life he'd so carefully built could crumble. "I've got things under control here, and I need to keep them that way. I'm all they've got. They're all I've got. I can't mess that up."

"No explanations necessary." Her voice had thickened. In a moment, she knew, it would begin to shake. "You made it clear from the beginning. Crystal-clear. Funny, the first time you invite me into your home, it's to toss me out."

"I'm not tossing you out, I'm trying to realign things."

"Oh, go to hell, and keep your realignments for your houses." She sprinted out of the kitchen.

''Nell, don't go like this.'' But by the time he reached the living room, she was grabbing her coat, and his boys were racing down the stairs.

''Where are you going, Miss Davis? You haven't—'' Both boys stopped, shocked by the tears streaming down her face.

''I'm sorry.'' It was too late to hide them, so she kept heading for the door. ''I have to do something. I'm sorry.''

And she was gone, with Mac standing impotently in the living room and both boys staring at him. A dozen excuses spun around in his head. Even as he tried to grab one, Zack burst into tears.

''She went away. You made her cry, and she went away.''

''I didn't mean to. She—'' He moved to gather his sons up and was met with a solid wall of resistance.

''You ruined everything.'' A tear spilled out of Zeke's eyes, heated by temper. ''We did everything we were supposed to, and you ruined it.''

''She'll never come back.'' Zack sat on the bottom step and sobbed. ''She'll never be the mom now.''

''What?'' At his wits' end, Mac dragged his hand through his hair. ''What are you two talking about?''

''You ruined it,'' Zeke said again.

''Look, Miss Davis and I had a . . . disagreement. People have disagreements. It's not the end of the world.'' He wished it didn't feel like the end of his world.

''Santa sent her.'' Zack rubbed his eyes with his fists. ''He sent her, just like we asked him. And now she's gone.''

''What do you mean, Santa sent her?'' Determined, Mac sat on the steps. He pulled a reluctant Zack into his lap and tugged Zeke down to join them. ''Miss Davis came from New York to teach music, not from the North Pole.''

''We know that.'' Temper set aside, Zeke sought comfort, turning his face into his father's chest. ''She came because we sent Santa a letter, months and months ago, so we'd be early and he'd have time.''

''Have time for what?''

"To pick out the mom." On a shuddering sigh, Zack sniffed and looked up at his father. "We wanted someone nice, who smelled good and liked dogs and had yellow hair. And we asked, and she came. And you were supposed to marry her and make her the mom."

Mac let out a long breath and prayed for wisdom. "Why didn't you tell me you were thinking about having a mother?"

"Not *a* mom," Zeke told him. "*The* mom. Miss Davis is the mom, but she's gone now. We love her, and she won't like us anymore because you made her cry."

"Of course she'll still like you." She'd hate him, but she wouldn't take it out on the boys. "But you two are old enough to know you don't get moms from Santa."

"He sent her, just like we asked him. We didn't ask for anything else but the bikes." Zack burrowed into his lap. "We didn't ask for any toys or any games. Just the mom. Make her come back, Dad. Fix it. You always fix it."

"It doesn't work like that, pal. People aren't broken toys or old houses. Santa didn't send her, she moved here for a job."

"He did too send her." With surprising dignity, Zack pushed off his father's lap. "Maybe you don't want her, but we do."

His sons walked up the stairs, a united front that closed him out. Mac was left with emptiness in the pit of his stomach and the smell of burned cocoa.

Chapter Ten

She should get out of town for a few days, Nell thought. Go somewhere. Go anywhere. There was nothing more pathetic than sitting alone on Christmas Eve and watching other people bustle along the street outside your window.

She'd turned down every holiday party invitation, made excuses that sounded hollow even to her. She was brooding, she admitted, and it was entirely unlike her. But then again, she'd never had a broken heart to nurse before.

With Bob it had been wounded pride. And that had healed itself with embarrassing speed.

Now she was left with bleeding emotions at the time of year when love was most important.

She missed him. Oh, she hated to know that she missed him. That slow, hesitant smile, the quiet voice, the gentleness of him. In New York, at least, she could have lost herself in the crowds, in the rush. But here, everywhere she looked was another reminder.

Go somewhere, Nell. Just get in the car and drive.

She ached to see the children. Wondered if they'd taken their sleds out in the fresh snow that had fallen yesterday. Were they counting the hours until Christmas, plotting to stay awake until they heard reindeer on the roof?

She had presents for them, wrapped and under her tree. She'd send them via Kim or Mira, she thought, and was miserable all over again because she wouldn't see their faces as they tore off the wrappings.

They're not your children, she reminded herself. On that point Mac had always been clear. Sharing himself had been difficult enough. Sharing his children had stopped him dead.

She would go away, she decided, and forced herself to move. She would pack a bag, toss it in the car and drive until she felt like stopping. She'd take a couple of days. Hell, she'd take a week. She couldn't bear to stay here alone through the holidays.

For the next ten minutes, she tossed things into a suitcase without any plan or sense of order. Now that the decision was made, she only wanted to move quickly. She closed the lid on the suitcase, carried it into the living room and started for her coat.

The knock on her door had her clenching her teeth. If one more well-meaning neighbor stopped by to wish her Merry Christmas and invite her to dinner, she was going to scream.

She opened the door and felt the fresh wound stab through her. "Well, Macauley... Out wishing your tenants happy holidays?"

"Can I come in?"

"Why?"

"Nell." There was a wealth of patience in the word. "Please, let me come in."

"Fine, you own the place." She turned her back on him. "Sorry, I haven't any wassail, and I'm very low on good cheer."

"I need to talk to you." He'd been trying to find the right way and the right words for days.

"Really? Excuse me if I don't welcome it. The last time you needed to talk to me is still firmly etched in my mind."

"I didn't mean to make you cry."

"I cry easily. You should see me after a greeting-card commercial on TV." She couldn't keep up the snide comments, and she gave in, asking the question that was uppermost in her mind. "How are the kids?"

"Barely speaking to me." At her blank look, he gestured toward the couch. "Will you sit down? This is kind of a complicated story."

"I'll stand. I don't have a lot of time, actually. I was just leaving."

His gaze followed hers and landed on the suitcase. His mouth tightened. "Well, it didn't take long."

"What didn't?"

"I guess you took them up on that offer to teach back in New York."

"Word does travel. No, I didn't take them up. I like my job here, I like the people here, and I intend to stay. I'm just going on a holiday."

"You're going on a holiday at five o'clock on Christmas Eve?"

"I can come and go as I please. No, don't take off your coat," she snapped. Tears were threatening. "Just say your piece and get out. I still pay the rent here. On second thought, just leave now. Damn it, you're not going to make me cry again."

"The boys think Santa sent you."

"Excuse me?"

As the first tear spilled over, he moved to her, brushed it away with his thumb. "Don't cry, Nell. I hate knowing I made you cry."

"Don't touch me." She whirled away and fumbled a tissue out of the box.

He was discovering exactly how it felt to be sliced in two. "I'm sorry." Slowly he lowered his hand to his side. "I know how you must feel about me now."

"You don't know the half of it." She blew her nose, struggled for control. "What's this about the boys and Santa?"

"They wrote a letter back in the fall, not long before they met you. They decided they wanted a mom for Christmas. Not *a* mom," Mac explained as she turned back to stare at him. "*The* mom. They keep correcting me on that one. They had pretty specific ideas about what they wanted. She was supposed to have yellow hair and smile a lot, like kids and dogs and bake cookies. They wanted bikes, too, but that was sort of an afterthought. All they really wanted was the mom.''

"Oh." She did sit now, lowering herself onto the arm of the sofa. ''That explains a couple of things.'' Steadying herself, she looked back at him. ''Put you in quite a spot, didn't it? I know you love them, Mac, but starting a relationship with me to try to please your children takes things beyond parental devotion.''

''I didn't know. Damn it, do you think I'd play with their feelings, or yours, that way?''

''Not theirs,'' she said hollowly. ''Certainly not theirs.''

He remembered how delicate she had seemed when they made love. There was more fragility now. No roses in her cheeks, he saw with a pang of distress. No light in her eyes. ''I know what it's like to be hurt, Nell. I never would have hurt you deliberately. They didn't tell me about the letter until the night... You weren't the only one I made cry that night. I tried to explain that Santa doesn't work that way, but they've got it fixed in their heads that he sent you.''

''I'll talk to them if you want me to.''

''I don't deserve—''

''Not for you,'' she said. ''For them.''

He nodded, accepting. ''I wondered how it would make you feel to know they wished for you.''

''Don't push me, Mac.''

He couldn't help it, and he kept his eyes on hers as he moved closer. ''They wished for you for me, too. That's why they didn't tell me. You were our Christmas present.'' He reached down, touched her hair. ''How does that make you feel?''

''How do you think I feel?'' She batted his hand away and rose to face the window. ''It hurts. I fell in love with the three of you almost from the first glance, and it hurts. Go away, leave me alone.''

Somehow a fist had crept into his chest and was squeezing at his heart. ''I thought you'd go away. I thought you'd leave us alone. I wouldn't let myself believe you cared enough to stay."

"Then you were an idiot," she mumbled.

"I was clumsy." He watched the tiny lights on her tree shining in her hair and gave up any thought of saving himself. "All right, I was an idiot. The worst kind, because I kept hiding from what you might feel, from what I felt. I didn't fall in love with you right away. At least I didn't know it. Not until the night of the concert. I wanted to tell you. I didn't know how to tell you. Then I heard something about the New York offer and it was the perfect excuse to push you out. I thought I was protecting the kids from getting hurt." No, he wouldn't use them, he thought in disgust. Not even to get her back. "That was only part of it. I was protecting myself. I couldn't control the way I felt about you. It scared me."

"Now's no different from then, Mac."

"It could be different." He took a chance and laid his hands on her shoulders, turned her to face him. "It took my own sons to show me that sometimes you've just got to wish. Don't leave me, Nell. Don't leave us."

"I was never going anywhere."

"Forgive me." She started to turn her head away, but he cupped her cheek, held it gently. "Please. Maybe I can't fix this, but give me a chance to try. I need you in my life. We need you."

There was such patience in his voice, such quiet strength in the hand on her face. Even as she looked at him, her heart began to heal. "I love you. All of you. I can't help it."

Relief and gratitude flavored the kiss as he touched his lips to hers. "I love you. I don't want to help it." Drawing her close, he cradled her head on his shoulder. "It's just been the three of us for so long, I didn't know how to make room. I think I'm figuring it out." He eased her away again and reached into his coat pocket. "I bought you a present."

"Mac." Still staggered from the roller-coaster emotions, she rubbed her hands over her damp cheeks. "It isn't Christmas yet."

"Close enough. I think if you'd open it now, I'd stop having all this tightness in my chest."

"All right." She dashed another tear aside. "We'll consider it a peace offering, then. I may even decide to..." She trailed off when the box was open in her hand. A ring, the traditional single diamond crowning a gold band.

"Marry me, Nell," he said quietly. "Be the mom."

She raised dazzled eyes to his. "You move awfully quickly for someone who always seems to take his time."

"Christmas Eve." He watched her face as he took the ring out of the box. "It seemed like the night to push my luck."

"It was a good choice." Smiling, she held out her hand. "A very good choice." When the ring was on her finger, she lifted her hand to his cheek. "When?"

He should have known it would be simple. With her, it would always be simple. "New Year's Eve's only a week away. It would be a good start to a new year. A new life."

"Yes."

"Will you come home with me tonight? I left the kids at Mira's. We could pick them up, and you'd spend Christmas where you belong." Before she could answer, he smiled and kissed her hand. "You're already packed."

"So I am. It must be magic."

"I'm beginning to believe it." He framed her face with his hands, lowered his mouth for a long, lingering kiss. "Maybe I didn't wish for you, but you're all I want for Christmas, Nell."

He rubbed his cheek over her hair, looked out at the colored lights gleaming on the houses below. "Did you hear something?" he murmured.

"Mmm..." She held him close, smiled. "Sleigh bells."

*   *   *   *   *

A Recipe from Nora Roberts

I do a lot of complicated baking at this time of year. Time-consuming treats that keep me in the kitchen for hours. I really don't mind, but there's something to be said for simplicity. One of my men's favorites is an old family recipe handed down through the Scottish branch of my family, through my father to me. It's wonderfully simple and old-fashioned, something that can literally be tossed together when you discover unexpected holiday visitors are coming to call. Best of all, since it's made in one dish, there's little to clean up. I should warn you, most of the measurements are estimates. Experiment. It's that kind of dish.

OLD-FASHIONED BREAD PUDDING

6 to 8 slices bread, torn into pieces
3 to 4 eggs, lightly beaten
1/4 cup margarine, melted
1/4 to 1/3 cup sugar
3 to 3 1/2 cups milk
About 1/2 cup raisins—it's up to you
Cinnamon to taste (I like a lot myself, maybe 3 tbsp or so. I really don't measure, I go by how it looks.)

Mix all ingredients, gently but thoroughly, in a casserole dish, pop it into the oven at 400° F for 1 hour. Can be eaten warm or cold.

A Very Merry Step-Christmas

BARBARA BOSWELL

A Note from Barbara Boswell

Dear Reader,

Christmas is my favorite time of year. I love the music, the decorations, sending and receiving cards from longtime friends scattered all over the country, and even the malls overcrowded with Christmas shoppers. Christmas is also a collection of wonderful memories. My two younger sisters, Monica and Mary Jo, and I still laugh about our cats climbing the Christmas tree every year and toppling it over. Our mother took it in stride; she made sure we had unbreakable ornaments. My husband, Bill, listened and learned from that story—we've had cats since we were first married, and he has always nailed our tree to the living room floor! The cats have climbed it over the years, and it has stayed firmly in place.

During the years our daughters, Susan, Sarah and Christy, were growing up, we enjoyed the fun of baking cookies and writing letters to Santa, the Children's Mass on Christmas Eve, and then the excitement of Christmas morning. The girls loved dolls, and I feel like a toy historian, looking back on those dolls that were under the tree.

Although the magic of Santa's visits is past now, Christmas remains special to our family. We enjoy being together and catching up on everybody's current interests and activities while feasting on too many cookies! During the holiday week, we visit Bill's family in Maryland, and my sisters and their families in West Virginia and New Jersey. It's a blitz trip, but definitely worth it. We have fourteen nieces and nephews at various stages of growing up, and it's always fun to be with them.

I wish each of you a safe, healthy and happy holiday.

Barbara Boswell

Chapter One

Detention at Port Mason High School was held every afternoon in Room 3, a long windowless basement room, between the chorus and the band rooms. During the months of November and December, detainees listened to the band practice and the chorus rehearse for the high school's annual holiday show. As the band struggled with "Silver Bells" and the chorus stumbled over the words of "Angels We Have Heard on High" over and over again, Brian Ritter decided that the two-hour imprisonment in cellblock 3 was not the real punishment. Having to hear Port Mason's band and chorus, day in and day out, was a far more effective torture.

Sighing, Brian slid into his seat at the front of the classroom, directly in front of Mrs. Crawford, the eagle-eyed teacher who was scowling and slamming desk drawers, a clear indication that band practice was taking its toll on her nerves, too. He would've preferred sitting in the back, but that coveted space was reserved for juniors and seniors, the lordly upperclassmen. Freshmen like Brian were doomed to sit in front; sophomores, a rung above, claimed the middle seats.

Brian took a quick glance at the back where bulking six-footers wearing ripped denim consorted with their women, babes in Spandex with enormously high hair and heavy makeup. They seemed astonishingly mature to Brian, who was still waiting for the manly growth spurt that his father kept assuring him would occur.

The regulars in detention were not the cream-of-the-crop students at Port Mason High; they tended to be a mixture of rebels, misfits and troublemakers who merely laughed when the teachers warned them that prison was in their future. Occasionally, a "good kid" like Brian was consigned to the lockup as a disciplinary measure for being late. For the past two months he'd been late so often that he was fast becoming a regular. Worse, his fellow inmates were becoming aware of his existence. Brian knew that being the son of the town's police chief was not going to be a factor in his favor in the eyes of this crowd.

"Were you late again?" A girlish whisper punctured his reverie.

Brian turned to see Natalie Nolan, a fellow freshman, slip into the desk beside him. He nodded his head. "Now I'm stuck here all week."

"Me, too," Natalie wailed in a low voice. "I've already been suspended from cheering at the next JV basketball game because I missed too many cheerleading practices. If this keeps happening, I could get thrown off the squad!"

"Then your life would be completely ruined," Brian said dryly. Natalie amused him. Pretty, peppy types like her normally did not bother with quiet, scholarly types such as himself, but they'd forged a friendship of sorts as the youngest detention mates. Both were outsiders among the usual hard core incarcerated here.

"Yes, it would." Natalie took him seriously. "If I get kicked off the junior varsity squad, I'll never make varsity cheerleader next year. That means I won't have a prayer of making the Homecoming Court as a junior and I can just kiss my dream of being Prom Queen senior year goodbye." She glanced at the hard, painted faces of the older girls in the back of the room. "If I keep getting sent here, I might end up like them!" she whispered in horror.

"So how come you're late all the time?" Brian asked, without much interest. He waited for her to complain about the amount of time it took to choose just the right outfit and to style her long blond hair, the pressures of achieving that incomparable Natalie Nolan look.

Her answer surprised him. "I have to get my brother and sisters to school and they're always late," she said grimly. "My little sisters Molly and Megan—they're first-graders— are like zombies in the morning. They move slower than the clock during hideous world history class. I have to pull on their clothes and do their hair and keep them awake while they eat. Today Molly fell asleep in her cereal. I'm not kidding, her face went right into the milk."

Brian chuckled, imagining the sight. "Good thing you were there to pull her out or she might've drowned."

Natalie scowled. She did not appreciate his joke. "And then there's my little brother, Ned. He's ten and he manages to lose everything he needs—his shoes, his book bag, his lunch money. We run around like maniacs every morning looking for his stuff. And so we almost always miss the bus and have to walk."

"And you're almost always late," Brian concluded. "That's so weird."

"Ned and the twins aren't weird," Natalie bristled defensively. "They might be slow and forgetful and drive me crazy, but they're not weird."

"I didn't mean that. I meant it's weird because my younger sister and brothers are what makes me late almost every day." In the presence of a fellow sufferer, Brian warmed to his subject. "The youngest, Ian, he's eight, is the forgetful one. He can lose his shoes going from one room to another. Justin is eleven and he's the sleepwalker in our family. But my sister Robin is the worst of all. She's twelve, in seventh grade, and she hates middle school this year. I have to drag her there in the morning. I mean, take her by the arm and pull her into the building and she's fighting me all the way. Lately, I've had to carry her in!"

"Why does she hate school so much?" Natalie asked curiously.

"She says the other kids make fun of her, especially the girls."

Natalie sighed. "I feel sorry for her. Girls that age can be very nasty."

"Yeah," Brian agreed with feeling. "Robin has it tough. *And* she's the only girl in our house. She says nobody understands what it's like to be her."

"Sounds like my brother," said Natalie. "He's the only guy in our house."

The fourteen-year-olds looked at each other.

"Doesn't your dad live with you?" Brian asked carefully.

Natalie shook her head. "He died six years ago when I was in third grade. What about your mom? Doesn't she live with you?"

"No. She died six years ago—when I was in third grade."

Natalie and Brian stared at each other, jaws agape, their eyes round with astonishment. "Wow!" Natalie breathed softly.

"It's, like, weird," murmured Brian.

"*Very* weird," Natalie agreed.

"Quiet!" Mrs. Crawford snarled. "This is detention, not a social gathering!" She pounded the desk top with a textbook to grab the attention of the rowdy crowd in the back of the room.

They didn't quiet down at all, but Natalie and Brian fell into an intimidated silence.

Though it wasn't quite five o'clock, the winter sky was already darkening as Brian Ritter and Natalie Nolan walked along High Street, the main avenue which ran through downtown Port Mason. A cold wind rustled the branches of the trees that lined the sidewalk, and Natalie pulled her scarf tighter around her neck, shivering.

"I can't believe old Crawford actually let us out of detention early. Maybe the Christmas spirit is getting to her," Natalie remarked as they approached the shopping district. The store windows were decorated for Christmas, each competing for the Chamber of Commerce's "Best Holiday Window" prize.

"I think it was the band and the chorus that was getting to her." Brian grinned. "'Silver Bells' never sounded worse."

"Hey there, Brian," a stout, red-cheeked police officer called a greeting.

Brian waved and hoped there would be no comment on his companion. A vain hope.

"Got a pretty little girlfriend there, Brian," the policeman said jovially. "Becoming a ladies' man, are you? A regular chip off the old block, huh?"

Mortified, Brian went crimson from the top of his head to the tip of his toes. He managed a weak smile and hurried up the street. Natalie hastened her stride to keep up with him.

"Don't mind him," Brian mumbled, his voice an embarrassed growl.

"I guess all the police in town must know you. Your dad being the police chief and all."

Brian nodded his head.

"Everybody seems to know everybody in this town," Natalie continued. "When we moved here over the summer, I couldn't believe how many people knew my mom's great-aunt Edith, the one who left us her house. So many people came by to welcome us to town. We got casseroles and cookies and cakes and pies."

"Yeah, Port Mason is a friendly place," Brian admitted grudgingly. "Sometimes too friendly."

"Too bad your dad didn't come by to meet my mom," Natalie said, slanting a glance at Brian. "She's really pretty, even if she is thirty-two and has four kids. Maybe they would've, you know, like started dating or something."

Brian stopped in his tracks. "My dad is thirty-six but he doesn't seem old. He's actually pretty cool." His eyes met Natalie's and he saw his own rising excitement mirrored in hers. He knew they were on exactly the same wavelength.

"If your dad married my mom, we'd both be free," Natalie cried. "Mom could quit her stupid job at the paper and stay home with the kids. *She* could get them *all* to school in the mornings. We'd never be late again. No more detention, ever!''

"Do you think she would cook dinner at night?" Brian was wistful. "My dad hates to cook, so we either have sandwiches or frozen stuff or take-out. I'm sick of all of it."

"My mom can cook," Natalie assured him. "Although I'm doing more of it since we moved here and she has those stupid deadlines at that stupid paper," she added darkly.

"My dad wouldn't let her work," Brian boasted. "Dad thinks a woman should stay home and take care of her family." So what if he'd never actually *heard* his father say this, Brian found the idea irresistible.

So did Natalie. "Cool!" she exclaimed. "I think they'll be perfect together. And my brother will be so glad to have a dad and some brothers around. I won't have to hear him whine about how awful it is to be the only guy in the house."

"And you could help my sister Robin with her hair and her clothes and stuff. She really could use it," Brian said fervently.

"Sure, I'll help her!" Natalie beamed. "With me for a sister, she'll be the most popular girl in her class."

Brian was thrilled. Natalie Nolan knew all about popularity. She'd taken their ninth-grade class by storm since her first day at Port Mason High in September. Robin's problems with those brats in her class would be solved, his detention days would be over, his little brothers would have a mother to take care of them.

And his father would have a wife. No more dating, he'd be at home like everyone else's father. The concept of his father dating had become intolerable to Brian this past year. He cringed at the thought of his dad behaving like a teenager, dancing and joking and kissing good-night. It was embarrassing!

But somehow the idea of his father dating Natalie's mother did not conjure up such disgust. After all, they were two parents who would behave respectably and marry and live quietly ever after. He breathed a sigh of relief. "We'll be like a normal family."

Natalie nodded excitedly. "Now, all we have to do is to get them to meet." She frowned, her enthusiasm wavering a bit. "How are we going to do that?"

"I know! My godparents have this caroling party every year. They have people over to decorate their tree and go around the neighborhood singing carols. Then everybody goes back to their place and eats and sits around the fire and sings some more. I'll ask Wayne and Annie to invite your mom."

"Will you and your sister and brothers be there?"

"No kids are invited. Just adults. Dad goes every year."

"I hope my mom will go." Natalie looked doubtful. "We didn't do stuff like that in Miami. Our neighborhood wasn't the kind of place you wandered around in at night."

"Well, Port Mason is safe." Brian grinned. "And your mom will be especially safe 'cause she'll be with the police chief."

Chapter Two

Standing on the doorstep, Claudia Nolan straightened the red bow she'd tied around the gift bottle of wine she was bringing to the Smiths' caroling party. She could hear party sounds inside the house, voices talking and laughing, Christmas music playing. She felt as nervous as a school-girl; but not a schoolgirl from *this* era, she silently amended with a smile. Claudia's smile widened at the thought of her daughter. Natalie had been more excited about this unexpected invitation than she was.

"I'm glad you're going out and meeting new friends, Mom," Natalie told her as she dressed for tonight. "And if you meet a cool guy there, drag him under the mistletoe."

Claudia assured her oldest child that she would do no such thing. After all, she was a thirty-two-year-old widow and mother of four, and she did not make a practice of kissing strange men, mistletoe notwithstanding. Her thoughts drifted. It had been years since she'd been kissed. Six years and three months to be exact, the day that her husband Jeff had kissed her goodbye and driven away, expecting to return from work that evening as usual. Except he hadn't. A trucker had fallen asleep at the wheel of his rig, crossed the median strip and crashed headlong into Jeff's car, killing him instantly.

Claudia forced herself to shake off the dark memory. She was not being disloyal to Jeff's memory by going to a Christmas party, she reassured herself. Still, it was odd to realize that this was her first party since Jeff's death, excluding family gatherings and children's parties. The first *adults-only* party.

Claudia was surprised she'd been invited. She didn't know Wayne Smith, though she knew from her job with the *Press* that he was a local attorney. She had met his wife Anne only once, when she'd gone into Annie's Flower Shop and Nursery this summer to buy potting soil and mulch. She'd introduced herself as Edith Cameron's great-niece, the one who'd moved into her old house on Hopwood Lane. Annie had known Great-aunt Edith and spoke fondly of her, recalling her zest for gardening.

It seemed everybody in town knew Great-Aunt Edith; she had been a fixture in Port Mason and Claudia knew she was reaping the rewards of the old woman's lifelong friendliness. Claudia had been hired as a reporter by the *Port Mason Daily Press* because the managing editor had been Great-Aunt Edith's paperboy as a youngster and still remembered the generous tips and Christmas bonuses over the years. There were countless other courtesies extended to her, courtesy of Great-Aunt Edith's benevolence. Obviously this invitation to the Smiths' party was yet another.

Claudia squared her shoulders, curved her lips into a determined smile and rang the doorbell. She wouldn't know many people at this party, but as Edith Cameron's great-niece, she would surely be welcomed.

The door was opened by a smiling, strapping hulk of a man, wearing a patently fake white beard and a red Santa Claus hat. His tie sported blinking Christmas lights that flashed red and green at intervals.

"Ho, ho ho! Hello, lovely lady!"

"Mr. Smith?" Claudia murmured hesitantly.

"Wayne," he insisted. "Also known tonight as jolly old Saint Nick." The man grabbed her in a suffocating bear hug. Claudia gulped for air and wondered if her host had been helping himself to an ample portion of liquid Christmas cheer.

"I'm Claudia Nolan," she managed to say. Her face was still pressed against his woolly red sweater. Claudia feared she would sneeze. Using the wine bottle she was carrying as leverage, she managed to pry herself out of the man's embrace. "This is for you."

She shoved the wine into his hands, her eyes sweeping the crowd behind him. It looked more like a mob scene than a party. People were packed into every square inch of the big living room. Claudia decided that she wasn't going to stay very long. As one among hundreds, her absence would not be noted and her presence would not be missed.

"Nolan. Claudia Nolan." Wayne Smith was mulling over the name, clearly trying to place her.

That would be impossible, of course, as they'd never met. Claudia had to smile.

Wayne studied the lights of his Christmas tie, then snapped his fingers. "Okay, now I got it!" He grinned hugely. "There is somebody here who is dying to meet you, Claudia. Positively demanded that you be sent an invitation! Annie and I were only too happy to oblige."

Claudia looked at him, bemused. She had no idea what he was talking about.

"Let me take your coat." It was more a command than an offer of assistance, as Wayne fairly pulled her coat from her shoulders. Claudia barely had time to straighten her pin, a whimsical cloisonné Christmas tree, last year's gift from her children, when Wayne grabbed her arm and began to push through the crowd.

They wound their way through the huge living room, down a few steps into a smaller paneled room with a fireplace that dominated one entire wall. This room wasn't as crowded, and it was rather dark, the firelight the only illumination. Several couples were seated on the couches placed strategically throughout the room, their heads close together in deep conversation.

Wayne Smith moved so quickly that Claudia, being dragged along after him, saw her surroundings pass in a blur. Her confusion was compounded when they came to a sudden halt directly in front of a big, dark green leather recliner chair near the fireplace.

A man was sitting on the chair, staring into the flames. "Well, here she is, Zack!" Wayne's voice boomed heartily, and the man in the chair glanced up. His gaze connected with Claudia's.

She found herself staring into a pair of the deepest blue eyes she'd ever seen.

"Claudia, Zack. Zack, Claudia," Wayne pronounced, then rushed off as quickly as he'd come.

Zack rose to his feet and surveyed the blonde standing before him. This must be the "babe who is hot to meet you"—Wayne's own words that Zack had been hearing all week. According to Wayne, this woman was so intent on meeting Zack that she'd angled an invitation to tonight's party.

Zack surveyed her lazily, liking what he saw. He guessed her age as mid-twenty-something, and she was tall and slender but not so thin as to lack enticing womanly curves, which were tastefully revealed by her red jersey wool dress. Her silky blond hair was cut in a smooth straight bob that framed her face, a pretty face with soft brown eyes, a firm little chin and wide, sexy mouth. She was an alluring package indeed, but he liked her mouth and her legs best. Her lips were full and mobile, her legs long and sleek. Zack allowed himself a second to fantasize her pleasing him with those lips and those legs. A pleasant rush of heat streaked through him.

Smiling rather wolfishly, Zack offered her his hand to shake. "Wayne isn't much on introductions. He provides the minimal information and then he's outta here."

Claudia nodded weakly, staring at him. From the moment her eyes had connected with his, the circuits in her brain had abruptly disconnected. What else could explain the physical riot going on within her? She felt stunned, as if a flaming cannonball had struck her in the stomach, leaving her breathless and hot and dazed.

She was totally disconcerted, she felt like a fool. This had never happened to her before, this astonishing lack of composure, this wild internal fire.

There is somebody here who is dying to meet you. Positively demanded that you be sent an invitation! Wayne Smith's words echoed in her ears. And this man was that somebody? Claudia gazed at his charming, disarming smile, his laughing blue eyes and thick dark hair. He was wearing jeans and a white shirt, open at the collar, the sleeves rolled to the elbow, his attire displaying not a single concession to the holiday, a sharp contrast to all the reds and greens and Christmas motifs worn by the other guests, herself included.

Her eyes swept over him compulsively, gathering details. He was about six feet tall with a hard, muscular build. Claudia was amazed at herself for noticing; she was not the type to ogle men's bodies. She never had before. But then, she had never before experienced such a fierce, primitive reaction to any man.

Her heart was racing now, every feminine instinct within her responding to his compelling masculinity. Belatedly she noticed his hand held out for her to shake. Flushed and flustered, she placed her hand in his.

Claudia almost groaned. She should have guessed that touching him would send currents of sensual electricity through her and it did.

Zack was feeling it, too. Tension stretched heavily between them. A chorus of bells resounded in his head, providing a surreal, otherworldly aura until he realized it was the stereo speakers blaring out a bell ensemble of "Carol of the Bells."

"I'm very glad to meet you, Claudia." His voice was low and husky. Fierce, undisguised lust burned in his eyes.

Her response to it went sharp and deep. Claudia wondered if her own turbulent feelings were so openly revealed to him and quickly dragged her eyes from his. "I—I'm pleased to meet you, too," she murmured, wincing at the inanity. But then, what words would suffice? What comment could one make about a cataclysmic upheaval such as the one they were mutually experiencing?

And it was mutual. Claudia could see it in his eyes, by the way he was looking at her, that he was feeling the same attraction, the same desire. The realization shook her so much that she jerked her hand from his. She hadn't experienced desire for so long, she'd almost forgotten what it was like. Looking into Zack's intense blue eyes, she vividly remembered.

"Do you like to sing?" Zack asked.

Claudia blinked, confused by the seeming non sequitur. At least she wasn't the only one making inane remarks.

"Because if you don't, we could leave here and go somewhere a little more quiet. And a lot more private." Zack glanced around the room, which was beginning to fill with the spillover crowd from the overpacked living room. "I personally hate to sing. I'm incredibly bad at it. I still remember the music teacher at school encouraging me to lip synch so my off-key singing wouldn't ruin the chorus."

Claudia laughed, but her amusement was tinged with nervous excitement. Leave the party and its cast of thousands to be alone with him? She was unnerved by how very much she wanted to. What if she were to say yes and go with him?

Apprehension shot through her as she realized that she was considering it. She was cautious by nature; being solely responsible for four children for the past six years did not encourage one to take risks.

A merry group of party guests noisily approached the fireplace, crowding her and Zack.

Zack grimaced and took her arm. "Let's go, Claudia."

Claudia didn't budge. "No, I—I want to stay. I enjoy singing, especially Christmas songs. I'd like to go caroling with the group."

Impatience rippled through him, coupled with frustration. What was her game? She'd wanted to meet him, had arranged to do so and definitely achieved her objective. She'd gotten his attention; he was interested. Zack's eyes swept over her. Oh yes, he was very interested. He wanted to take her to bed as soon as possible.

And she wanted to stick around here and sing about Santa Claus and the little town of Bethlehem?

Claudia nervously balled her fingers into fists. He looked annoyed. Because she wouldn't leave with him? Had her behavior given him cause to believe that she would? She flushed as scarlet as her dress. She'd been standing here, gazing at him like some raptly dazed adolescent in the presence of a rock idol. Naturally he thought she would be willing to follow him wherever he wanted to take her.

To bed? Her pulses roared, echoing in her ears like thunder.

"I'd better find Annie and say hello." Claudia began to back away from him, her eyes darting around the room in an all-out effort to avoid his intense blue gaze. "I haven't seen her yet. I'd better start looking for her now. With the size of this crowd, it'll probably be like trying to find somebody in Times Square on New Year's Eve."

She hurried from the room, not pausing to look back, though she wondered if he were following her. Part of her actually hoped that he was, and Claudia berated herself for it. She was clearly not ready for the world of adult socializing, not when she could be so shaken upon simply meeting a man.

She never did find Annie Smith. A group of guests were organizing themselves to go out into the neighborhood to sing, and Claudia followed them to one of the bedrooms, where the coats were piled high onto a double bed. She found her coat, slipped it on and fled.

Fifteen minutes later, when she was inside her own home, she breathed a sigh of profound relief.

"Mom?" Natalie came into the small vestibule where Claudia was hanging up her coat in the crowded closet. "What are you doing home so early?"

"I decided I'd rather be here." Claudia smiled at her oldest.

Who did not return her smile. "Why?" Natalie demanded.

"Oh, Natalie, what a question! Of course I'd rather be at home with my family instead of stuck with a horde of strangers. Where are the kids?"

Natalie frowned. "Ned's sulking in his room because he wanted to play his video games, and I let the twins watch that Christmas special that's on TV tonight. I wish we had another TV set where he could permanently play his stupid games and we wouldn't have a war about—"

"One television set per household is plenty," Claudia cut in. She hated when Natalie turned materialistic. "I grew up with one black-and-white TV and was perfectly happy with it. You kids are lucky—you have color."

"Mom, everybody in America has color TV, it's no big deal." Natalie was clearly exasperated. "In fact, lots of people in America have at least *two* color TVs—especially if they have a ten-year-old boy in the family who hogs the set with his—"

"Stupid video games," Claudia chimed in, and they ended up chorusing it together.

Claudia laughed. Natalie scowled.

"So you didn't meet anybody at that party tonight worth staying there for?" Natalie pressed, looking even grimmer.

A vivid image of blue-eyed, smiling Zack flashed before Claudia's mind's eye. She saw the hot fire in his blue eyes, the sensual curve of his lips. *We could leave here and go somewhere a little more quiet. And a lot more private.* His voice, husky with sensual promise reverberated through her head. A hot, honeyed stab of desire sliced through her.

Claudia flinched. Her body had turned traitor on her, succumbing so thoroughly to Zack's sexual magnetism that the mere thought of him aroused her. Her cheeks flamed.

"You know me, honey, I'm not what you'd call a party animal." She tried to keep her tone light and hoped her daughter didn't notice the betraying quaver in her voice.

"That's for sure," Natalie grumbled. She was aware of nothing but her own disappointment. Her dreams of a father to provide for the family—which would definitely include a second TV set—and a stay-at-home mother to send the kids off to school in the mornings and liberate her from detention suddenly seemed as hopeless as her fantasy of Seth Albans, senior class president and quarterback of the football team, dumping his girlfriend who happened to be the secretary of the senior class, cheerleading captain and Homecoming Queen, to invite freshman Natalie Nolan to the Port Mason High Holiday Dance.

"Mommy! You're home!" Six-year-old Megan came running into the vestibule and hurled herself into her mother's arms. "I missed you, Mommy!"

Claudia picked up the little girl and hugged her tight, burying her face against her child's soft, silky, blond hair. "Well, I'm here now, sweetheart."

She shouldn't have gone out tonight, Claudia reproved herself. She belonged here at home with her children, safe from tempestuous feelings, free from temptation evoked from a tall, blue-eyed—Claudia shook her head slightly, as if to shake off the disturbing thought. "What show are you and Molly watching tonight, Megan?"

"It's about Rudolf the Red-Nosed Reindeer. It's got puppets." Megan wriggled out of her mother's arms. "Would you make us some popcorn, Mom?"

"I made them some popcorn earlier. They ate half and spilled the rest all over the floor." Natalie heaved a long-suffering sigh. "So then I had to vacuum, and they complained it was making too much noise and turned up the volume on the TV so loud that my ears are still sore from—"

"I'll make some more popcorn," Claudia interrupted Natalie's diatribe.

"If they spill it again, I'm not vacuuming it up," Natalie warned.

"She's as grouchy as the Grinch tonight." Megan stuck out her tongue at her big sister.

"Like I don't have every right to be," Natalie said darkly and stalked upstairs.

Chapter Three

"Don't show it to him," warned Gail, secretary to Chief Zachary Ritter and the Port Mason police department. Two police officers, Kowalski, a rookie fresh from the police academy and his partner O'Neil, a veteran officer nearing retirement age, crowded around her desk, an open *Press* in hand. "He's in a rotten mood this morning and—"

"Don't show me what?" Zack strode out of his office, his black brows narrowed, his expression dark as a thundercloud. "If you don't want me to hear every word you're saying, you should make sure the office door is closed, Gail," he added, throwing the secretary a reproving stare. "And I'm not in a rotten mood. Far from it. I feel great, filled with holiday spirit." His glower was directly at odds with his proclamation of good cheer.

Gail was undaunted. "Well, you won't after you read this, which is why I tried to keep Batman and Robin here from showing you."

Zack snatched the paper from Kowalski's hands.

"It's another smear by that pest of a columnist who calls himself the PM Observer," O'Neil said, pointing to the column.

"Blasting the speed trap again," Kowalski added. "Er, I mean our vehicular velocity restraint zone." He knew the chief preferred that particular term—coined by Zack himself—to the more inflammatory *speed trap*.

Zack's eyes perused the column. A dark flush spread from his neck to his face as he read aloud. "Chief Ritter's insistence on entrapping motorists by imposing the ridiculous twenty-five-mile-an-hour speed limit on the well-traveled quarter-mile stretch of road connecting highway 8 with the Interstate is as unfair as fishing with dynamite.''

"Ouch," muttered Kowalski.

"Fishing with dynamite?" Zack roared, throwing down the paper. He was an avid sportsman with a passion for fly-fishing, thus the analogy hit its mark and stung badly. "Of all the cheap shots! As if I would ever—"

"I told you he'd go ballistic," Gail observed, picking up the paper from the floor. "Fishing and that speed trap are practically sacred to him."

"It is not a speed trap, it is a vehicular velocity restraint zone," Zack retorted.

"Of course, the VVRZ," Gail said sarcastically. "I keep forgetting that one."

Zack threw her a speaking glance, then stormed into his office, snatched his jacket from the hook behind the door and headed down the hall, pulling on his coat as he marched past the departmental offices.

"Where are you going, Chief?" O'Neil called after him.

"I'm going to pay a visit to the comrades down at the *Port Mason Daily Press,*" Zack shouted, loud enough for everyone in the department to hear. "I understand all about their First Amendment rights and freedom of the press, but this time they've gone too far!"

A short time later he told Manny Fisher, the managing editor of the *Press,* the same thing. Zack had known Manny for years, since their football-playing days together at Port Mason High.

"This is the third column written by that idiot slamming the police department's attempts to enforce the speed limit," Zack snarled, pacing Manny's office like an enraged jungle cat. "All have been written anonymously under the pseudonym PM Observer because the nitwit doesn't even have the balls to use his own name."

Manny's lips twitched. "I, er, wouldn't exactly say that, Zack."

"Well, I would. And I want to say it to his face. There are a number of things I want to tell this self-righteous twit who's deliberately trying to incite the public against the police department! I demand to talk to this PM Observer, man-to-man." Zack stopped pacing and stood in front of Manny's desk, his arms folded in front of his chest. "And I'm not leaving here until I do. So, unless you want me camped out here, you'll arrange for me to meet this guy right now."

"I'll arrange it." Manny tried to suppress a grin. He failed. "But I think I ought to tell you that this guy happens to be a gal. The PM Observer is a woman, Zack."

Zack threw up his hands in the air. "Well, that explains everything," he growled. "I should've guessed. No man would write anything as—as insulting as that fishing-with-dynamite crack. I recommend that you rename her ditsy column the PMS Observer."

"Ditsy," Manny echoed. "When you thought it was a guy you accused him of inciting the public but now the column is merely ditsy? Because a woman writes it?"

"Skip the political correctness lecture and send in Brenda Starr, girl reporter. After I'm through with her, she'll beg to be reassigned to the cooking and party pages in the women's section. Where you should've kept her all along, Manfred."

"It's called the Life-style section, Zack," Manny corrected him patiently. "The articles are of broad mainstream interest not solely devoted to women's—"

"Yeah, yeah," Zack interrupted, grinning. "Ask any man if he reads that section and you'll get a resounding no, old pal."

"You're a hopeless chauvinist, Zack. How have you managed to avoid getting your consciousness raised? Well, just wait here and I'll send your nemesis in." Manny left the office, chuckling.

"Police Chief Ritter is in my office, demanding to speak to you," Manny told Claudia a few minutes later. "I think I ought to warn you that he's plenty steamed. He's an avid fisherman who would never use sticks of dynamite to blow fish out of the water, and he didn't take kindly to your column about the speed trap, either."

"Well, the motorists who are stopped, at the rate of 120 cars during a six-hour checkpoint, on a clear, wide straight stretch of road that presents no threat to pedestrians or other vehicles don't take kindly to Ritter's cash cow of a speed trap." Claudia's chocolate brown eyes flashed with indignation. "I think it's both unfair and reprehensible that—"

"Hey, don't lecture me! I'm on your side in this one," Manny protested. "I've been nailed three times in that cursed speed trap. Go tell it to Ritter."

"I will. Thanks for your support, Manny." Claudia stood up, left her cubbyhole and strode through the newsroom, heading for the editor's office on the floor above.

Manny watched her leave, an unholy gleam lighting his eyes.

In Manny's office, Zack mentally outlined exactly what he intended to say to this addle-brained female who was so clearly out of her depth writing about traffic and law enforcement.

On her way to Manny's office, Claudia rehearsed her rebuttal to the self-serving argument, which the avaricious chief of police undoubtedly planned to deliver.

She walked forcefully into the office, firmly closing the door behind her. She was on the side of the angels in this fight, and she intended to display no apprehension or doubt.

"Chief Ritter." She addressed the shiny badge first, before focusing her eyes on the man himself.

And then she focused. Standing before her in policemen's blues was none other than Zack from the Smiths' party the night before.

Zack—Zachary. Zachary Ritter, Port Mason's police chief. She made the connection instantly, though she certainly hadn't last night. But then Wayne Smith had not supplied surnames in his two-second introduction. Claudia stared at Zack, her eyes round with astonishment, her mouth suddenly dry.

"You!" Zack practically gasped. He was gaping at her. The lady in red from the party last night! The one who'd been hot to meet him, made him hot when she had, and then disappeared, leaving him unaccountably restless and irritable all evening long.

The sight of her brought back that surge of hungry urgency she'd evoked in him last night, that knife-sharp desire that had gone unslaked. He had tossed and turned in his lonely bed and awakened testy and tired, only to have his morning ruined by that damnable column.

Which had been written by his sexy mystery lady in red. Who looked just as desirable in her no-nonsense gray pleated skirt and her starched, high-collared gray-and-white blouse. Why did she have to look so soft, so touchable? Zack silently lamented. His body seemed to be expanding with sexual tension. She was dressed primly as a Pilgrim, sans bonnet, so how in the world could she turn him on so fast and so hard?

"You're angry about my columns." Claudia swallowed, forcing herself to speak, when all she wanted to do was run from the office and hide. "That's why you asked Wayne Smith to introduce you to me last night. So you could vent your spleen." She remembered her adolescent reaction to him, right down to the tongue-tiedness and sweaty palms, and cringed.

"*You* were the one who wanted to meet *me*," Zack corrected hastily. "You even weaseled an invitation to the party so the Smiths could introduce you to me. Why? Did you hope I'd fix a ticket you'd—"

"I did not weasel an invitation to that party!" Claudia flared. "According to my sources, *you* demanded that the Smiths invite *me*."

"Your sources are totally erroneous, which is obvious by the dreck you churn out and call a column. I didn't ask Wayne and Annie to invite you so I could confront you. I didn't even know who you were. I'd seen your earlier columns and found them annoying, but I didn't read your latest work of propaganda until this morning. You went from annoying to outrageous in that one, lady. It wasn't till then that I wanted to tell you in person that what you've dredged up is nothing but unfair, irresponsible yellow journalism. Imagine my surprise when Ms. PMS Observer turned out to be you!''

"PMS Observer," Claudia repeated icily. "I suppose that is a pathetic attempt at humor on your part?"

"I wouldn't expect you to get the joke. Or any joke."

"Your speed trap is a joke, a bad joke, and I got that one. Setting up a checkpoint where you clock drivers and pull them over for going even five miles above a ridiculously low speed limit on a stretch of road that doesn't warrant it—ha! ha!"

"Your references to our VVRZ—"

"Your what?" Claudia interrupted. "In English, please."

Zack cleared his throat. "The vehicular velocity restraint zone," he said, bracing himself for her reaction. He had a strong feeling that she was going to be as critical as Gail when it came to his updated terminology.

"Vehicular velocity restraint zone?" Claudia's expression and tone were as derisive as he'd expected. "Who dreamed that one up?"

"The term is mine," Zack said tightly.

"Congratulations. I always thought the government had a lock on inventing ridiculous, euphemistic doublespeak but you've managed to top them."

"I have no intention of holding a linguistics debate with you," Zack snapped.

"Yes, you've come to defend, protect and uphold your speed trap."

Zack managed to hang on to his temper, but just barely. "The VVRZ happens to net the Port Mason Police Department nearly a quarter of a million dollars a year in fines," he said tightly.

"My point exactly," Claudia was triumphant. "That's an obscene amount of money. You've got yourself a regular roadside hustle going on in this town."

"A hustle?" Zack echoed, outraged. "Enforcing the speed limit is certainly legal. And there is nothing obscene about collecting those fines which are an invaluable addition to the police department budget."

"Addition? It's enough to *be* the police department budget!"

"Why am I even bothering to try to explain this to you?" Zack seethed. "You are one of those dour, misinformed, sanctimonious crusaders who foists your half-baked opinions on the public without bothering to get the facts straight or to consider the ramifications and the consequences of the garbage you write."

"It seems to me that the police chief doth protest too much," Claudia retorted coolly. "All this fury over a column criticizing a notorious speed trap? It leads me to believe that you know I'm right and—"

"Believe me, baby, you don't know right from left, let alone right from wrong," Zack cut in hotly.

Claudia raised her brows and eyed him condescendingly. "I think you feel guilty about fleecing the hapless drivers unfortunate enough to get caught in your trap, Chief Ritter. That's why you changed its name, a typical bit of propaganda. That's why you're trying to justify yourself to me."

"I have no interest in justifying myself to you—*or* to anyone!"

"That's typical. Fascists never do consider any viewpoint but their own."

"You're calling me a fascist?" The charge empurpled him. A pulsing vein stood out in his neck, signaling the force of his fury.

Claudia knew she'd gone too far. "I didn't mean that," she hedged. The tip of her tongue darted out to quickly, nervously lick her lips. "Uh, not exactly."

Zack's blue eyes, narrowed and piercing, focused on her mouth.

"Then what exactly do you mean?" He started to walk toward her and she instantly, instinctively began to back away from him. "You compare me to a fascist and then *not exactly* renege. What's next? Charges of police brutality?"

"If I learn of any police brutality in this town, you can count on me writing about it," she said shakily. Her eyes darted anxiously toward the door. If she turned and made a dash for it, she could be out of here in less than ten seconds.

"If you learn of any police brutality in this town, I'd be interested in hearing about it myself. But I can assure you that you won't find any such thing. I run a clean, professional department."

He'd moved too fast for her; she had run out of time and space. Claudia found herself backed flat against the closed door. There was nowhere else to go and Zack Ritter was only a hairbreadth away.

"I didn't mean—that is, I mean I—" She was breathless and her words became choked in her throat. Somehow her palms were flattened against the broad expanse of his chest. She felt the warmth of his body heat under her fingertips. The spicy masculine scent of his after-shave filled her nostrils, sensually drugging her.

"I don't think you know what you mean," Zack said huskily. He laid his hands briefly over hers, then lowered them to her waist, pulling her slowly against him. "But I do know what you want because I want it, too."

Claudia's paltry resistance crumbled as spirals of heat began to uncoil in her belly, unleashing a hot syrupy warmth, which flowed seductively through her. Her lips parted, and Zack thrust his tongue inside to probe the warm wet hollow of her mouth.

The kiss grew hotter and wilder and deeper. His big hands moved firmly, smoothly over her back and the curves of her waist, her hips, to intimately cup her bottom, then mold her into the hard male planes of his body.

Something within her went weak and soft. Claudia made a small hungry sound and clung to him. She allowed her tongue to slip into his mouth and rub seductively against his while her fingers stroked his neck and feathered through the dark springy thickness of his hair.

He tasted wonderful, he felt wonderful. It was wonderful to be in his arms. She was drunk on the taste and the scent and the feel of him. The powerful male strength of him pulsed against her, arousing a clamor of long-dormant feminine needs that she'd kept locked tightly inside her. Claudia shuddered on a soft moan of pleasure. Zack had released her self-imposed restraints and she'd broken free to soar into the dizzying stratosphere of sensuality.

Zack's need was as urgent as hers, and he lifted his mouth slightly, providing them with a moment to gulp for air. "I wanted to do this from the moment I saw you last night," he rasped hoarsely. "You wanted it, too, but then you took off."

He didn't give her time to explain, he wasn't really interested in hearing an explanation, anyway. He wanted to feel her lips against his, her mouth opening to him, to feel her warm feminine body squirming sensuously under his hands.

His mouth closed over hers again with compelling possession. Her senses reeling, Claudia surrendered to the languorous heat enveloping her, sinking into the warm velvet mists of sensation.

Passionate ardor flared like wildfire between them, and both lost all sense of time and place as they gave themselves up to the thrilling sensations erupting inside them.

Zack's hand closed over her breast and he fondled it gently, one long finger finding the taut nipple beneath the layers of her blouse and bra and stroking with deft expertise. Claudia whimpered and pressed herself more tightly against him. She wanted his touch, needed it. The barriers of clothing were a frustrating impediment, and she wanted to pull them off, to feel his bare skin against hers. To feel his mouth there, on her breast, his tongue soothing her throbbing, aching nipples....

Groaning with urgency, Zack thrust his thigh between hers and rubbed against her. The pressure was exquisite and Claudia strained closer, wanting more.

And then...

"Hey, it's awful quiet in there!" Manny's ear-splitting voice outside the door ricocheted through the room like a gunshot.

Claudia and Zack sprang apart, as if they'd been doused by a bucket of icy water. Manny's loud, hard raps on the door were certainly a likely equivalent.

"Have you two killed each other or what?" Manny bellowed. He rattled the doorknob.

Zack blocked the door with his body, holding it closed. "Give us another minute, Manny." He reached out to try to smooth Claudia's tousled hair back into place. "We're, uh, in the midst of working things out."

Claudia fought back a dreadful, nervous urge to giggle. Zack's lips bore noticeable traces of her lipstick, and she tried to rub it off with her fingers. Stifling a groan, he caught her hand and pressed his mouth against her palm.

"I have to see you again," he murmured urgently. "When can I call you?"

Claudia's heart seemed to somersault in her chest. She wanted to see him, too. "Tonight, after ten," she whispered. The kids would all be in bed, she would be free to talk, to make plans.... She shivered with anticipation.

"Are you in the phone book?"

She nodded her head.

"I'm coming in," warned Manny, making good on his threat. He appeared in the office and gave both Claudia and Zack a thorough and amused once-over. "I presume the speed trap debate has been resolved?"

Zack grimaced. "If you are referring to the VVRZ, I think she understands my point of view on the matter."

"We agreed to disagree," Claudia put in. Her voice sounded husky and thick, and she blushed.

"Glad to hear it," Manny said dryly. "You explained to her that you're not the sort who would fish with dynamite, Zack?"

"She promises never to use that repulsive analogy again, don't you, Claudia?" Zack slanted her a heavy-lidded stare and stepped closer to her.

There was a very masculine gleam in his eyes, and it was having an astonishing effect upon her. Her body felt hot and turgid and weighted down. She couldn't seem to move away from him, though she knew she should. Manny Fisher was watching them carefully, no doubt drawing his own conclusions.

"I don't remember making any promises of any kind," she said faintly. She knew she was in deep trouble when Zack Ritter could immobilize her with only a look.

"Ah, but you did." Zack's sexy, assessing gaze deepened her blush. "I'll be only too glad to remind you when the time is right."

"Are you talking in code?" Manny demanded.

Claudia's nerves were stretched tight; she felt jittery and on edge. "I have to get back to my desk," she said quickly. What she really had to do was to get away from Zack and try to regain her lost emotional equilibrium. "If you'll both excuse me . . ." She headed out the door.

"Just a minute." Zack's tone, strict and authoritative, halted her automatically.

She turned, annoyed by her instant compliance. "Is that your police chief voice? The one you use to stop criminals in their tracks?"

"Worked on *you,* didn't it, honey?" Zack smiled lazily. "You didn't tell me your last name, Claudia."

Claudia was suddenly in the throes of a churning sexual panic. He wanted her last name so he could look up her number in the telephone directory. So he could use her again—perhaps tonight? And pick up where they'd left off here in the office? She was suddenly scared. Things were moving too fast, she wanted him too much.

"I'm waiting, Claudia," Zack said, all smug masculine arrogance. He knew how flustered she was and credited himself for it!

Claudia felt a perverse impulse to refuse to answer him. "Maybe I'll just plead the Fifth on that one, Chief."

"I think she's going for some police department humor," Manny interjected. "Your turn, Zack. Going to cuff her and read her her rights?"

"Handcuffs," Zack said. "Hmm, interesting thought."

His eyes met Claudia's, and she had no trouble conjuring up the images he was not-so-subtly taunting her with.

"Are you going to tell me your last name or am I going to have to get it from Manny?" Zack asked her, with a calm she both envied and resented.

"I have a column to write," she announced, bolting from the office.

"It's Nolan," Manny Fisher said before Zack turned to ask. "She's old Edith Cameron's great-niece. Moved up here from Florida this summer. Edith left her her house on Hopwood Lane."

"I always liked old Miss Cameron," said Zack. "She sure had a lead foot when it came to driving, though. I wonder if Ms. Nolan knows that her great-aunt was stopped regularly during our traffic checks? Always clocked doing about sixty. I think Miss Cameron's fines paid for half a police car one year."

"Let's hope you don't have cause to stop Claudia again." Manny grinned. "Or the PM Observer will be back on the warpath."

"Again? That means she was pulled over?"

"By O'Neil. He clocked her doing thirty and wrote her a ticket. Boy, was she mad!"

"And so she chose to use the power of the press to avenge herself." Zack shook his head thoughtfully. "She is an intriguing lady, Manny."

"And you're intrigued by her?"

Zack laughed. "I plead the Fifth on that one."

Chapter Four

Natalie was already in her seat in the front row when Brian shuffled glumly into detention later that afternoon.

"You were late again?" he asked, and Natalie nodded her head.

"Later than usual. The way things are going I'll be in detention till I graduate," Natalie muttered grimly. "Your plan didn't work. My mother didn't even stay at that party for an hour last night. She couldn't have met your dad."

"Tell me something I don't know." Brian gazed morosely at his stack of books. "I saw who my dad hooked up with last night and it sure wasn't your mom."

His aura of despair roused Natalie's curiosity. "Who was it?"

Brian looked pained. "Miss Pierson."

"Señorita Pierson, the Spanish teacher? The really pretty redhead?" Natalie stared at him, astonished. "I have her for Spanish one."

"So do I," Brian said, aggrieved. "My dad met her at the Smiths' party and brought her home afterward. I sneaked downstairs when I heard voices 'cause I thought it would be your mom and I wanted to check out the situation. And there they were—my dad and Miss Pierson."

"Were they kissing?" Natalie whispered.

Brian shook his head. "They were talking and laughing and joking around." He shuddered. "Like they were *our* age!"

Natalie's dark eyes reflected both sympathy and horror. "Oh, gross!"

"My father is thirty-six years old. He has four kids. He shouldn't be dating! And Miss Pierson is way too young for him, anyway. She told our class she was twenty-four on her birthday, the day after Halloween. We threw a birthday party for her."

"Our class did, too. Jessica and I brought in cupcakes." Natalie frowned. "What if your dad decides to marry her? Señorita Pierson would be your stepmother!"

"No way is that going to happen!" Brian pounded the desktop with his fist. "The kids need a real mother, not a babe like Señorita Pierson. My dad has to get married and settle down and it has to be with someone who's not—who's not—"

"A babe," Natalie finished. "He needs someone in her thirties who already has kids. Someone who won't act all young and stupid."

"Right." Brian nodded fervently. "Someone like your mom."

"Do you have two TV sets?" Natalie asked suddenly.

Brian looked confused, but replied anyway. "We have three. Two for us kids, one to watch and one to play video games on. And one in my dad's bedroom."

"It's even better than I hoped! When your dad and my mom get married, we'll have four TV sets!" Natalie rhapsodized. "We'll be able to watch whatever we want while the kids play their games and our folks watch what they want!"

Our folks. It sounded good to Brian. "But first they have to meet," he reminded her.

"They will, tonight at the mall. Now it's *my* turn to plan. Here's what we'll do..."

"Me and Megan want to sit on Santa's lap and get our picture taken, Mommy!" Molly exclaimed, tugging on Claudia's arm. "Right now! Please!"

"Megan and I," Claudia automatically corrected. "Natalie, why don't you go into the office supply store and get that poster board for your art project while we—"

"Let's get something to eat first," Natalie said quickly. She surveyed the Port Mason Mall food court with a speculative glance. "I'm hungry, Mom."

"How could you be hungry?" Claudia was exasperated. "We finished dinner less than half an hour ago."

Their impromptu trip to the mall tonight had been forced on her by Natalie's panicky request for a red poster board, due for tomorrow's art class for a holiday collage. She'd scolded her daughter for letting things slide until the last possible moment, which actually was most unlike the usually well-organized Natalie.

But then she'd given in and bundled all four kids into the car for the fifteen-minute drive across town. At least the mall wasn't crowded this evening. Undoubtedly the cold, rainy weather had been a factor in that.

"I'm hungry, too," Ned chimed in. Anytime anyone mentioned food, Ned was ready to eat. "Can I get chicken nuggets and fries?"

"On top of a full spaghetti dinner? Certainly not," Claudia replied firmly. "Since we didn't have dessert, you can each have a frozen yogurt."

"Thanks, Mom!" Natalie flashed a wide grin. "Molly, Megan, what kind of yogurt do you want? They have fifteen different flavors."

"Don't tell them that!" Claudia groaned. She was well aware that the six-year-olds would insist on hearing the name of each available flavor and then have a lengthy debate over which to choose. "We'll be lucky to get out of here by Christmas!"

Ned laughed; he thought she was joking. "I'm having vanilla," he announced.

"Boys are so easy," Claudia murmured, and Natalie paused in her recitation of flavors to smile sunnily at her mother.

"I bet you wish you had more boys, huh, Mom? Like maybe three more?"

"I wouldn't trade you three girls for anything," Claudia affirmed, misinterpreting her completely.

"Oh, you won't have to," Natalie assured her. "Pineapple, lime, black raspberry," she continued with the litany of flavors.

"Food court! Food court!" Ian and Justin Ritter chanted in unison, rushing ahead of their father and older brother and sister.

Brian glanced at his watch. They were over ten minutes late; Natalie was probably going crazy wondering where they were. What if she and her mother weren't there? He shot a covert glance at his father. It hadn't been easy talking Dad into coming to the mall tonight. He'd been willing to let Brian take the mythical F on the mythical art project instead of driving out to buy the mythical required poster board. Luckily, Robin and the boys had taken up his cause, begging to go to the mall for dinner at the food court, a collections of fast-food stalls surrounded by tables overlooking the ground-floor plaza.

Zack Ritter had a harder time saying no to four kids than to just one. He'd caved in and here they were.

Luck was on their side, Brian thought gleefully. He spotted Natalie the moment they entered the open spacious food court. She was talking to two cute little identical twin girls who wore short red dresses and red tights and had long blond braids tied with red ribbons. A blond-haired boy sat at the same table crunching on the remains of a cone.

"Hey, there's a friend of mine from school!" Brian said, just as he and Natalie had rehearsed it during detention. He sped away from his family, heading straight to the Nolan table. "Hey, Natalie!"

"Old World chocolate with white chocolate is really good, Molly. It tastes like chocolate marshmallow..." Natalie looked up, relief written on her face as she spied Brian. She wasn't sure how much longer she could drag out the twins' frozen yogurt debate. "Hey, Brian," she called, waving to him.

Claudia saw the cute dark-haired boy making a dash for their table, and a knowing smile crossed her face. She strongly suspected that Natalie's reason for coming to the mall had less to do with an urgent need for poster board than meeting young Brian here.

Natalie stood up, smiling at the boy who stood before them, panting from his run. "Mom, this is Brian Ritter, he's in my class at school. Brian, this is my mom," she added proudly.

"Hi, Mrs. Nolan," Brian greeted her politely, then sent Natalie a look of approval. Her mother was perfect. Pretty but not a babe, wearing just the right clothes, dark blue slacks and a blue-and-green sweater, clothes a respectable mother in her thirties would wear. Very different from the shockingly brief and tight gold-spangled dress Señorita Pierson had on last night.

"Hello, Brian." Claudia was amused. Natalie and Brian looked so pleased with themselves. She felt a sentimental pang as she gazed at the girl and boy. They made a darling couple. "I'm going to take a wild guess that you're here for poster board, too."

"For the art project," Brian agreed. He glanced over his shoulder to see his father approaching them with the three younger kids.

Claudia saw them, too. Her eyes widened at the sight of Zack Ritter, in jeans and a gray sweatshirt, walking toward them accompanied by three preteen boys, all wearing ripped jeans, oversize jerseys bearing various sports team logos, and beat-up, high-top sneakers.

"Claudia?" Zack arrived at their table. He was stunned to see her. His gaze swept over the four blond, brown-eyed children gathered around her. Their resemblance to her was unmistakable.

"Hello, Zack," she said, her voice slightly tremulous. The four dark-haired, blue-eyed kids had to be his. Their resemblance to him was undeniable.

"You know each other?" Brian was incredulous.

"How?" Natalie demanded to know.

Zack ignored them, his attention focused on Claudia. "These are your kids?" he asked, hoping they weren't, knowing they were. He hadn't speculated at all on her past, aside from assuming that her marital status was single and available. Now he found himself searching her left hand for a wedding band. He didn't see one.

"Yes, these are my children, Natalie, Ned, Molly and Megan," Claudia said with noticeable maternal pride. "Kids, this is Police Chief Ritter."

"Do you have a gun, Chief Ritter?" Ned asked, impressed.

"Of course he does," Justin Ritter replied for his father. "All cops have guns."

"Do you shoot bad guys?" asked little Megan, awed.

"He kills them," boasted young Ian. "Every day."

Molly looked alarmed and took a step behind her mother.

"I do not go around shooting and killing people." Zack felt obliged to defend himself and his profession.

His eyes met Claudia's and he quickly averted them. He'd spent a good portion of the day redirecting his thoughts away from that wild little interlude they'd shared in Manny Fisher's office this morning. He had looked up her phone number, written it down and planned to call her tonight, after his kids went to bed. Hoped to see her tonight, after his kids were in bed.

He stared at the eight children standing around the small table in the food court. His kids. Her kids. *Between them they had eight kids!* Zack paled. He knew he would not be making that phone call to her tonight—or ever.

Since his father was standing mute and bug-eyed, Brian took it upon himself to complete the introductions. "This is my sister Robin and my brothers, Justin and Ian,'' he announced to Claudia and the rest of the Nolans.

Molly stared from Justin to Robin to Ian. "Who's your sister?" she asked, puzzled. "They all look like boys to me."

At first glance, they did to Claudia, too, but after a closer look, she noticed that the girl's build was slighter, her features more delicate and feminine than the other two. But Robin's haircut was dreadful, chopped short like her brothers, no doubt by a barber who made no allowances for gender or style. And in Claudia's opinion, the three youngest Ritters' attire was more suitable for cleaning out the garage than a trip to the mall.

Robin flushed and glared at the Nolans. Zack, however, seemed oblivious to the underlying tension. "Rob hears that a lot," he said with a fond chuckle. "And she's as tough and as strong as any boy."

"Tougher and stronger," Ian claimed in a vicarious boast. "Robin can beat up Justin and his friends."

"Can not!" growled Justin, taking a swing at his younger brother. "Shut up, Puke Breath."

"*Puke Breath?*" The twins repeated, clearly relishing the insult.

Natalie and Brian exchanged worried glances.

"No fighting, guys," Brian announced. He didn't want his brothers' antics to scare off Natalie's mom. "They're just kidding around, Mrs. Nolan. They're really best friends with each other," he added.

"You have beautiful blue eyes, Robin," Natalie said sweetly, trying to make amends for her little sister's tactlessness. "I always wished my eyes were blue."

Robin said nothing. She scowled and stared at the ground, stuffing her hands deep into her pockets.

"Do you guys want to play some video games?" Brian asked, after another swift glance at Natalie. She'd nodded almost imperceptibly, his cue to get them moving, away from their parents so the two could have some time alone.

Predictably, Justin, Ian and Ned all enthusiastically endorsed a visit to the mall's video arcade on the ground floor. "I'll take the twins to see Santa," Natalie injected quickly. "Want to come with us, Robin?"

"To see Santa Claus?" Robin gave a derisive hoot. "No way! I'm going to the arcade with the guys."

"Kids, I really don't think you—" Zack began.

"Kids, we really don't have time for—" Claudia said at the same moment.

"Let's go!" exclaimed Brian and took off like a bank robber making a getaway. Robin and the three younger boys raced after him. Natalie caught a twin by each hand and dashed to the escalator.

It happened so fast that Zack and Claudia were caught unawares. They were left alone at the table, staring at the backs of their fleeing offspring.

Claudia cleared her throat. "I think we were set up," she murmured. "It's very obvious that my Natalie and your Brian made plans to meet here this evening. I don't think they counted on having the two of us and all the other kids around, though. They both got flustered and couldn't cope. Thus, their sudden take-off."

"You have four kids," Zack marveled mournfully. "Are you divorced?"

"Widowed," Claudia murmured. "Six years ago. My twins were just a month old at the time," she added. She always felt compelled to add that sad, heartrending detail, which was such a part of the tragedy of Jeff's death.

Zack made a whistling sound. "Tough."

"Are you divorced?" Claudia asked, feeling uneasy. She hadn't given a thought to his marital status until she'd seen him with his children. He'd better not be married, not after those hot glances last night and that passionate kiss in Manny's office!

"My wife died six years ago," Zack said reluctantly. He found it difficult to discuss Sharon with anyone.

"I'm sorry." Claudia's voice was quiet and soft. "I know exactly how difficult it is to raise four children alone."

Zack felt a creeping apprehension. She had four kids, and there was no father in the picture at all. He looked into her big velvety brown eyes and felt a self-protective urge to flee. But something even stronger, more elemental, kept him standing beside her.

"I haven't had to do it alone," he heard himself say. "My mother lived with us until this past summer. Then she remarried and moved to Florida with her new husband. We're doing fine," he added heartily. "My kids don't need coddling. They are very self-sufficient and independent."

Claudia was doubtful. Brian was well turned out, but the two younger boys looked like ragamuffins. And poor Robin! As a former adolescent girl herself and the mother of a current one, Claudia could guess how badly Robin must be faring among the style- hair- and clothes-conscious girls of her age.

She held her tongue, however. It was within her rights to criticize his odious speed trap in column, but how he chose to raise his children was really none of her concern.

"After Jeff died, I lived with my parents in Florida until this summer." She offered personal information instead of advice. "They wanted to move to Arizona and invited us to go along, but I didn't think it was fair to take up any more of their retirement years. Great-aunt Edith left me this house, and Manny Fisher offered me the job with the *Press* so the kids and I moved here in June."

"My mother retired *to* Florida and your folks retired *from* Florida," Zack observed. "Funny, huh?" It wasn't, not particularly, but he did not want the conversation to take a more personal turn.

"Zack, about this morning," Claudia began, and Zack winced. Their little scene in Manny's office was about as personal as two could get.

"I want to apologize for that," he said quickly, determined to keep his distance. "I reacted without thinking, and that is unusual for me."

"I . . . wasn't looking for an apology," Claudia said quietly. "I just wanted to say—"

"And while we're on the subject of, uh, this morning." Zack drew in a deep breath. "This is going to be awkward but it has to be said, Claudia. I pride myself on my honesty and it would be unfair of me to let you—" he coughed slightly. She was watching him, those lovely brown eyes of hers wide and wary.

"To let me what?" Claudia asked stiffly.

Awkward? This was excruciating. But fair was fair. Zack pressed on. "I said I'd call you tonight, and it wouldn't be fair to let you wait for that call, because—" another sharp inhalation "—I'm not going to call you, Claudia. Not tonight, not ever."

Chapter Five

Claudia didn't move or show any expression. "I see." Her words were slow and precise.

Zack ran his hand through his hair, tousling it. This was not getting any easier. "Claudia, I can't get involved with you."

"I don't recall asking you to," she retorted, anger kindling within her.

"I can understand why you're angry," Zack said earnestly. "After that kiss in the office, it's only natural that you expected—"

"I expect nothing from you," Claudia interrupted coldly. The insensitive clod! How dare he humiliate her like this! If he didn't want to call her, then why didn't he simply not call, rather than rub his rejection in her face this way?

"I intended to call you, Claudia, I really did, I was looking forward to it, but after seeing you here—" He was bungling badly, Zack thought, feeling sweat bead on his brow. He'd handled career criminals with more finesse than this!

"Claudia, I do not date women with children," he blurted out. "I've made a point of that, and I have to stick to it. I have four kids of my own and I can't—I won't—"

"What a coincidence," Claudia cut in. "It just so happens that *I* don't date men with children."

It was a lie. She hadn't dated anyone since she'd been widowed, and until now had never thought to ban men with children as potential escorts. But he'd wounded her pride, and she was determined to strike back.

"Since you have four kids, you're out of the running, Chief. I wouldn't go out with you, even if you got down on your knees and begged."

She looked haughty as a queen. And as desirable as a model in a perfume ad. Heat surged through him, and Zack swallowed hard. He wanted her, kids or not. He'd wanted her the moment he had first laid eyes on her at the Smiths' Christmas party. She wanted him, too. He knew it. The way she had responded to him this morning convinced him that the attraction was definitely mutual.

But according to his own rules—and hers, too, it seemed—he couldn't have her. Frustration clawed through him.

Claudia didn't stick around for his mental meanderings. She walked away from him, shoulders squared, her chin held high, to stand by the railing and look down at the fantasy North Pole headquarters constructed in the open plaza area on the level below. A child-size train encircled scenes of Santa's workshop where animated figures of elves worked on toys, and Mrs. Claus baked an assortment of colorful holiday goodies for cute little stuffed reindeer. One of them had a red nose that glowed brightly, and the children riding in the train inevitably pointed to it, exclaiming with delighted recognition.

At the center was a red thronelike chair where a jolly Santa Claus held court, holding children on his lap while they apprised him of their wishes. Photographs and videotapes of the event were available for a price, and a girl in a green elf suit stood beside a red-and-white candy striped booth collecting fees from the doting parents.

Molly and Megan were sitting on Santa's lap, one on each knee, looking adorable as they chatted happily with their idol. Natalie stood beside the booth, Brian at her side. They were talking together as vivaciously as the twins with Santa Claus.

"Your little ones are having quite a talk with Santa." Zack was beside Claudia, his eyes focused on the twins. He'd followed her because he was strangely unable to walk away from her. "They're very cute, Claudia."

"They're about as appealing to you as typhoid carriers working in the kitchen are to a restaurant owner." Claudia did not look at him. "Don't bother tossing out compliments that you don't mean, Chief. You've already made it quite clear you don't like children, and I don't expect you to make an exception for mine."

"I like kids!" Zack protested. "I have four of my own and I enjoy them very much."

"Then go enjoy your own kids." She lifted her chin a fraction higher. "And let me alone to enjoy mine."

Having been ordered away, perversely, Zack was determined to stay. "Look, we've had a . . . misunderstanding. There is no need for us to be enemies."

He glanced down at his son who was standing next to Claudia's older daughter, talking and laughing. He had never seen Brian, who was usually quiet and reserved, so at ease in a girl's company. "Can't we be friends, Claudia? For our kids' sake? It looks like they're really hitting it off."

"I am not interested in your friendship, Chief Ritter. Just because Natalie is Brian's friend doesn't mean I have to befriend his blockhead of a father." Claudia walked away from him, heading for the escalator.

Zack found himself right behind her. It was as if he were some sort of pull toy and she held the string, dragging him along with her. He stood on the step above her on the descending escalator, looking down at the top of her silky blond head. It would be so easy to place his hands on her shoulders and pull her back against him, to bury his lips in the soft curve of her neck. A hot rush of sensual need spiraled through him.

"Claudia," he began hoarsely.

"Go away," she said succinctly, keeping her eyes straight ahead.

"You're deliberately being unreasonable, Claudia."

"What I'm trying to do is to ignore you, but you're not making it easy. Is there an antistalking law in this state? If there is, you're breaking it."

"Why won't you understand?" Zack heaved an exasperated groan. "I don't want to have stepchildren. Is that such a crime? Just check out the statistics. More second marriages than firsts break up, and one of the main reasons is the inexorable presence of stepchildren. Life is not an episode of "The Brady Bunch," Claudia. And you and I—my God, we have eight kids between us! That's an incomprehensible amount of children."

"I don't remember agreeing to marry you," Claudia snapped. "In fact, I believe I told you I wouldn't even go out with you. So will you please stay away from me and stop insulting me!"

"I wasn't insulting you, I—"

They stepped off the escalator. Claudia whirled around to face him. "You weren't insulting me?" she repeated incredulously. "Well, it just so happens that I have never been so insulted in my entire life, Zachary Ritter."

She stalked over to the booth just as Molly and Megan came skipping down the red-carpeted path from Santa's throne.

"We told Santa Claus we wanted Barbie's Mermaid Sea Castle, Baby Skates and Wets, and Mother Cat with Kitty Cutie," sang out Megan.

"Santa gave us candy canes and said he knew we were good!" cried Molly.

"You owe for their picture, Mom," Natalie said. "I ordered two, one for you and one to send to Grandma and Grandpa in Arizona."

"Where's my dad?" asked Brian.

Their voices swirled around Claudia's head. Her heart was still pounding from her encounter with Zack, her stomach churning with tension. Even worse was this sick feeling of disappointment. She realized just how much she'd been looking forward to his call tonight, to the possibility of—something—happening between them.

Something had happened, all right. Zack Ritter wanted no part of her because she was a mother. He'd rejected her and her children out of hand because he didn't want to run the risk of stepchildren!

"Your father was on the escalator, Brian," she replied. "Then I lost track of him." She tried to keep her voice steady but was unable to prevent a note of coldness from creeping in. "We have to be on our way now. Brian, will you please go to the video arcade and tell my son to meet us here immediately?"

Natalie and Brian looked at each other.

"Strike two," he muttered under his breath, and hurried off in the direction of the video arcade.

A few moments later Zack joined Claudia and her daughters beside the small white wooden gate leading to Santa's throne. Claudia, who was writing a check to the elf in the candy-striped booth, did not deign to acknowledge his presence. The three girls stood together, watching the animated figures in the fluffy faux snow.

"Where did Brian go?" asked Zack.

"He went to get the kids at the arcade, Chief Ritter," Natalie replied with a thousand-megawatt smile at him. There was a moment's silence.

Zack watched the small twins watch the animated scenes, their brown eyes round with the delight of children enjoying the special sights and sounds of the holiday season. He remembered his own kids' Christmastime excitement and felt a nostalgic tug. It was different now; no one in his family believed in Santa Claus anymore, not even eight-year-old Ian who'd been told the truth this fall by his classmates.

"Have you started your Christmas shopping yet, Chief Ritter?" Natalie asked pleasantly, using the tone she'd developed for making adult small talk.

Zack was grateful for the girl's conversational sally. He knew he wasn't going to get one from her mother. "Not yet," he confessed. "Just the thought of Christmas shopping overwhelms me."

It was true. Finding out what the kids wanted, trying to find the stuff, hide it and get it under the tree by Christmas morning had him totally flummoxed. His mother had handled all that since Sharon's death. This was the first year he would be doing it alone.

"Maybe my mom can help you," Natalie suggested ingenuously. "She's a super shopper. And so organized, too! She mailed out all our Christmas cards already."

"She would," grumbled Zack, who hadn't even bought his cards yet.

"Molly, Megan, tell Chief Ritter what you want for Christmas," Natalie prompted the twins.

She was well aware that identical twins were crowd pleasers. Since the twins' birth, even perfect strangers had been admiring the two little look-alikes. Natalie decided she might as well use the twins' seemingly universal appeal to captivate Zack Ritter. Their mother certainly wasn't helping much in this campaign; she was taking an awfully long time to write the check for the Santa pictures, ignoring the chief completely.

Zack leaned down, smiling at the two little girls. Claudia must've looked like them as a child, he guessed. They shared her coloring, her features, her beautiful soft brown eyes. "What did you tell Santa you wanted?" he asked them, his tone indulgent.

"A daddy," Molly said without hesitation.

Her clear young voice seemed to resonate throughout the mall. At least it seemed that way to Claudia, who flushed scarlet. Of all the things to say to a man who most definitely did not care to be a daddy to anyone else but his own flesh-and-blood foursome!

"You didn't say that, Molly!" Natalie exclaimed. She was blushing, too, recognizing that Molly's answer was less than subtle. "You know you said you wanted Barbie's Mermaid

Sea Castle, Baby Skates and Wets, and Mother Cat with Kitty Cutie. Megan said so."

"That's what Megan told Santa we wanted," agreed Molly. "But I told him we wanted a daddy."

"She did," Megan affirmed. "We've been wanting one for a while now. Neddy has, too."

Claudia was aghast. The way this was going, next the twins would ask Zack to be their daddy! She could just imagine his reaction to that! Even worse, he probably thought she'd put them up to this, that she was so obsessed with finding a man that her children had picked up her rallying cry and were helping in her quest.

She caught a glimpse of Natalie's face. The fourteen-year-old looked horrified; she was old enough to realize how embarrassing the twins' innocent remarks sounded.

"You have a daddy, girls. He is in heaven and he loves you very much," Zack said, surprising Claudia.

She realized, then, that he must've dealt with his own children's remarks about the lack of a mother in their lives. Claudia warmed to him a bit. At least he'd handled the twins sensitively and not run from them as if they were abhorrent extraterrestrials. Given his take on children with marriageable mothers, it had been a distinct possibility.

"But a daddy in heaven can't belong to Indian Princesses with us," Molly said plaintively. "Six girls in our class belong to Indian Princesses with their dads. They get Indian names and make neat stuff and go places. This week, they're going to make reindeer ornaments out of clothespins at Brittany's house and have a big Christmas party at the 'Y' with all the other tribes in Port Mason."

"We can't go because we don't have a dad," added Megan.

"We'll make reindeer ornaments at home," Natalie said quickly. "I know how."

"It's not the same thing," complained Megan.

Zack sneaked a covert glance at Claudia. Their eyes connected for an instant, and then she coldly looked away. He felt oddly bereft, as though he'd lost something special that he didn't even know he'd wanted.

"Maybe I should take them to get their frozen yogurt now," Natalie offered, a bit desperately.

"Dad! Dad!" At that moment Justin and Ian came charging through the mall, shouting at the top of their lungs. Brian and Ned were right behind them.

"I know, I know, you guys are starving," Zack said, laughing with relief. Their presence provided a most welcome reprieve from the emotional tension pulsing through him. "Come on, let's go get some dinner."

"Dad, in case you didn't notice, Robin's not here," Brian said reproachfully.

Zack's eyes scanned the group of four, consisting of his three boys and Claudia's son. He felt a telltale surge of color stain his neck. "I did notice, Brian," he said a bit more sharply than he intended. But he didn't appreciate the boy's tone—and in front of Claudia, too! "Go back to the arcade and tell your sister that she has to come for dinner right now."

"She's not there!" Ian blurted out. "We don't know where she is!"

"What?" Claudia and Zack chorused together. Their eyes met again, this time in mutual apprehension, as fellow parents who recognized that phrase as one of the most terrifying a mother or father could hear.

Zack immediately suppressed the sickening surge of panic that welled up within him. Port Mason PD handled as many lost child cases as any city its size, and every one of those children had turned up, safe and well. He refused to let himself think about those rare and terrible cases elsewhere, where despite the best efforts of the police and the community, the missing child was gone forever.

"She probably went into one of her favorite stores," he said. In police work, as in life, he'd learned that Occam's Razor usually applied—that the simplest explanation is usually the most likely. He knew his daughter was partial to the candy store, the toy store, the music store.

"She didn't say, she just ran away, Dad," Justin said solemnly. "On our way to play video games we stopped to look in the pet shop and these stupid girls from her class were there."

"The ones who are so mean to her?" Natalie asked.

Justin nodded glumly.

Brian grimaced. "Uh-oh."

"They were laughing and they said something to her," Ned reported. "I didn't hear 'cause I was watching the puppies, but all of a sudden she ran out of the store."

"We thought she'd go to the arcade but she didn't," added Ian. "Where'd she go, Dad?"

Chapter Six

Zack didn't have an answer to Ian's question but he did have a question of his own. "What girls are mean to Robin?" he demanded.

"There are some nasty little snots in her class who pick on her," Natalie informed him. "Middle-school girls can be horrible," she added with a world-weary sigh.

Zack stared, uncomprehending. This was the first he'd heard of Robin being picked on by anyone. "How long has this been going on?" And why did Natalie Nolan know all about it when he didn't?

"A few months," Brian said grimly. "Almost from the first week of school."

"It's getting worse, though," Justin piped up. "At first Brian just had to drag her to the school, but this week he had to carry her all the way."

"Brian is really strong," Ian said admiringly. "He carries Robin, and me and Justin take turns carrying her backpack and stuff."

"We're always late though," sighed Justin. "Brian gets detention all the time for being late. I'm glad my school doesn't have detention or I'd be in it, too. But I get hollered at a lot," he added glumly.

Zack stood rooted to the spot, as ever-increasing waves of horror swept through him. He felt as if he'd walked into a play, and having missed the first crucial act, was trying to catch up with the plot. But this was real. These were his children describing a situation he'd never even remotely suspected existed.

"What do the mean girls say to Robin?" Megan asked.

"They make fun of her hair and clothes and stuff," Natalie replied. "Remember back in Florida in my gymnastics class when those nasty girls from the other school said my clothes were stupid and I looked like a poor girl? Remember how bad I felt?"

The twins nodded solemnly. "Poor Robin," said Molly.

"Why didn't anyone tell me what was going on?" Zack felt winded, as if someone had heaved a bowling ball straight into his solar plexus.

The three Ritter brothers looked at each other and shrugged.

"You couldn't do anything about it, Dad," Justin said. "I mean, you couldn't put those stupid girls in jail or shoot them or anything."

"You could put bubble gum in their hair," Ned offered a suggestion. "That's what me and my friends did to those girls who made Natalie cry. Boy, did they scream!" He grinned at the memory.

Justin brightened. "Cool!"

"You put bubble gum in those girls' hair?" Claudia was astonished. "That's the first I've heard of that."

"There are some things you just don't tell your parents," Natalie explained. "Especially if there is only one." She looked from her mother to Zack. "We know you have it hard enough without having to worry about all your kids' problems."

Brian nodded his head. "So we try to take care of stuff on our own."

Claudia looked stricken. "But we want you to come to us for help!" She addressed all seven children, her brown eyes filling with emotional tears. "We're your parents and we love you. We don't want you worrying about us, we want to know all about your problems and to help every way we can. Isn't that right, Zack?" She turned to him.

"Of course," he muttered, looking grim.

"Then is it okay to tell that we're late every day, too?" Megan asked, looking uncertainly at Natalie, who gave her head a warning shake.

But it was too late, the words were out. "You're late to school *every day?*" Claudia repeated faintly.

"Me and the twins are hopeless in the morning," Ned said, quoting his older sister's oft-repeated lament. "So we miss the bus and Natalie has to walk us to school and then walk to high school. That's why she gets detention all the time."

"I wish I had a great big brother like Brian to carry me to school," Molly said, gazing raptly at Brian. "Neddy would never carry me."

"You got that right," scoffed Ned.

Claudia looked at her oldest daughter. "You never mentioned being in detention, Natalie."

"It's not something I like to brag about," Natalie said sullenly. "Anyway, the kids are in after-school daycare so it doesn't matter where I am—at cheerleading practice or detention."

"It matters to me," Claudia replied. Did Natalie think that her only worth to her mother was as a baby-sitter? Claudia felt like crying.

"That's where we met, in detention," Brian said. "We decided to help each other come up with a solution to our problems. We haven't had much luck so far," he added, glancing from his father to Natalie's mother. He was exasperated. Why couldn't the two adults see that *they* were the solution? It was so clear, so obvious to himself and to Natalie.

"We'll discuss all this later," Zack growled. "Right now I want to find Robin. We'll check all her favorite stores first and—"

"Didn't you say that the boys haven't eaten dinner yet?" Claudia cut in.

"We didn't!" cried Ian, throwing her a grateful smile. "And we're starving to death!"

"Why don't they get something to eat?" suggested Claudia. "All the kids can go to the food court while you and I search the mall, Zack. When Brian has finished his dinner, he can help us look for Robin if she hasn't turned up yet. Natalie will stay with the younger kids."

"That sounds like a real good plan to me," Brian seconded enthusiastically.

Without a word, Zack handed his oldest son some money and the seven kids took off together. Claudia and Zack faced each other.

"Dinner completely slipped my mind," he said, a little awkwardly. "Thanks for reminding me."

"I know from my son that boys are pretty useless when they're hungry."

"Not to mention irritable," Zack added.

"Possessing all the amiability of ravenous jungle beasts."

"Yeah." He met her eyes. "I told you my kids were independent and self-sufficient," he said quietly. "Maybe what's closer to the truth is that they don't feel comfortable confiding in me or asking for my help. Or maybe they don't think I have a clue as to what to do." He shrugged, his expression rueful. "They might just be right."

"I know how you feel." Claudia gazed into space. "I keep picturing my kids walking that long distance to school in the cold weather and the rain, when all the time I thought they were safely riding the school bus. And for them to believe that I couldn't be told! It's shattering to learn how much confidence our kids don't have in us."

"Well, I can't picture Brian having to carry Robin to school because she refused to face some bratty little girls." Zack scowled. "It just doesn't fit with what I know of Rob."

"Who's stronger and tougher than any boy," Claudia repeated his own description of his daughter to him. "The problem is that when girls get older, they fight verbally. And a group of sharp-tongued adolescent girls can annihilate the confidence of their particular target."

"But why would they target Robin in the first place?" Zack was clearly baffled. "She's smart, she's tough, she can run fast and shoots baskets one-on-one better than any of her brothers."

Claudia found his naiveté rather touching. And depressing. "Unfortunately, seventh-grade girls use different criteria to judge other girls, and hair and clothes top the list. It's a shallow age but they do outgrow it, that's the good news. The bad news is that there are a lot of hurt feelings until they do."

"There's nothing wrong with Robin's hair and clothes," Zack insisted.

Claudia knew this was not the time to deliver a fashion update. "I'll check out all the women's rest rooms," she volunteered. "There is a public rest room downstairs and another by the food court. Then I'll check the department stores."

He nodded briskly. "I'll go to all her favorite stores. We'll meet back here in twenty minutes. And Claudia?"

Already on her way, she paused and turned to look at him.

"I appreciate your help. I couldn't enter the women's rest rooms to look for Robin." He drew a deep breath. "Thanks."

"I'd help anyone look for a lost child," Claudia replied with a shrug of dismissal. She was not going to lose her head over that intense blue-eyed gaze, not again. "Who wouldn't?"

Moving at a rapid pace, Claudia checked every women's rest room in the Port Mason Mall. Robin Ritter wasn't in any of them. She glanced at her watch. She had nearly ten minutes before she met Zack. She wondered if he'd had better luck in his search and hoped so. How much time had elapsed before a lost child became a missing child? The thought chilled her.

The sound of a bell ringing caught her attention, and she glanced toward the big glass door leading to a side entrance to the mall. She remembered hearing that last year the Port Mason Mall managers had banned traditional bell-ringing Salvation Army members from seeking donations inside the mall and refused to let them stand outside any of the main entrances, either. They'd been banished outside to those doors which had less usage, and spontaneous donations had fallen off sharply, hurting those who were served by the organization.

Apparently, the same rules applied this year as well.

Frowning, Claudia made her way outside, the idea for an article forming in her head. She would interview the bell-ringers and the mall managers. She planned her angle, something along the lines of dedicated charity workers trying to bring Christmas cheer to the less fortunate versus the Scrooges of Port Mason.

"But why can't I join up now?"

Claudia heard the childish voice the moment she stepped outside. A gust of wind blew a cold blast of rain in her face.

The bell-ringer was not alone. Robin Ritter stood beside her, demanding immediate admittance to the Salvation Army.

"Robin!" Claudia exclaimed, rushing to the girl's side. "We've been looking for you."

"Robin wanted to come back to the mission with me tonight," the bell-ringer said. "I told her she belonged at home with her family."

"I don't want to go home! And I don't want to go back to school!" Robin cried defiantly.

"Why don't we go back inside and get something to eat? I know you must be hungry for dinner, Robin." Claudia placed a donation in the shiny red kettle, before shepherding Robin inside.

Robin did not protest. Claudia guessed the girl was tired and hungry and quite ready to be found. "Your father is worried about you, Robin," Claudia said quietly. "Your brothers told him about the girls from school and how they've been making you miserable."

Robin groaned. "Daddy won't understand. He'll just say, 'Don't pay any attention to them. Sticks and stones can break your bones but names will never hurt you.'"

"Well, he's dead wrong there." Claudia grimaced. "In many ways, words can hurt even worse than sticks and stones."

"I know." Robin's blue eyes filled with tears. "Especially if you look like me." She blinked the tears back and glowered up at Claudia. "And don't tell me that I'm pretty on the inside and that's all that matters, like my grandma used to say. 'Cause inside I'm just a bunch of that gross stuff we learned about in science class and outside I'm still ugly!"

"You're not ugly, Robin," Claudia countered. "You do have a bad haircut, but that can certainly be remedied. I found a good hairdresser here in Port Mason named Paula, and I could make an appointment with her for you, if you'd like."

Robin stared at her thoughtfully. "My haircut really is bad," she agreed.

"Your younger brothers could use good haircuts, too, and Paula cuts boys' hair. Do you think I should make appointments for them?"

"Maybe for Ian," Robin said slowly. "But not Justin. I'm glad he has bad hair! We always fight. He hates me and I hate him."

"Justin doesn't hate you, Robin. He was very concerned when you ran off, and he sounded upset when he talked about those rotten little creeps making fun of you."

"They are rotten little creeps." Robin brightened a little, then scowled again. "But they're right about my geeky clothes. Even if I have nice hair, I'll still be ruined by my clothes."

"Then it's time to get some new ones," Claudia said briskly. "Stuff that's not interchangeable with what your younger brothers wear."

"I won't know what to get. And there's nobody to go shopping with, anyway." Robin's shoulders drooped. "And don't say my dad 'cause he won't know, either, plus he hates to shop."

Faced with the despondent twelve-year-old, Claudia said the only thing she could have, given the circumstances. "Well, my daughter Natalie and I could go with you, if you'd like. We both like shopping."

"Your daughter wouldn't go with me. She's cool! She wouldn't go anywhere with a geek like me."

It was the ideal lead-in for Claudia to relate Natalie's troubles with the girls from the gymnastics class back in Florida. When she added the part she'd just learned tonight, about Ned and his bubble gum vigilantism, Robin actually laughed.

The two were laughing together when Zack joined them beside the North Pole headquarters. A tidal wave of profound relief surged through him at the sight of his daughter, instantly followed by a scalding anger.

"Don't you ever pull a stunt like this again, young lady!" he roared.

Several toddlers, walking with their mothers to visit Santa Claus, cast alarmed glances at him.

Claudia saw Robin stiffen. The father-daughter reunion was off to a miserable start. What else could she do but intervene?

"Zack, Robin needs to eat her dinner," she said, admitting to herself that her tone was officious. "Let's walk her up to the food court, and then I want to talk to you. Alone, Chief," she added pointedly. She walked off, with Robin right at her side.

Zack had no choice but to follow. Claudia deliberately kept ahead of him, but she could practically feel the tension emanating from him as they dropped Robin off with the other kids. He followed her to a less-crowded corridor of the mall where several benches were placed.

Claudia stopped walking. "Okay, go ahead and yell at me." She gazed up at him, her brown eyes challenging. "I know you're ready to explode, and I can take anything you can dish out. Robin can't, not right now. So come on, let me have it, Chief."

She was right, the explosive feelings within him were building to flash point, and her disdainful challenge acted as the detonator. "You want it? Baby, you'll get it!" He caught her wrist and propelled her into his hard body. "But I prefer action to words."

"Zachary!" she protested, struggling. She noticed a few shoppers casting frankly curious glances at them. One young man actually turned around and began to walk backward, the better to observe the action. "Zack, we're in a shopping mall, for heaven's sake!"

"I don't care." He held her closer, gazing down at her, scanning the delicate features of her face. His eyes lingered on the tempting fullness of her lips. The touch of her hands on his chest—even though she was pushing against him— seemed to turn his blood into hot lava as it pumped through his veins. He felt his body going rigid and knew he should release her at once. But he didn't. He couldn't. "I don't care!" He groaned.

Claudia felt him against her and froze. "You can't want me," she reminded him. "I have *four children,* remember? According to your self-imposed standards, that makes me taboo."

"You are most definitely taboo," he gritted. "I don't want to want you." His possessive blue gaze traveled from her face to the soft curve of her breasts crushed against his chest. The sight struck him as incredibly erotic. He wanted to see more, to see her breasts full and bare against his skin.

"Unfortunately I can't remember ever wanting a woman more," he confessed, burying his face into the sensitive curve of her neck. He drew in several uneven breaths.

Claudia felt a warm liquid sensation deep inside, and the fight drained out of her. "Poor Zack," she sighed, and leaned into him. She put her arms around his waist and relaxed against the hard wall of his body. "This has been a very trying day for you, hasn't it?"

"Very." He held her tight, his heart pounding against his ribs. He was not an advocate of public displays of affection, but holding Claudia felt so good—an irresistible combination of excitement and abiding comfort—that he broke his own rules. He wished they were alone, he particularly wished they were not in Port Mason's major shopping mall.

"I awakened this morning after a lousy night's sleep because I kept tossing and turning and thinking about the sexy lady in red who'd fired my imagination and then disappeared from the Smiths' party. Then I read a column written by Port Mason's crusading crackpot blasting my VVRZ."

"A speed trap by any other name is still a speed trap," Claudia paraphrased boldly.

Zack threw her a mock scowl of disapproval. "Imagine my surprise when the crackpot and the babe who was hot to meet me turned out to be one and the same."

"Imagine *my* surprise to be standing in a mall being groped by the chauvinist blockhead who refers to me as a crackpot and a babe," Claudia said archly.

Zack grinned and reluctantly dropped his arms and stepped away from her. "I was simply holding you. When I'm groping you, you'll know it. *Babe,*" he added, his blue eyes teasing.

Claudia laughed, she couldn't help it. She liked him, she admitted to herself. And she was very attracted to him. It seemed a shame that there was no possible future for them, except friendship. Because Zack did have a point—eight was an incredible number of children. And though Zack seemed overly zealous against the idea of stepchildren, in all honesty, she herself was not champing at the bit to take on four more children, either.

They walked back to the food court, side by side, talking easily together. Claudia told Zack about Robin's plans to sign up for the Salvation Army and her own promises to help the girl.

"No strings attached," Claudia added, just to make things clear. "I don't want you to think I'm spending time with Robin to get close to you. I would never use a child that way."

Zack felt a peculiar pang at the finality of her tone. He was appalled to realize that he wouldn't mind Claudia trying to get closer to him. Confusion swept over him like a thick blanket of fog. He did not want to become involved with a woman who had children, he reminded himself, especially not four children! Perhaps if Claudia had just one child—all right, he mentally conceded, maybe even two—he could reconsider his vow against fatherhood. But *four?* Double his family with just one stroke? No, it was absolutely out of the question.

Claudia seemed to feel the same way. When they parted at the food court after collecting their respective offspring, she made plans to go shopping with Robin, but there was no mention of her seeing or talking to Robin's dad.

Chapter Seven

"The band is getting better, isn't it? You can actually recognize 'Silver Bells,'" Natalie exclaimed brightly as Brian took his usual seat beside her in the cheerless basement detention room the next day. Next door the band played on, while the chorus practiced on the other side. "I think they'll have it right in time for the holiday program. And I like the way the chorus sings 'We Wish you a Merry Christmas.' They sound almost good."

"You're sure in a good mood today," Brian observed.

"I know. Because after my sentence is up at the end of this week, I'm out of detention for good!"

"Not going to be late anymore, huh?"

Natalie shook her head. "My mom called her boss and said she couldn't come to work until after she got the kids on the school bus. She said she'd make up the time in the afternoon. This morning was great!"

Natalie beamed with pleasure. "Mom was the one chasing after Ned's book bag and coat and shoes, and she had to get those pokey twins moving, too. And when I was leaving she said she was sorry that she'd left me to do it all, that this was the first school term we didn't have Grandma to help in the mornings plus the first time the twins had to get up for school. She said she had no idea what a hard time we'd been having, and she's going to buy me a new Lemonheads tape to make up for my time in detention!"

"Sounds like everything worked out for you." Brian was happy for her, but his voice held an unmistakable note of gloom.

"What about you?" Natalie asked. "Were things any better at your house now that your dad knows what's been going on?"

"He stuck around this morning, though he won't be able to every day. And things were as bad as ever, except Dad was there for it all—Justin being slow, Ian losing everything and Robin throwing a fit and refusing to go to school. I felt guilty when I left the house on time, leaving Dad to cope with it all alone."

"He's probably worse at it than you," Natalie commented, and Brian nodded his head.

"My dad still needs a wife, but I guess you don't care if your mom is married or not since you won't be stuck in detention anymore." He heaved a sigh.

"Brian, I don't think we should give up on our plan." Natalie leaned closer and lowered her voice. "Your dad and my mom should be together. The kids need both a mother and a father. And I could really use another TV set. Tonight I'm going to miss the *Billboard Music Awards* because the twins will be watching the *Frosty the Snowman Special.*"

"You could come over to my house to watch it," Brian suggested immediately. "Your mom could drive you over."

"No, she won't leave Ned and the twins alone, even for a little while. They'll have a monster fight over the TV. You can see why we just can't go on with just one set."

"Then I'll ask my dad to pick you up. But you'll have to figure out a way to get him into your house to see your mom."

"Don't worry." Natalie's jaw was set with a determination he was beginning to know well. "I'll think of something."

Leaving Robin in charge of the two younger boys, Zack drove Brian to the Nolans' house to pick up Natalie. It was a cold, clear night, and Zack slipped a cassette of Christmas songs into the tape player as they rode along the brightly lit streets of Port Mason. In the downtown area, a large wreath with weatherproof red ribbon was hung on every streetlight. As they moved into the residential areas, most of the houses sported Christmas lights, varying from single white candles in the windows to dazzling displays of multicolored lights that changed sequences every few seconds.

"Natalie lives on Hopwood Lane?" Zack asked Brian. He knew she did, of course, because he'd looked up Claudia's number and address in the phone book. He cast a sidelong glance at his son. This was the first time Brian had ever invited a girl over to the house, and he supposed the evening constituted his son's first date.

He viewed the situation with a certain amount of nostalgia. It seemed like only yesterday Brian was a toddler, and now he was dating! Next came definite misgivings. He was uncomfortable with the fact that he was lusting after his son's little girlfriend's mother. Poor Brian would be horrified if he even suspected such a thing!

Of course, nothing could result from his feelings for Claudia Nolan, nothing but a lack of sleep. Zack yawned, courtesy of another restless night of wanting her and not having her. He had to get over this, he admonished himself.

"There's Hopwood Lane," Brian called. What sort of plan had Natalie come up with? he wondered. Would they be able to carry it off?

Zack heard the note of apprehension in his son's voice and misinterpreted the source of the boy's anxiety. He remembered back to his own early days of dating, the excitement and abject fear of being alone with a girl. Wondering when, if and how to make a move on her....

Zack coughed. "Brian, we've never really had a...talk about, uh, dating and the, er, responsibilities that a boy—"

"Dad!" Brian cut in, aghast. Surely his father wasn't about to launch into a father-son talk about sex! "Natalie's just a friend," he added hurriedly. He could never think of her in any other way, not now. She was going to be his sister!

"There's the house—433," Zack boomed heartily. He was disconcerted but determined not to show it. He'd always prided himself on having an open easy relationship with his kids, yet for the second time in as many days, he'd been rebuffed by them. First by Robin's refusal to confide her middle-school problems and now by Brian, cutting off what was to have been their first adult male-to-male talk about the opposite sex.

"Natalie's up on that ladder." Brian leaned forward in his seat and gazed out the windshield.

Natalie stood on a ladder, trying to string Christmas lights around a window. Claudia and Ned were busy draping strings of lights around a cluster of evergreens that surrounded the front of the house.

Just as Zack pulled into the driveway, the ladder began to sway precariously, and suddenly Natalie fell off.

"She fell!" Brian shouted, horrified.

Claudia screamed, dropped the lights and ran over to her daughter. Zack screeched the car to a stop and bolted from the car. Seconds later, he and Claudia were kneeling beside Natalie, who lay on the ground, moaning.

"Is she okay?" Brian asked worriedly.

"I don't see any blood," Ned sounded almost disappointed.

"Natalie, honey, are you all right?" Claudia touched her daughter's head, her neck, feeling for breaks or bumps or open wounds.

"Can you move your arms and legs, Natalie?" Zack asked worriedly.

Natalie gingerly moved her fingers and her feet, then carefully bent her elbows and her knees. "I can move them," she said faintly. She glanced up and caught Brian's eye.

Brian was taken aback. He could've sworn that she had almost grinned at him. His eyes narrowed. Could it be? Was it possible? Was falling off the ladder part of Natalie's plan?

"Try to sit up, sweetheart," Claudia urged, helping her daughter to half sit, half lean against her. "Are you dizzy?"

"How many fingers am I holding up?" Zack asked, thrusting three fingers in front of Natalie's face. "Do you know what day this is?"

Natalie answered the questions correctly. "I guess that means my brains aren't scrambled," she said, smiling a bravely sweet smile.

"Try to answer these." Brian knelt down beside her. "What famous Christmas song do we hear the band trash day after day while we're in detention? And while we're on the subject of detention, is Shonna's new nose ring silver or gold? And what serpent is on Smash's tattoo?"

He watched Natalie struggle to maintain her wounded waif look and suppress her laughter and realized that the fall was indeed part of her plan. Her dedication to their cause awed him.

"I think I can stand up now," Natalie said in a commendably weak voice.

Claudia helped the girl to her feet. Her heartbeat was beginning to return to a rate compatible with life; she'd nearly fainted with fright when she'd seen her oldest child hit the ground. "I think we ought to take you to the hospital and have a doctor look at you, honey. Maybe you should be X-rayed, too."

Zack nodded. "Good idea." He looked at Claudia's pale face. She was shaken and trembling and he felt parentally empathetic toward her. "I'll drive you," he added.

"Oh, I couldn't let you—" Claudia began.

"I insist," Zack said, interrupting. "Brian can stay with the younger kids while we're at the hospital. And be sure to call your sister to tell her where we are, son."

"I don't want to go to the hospital!" Natalie pouted. "And it's not fair to make Brian stay here and watch *Frosty* with the twins."

"Brian doesn't mind," Zack said firmly. "We're taking you to the hospital, Natalie, and that's that. Can you walk to the car or shall I carry you?"

"I can walk," Natalie grumbled. "But maybe you should carry my mom. She looks worse than me."

Zack put a friendly arm around Claudia. "Yes, she does, doesn't she?" He hugged her closer to his side. Strictly friend-to-friend, he assured himself. "Don't worry, you're both going to be fine."

Brian walked Natalie to the car while Zack went inside the house with Claudia to explain the situation to the younger children.

"I can't believe you fell off that ladder on purpose!" Brian scolded his cohort as they sat in the back seat of the car. "Are you crazy? You really could've gotten hurt!"

"Nah!" Natalie shrugged. "I've been taking gymnastics since I was six. One thing I know how to do is land. And that wasn't really a fall. It was sort of like a dismount off the parallel bars, except I made sure I didn't land on my feet. I'm fine, and our plan worked!" She clutched Brian's arm excitedly. "They're together! Did you see him hug her?"

"But you have to go to the hospital," Brian reminded her.

"*That* wasn't part of the plan. I could've talked my mom out of going, but your dad wouldn't let me."

"My dad is the police chief. He's used to being in charge. He expects people to do what he says and they almost always do."

Natalie sighed. "So now we'll both miss the music awards. Sorry that you're stuck here baby-sitting."

"It's okay." Brian shrugged. "I kind of like those old cartoons. Good luck at the hospital."

Their parents joined them, Zack solicitously helping Claudia into the front seat. "Natalie looks fine," he murmured gently, leaning down to buckle her seat belt. "Don't worry, Claudia. Taking her to the hospital is strictly a precautionary measure. I'm sure they'll verify that she wasn't hurt.''

Claudia was fully capable of fastening the belt herself, but she allowed Zack to do it for her. There was something comforting in being taken care of, and she realized that it had been a very, very long time since a man had even attempted to do so.

''Thank you, Zack,'' she said softly. Her face was very close to his. They gazed deeply into each other's eyes for a long moment. ''This is very kind of you.''

Zack swallowed. The urge to touch his mouth to hers in a gently soothing kiss was almost overwhelming. His heart thudded against his ribs, and he had to summon a surprising amount of willpower to make himself straighten and move away from her.

The drive to the hospital was quick, the wait in the emergency ward quite long. Natalie immersed herself in a fashion magazine and sat on the opposite side of the waiting room from her mother and Zack.

''Natalie is pretending not to know us,'' Claudia murmured to Zack, who sat beside her. ''She's in one of her I-don't-have-parents-I'm-living-single-on-my-own moods.''

''Ouch.'' Zack laughed. ''My kids haven't pulled that yet.''

''Just wait. One day you'll offend their sense of what is cool and what isn't, and suddenly you'll be banished. For a while, anyway.''

Zack glanced at Natalie. ''She looks bored. We might not be cool, but at least we're having a good time, hanging out together. She's stuck with her own company.''

''A definite hazard of the living-single state.'' Claudia grinned at him.

''We ought to know,'' murmured Zack. Despite all their children, he and Claudia were essentially ''living single.'' And having all the kids set them apart from other single adults who weren't parents. He acknowledged that their circumstances were astonishingly similar.

"Having four kids, we're never alone but sometimes it gets awfully lonely," Claudia said softly.

A stunning insight, Zack decided, giving her full marks for perception. How pleasant it was to have another adult around to share things with, to laugh with. An adult who understood kids, who wasn't unnerved by them or didn't idealize them. All the women he'd dated in the past seemed to do one or the other. Of course, the women he'd dated in the past were younger, in their early or mid-twenties, and had no children of their own.

Natalie was examined by the doctor and sent to X ray; she insisted on being accompanied only by the aide. That left Claudia and Zack alone in the waiting room where they passed the time, chatting companionably.

Zack told her all about Port Mason. Being a fourth-generation native of the town, he knew much of its history and interesting scandals, and Claudia soaked up the information, as a newspaper reporter and new citizen eager for knowledge about her new hometown. She loved listening to him; he was funny and shrewd and insightful. The usual tedium of a hospital waiting room was transformed into something else entirely.

When Zack bought sodas and snacks to eat and drink as they talked and laughed together, it was almost as if . . . as if they were spending time getting to know each other on a date! Claudia felt an immediate pang of guilt. Her child was being poked and probed and X-rayed, and she was carrying on like a giddy teenager right here in the waiting room with Zack. She berated herself for her unmaternal behavior.

Zack sensed her withdrawal immediately. And he didn't like it. "Don't," he said gruffly.

Claudia looked at him. "Don't what?"

His blue eyes glittered. "Suddenly turn cool on me. I won't put up with that kind of moodiness, Claudia. Friendly and warm one minute, cold the next."

Claudia bristled, about to launch a counterattack. But some instinct stopped her. "I was thinking about Natalie," she said frankly. "And feeling guilty that I'm out here having fun with you while she's in there with the doctor, missing her TV show with Brian. And that's the lucky part. She could've been seriously hurt in that fall."

Zack felt the sudden tension drain from him. He'd been poised for an argument that didn't come. "I'm sorry." He mumbled the words, feeling foolish.

"Who was the moody person in your life that set off that alarm?" Claudia asked lightly. She wondered how she'd become so attuned to him that she knew there was such a person. "Your mom?"

"My mother was the most levelheaded, even-tempered woman I've ever known," Zack said after a pause. "I guess that's why Sharon—my wife's—temperament came as a shock. Her moods were as unpredictable and fast-changing as the weather." He gave his head a shake. "It was hard on the kids, she was so inconsistent. Screaming at them for doing something one time and then laughing about it the next."

Claudia guessed at what went unsaid, that Zack's late wife was equally inconsistent and unpredictable in her responses to him.

Zack drew in a deep breath. "Sharon and I didn't have a happy marriage," he admitted grimly. "Things seemed to go sour almost right from the start. We thought maybe having a family would bind us closer but it ended up driving us even further apart."

He wasn't sure why he was telling her this; his marriage was the one subject that he took care not to discuss with anyone. But somehow it felt right, even necessary, to share this piece of his past with Claudia.

"Sharon had already filed for divorce when her liver cancer was diagnosed. I talked her into withdrawing the petition, and we tried to work things out, but it wasn't to be.

She got very sick very fast. In less than six months she was dead."

"I'm sorry," Claudia said quietly. "It must have been terrible for you." She realized how lucky she was to have had so many warm memories of Jeff to sustain her.

Zack rose to his feet, giving a forced false laugh. "I don't know why I'm dumping all this on you." He stared uncomfortably at the floor.

"Because we're friends." Claudia stood up, too, and impulsively slipped her hand into his. "And friends tell each other things." She squeezed his hand. "They also do things for each other, like sitting for hours in a hospital emergency waiting room. Thank you for being my friend, Zack."

Natalie came through the doors at that moment followed by a nurse. The girl's brown eyes gleamed with glee when she spied her mother holding hands with Zack Ritter.

"Mrs. Nolan, Natalie is just fine," the nurse announced. "We did warn her against climbing on ladders, however."

The three were driving back to the Nolan house when Natalie made an announcement of her own. "I can't stay off ladders just because of one little fall. I'm going to climb that ladder tomorrow and finish putting up the lights."

"No!" Zack and Claudia chorused together.

"Well, somebody has to put up those lights and I don't want my mom falling off the ladder," Natalie said calmly. "So I'm going to—"

"Natalie, *I'll* put up the lights," Zack said firmly. "You stay away from that ladder, do you understand?"

"Yes, sir," Natalie said demurely. "Mommy, if Chief Ritter is going to put up the lights for us, could he and the kids come to our house for dinner tomorrow?"

"I think that's a wonderful idea, Natalie." Claudia turned to smile at her daughter, then glanced over at Zack. "That is, if you'd like to come, Chief Ritter."

Zack grinned. "And I'll be sure to bring Brian along," he said, his voice teasing. "Your mom and I weren't born yesterday, Natalie. We recognize a setup when we see one."

"I don't know what you mean," Natalie said innocently.

"He means that we both know you want to spend some time with Brian, since tonight didn't work out," Claudia said.

"Gee, parents are so smart," said Natalie. She almost laughed out loud. *Herself and Brian?* Why, they were practically sister and brother! Soon they would be; she was absolutely certain of that.

"Absolutely," Zack agreed. "Keep in mind that your mother and I will always be one step ahead of you kids."

"After all, you were our age once," Natalie added helpfully. "Oh, turn up that song!" she commanded. "I love it. The chorus has never sung it. Maybe that's why I like it so much."

Zack obligingly turned up "We Need a Little Christmas."

The accompanying chorus of bells filled the car. Zack and Claudia cast quick smiles at each other. Keeping one hand on the steering wheel, his other hand found hers and closed over it.

Somehow their fingers interlocked and stayed that way. After all, why shouldn't a couple of friends hold hands? Especially during this time of year, the season of peace and joy and good cheer?

Claudia was filled with a melting warmth as she felt the strength of his hand clasping hers. By the time they arrived home, the song was over, but bells seemed to be ringing in her head. Every time Zack smiled at her, they grew louder.

Chapter Eight

The Ritters were the most enthusiastic, appreciative dinner guests Claudia had ever entertained. They adored her beef stew, which had been simmering all day in the slow cooker, they raved about her quickie refrigerator biscuits and devoured the red-and-green Jell-O fruit salad. Their compliments on her cooking made her feel like a five-star chef.

Claudia was astonished. Among her children, Ned had a hearty appetite, but the girls were picky eaters. It made cooking for the family less than a joy, but the Ritters reversed all that. She was so inspired that she suggested baking cookies for dessert. "By the time Zack and Brian are finished putting up the lights, the first batch will be ready."

"Let's make gingerbread people!" cried Molly.

Megan ran to the cabinet to retrieve the cookie cutters.

"There are men and women and boys and girls," Zack observed, lifting the metal cutters from the box. "I thought she was being politically correct when she said *gingerbread people* instead of the traditional *men,* but there really are both sexes and different ages represented here."

He caught Claudia's eye. "Did you expect anything less from the daughter of the PMS Observer?" she demanded saucily.

"You're not going to let me forget that one, are you?" Zack moved closer, giving her a smile that sent her pulses into overdrive. His blue eyes held hers.

"Not likely."

Her smile had an equally potent effect on him. His eyes darkened and he sucked in his breath, wishing they were alone. If they were, he would pull her into his arms, taking her up on what that sexy, suggestive smile of hers suggested. He temporarily forgot that such behavior was not the norm between good pals like Claudia and himself.

"We like to make whole gingerbread families," Natalie was explaining to the Ritters. "The dad, the mom, the brother, the sister."

"The twins," put in Megan.

"The grandparents?" suggested Robin, rummaging through another box which contained tubes of many different colored icings.

"There's even a dog and a cat in here!" enthused Ian, grabbing the animal-shaped cutters. "I'm going to make a whole family of dogs and then a whole family of cats."

"I'm going to make a football team," Justin declared. "I can use these green and orange colors to make them uniforms. I'll put numbers on them. My number is seventeen," he added proudly.

"I thought you guys would play video games with me," said Ned.

Justin shook his head. "We can do that anytime. We want to do this now."

"I'll get out the ingredients," Natalie said quickly, moving toward the refrigerator.

"I'm in shock," Zack murmured to Claudia as they watched the children settle themselves around the table. "Justin and Ian haven't turned down an offer to play video games since they picked up the controls at the ripe old age of four or five. And now they want to *bake?*"

"Stick around us and we'll make multifaceted nineties' men of your sons yet," Claudia teased.

"I think I'll help you with the lights, Chief Ritter," Ned decided, sidling up to Zack. "You and me Brian can work while they—" he glanced disdainfully at his mother and sisters. Clearly, he did not share the other Ritters' fascination with a kitchen project "—bake cookies."

Claudia suppressed a grin as Ned, affecting a macho swagger, followed Zack and Brian outside. It was nice to have other males around to rescue Ned from the all-female atmosphere normally surrounding him.

Meanwhile, the three youngest Ritters seemed to bask in that same atmosphere that Ned was eager to escape. Having strung the lights outside, Zack returned to watch the kids in action in the kitchen. There was much hilarity as the cookies were cut, cooked—occasionally burnt—and decorated with a wild assortment of icing colors and garbs.

Ian and Justin continually sought Claudia's opinion and her assistance, much more so than the twins who were smaller and younger. Zack was about to make some crack about the boys being out of their element in the kitchen when it occurred to him that his sons weren't so much incompetent as avidly seeking Claudia's attention. They talked with her and made stupid jokes that she chuckled over. When she laid her hand on Ian's shoulder, he actually leaned against her like a small puppy seeking warmth. The sight stirred Zack. He was not particularly physically demonstrative, nor had his mother been. Ian seemed to soak up Claudia's natural gestures of affection like a sunflower turning toward the rays of the sun.

There were other revelations. Robin was actually being helpful and sweet with the twins, Robin who spent most of her time at home at war with her younger brothers. Zack had been convinced his daughter hated younger kids, but she didn't seem to hate the two little Nolan girls at all. They were getting along splendidly. And Natalie was kind to Robin, joking around with her, treating her as a peer and not a pariah.

Claudia presided over the scene like a maestro conducting an orchestra. There was less noise and confusion and chaos in this kitchen with six children than at his own house with just four. In the other room Brian played a video game with Ned who showed Brian a respect he didn't get from his own siblings. Their young male bonding was actually heartwarming to observe.

"Eight kids, and there hasn't been a single fight, no shouts, no blows, no endless rounds of recrimination," Zack murmured to Claudia as he came to stand beside her. "What did you do, cast a spell on them?"

"Of course," Claudia agreed cheerfully.

Her spell was a potent one, extending to himself, though Zack was careful not to mention that. His hand slipped to the nape of her neck and he began to knead with strong fingers.

"You're not even tense," he accused mildly. "How can I suggest slipping away upstairs for a soothing massage when you're already so relaxed?"

Claudia glanced up and saw that Zack was watching her intently. There was a tension in his eyes, in his face, that made her catch her breath. "I'm not really good at this sort of thing, Zack," she said in a voice that she wished weren't so tremulous.

"No?" He dropped his hand from her neck to lightly brush his knuckles down the smooth, flushed skin of her cheek. "I'd say you are a premier cookie baker, organizer and adviser," he said lightly.

"That I am." She nodded her head, summoning a shaky smile. "But I'm out of my depth when it comes to trading sexy banter and innuendos with a man who has already made it clear that friendship is all he wants from me."

She moved away from him, stepping carefully beyond his reach. "I like knowing the rules and playing by them," she said in a low voice. "Being a policeman, I thought you did, too. Friends don't let friends cross over the line," she said, paraphrasing succinctly.

She was nervous and confused, though she tried hard not to show it. Just the touch of his fingers on her skin sent shivers of excitement through her. No other man had ever raised such an immediate and intense response in her, not even her long-lost beloved Jeff.

When Zack was close, she wanted to touch him, when he was touching her, she wanted to lean into him and melt against him, to feel his lips on hers, his hands moving over her, pressing her closer, making demands she was only too eager to meet.

But Zack didn't want to be involved with a woman with children, and she could never be sexually involved with him without the full spectrum of emotional demands and needs and promises that exist between an intimately involved man and woman. For her own sake they must let their attention dissolve into the nonsexual realm of friendship.

I like knowing the rules and playing by them. Zack stifled a sigh. Claudia was right, of course. He was sending out mixed signals, claiming one thing, seeking another. He wished it were possible for him and Claudia to be both friends and lovers, but of course, that could never be.

So he tamped his desire and turned himself into Good Buddy Zack. "I want to make some policemen," he announced, commandeering several of the undecorated gingerbread men from the cooling tray. "Where's the blue icing for their uniforms?"

"Too bad there isn't a car cookie cutter," Natalie said. "You could make them a gingerbread police car."

"And set up a VVRZ to nab all the hapless gingerbread shoppers driving home from the mall," Claudia put in. "Bring in a little extra cash for the gingerbread policemen's ball."

"There is no policemen's ball in Port Mason, gingerbread or otherwise," Zack shot back. "But I'm delighted that you've finally mastered the correct terminology."

"I think you mean doublespeak. And I've mastered it so well, I'm planning to write a column on what I've learned. You know, that *revenue enhancing* is *raising taxes,* an *interdimensional communications device* is a *newspaper ad.* I thought my grand finale would be *VVRZ* equals *speed trap.*"

"Oh, I'll be looking forward to that," Zack said dryly. He tried to summon the outrage such a column—an unabashedly mocking one—ought to arouse in him. But he felt no outrage, not even mild annoyance. Writing columns was Claudia's job just as enforcing the law—and the speed limit!—was his. Neither seemed to have anything to do with their relationship. Their friendship, he amended quickly to himself.

"A Christmas tree farm?" Molly was puzzled. "Do they have reindeers here, too?"

"No animals, cookie," Zack explained. He'd taken to calling both twins cookie because it seemed a tactful way to disguise his inability to tell one from the other. In addition, the Nolan kids had insisted that the Ritters join them for more cookie baking for four separate evenings after the initial gingerbread people baking spree. Christmas cookies and the Nolans were irretrievably linked in his mind. "There are just Christmas trees here."

"It can't be a farm without animals," Megan pointed out. "Old Macdonald had pigs and cows and lambs and stuff on his farm, not Christmas trees."

Natalie sighed. "Those two have been obsessed with this Christmas tree farm business ever since you invited us to come along and cut down our tree with you."

"Not obsessed, excited," Claudia corrected, putting a more positive light on her youngest daughters' relentless fixation with the concept of a Christmas tree farm.

"I can't believe we're going to go into the woods and cut down our own tree!" Ned exclaimed. "Chief Ritter, can I swing the ax?" He cast an admiring glance at the big, shiny, sharp-bladed ax that Zack was holding.

"I don't think—" Claudia began worriedly.

"Yes, Ned, you certainly can," Zack cut in. "I'll show him how, Claudia, he'll do fine."

"I don't like axes," announced Ian, standing closely beside Claudia. "I'm scared I'll chop myself up instead of the tree."

"Well, you don't have to touch the ax if you don't want to," Claudia soothed, putting a protective arm around the little boy's shoulders. "You can stand with me well out of the way, Ian."

Smiling his relief, Ian leaned against her, reaching up to take her hand.

The Ritters and the Nolans were on a joint trip to the Emersons' Christmas tree farm, fifteen miles west of Port Mason. The Ritters went every year to tramp into the woods, select their tree, chop it down and then drag it back by sled to the big barn, where a roaring fire and cups of hot cider and donuts awaited as a reward for their hard work.

During one of their cookie-baking evenings—they'd done sugar cookies, green Christmas trees with colored nonpareils that night, which had prompted the subject of trees—the Ritters had explained their tradition to the entranced Nolans who'd made do with an artificial tree all those Christmases in Florida.

"A fake white one with white lights and white balls," Ned grumbled while the Ritters shuddered in horror at the very idea.

"It was Grandma's," Natalie added. "She thought it was beautiful, and we had to put it up every year."

Claudia laughed at her disgruntled offspring, well remembering their annual outrage with their grandparents' all-white tree. "We were looking forward to this year when we could buy a *green* artificial tree."

"Dad will arrest you if you put up an artificial tree, no matter what color it is," Brian joked. "We'll chop down a real tree for you, right, Dad?"

"They can come along with us and pick out their own," Zack decreed. "Although we will help them with the chopping."

So the two families were here, and the excitement among the children was running high. It began to snow as they tramped into the woods, the boys pulling sleds to carry back their cut-down trees. The kids charged ahead while Claudia walked with Zack who was moving more slowly, the better to assess the attributes of the various trees along the way.

"This is so beautiful," she said, gazing around the ever-green forest, as thick white snowflakes fell around them. "It's like we're in a Christmas movie or something. The scenery is just perfect. Thank you for inviting us along, Zack."

Zack glanced down at her. She was wearing a bright blue jacket and matching earmuffs, and snowflakes were begin-ning to fall and glisten on her pale hair. She looked beauti-ful, a perfect complement to their glorious wintry surroundings. He felt the familiar quickening in his blood at the sight of her, along with another deeper rush of emo-tions.

"My pleasure," he said thickly. Which it was. He wanted to say more, but here in the woods in the snow with eight kids and an ax, did not seem the right time and place.

He halted in his tracks. "Kids, here's a good tree. And another nice one right behind it. Come over and take a look."

All eight children clustered around the trees and pro-nounced them perfect. The chopping began.

"Cutting down two trees is hard work," complained Justin a long while later, as they dragged the two trees back to the barn on the sleds. "We should've just cut down one and shared it."

"But whose house would it go in?" demanded Robin. She reached into her coat pocket and pulled out a comb, run-ning it through her newly cut, newly styled hair. It was a flattering cut and had done wonders for the girl's appear-ance and self-confidence. Her new clothes, purchased on a shopping trip with Claudia and Natalie, had worked a similar magic. "If there was only one tree, then one house wouldn't have a tree," she added logically.

"It could go in Claudia's house," Ian piped up. "And then we'd go live there, too."

"You can't live in somebody's house just because you're sharing a Christmas tree, Ian," Natalie explained patiently. "To live together, the two families would have to become one. Like if your dad married my mom."

"Okay," Ian agreed. "When?"

"Subtle, Nat," Brian murmured wryly. "Real smooth."

Claudia and Zack remained still and silent throughout the exchange. They took great care not to glance in the other's direction.

"Well, I think it's a good idea," Ned exclaimed. "We need a dad and the Ritters need a mom. How about it?"

"Neddy, you know that Chief Ritter and I are just friends," gritted Claudia.

"Oh, Mom, no you're not." Natalie heaved an impatient sigh. "Brian and me are friends but you and Chief Ritter are more than that. Why don't you just admit it and go for it?"

Zack felt compelled to speak up, for Claudia was crimson with embarrassment and apparently silenced from it as well. "Natalie, I think this is strictly a smoke screen you're sending up because your mother and I are very well aware that you and Brian—well, how shall I put this?—have a crush on each other?"

"Oh, *puh-leeze!*" Natalie rolled her eyes. "I prefer older men. Like Seth Albans. I just wish he preferred me."

"And I'm not ready to settle down with a girlfriend," Brian said, displaying his best man-of-the-world air. "I'm too busy enjoying my freedom."

"Brian and I are like sister and brother. Which we want to be and *soon!*" Natalie blurted out, exasperated. "Why do you think Brian asked the Smiths to invite Mom to their party? So she could meet you, Chief Ritter," she added, in case the adults were too dense to guess the reason why.

"You were behind that invitation?" Claudia gasped at the pair.

"It didn't work," Brian said ruefully. "Dad ended up with Señorita Pierson and we had to come up with another plan to get you together. Like Natalie and the lad—"

"Shut up, Brian," Natalie warned, then flashed a sweet smile at her mother and Zack. "It doesn't matter how you got together, now you finally are, and we're all going to be a family."

"Kids, you're way, way off base on this one." Zack was beginning to perspire, though it was certainly not warm outside. In fact, the weather was grower colder as the wind picked up and the snow began to fall faster and heavier. "Not to mention way out of line," he added tersely.

"I'm tired of walking," Megan complained. The three youngest children were the only ones not paying attention to the critical conversation going on around them. "I'm cold. My boots are wet. Can I ride on top of the tree on the sled?"

"No!" everybody but Molly and Ian said at once.

Megan began to wail piteously. Claudia picked her up, and the little girl wrapped her arms and legs around her mother and held on like a small monkey.

"Why don't you want to marry Claudia, Dad?" whined Justin. "We want you to."

"Don't you like my mom, Chief Ritter?" Ned asked, sounding hurt.

"I think we've said enough on this subject," Claudia interjected. She managed to keep her voice commendably light and jolly. "Let's talk about something else."

"Like your date to the the *Port Mason Daily Press* Christmas party?" Natalie asked artlessly. "What's his name again, Mom? Owen Something? Or Something Owen?"

"Owen Wexler," Claudia murmured, trying to silence Natalie with a sharp maternal glance.

"He reviews books and movies for the paper and gets free movie passes, isn't that cool?" exclaimed Natalie, catching Brian's eye. "What are you going to wear on your date, Mom?"

"A date?" Robin gasped. "What about Daddy?"

"Dad can go out with Señorita Pierson," said Brian. "Who cares if she's too young and wears clothes that are too tight and my life will be miserable because everyone at school will be making jokes about it?"

"There's the barn!" Claudia called out. She was still carrying Megan who had finally stopped howling. "I bet everybody is ready for some hot cider and donuts." Her gaiety had a desperate ring to it.

"You have a date for the *Press* Christmas party?" Zack was at her side, his teeth clenched, his voice low. He was reeling in the throes of a sexual jealousy as fierce as the snowstorm swirling around them. "You didn't say a word about—"

"I don't recall you mentioning Señorita Pierson, either," Claudia retorted. She tried to pick up her pace and get away from him, but lost her footing. She stumbled, tried and failed to right herself, then she and Megan tumbled to the ground.

Megan began to cry loud and hard. Zack grimly scooped her up with one arm and yanked Claudia to her feet with the other.

"We can manage, thank you," Claudia said stiffly, reaching for Megan.

"Yeah, sure." Zack was surly. Keeping a tight hold on her arm he half dragged her toward the barn, holding Megan just as firmly under his other arm.

"I think they're having a fight," Natalie remarked to the others as they all trudged toward the barn. "Or about to."

"Mentioning that your mom had a date sure was dumb," Justin muttered. "Dad's mad, I could tell."

"I think it's because he's jealous," Robin said.

"And if he's jealous, that means he cares. It could even mean he's in love!" Natalie added exultantly. "It better mean that!"

Brian stared at his father, now warming his hands over the fire, looking angry and impatient, but clearly not like a man in love. Claudia was already helping the younger children get their refreshments.

Brian approached his dad cautiously.

"Dad, are you going to that party Claudia is going to with her, uh, date?"

"No!" Zack snapped. "It's a company party for the *Press* employees. And don't try to wangle an invitation out of Manny Fisher for me, either," he warned. "I think you and your young accessory have done enough already."

"Natalie's the main perpetrator," Brian defended himself. "*I'm* the accessory after the fact. We just wanted—"

"I don't want to talk about it," Zack said in such a forbidding tone that Brian wondered if he should request to be read his rights.

He wandered over to where Claudia stood, surrounded by kids, hers and Zack's. "Are you mad at me and Natalie?" Brian asked her bluntly. She didn't seem angry or upset, but he thought it best to check.

"Natalie and me," Claudia corrected. She sighed. "No, I'm not mad, Brian. I'm glad I met you and your sister and brothers. I want you to know that the four of you are always welcome in our house."

"But not my dad?" Brian glanced across the barnyard to where his father stood alone, glowering into the fire.

"Your father, too. He and I are friends," Claudia insisted. She stole a glance at Zack who was staring hard at her. He did not look the least bit friendly. A small devil imp seized her, and she raised her hand and waved at Zack, flashing her warmest, friendliest smile.

She was not in the least surprised when he did not smile or wave back.

Chapter Nine

The snowstorm was showing signs of turning into a full-blown blizzard. Visibility was terrible, and not even setting the car's windshield wipers at warp speed kept the glass free from the fast-falling blanket of snowflakes. Zack muttered and cursed under his breath as the car inched along the increasingly slippery road. Claudia's car was supposed to be directly behind his, but he kept losing sight of it. The heating element in the back of his car, supposedly designed to keep it free of precipitation was, well, out of its element in this fierce, driving storm.

The kids were quiet, sensing his tension. Occasionally Zack cast quick glances at them, Brian beside him, the younger three in the back seat. They looked downcast and glum, and he knew it had nothing to do with anxiety over being trapped in the car in this storm.

They thought their little idyll with the Nolan family was over, and they were blaming him. Zack wanted to protest at the unfairness of it all. It wasn't *his* fault that Claudia chose to date another man! He pictured her that first night they'd met at the Smiths' party. She'd been wearing the red dress, looking sexy and gorgeous, smiling and bright, her brown eyes sparkling. Maybe she would wear that same dress to the *Press* party where she would smile and sparkle for her *date!*

He clutched the steering wheel so tightly his knuckles turned white. His mouth was a taut, thin line. The thought of Claudia with another man was intolerable, and he was furious with her for daring to date that Owen person and even more furious with himself for minding. Observing the code of friendship, he should be congratulating her for landing a date with an eligible man! One who got free movie passes! Zack seethed.

In the car behind him, Claudia clung to the steering wheel in a state of abject terror. Having spent her entire life in southern Florida, she had never before driven in snow, and this storm was a challenge for winter-weather veterans. The windshield wipers made a valiant effort to keep the glass clear but they were fighting a losing battle. She couldn't see anything in front of her, not even Zack's car which she was supposed to be following.

In the back seat, Molly and Megan were singing their thirtieth round of "Jingle Bells" while Ned peered out the window uttering comments like "awesome" and "cool." He'd never been in a blizzard before and was thoroughly enjoying the experience from within the warm confines of the car.

Natalie sat quietly in the front seat, beside her mother. "This is scary, Mom," she whispered at last, keeping her voice low so as not to alarm the younger kids.

"It would've been nice to have eased into driving in snow," Claudia said lightly. She did not want to convey her own fear and further alarm Natalie. "You know, first a few flurries, then perhaps an inch or two, so I could've gained some experience instead of having my very first time be a blizzard."

The wind howled and gusted, sending snow spiraling around the car. "Mom, what is worse, a blizzard or a hurricane?" Ned asked curiously.

Claudia had no time to answer. A fierce gale of wind shook the car and a blinding swirl of snow completely blocked all visibility. A moment later they struck something.

"Mom, there's a tree in the middle of the road!" Natalie cried, at the very moment their car plowed into it. The evergreen lay across the road, blocking it. There was no way around it, even if they'd seen it beforehand.

Claudia might have been able to keep control of the car after it impacted with the tree if the road hadn't been so slippery. But the ice rendered the surface as slick as glass, and the vehicle went spinning around like a top before skidding off the road.

"This is fun!" squealed Megan.

The car slid into a ditch, landing almost on its side. Since all the passengers were belted in, they remained safe and stationary, though sideways in the oddly angled car.

"Fun?" grumbled Natalie. "It's about as much fun as sitting in detention and listening to the band murder 'O Holy Night.'"

"This is like a ride at Disney World!" enthused Molly. "We get to sit sideways."

"How are we going to get out, Mom?" asked Ned.

Claudia grimaced. "Carefully. Very carefully."

"Something happened, Dad," Brian said as the gale-force wind rocked their car. There was a bump, followed by a couple of thumps, then utter silence, except for the eerie howling of the wind.

"I know." Zack pumped the brakes to a stop. As the car idled, he opened his door, and wind and snow blew inside, to the mingled protests and shouts of glee from the riders in the back seat. Gripped with a sickening anxiety, Zack glanced at the top of his car where, shortly before, their newly cut Christmas tree had been secured to the rack. It wasn't there now.

He got back into the car. "The tree blew off the roof."

"Oh, no!" wailed Ian.

"Do we have to cut another one?" Justin was appalled.

"Let's go back and find it, Dad," pleaded Robin.

"Dad, what if the tree fell in the road and Claudia ran into it?" Brian whispered to his father.

"That's what I'm afraid of," Zack growled. Worry pulsed through him with every heartbeat. He could not see a foot in front or back of him, and neither Claudia's car nor the missing tree was visible in the storm.

Slowly, carefully, and after what seemed to take an inordinate amount of time, he managed to turn the car around on the snow-covered, slippery road and retrace their route.

"I don't like this anymore," whimpered Molly, trying to sit upright in the car. It was an impossible feat. The movements of the passengers inside had caused the car to tilt further, and it now rested firmly on its side.

Ned stuck his head out the side window. "This is like a submarine and I'm the periscope," he said cheerfully. "Boy, is it ever snowing out there!" He lowered his head, his hair covered with snow and struggled to close the window. At that angle, it was an awkward feat.

"Mom, why doesn't Zack come back for us?" demanded Natalie. "It was his stupid tree that made us go off the road. The least thing he could do is to rescue us!"

"He probably doesn't even realize what happened," Claudia explained, her heart sinking. "The visibility is so terrible that he probably couldn't see us."

"What if he knows darn well what happened and isn't coming back because he doesn't care where we are?" Natalie wondered aloud. "I guess I shouldn't've mentioned your date for the party. I thought it would make him jealous, but what if it made him not care? Or hate us? Maybe he *hopes* we'll all freeze to death here."

"Natalie, please save your theory of impending doom for some other time," Claudia said impatiently. "I wonder if we should stay in the car or get out and try to find help?"

"There is nothing but woods and farm for miles," added Natalie gloomily.

"Then we'll stay here and wait for help," Claudia decided. "This is certainly an adventure," she said with bracing maternal brightness. "Our very first blizzard!"

Megan didn't buy it. "I want to go home!" she wailed.

* * *

First, the Ritters came across the Scotch pine lying in the middle of the road, looking rather the worse for wear. Zack and Brian dragged it off to the side, then returned to their car to continue their search for the Nolans.

"They have to be very near," Zack stated. The car inched along the road through the storm. "We'll have them in no time at all."

And he would never be so cavalier with their safety again, he promised himself. If he hadn't been acting like a jealous idiot, he would've realized that Claudia shouldn't have been driving that car—her a native Floridian braving her first Port Mason winter! Oh, she might've protested if he'd bundled them all in his car, she might've called him overly macho and chauvinistic but from now on she was going to have to learn that under certain circumstances *he* called all the shots and could not be overruled. It would probably take a long, long time to teach her that lesson, maybe even a lifetime, but Zack decided he was more than up for the task.

"Dad, I think I see their car!" Brian called a few minutes later. He was leaning out the window, braving the wind and the snow, to keep an eye out for the Nolans. "It's sideways in the ditch, down off the road!"

"What if they're dead?" Robin whimpered.

Ian burst into tears.

"You kids stay here," Zack ordered. He climbed out of the car and fought his way across the road to the upturned Nolan car. His blood was roaring in his ears, his own anxiety and his kids' teary fears reverberating in his head. He couldn't see inside as he rapped on the window of their car, searching his mind for a plan, in case no one inside was able to assist him in getting them out.

The window slowly began to unwind. Ned was struggling manfully with it. "Zack!" he cried joyfully. It was the first time the boy had called him by his first name. "I knew you'd come for us!"

"Natalie said you hoped we'd get frozen to death," one of the twins sniffled, reaching her arms up to him.

"I'm not going to let anything happen to you, cookie," Zack promised, hauling her out of the car. "I can promise you that."

He wrestled open the car door and pulled the Nolans out, one by one. Brian had defied his orders to stay in the car and joined him in the rescue.

"Brian, Natalie, get the kids into our car," Zack ordered, extending a hand to Claudia, who was attempting to scramble out on her own.

She gave a startled gasp as he clasped her under her arms and lifted her from the car, as easily as he'd plucked the kids out. Suspended above the ground, the wind blowing fiercely, she instinctively grasped for something strong and steady to hold on to.

Zack. Her arms went around his neck.

"Now wrap your legs around me, and I'll carry you to the car," he ordered.

Claudia was hesitant. Blizzard or not, there was something intensely sexual in that position. She immediately admonished herself for being ridiculous. He was a policeman implementing a rescue, for heaven's sake!

She wrapped her legs around his waist. Her eyes happened to meet his, and what she saw in his burning blue gaze was a desire that was intently sexual indeed.

"You are not going anywhere with any other man," Zack said fiercely as he carried her across the road. "If you want to go to the party, I'll take you."

The wind was blowing snow in her eyes, making them water. She rested her forehead against his chest, seeking protection from the icy precipitation. And from the possessive intensity of his stare. "Isn't that carrying friendship above and beyond the usual limits?" she murmured into his coat.

Zack heaved a sigh. "You're going to make me say it, aren't you?"

"Say what?" Her lips curved into a secret smile.

"Oh, yeah, you're really going for broke." Zack laughed softly. "Okay, Ms. Nolan, you win this round. I'll admit it. My feelings for you go a lot deeper and further than friendship. I want you, and you know it. Even in the midst of a blizzard with eight kids going bananas in the car three feet away from us, I want you so badly I feel like a stick of dynamite ready to explode."

Her limbs tightened around his. A sweet honeyed warmth was flowing through her. She wanted him as much as he wanted her, despite said blizzard and the very conspicuous presence of eight children. But she wasn't ready to concede so easily.

"You want me even though I have four children and you made a sacred vow to avoid women with children to protect yourself from the dangerous specter of *stepchildren?*" She lifted her head to meet his eyes.

"I want you," Zack repeated, gazing at her hungrily. "And somehow the kids have become a bonus instead of a penalty." They'd reached the car, and he set her on her feet.

"You... aren't angry that your oldest son and my oldest daughter have been manipulating us?" Claudia asked, a little nervously. Zack was a man who was accustomed to exerting control, but he'd been bested by the pair of junior matchmakers. "Deep down, do you resent—"

"Deep down, I'm grateful to the little connivers. Although I firmly believe that eventually we'd have found each other on our own."

"Like we were fated to meet?"

He smiled. "I'm not so hard-boiled that I don't believe in miracles, especially during this time of year."

They were standing closely together, the snow blowing around them. Almost imperceptibly, she raised her face, her eyes fastened on the hard curve of his lips. Zack reacted at once. He pulled her against him, and his mouth came down to cover hers.

His kiss was long and slow and thorough. Claudia went weak all over, clinging to him, her lips moving against his as she kissed him back, giving in to his hungry demands while making promises and demands of her own.

"They're kissing!" Natalie exclaimed from within the overcrowded confines of the Ritters' car. She wiped away the steam from the windows with her mitten, the better to observe the satisfying sight. "This really is the season to be jolly!"

"Ho, ho, ho," Brian added for good measure. He and Natalie exchanged mittened high fives.

"Let's sing 'Jingle Bells'!" Megan suggested happily.

"No, let's bark it, like those dogs on the record," countered Ian.

"Cool!" enthused Ned, who joined Megan and Ian in the barking chorus. It took only a moment or two for Molly, Robin and Justin to bark along.

Natalie and Brian exchanged glances. "Well, I guess they don't sound much worse than the chorus's version of 'Here Comes Santa Claus,'" Brian said resignedly.

Outside the car, the need for oxygen and the stinging bite of the wind and snow caused Zack and Claudia to reluctantly draw apart.

They looked at each other, their faces flushed and their mouths damp and slightly swollen from the passion of their kisses.

"What an effect you have on me!" Zack grinned. "I can hear bells ringing."

Inside the car, Ian had a small string of colored bells that he was enthusiastically shaking, providing musical accompaniment to the group's doggy chorus.

"I hear dogs barking." Claudia arched her brows. "Strange, off-key dogs who sound alarmingly like our musically untalented offspring."

They laughed, falling back into each other's arms for a quick, affectionate hug.

"This is going to be an interesting courtship," Zack remarked.

"So you're planning to court me?"

"I think I've been doing it from the first moment we met. But I intend to do a much more thorough job of it. A thoroughly *romantic* job," Zack added. "Beginning right now." He opened the car door for her. "It's not a one-horse open sleigh, but we'll do that next weekend. Just the two of us— and not in a blizzard."

She climbed into the car and snuggled close against him in the front seat. "I can't wait."

Chapter Ten

One year later

Claudia and Zachary Ritter's wedding ended with the church bells pealing, as the couple emerged from the church into the sunny winter day. A stirring rendition of "Joy to The World" resounded throughout the neighborhood, and everybody was smiling as they watched Claudia and Zack make their way through a throng of well-wishers to the waiting limousine.

"It's highly unusual for the bride and groom to skip their own wedding reception," Claudia's mother remarked to Zack's mother as they stood on the church steps. The combined eight grandchildren lined the curb, waving wildly as the limo pulled away. The four girls looked beautiful in their long, red velvet dresses and the four boys were handsome in their rented tuxes with bright red ties and cummerbunds.

"I tried to talk them into staying for just an hour or so, but Zack was adamant about letting the guests enjoy the reception while they flew off to Key West," said Zack's mother. "They didn't even ask us to save them a piece of wedding cake!"

"Can you blame them for wanting to take off as quickly as possible to grab some time alone together?" Claudia's father asked. "They've spent the past year courting with eight kids tagging along! I'd say that's far more unusual than a couple wanting to begin their honeymoon immediately!"

"I don't blame them in the least," Zack's stepfather said dryly. "Eight children! The concept is mindboggling!"

"And from what Zack has said it sounds like he and Claudia would love to have one more." Zack's mother looked dazed. "They'll be a regular yours, mine and ours household."

"They're so in love." Claudia's mother wiped away a sentimental tear. "I'm so happy for them! Although I wish they'd have had a summer wedding. I do hate this cold weather."

"Mom and Zack said that the Christmas season was such a part of them meeting and getting to know each other that their wedding just had to be now, two weeks before Christmas," Natalie chimed in knowledgeably. She had joined the grandparents on the steps. "Wasn't the wedding romantic and beautiful?" she asked with a happy sigh.

Everyone agreed that it was indeed.

"A toast, Mrs. Ritter?" Zack popped the cork on the bottle of champagne that was cooling in an ice bucket in the back seat of the limo. It had been thoughtfully provided by the staff of the *Port Mason Daily Press* while the limousine and motorcycle escort was courtesy of the Port Mason Police Department.

They clinked glasses and sipped at the champagne. "Our mothers were slightly scandalized that we opted to skip the reception," Claudia observed.

"I think everybody else understood, though." Zack set their empty glasses down and took her in his arms. "I can't wait to have you alone for an entire week without going through all the usual logistics required for a few hours of privacy."

"We have been very creative this past year," Claudia agreed, stroking his cheek with her fingertips. "Remember the first time we made love?"

Zack grinned rakishly. "We worked out every last detail. All the kids over at my house so we could have your house to ourselves."

"We told them we were going to dinner and a movie."

"But we spent all four and a half free hours in your bed."
Zack's blue eyes gleamed. He chuckled. "Our kids think
we're avid movie fans, we tell them we're catching a movie
a few times a week. Good thing they don't quiz us on the
plots. Except on our joint family outings when the ten of us
troop in and buy enough popcorn to supply half of Port
Mason, I haven't seen a single flick all year."

His lips took hers in a kiss that made her throb with
helpless longing. "I'd much rather be alone with you,
Claudia. You interest me more than anybody on any movie
screen."

His fingers moved to gently caress her breast, and Claudia closed her eyes as sensual shivers tingled along her spine.

She thought back to the first night Zack had made love to
her and all the many thrilling and erotic times since. Zack
was an exciting, passionate lover who aroused and satisfied
her completely. She'd never known it could be like that, the
wild urgency of desire and need, the fusion of giving and
taking, of pleasure and demands sought and well met. She'd
never known she could want like that, and knowing Zack
wanted her just as much freed her to explore the deepest
sensual side of her nature—and his.

"My own sweet wife." Zack's lips moved tenderly across
her forehead, her cheek, before brushing her lips. "Have I
told you how beautiful you look today?" He smoothed his
hand possessively over her shoulders, along the curve of her
waist, to her thighs.

Claudia watched his big hand move against the soft white
wool of her dress and felt a delicious sensual weakness grow
within her. She touched him, loving the feel of him so solid
and muscular and strong. Intimate memories of his hair-
roughened skin against her own smooth skin and the exciting contrast, the sensually abrasive arousal, shuddered
through her.

Her eyes drifted from the brand-new gold wedding band
he wore on his left hand to the matching one she wore on

hers. He was her husband. A deeply feminine possessive ache clutched her.

"Oh, Zack," she whispered, her voice catching in her throat. "I love you so much."

"And I love you, sweetheart." He pulled her onto his lap, wrapping her completely in his arms, rocking her in his warm embrace. "How long is our flight to Key West?" he murmured, nuzzling her neck.

"A few hours, not counting waiting time in the airport."

Zack groaned his impatience. "I don't know if I can wait that long to get you into bed, Mrs. Ritter." His hand slipped audaciously under her skirt and desire flashed through her sharp and swift.

He touched her intimately, and she was trembling when she forced herself to slide reluctantly off his lap.

"We'd better try to distract ourselves or our limo driver will have quite a tale to tell the Port Mason PD." Claudia flashed an enticing, charming smile. "I know, let's try to recite all the gifts mentioned in the 'Twelve Days of Christmas.' I'll start. The first is a partridge in a pear tree. Now it's your turn."

"Two golden hens? Two French horns?" Zack frowned. "I don't know. I don't care, either. If you really want to distract me, ask me about the NFL play-off standings."

Claudia caught his hand and carried it to her mouth, pressing her lips against his palm. "I have an even better idea. Tell me when you first knew you loved me and were going to marry me."

"I can't remember *not* knowing it, Claudia," Zack replied seriously. "And this past year with you and all our kids simply reinforced it. You're the love of my life."

She laid her head on his shoulder, keeping hold of his hand and interlacing her fingers with his. "Jeff and I married right out of high school and spent our whole marriage working hard to make something of ourselves and give our kids a good life. When he was killed, I was devastated. I never thought I could ever love another man. I didn't want to even try. And then I met you, Zack. And I didn't have to try to love you, it happened with the force of a—a nuclear explosion.''

She smiled dreamily. "I never knew love could be like this, the way it is with you, Zack."

"Which is a tactful but rather circuitous way of telling me that *I'm* the love of your life," Zack finished for her.

"Yes. And marrying you right before Christmas and gaining four bright, adorable children is the very best Christmas present I've ever received, Zack."

"I feel the same way, my love."

They arrived in Key West in time to enjoy a seafood dinner in an oceanside restaurant that was decorated with blue-and-white artificial garlands and twinkling blue-and-white lights.

"The kids would not approve," Zack noted, as he finished the last bite of key lime pie. "In fact, the day after we get home I promised to take the whole gang out to Emersons' Christmas tree farm to continue our tradition begun last year."

"Of losing your tree in the middle of the road and getting caught in a blizzard?" Claudia asked innocently.

"That was the day I knew I'd met my Waterloo." Zack smiled in remembrance. "I saw the future and it was you." A small dance band began to play a romantic standard and he caught her hand. "Dance with me, Mrs. Ritter."

Claudia was eager to oblige. Zack led her onto the small, tiled dance floor, and she fairly glided into his arms. He held her tight and she cuddled close to him as they moved slowly to the music.

"This feels so right," she whispered, swaying against him.

"Overwhelmingly right, my darling."

They danced to a few more tunes, then strolled hand in hand through the streets back to their hotel. A warm tropical breeze rustled the palm fronds high above them. Though Christmas lights shone brightly in nearly every store window, the contrast to the winter setting of Port Mason was dramatic.

"Do you miss your year-round warm weather?" Zack asked, glancing down at her cotton dress and his own short-sleeved sport shirt. At home, they'd have been ensconced in heavy, goose down coats.

Claudia shook her head. "Not really. The change of seasons is still new enough to me to be exciting. And snow still seems like something out of a fairy tale!"

"A cold, grim one." Zack did not romanticize snow. "*The Little Matchgirl* comes to mind."

Claudia actually giggled. She was floating on a romantic cloud, exhilaration and joy streaking through her. This was their wedding night! She felt as if she were the heroine in a fairy tale—not a cold, grim one—and was in the midst of the happily-ever-after with her hero. A police chief made a marvelous Prince Charming.

Zack proved his own romantic streak by picking her up and carrying her over the threshold of their hotel room where he gently deposited her on the big wide bed of the honeymoon suite. They were delighted to find the room decorated with a small Christmas tree—artificial but green—twinkling with multicolored lights.

And then their thoughts turned exclusively to each other as they celebrated the vows they'd made to each other that morning. They kissed and kissed with hungry demand, their desire building and growing to an almost painful urgency. Her need was as compelling as his, and they merged together in love and passion, their union bonding them physically as well as strengthening the emotional bond between them.

Together they spiraled higher and higher until both went spinning over the edge of rapture into a dimension of profound pleasure, finally drifting down into the warm seas of sexual satisfaction.

Afterward, they lay together, sated and replete, watching the colored lights shining in the small tree.

"We're so good together," Claudia murmured, brushing a stray lock of hair from Zack's forehead.

"The best," Zack agreed. He covered her hand with his, and they smiled lovingly into each other's eyes for a long, intimate moment.

"Do you think next Christmas we'll be waiting for our baby to be born?" Claudia asked, her brown eyes dreamy with love. Making a soft sound of yearning, she arched her body against his. "If it's a girl we could name her Holly or Joy or Noelle or Christy."

Zack kissed her lingeringly. "And if it's a boy, we could name him Zachary, Jr."

"So very seasonal." Claudia grinned. "But I happen to love that name. And Zachary, Sr."

"And I love you, my angel. Merry Christmas, Claudia." She held him tight. "Merry Christmas, Zack."

* * * * *

A Recipe from Barbara Boswell

CHOCOLATE KISS YO-YO COOKIES

½ cup butter or
   margarine
¾ cup plus 2 tbsp sugar
1 egg
½ tsp vanilla
½ cup sour cream

2 cups sifted all-purpose flour
½ tsp baking powder
½ tsp baking soda
¼ tsp salt
1 11-oz pkg milk-
   chocolate kisses

Cream butter and sugar until fluffy. Add egg and vanilla. Mix well. Sift dry ingredients together. Add alternately with sour cream into the butter-sugar mixture and chill batter.

Measure level teaspoons of dough into round balls. Place on greased cookie sheet. Bake at 425° F for 6-7 minutes until firm and lightly browned. Remove half of the cookies from the tray. Put a chocolate kiss on each of the cookies still on the tray and place back in oven for 20 seconds.

Remove, and put the other cookies on top of each kiss, melting it and making a yo-yo shape.

Jack's Ornament

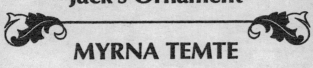

MYRNA TEMTE

A Note from Myrna Temte

Dear Reader,

When I grow up, I want to be one of those women who finish their Christmas shopping by Halloween, decorate their homes the day after Thanksgiving, mail their Christmas cards by December 1 and then bake fifteen batches of cookies, make four kinds of fudge and throw a party. After twenty years of marriage, however, I'm beginning to doubt I will ever be that organized.

The holidays tend to be a little...flexible at my house. Well, all right, I'll admit it. Our tree usually gets decorated after December 15, my kids have to nag me to bake cookies (we use a mix and they have to clean up the mess), and I finish my shopping at five o'clock on Christmas Eve. I've never thrown a party, and I've been known to mail Christmas cards in March.

That's not to say we don't observe traditions. Things may not get done on a schedule, but the important ones eventually do get done, and we usually have a wonderful time. Christmas isn't about perfect houses or food, presents or cards, spending money or having snow. It's about generosity of the spirit—people sharing laughter and hugs, memories and music, peace, hope and love.

So join me this year. Relax. Spend an afternoon curled up with a good book and a hot-buttered rum or a cup of tea. No matter what doesn't get done, Christmas will still happen.

Wishing you all the best for a stress-free holiday season,

Myrna Temte

P.S. If you see a harried, demented woman charging through the mall on Christmas Eve, please be kind to her. It could be me.

Chapter One

"Sing it again, Wizabet," two-year-old Charlotte Stone demanded.

Smiling at the toddler's inability to pronounce her name, Elizabeth Davies-Smythe glanced over her shoulder at Charlotte and her five-year-old brother, Nathan. Both children were buckled into safety seats in the back of the car she had rented in Jackson Hole, but after three hours of driving, they were bored and restless. Elizabeth didn't blame them.

At the moment, however, she could do little to help the children other than sing songs and pray neither would have to go potty again until they arrived at their uncle's ranch. Though she was an avid skier, she had never seen snow fall as thick and fast as it was falling now. Nor had she ever seen a road this narrow, nor driven such a long distance without encountering another human being.

She had never been to Wyoming before, either, and the longer she drove in this blizzard, the more she missed Connecticut, where they had modern conveniences, such as paved roads. Frequent gas stations. Heated rest stops.

"Yeah, c'mon, Lizbeth," Nathan coaxed. "Let's do 'Jingle Bells' again."

"Okay, Nathan. Dashing through the snoo-oow..."

The windshield wipers swiped over the glass, and through the cleared patch, Elizabeth thought she saw something in the road at the bottom of the hill. A fresh layer of snow instantly blurred her view. Tightening her grip on the steering wheel, she eased off on the accelerator and leaned forward, straining to see if the dark shape was still there when the wipers made their next swipe. It was an animal. A big one.

"Sing, Wizabet," Charlotte whined.

It was difficult to sound soothing when her heart was pounding with fear, but Elizabeth tried. "In a moment, darling. I'm a little busy right now."

The hill was so long and steep, tapping the brakes barely slowed the car. Elizabeth shifted into a lower gear and pressed harder on the brake pedal. The vehicle slowed, but not enough. With every swish of the wipers, the cow—at least she thought it was a cow—loomed larger and larger.

"Wizabet! Sing wif us!"

"Not now, Charlotte," Elizabeth said, anxiety sharpening her tone more than she had intended.

Shifting down again, she pumped the brake pedal in short, hard thrusts. The vehicle's back end swerved. She pounded the horn and flashed her lights. The animal simply stood there, gazing at the car with an expression of bored indifference, not unlike the expressions she often noted on the faces of the people attending her mother's charity functions.

The animal was so huge, she couldn't drive around it. She continued to brake and honk, and shot frantic glances at the ditches on either side of the country road. No escape there; she couldn't risk rolling the car.

"Move, you stupid beast," she muttered, trying not to imagine the damage a head-on collision with a cow might cause.

With disaster literally staring her in the face, however, it was impossible to repress such thoughts. The car had a driver's-side air bag, and the children's car seats should protect them, but that poor, stupid cow would undoubtedly perish. Oh, God, there was no time to think, nowhere to go.

In a last, desperate act, she smashed the brake pedal to the floor. She turned into the skid, released the brake for an instant, then smashed it again. Turning into the next skid, she repeated the procedure until, finally, the rear tires cut through the snow to the gravel underneath, bringing the vehicle to a shuddering halt two feet from the cow.

A sudden, deafening silence filled the car. Inhaling deep, ragged breaths, Elizabeth opened her eyes and found herself in a stare-down with the wretched beast, who hadn't budged so much as an inch. A quiet sniffle from the back seat forced her to forfeit the contest.

She turned to look at the children, and discovered her fingers were locked around the steering wheel. When she spoke, her voice was little more than a thin squeak. "Nathan? Are you and Charlotte all right?"

"I—I—I . . . th-think s-so," the little boy stammered.

The lingering fright in his voice broke through Elizabeth's momentary paralysis. Prying her fingers loose, she unfastened her safety belt and leaned over the seat. Tears glistened in Charlotte's big blue eyes. "I w-want M-mommy!"

Freeing Charlotte from the child restraint, Elizabeth lifted her into the front seat and cuddled her close. "I know, sweetie. Everything's okay now. Please, don't cry so hard, baby."

Charlotte rubbed her eyes with her fists and poked out her lower lip. "I not a *baby,* Wizabet."

"Oh, silly me. I forgot, you're a big girl now." Elizabeth affectionately ruffled the little girl's golden curls.

Nathan climbed into the front seat and knelt beside them. Elizabeth opened her eyes wide in feigned shock. "My goodness! How did you get out of your car seat?"

He gave her a mischievous grin. "I figured out the latch all by myself."

Shifting Charlotte to her left arm, she hugged Nathan with her right. "That was very clever, Nathan, but you could have been badly hurt if you hadn't been strapped in. You must promise never to unlatch it again without permission."

"Okay, I promise." He shifted around on his knees until he could see out the windshield. "What're we gonna do about that bull, Lizbeth?"

Elizabeth glanced at the animal, then looked back at Nathan. "How do you know it's not a cow?"

He shot her a don't-you-know-anything look. "It's too big to be a cow, an' it gots...you know, those big hang-down things so it can be a daddy. Uncle Jack showed me when we were here last summer."

Choking back a laugh, she ruffled his hair, which was the same color as Charlotte's. "Excellent observation, Mr. Stone. I'm afraid I didn't have time to look when I was trying to avoid crashing into him."

Since Nathan had mentioned it, however, the animal's "hang-down things" were a bit difficult to miss. And wasn't it just like a male to stand in the middle of a road, arrogant as a king, and refuse to give ground, even if it meant annihilation? Her father and that bull had a great deal in common.

Now that the danger was over, Nathan's brown eyes glittered with bravado and excitement. "Yeah, that was really cool. It was just like a carnival ride."

Charlotte laid her head on Elizabeth's shoulder and sighed. "I hungwy, Wizabet."

"According to your mommy's map, it shouldn't be too far to your grandmother's house, sweetie. Maybe if you and Nathan honk the horn again, Mr. Bull will move."

The children assaulted the animal with noise. No reaction. Elizabeth helped them back into their car seats and tried inching the car forward while honking at the bull. No reaction. She rolled down her window and shouted at him. No reaction.

She sincerely hated the thought of getting out of the vehicle. For one thing, although he looked as if his hooves had been frozen to the road, the bull might charge her. For another, since the snow had barely started when they'd left

Jackson Hole this morning, she'd packed her boots in the trunk.

But they couldn't sit here all day. Besides the potty and the food issues, she had no idea how long the remaining gas in the car's tank would last. Well, there was no help for it. She pulled on her ski jacket and, sadly eyeing her designer loafers, stepped out into the cold.

Six inches of snow swallowed her feet and ankles. The frigid wind stole her breath and nearly jerked the car door out of her hand. She managed to slam it shut, then waved her arms at the animal.

"Shoo, bull! Get along little dogie! Scram!"

Though his expression held more interest than it had before, the bull refused to budge. Elizabeth clapped her hands at him.

"Beat it! Go away! The cows are calling you!"

Steam poured from the beast's nostrils, but he didn't move. She stepped closer again. Good Lord, he was huge! Did she have the nerve to swat his nose or whack his bottom the way cowboys did in the movies? And for heaven's sake, shouldn't there be a cowboy around somewhere looking after this creature?

As if she had conjured him with her thoughts, a man rode out of the swirling snowflakes on a big chestnut horse. Convinced she was hallucinating, Elizabeth blinked and shook her head, but he was still there, the quintessential cowboy, complete with chaps, boots, a heavy, fleece-lined coat, a Stetson hat and a coiled rope in his gloved right hand. He looked so big and muscular and . . . well, cowboyish that the phrase "tall in the saddle" took on new meaning.

Snow clung to his eyebrows and mustache. His cheeks and ears were reddened from the cold. His features were as rugged as the Wind River Mountains to the east. The only thing even vaguely soft about him was his wide, friendly smile.

"Howdy, ma'am. Everyone in the car okay?"

That voice! She *must* be hallucinating. He couldn't look so gorgeous and have such a deep, sexy voice, too. Reining the horse a to halt, he dismounted and walked toward her, a worried frown creasing his forehead.

"Ma'am? Are you all right?"

Fearing her own voice would come out in a thin squeak again, Elizabeth nodded. He extended his right hand to her. She shook it automatically.

"I'm Jack Zorn. Sorry about Buster," he said, tilting his head toward the bull. "Any time he finds a fence down, he comes out here and stops traffic."

"Excuse me, did you say 'Zorn'?" She studied his face intently. Yes, he had Charlotte's blue eyes. He must be her best friend Mary's brother, the Uncle Jack who had shown Nathan the bull's "hang-down things."

"Sure did, ma'am," he drawled. "I run the Bar Z Ranch. It's just up this road a little way."

"It's a pleasure to meet you, Mr. Zorn." She offered her hand, enjoying immensely the firm shake he gave it. "I'm Mary's friend, Elizabeth Davies-Smythe. Your niece and nephew are in the car."

His smile widened. "Call me Jack, Elizabeth. We're not real formal around here." Still leading the horse, he walked over to the car and knocked on Charlotte's window. "Hi there, kids. You all right? Well, good. Sit tight and I'll get ol' Buster out of your way. Grandma's waitin' for ya at the house."

He walked back to Elizabeth. She shivered as he approached, whether from the cold or the pleasurable anticipation of having his attention again, she couldn't say. The next time she spoke with Mary Zorn Stone, however, her friend was going to receive a scolding. She had said her older brother was a bachelor, but she hadn't mentioned how attractive he was.

With a gallantry she hadn't seen in years, Jack opened the car door, helped her climb into the driver's seat, then closed it when she was safely inside. She rolled down the window.

"Soon as I get Buster off to the side of the road, just head on up another mile and take your first right," he said. "You can't miss it."

He tipped his hat to her, then led the horse away from the car and swung himself up into the saddle. Elizabeth sighed in admiration, chuckling when she realized she'd sounded like a teenager daydreaming over a rock star.

A piercing whistle rent the air, then Jack rode straight at the bull. Obviously having more respect for a horse than a vehicle or a woman, Buster made a slow, ambling turn. Jack waved his rope and shouted. "Come on, you old knothead, get movin'!"

The bull broke into a lumbering trot. Jack turned in the saddle, smiled at Elizabeth and motioned for her to pass him. She started the engine and carefully drove ahead, sighing again—with disappointment this time—when the cloud of steam from the exhaust obscured her view of him in the rearview mirror.

"Are you okay, Lizbeth?" Nathan asked.

"I'm fine," she assured him.

She wasn't certain that was strictly the truth, however. Hoping to avoid Warren Jameson III, the most persistent in a long line of suitors her parents had chosen for her, Elizabeth had volunteered to deliver the children to the Bar Z Ranch for Mary and her husband, who were taking a six-week trip to Europe. The last thing she needed or wanted was a romantic entanglement with a man, no matter how attractive he might be. But, Jack...

Well, it didn't matter. She would deliver the children, help them get settled with their grandmother and drive straight back to Jackson Hole. By this time tomorrow, she'd be zipping down the slopes above Teton Village, and Jack Zorn would be nothing more than a pleasant memory.

If she hadn't found Mr. Right among the hundreds of wealthy, sophisticated men her parents had found for her across the east coast in the past ten years, the chances were zero to none she herself would find him on a ranch outside of Pinedale, Wyoming. Weren't they?

here and there at random... he checked at the memory of Gina... standing out in the road, pointing a gun, but... ed blazing.

"Do... the money?"

Emilio... been by... to see that... fact, and the... weather it's...

They probably... would. That... wouldn't ask for you, but... then they wouldn't... and...

Chapter Two

"Git goin', Buster," Jack shouted when his prize Hereford bull dodged the gate. "You've had your fun."

Buster obediently swerved the other way and ambled right past the opening as if he didn't know what he was supposed to do. Swearing under his breath, Jack nudged his quarter horse, Rebel, with his knees, not that the gelding needed instructions. They'd played this game with Buster so many times, they both knew every one of his tricks.

When they finally got the bull back into the pasture, Jack shut the gate and rode ahead to fix the fence before the wily old devil could escape again. By the time he'd finished, his hands and ears felt frozen. He shot a worried glance at the sky, hating to see the weather get so bad when it was only the second week of November. If it stayed this cold, they'd have to feed the stock twice a day, which would play hell with the ranch's profit margin.

On the way back to the house he spotted his elderly uncle, Billy Zorn, pitching hay from the bed of his pickup to the eager cows crowding around for their rations. Dammit, he'd told that stubborn old coot to wait until he could help, but as usual, Billy hadn't listened.

"I see ya found ol' Houdini," Billy said when Jack rode up. "Heard a lot of honkin'. Who was he terrorizin' this time?"

"That heiress friend of Mary's and the kids."

Billy cut the twine on another bale. "Yeah? What's this heiress gal like?"

Jack herded the cows back so his uncle could spread the hay out more evenly. "There's not much of her, but what there is, is mighty pretty." He chuckled at the memory of Elizabeth standing out in the road yelling "Shoo, bull!" at Buster.

"Is she snooty?"

"Didn't seem to be. She's got long black hair and the greenest eyes you ever saw."

Billy scowled at him. "That kinda woman ain't for you."

"Uncle Billy, you hate women so much, I'll die of old age before I find one you approve of."

"I don't hate 'em," Billy said. "But them city gals are too damn soft and they got no stayin' power."

"Tell that to Sam Dawson," Jack said, referring to their nearest neighbor who'd married a woman from Chicago a few years ago. She'd already given Sam a son and was expecting another baby in the spring.

"Humph. Dani Dawson's the exception that proves the rule."

Jack shrugged. Uncle Billy had been married to a woman from Seattle, but she hadn't been able to tolerate Wyoming's harsh winters or the isolation of the ranch. The old man had never forgiven her for deserting him.

"That should do it," Billy said a moment later. "I don't even want to meet that gal. I'll eat in my trailer."

Nodding, Jack turned Rebel toward the barn. The gelding didn't waste any time getting there. Jack took care of him, then headed for the house, smiling when he saw Elizabeth's car parked by the back door. So, she was still here.

He glanced up at the sky and smiled even more. While he was worried about his profit margin, it wouldn't hurt his feelings a bit if Elizabeth got snowed in at the Bar Z for a few days. Uncle Billy was right that a city gal wasn't for him, but he didn't have to fall in love or marry her. It sure would be fun to have a little flirtation with her, though.

"Don't be bashful now, Elizabeth. Have another cookie."

Elizabeth smiled at the children's grandmother. The plump, gray-haired woman had welcomed her and the children with chocolate-chip cookies fresh from the oven. Elizabeth had thought such grandmothers had become extinct. For the past half hour, Hazel Zorn had systematically plied her with coffee and pumped her for information about Mary's trip to Europe and Elizabeth's own plans to hit every ski resort in the Rockies before she returned to escort the children home on the sixteenth of December.

Like her daughter, Hazel didn't know the meaning of the word *pretentious*. She wore jeans, a baggy red sweatshirt and a pair of slippers designed to look like shaggy dogs. Her house had obviously never seen an interior decorator. She made her coffee in an ancient percolator on the stove and served it in cheap stoneware mugs. But there was a warm coziness about this old house and Hazel that made Elizabeth want to linger. The back door opened and Jack stepped inside. While he stomped the snow from his boots, Hazel dragged a chair across the room for him. He bent down, kissed her cheek and hung his hat on a peg mounted by the door. Then he raked one hand through his thick blond hair and grinned at Elizabeth.

"Does she know your whole life story yet?" he asked, inclining his head toward his mother.

Chuckling, Elizabeth shook her head. "Almost."

Hazel swatted Jack's shoulder. "Quit teasin' me. And keep your voice down. Charlotte's asleep on the couch, and Nathan's zonked out in front of the TV. Where's Billy?"

"Said he'd eat at his trailer today."

Hazel rolled her eyes in exasperation. "It's probably just as well. That ol' curmudgeon can't hardly be civil anymore."

Jack peeled off his coat and hung it next to his hat. Elizabeth's mouth went dry. Even without the big coat, his shoulders were nearly broad enough to span the doorway. His royal blue flannel shirt outlined a muscular chest that narrowed to a trim waist, circled by a hand-tooled leather belt.

The snug fit of his jeans revealed long, well-muscled legs and a couple of other attributes she didn't dare dwell on. Telling herself she'd ogled the man quite enough, Elizabeth sipped her coffee. Then he sat on the chair, drawing her attention again as he yanked off his boots. While she knew he was simply protecting his mother's clean floor, it seemed like an awfully intimate thing to do in front of a stranger.

Jack carried his chair back to the table and sat down across from Elizabeth. Hazel retrieved the coffeepot from the stove, got another mug from the cupboard and filled it for him. Elizabeth shook her head when she offered her a refill.

"No, thank you, Hazel. I should leave soon."

"Better call for a road report before you go anywhere," Jack said. "The way it's comin' down out there, I'll bet the road to Jackson's closed."

"Phone's right over there." Hazel pointed to a cluttered, rolltop desk behind the table. "Number's tacked on the bulletin board."

Elizabeth went to the phone and dialed the number. A recorded voice painted a gloomy picture of road conditions for the entire state. The road between Pinedale and Jackson topped the list of closures. Returning to the table, she held up her hands in surrender.

"You were right, Jack. Is there a motel in Pinedale you could recommend?"

"Nonsense," Hazel said. "You're welcome to stay with us whether the road's closed or not."

"Oh, I couldn't impose on you—"

"Now, don't start that," Hazel scolded. "Any friend of Mary's is a friend of ours, and I'll be glad to have some help keepin' track of those kids. It's been a long time since I've had little ones underfoot. I'd better go check on 'em."

When Hazel had left the room, Jack said, "That was some pretty fancy drivin' you did out there."

Elizabeth felt her face grow hot. "You saw that?"

His eyes glinted with amusement. "Oh, yeah. I'd just found the downed wire when you started honkin' at Buster. If you hadn't been so busy, you'd have seen me high-tailin' it for the gate right along the fence line." Then his expression sobered. "I wouldn't have blamed you if you'd plowed right into him."

"I almost didn't have a choice," she said. "I thought 'bout driving into the ditch, but—"

Jack cut her off with a vigorous shake of his head. "No. You did exactly the right thing. One of our neighbors lost her brakes at the top of that hill one day when Buster was out there, went for the ditch and rolled her pickup twice."

"Was she badly hurt?"

"Nah. Just got a concussion. But if Becky hadn't had her seat belt on, she might've been killed. I should've gotten rid of Buster back then."

"Why didn't you?"

Jack glanced away, hesitating so long Elizabeth thought he wasn't going to answer her question. Then he gave her a sheepish grin that charmed her completely.

"Well, see, Buster's a mighty good bull," he drawled. "His calves are great and he's not too aggressive. He just doesn't like bein' cooped up behind a fence. I've always admired his determination to get out and see what's goin' on in the world."

"It sounds as if you might like to do that yourself."

He shrugged. "I used to think about it some, but when my dad died, I knew Mom and Uncle Billy couldn't handle the ranch by themselves. So, I'm still here."

Hazel came back, holding Charlotte in her arms. Nathan walked sleepily beside her. The instant he spotted Jack, however, his eyes lighted up and he charged across the room. Jack grabbed the boy under his arms and tossed him into the air. Shrieking with laughter, Nathan gave him a big hug.

"It's good to see ya, pard," Jack said, ruffling the boy's hair as he settled him on his lap. "I think you've grown a foot since summer. What's your mama been feedin' you?"

"Vegetables." Nathan made a face and a gagging noise.

Jack threw back his head and laughed, a rich, carefre sound that made Elizabeth's heart turn over. Then he pulle the plate of cookies in front of Nathan. "Maybe you'll lil these better."

Charlotte pulled her thumb out of her mouth. "Wai Wizabet."

Hazel handed Charlotte over, went to the stove and stirre a bubbling pot of soup. Elizabeth's throat tightened wit emotion when the little girl poked her thumb back into he mouth and snuggled against her breasts with the comple trust only a well-loved child can give. Smoothing Cha lotte's tousled curls, Elizabeth hoped Mary knew how luck she was to have married for love and then been given thes adorable children. If only...

Telling herself if-only's were a waste of time, she glance up and found Jack staring at her with such intensity sh couldn't look away. He blinked, smiled, and the disturbin moment passed, but she couldn't help wondering what h had seen when he'd looked at her that way.

Feeling like an idiot, Jack forced his gaze away fror Elizabeth and Charlotte. What the hell was the matter wit him? At thirty-six, he'd been attracted to his share o women. Elizabeth was such a pretty little thing and so eas to talk to, it wasn't surprising he'd feel attracted to her.

But when she'd taken the baby into her arms, he'd felt th strangest...connection to her. Time had paused, and for heartbeat or two he'd entertained the crazy notion he wa glimpsing the future, and that baby belonged to Elizabet and him. The whole thing was ridiculous.

In the first place, unless Elizabeth carried a recessive gen for blond hair, the two of them would never produce golden-haired child like Charlotte. In the second place, h didn't know the woman well enough to kiss her yet, muc less get her pregnant. And in the third place, Mary had tol

he family enough about Elizabeth's background to con-
ince him he had nothing to offer her.

This woman lived in a mansion, vacationed in Europe,
ocialized with movie stars, U.S. senators and industrial-
ts. She probably gave more money to charity every year
han he earned in ten. Contemplating a little flirtation with
er was one thing. Imagining having a kid with her was
ownright insane!

He glanced at her again. Oh, God. As she sat there ten-
erly holding Charlotte, her eyes closed as she rubbed her
heek against the baby's soft curls, all he saw was a beau-
ful woman—sweet, sexy and maternal all at the same time.
nd he wanted her so bad at that moment, he ached.

Chapter Three

The snow continued to fall for the next five days. Eliza
beth was having so much fun at the Bar Z, she honestl
wouldn't have minded if the storm had lasted for months.

She romped with the children and made Christmas tre
ornaments for a church bazaar with Hazel. She acquainte
herself with the horses, the barn cats and both of the dogs
She learned how to play poker, and even coaxed a few smile
and chuckles out of Mary's crotchety Uncle Billy.

The old man hadn't seemed to like her much at first, bu
she had won him over by playing his favorite songs on th
ancient upright piano in the living room.

One afternoon the wind died down a bit, and Jack in
vited her to tour part of the ranch with him on horseback
To someone used to an English saddle, the big Wester
saddle felt strange. The breathtaking scenery she saw mor
than compensated for any discomfort, however, and she fe
a smug pleasure in surprising Jack with her ability to han
dle a horse.

Returning to the barn, she was thrilled to discover Ha
zel's Irish setter, Bridget, feeding a brand new litter of pup
pies in one of the stalls. Her heart went out to the tiny runt
whose greedy siblings pushed him aside whenever he trie
to nurse. Despite Jack's prediction that he wouldn't sur
vive the night, Elizabeth insisted on taking the pup to th
house. She stayed up all night, feeding him milk with a
eyedropper and cuddling him to keep him warm. To he
delight, he grew stronger with each feeding, and she love
him fiercely. The Zorns observed her devotion to Runt wit
amused tolerance, helping her whenever they could.

During those five days, Elizabeth wallowed in the cozy, relaxed atmosphere of their home. For the first time in her life she felt accepted for herself. If the Zorns knew she had a fortune, they didn't mention it, nor did it appear to impress them. Hazel mothered her. Uncle Billy grumbled at her whenever he felt like it. Jack teased her and called her Beth. Elizabeth grew extremely fond of them all.

But Jack was her favorite.

She had never met anyone like him. At times his speech was almost painfully blunt; he held strong opinions about a lot of things and didn't hesitate to express them. He respected the opinions of others, however, and though he showed no signs of being a mama's boy, he shared an enviable bond of affection with Hazel. Invariably gentle and patient with the children, he also appeared to enjoy spending time with them.

Jack seldom talked about himself, which, in Elizabeth's experience, made him a rare man, indeed. Though he'd had little formal education beyond high school, he was well read and possessed an amazing store of practical knowledge.

He was comfortable in his own skin, confident without being boastful, and sexy as sin without the aid of designer clothes, elite hairstylists or hours spent at the gym. He was also an outrageous flirt, but he was so charming, she felt flattered rather than put-upon.

If she were ever stranded in the wilderness, shipwrecked or caught in a war zone, she would want a man like Jack at her side.

While Elizabeth didn't mind admitting she had an intense crush on him, she kept her feelings to herself. Alone in her room, however, she enjoyed fantasizing about him.

The longer she stayed at the Bar Z, the longer she wanted to stay. Unfortunately, it couldn't snow forever. On the evening of her fifth day with the Zorns, the wind died completely, the snowflakes stopped falling and the radio announcer said the snowplows were out in force.

At dinner, Uncle Billy looked up from his bowl of stew and smiled at Elizabeth. "Road to Jackson'll be open by morning. Guess you'll be on your way to the slopes now, huh?"

"Billy!" Hazel scolded. "You show some manners at this table or you can eat in the barn."

"I was just makin' conversation," the old man grumbled.

Ignoring him, Hazel turned to Elizabeth. "You're welcome to stay here as long as you like."

Elizabeth shook her head. "Thank you, but I've imposed on your hospitality long enough. I really should be going."

"Well, it's your decision, and I know you have a vacation all planned."

The evening progressed as the others had. While Hazel cleaned up the kitchen, Elizabeth gave Charlotte and Nathan their baths and read them three stories. Jack and Hazel came in to help tuck them into bed. Then Hazel went to her own room, leaving Elizabeth alone with Jack in the upstairs hallway.

Painfully aware he hadn't seconded his mother's invitation for her to stay longer, she suddenly felt awkward in his presence. Had she only imagined those long, admiring looks he'd given her? Or misinterpreted them? Perhaps he was as eager as his uncle to be rid of her. The thought hurt.

Sidling past him, she forced a bright smile onto her face. "I'd better pack my bags. If I don't see you in the morning, thank you for everything. I've really enjoyed getting acquainted with all of you."

Jack reached out and grasped her elbow. "Come downstairs when you're done and I'll make you a hot buttered rum."

His gentle touch, his husky voice, and the undisguised heat in his eyes told her she hadn't imagined or misinterpreted anything. She gazed up at him, feeling her heart contract at the prospect of leaving without ever having kissed him. Her throat too tight to speak, she nodded, then hurried to her room.

Twenty minutes later she paused at the top of the stairs, inhaling deep breaths to still the pounding of her pulse and hoping he wouldn't notice she had spent more time primping than packing. Oh, she was acting utterly ridiculous for an experienced, thirty-year-old woman. It wasn't as if she'd never been kissed before, and Jack might not even kiss her. But she desperately wanted him to.

Telling herself nothing at all would happen if she dithered up here all night, she straightened her shoulders and descended the stairs. Except for a small lamp burning in a far corner and the fire burning on the hearth, the living room was dark. Soft music poured from a radio sitting on top of a bookshelf.

Jack came into the room carrying a tray with two mugs and an insulated carafe. His smile when he saw her was friendly and seductive. A pure, golden warmth ignited in the pit of Elizabeth's stomach.

She wasn't the only one who had been primping, either. Jack had changed from his work clothes into clean jeans, moccasins, a denim shirt and a blue-and-gray sweater that brought out the color of his eyes. His hair looked freshly combed and slightly damp, and she would wager her trust fund there wasn't a whisker left on his face other than the ones in his mustache.

With feigned nonchalance, she took a seat on the sofa. He set the tray on the coffee table and sat beside her, explaining the finer points of making hot buttered rum while he mixed their drinks. Then he handed her one of the mugs, picked up the other and clinked it against hers in a toast.

"To friendship."

"To friendship," she repeated, studying him over the rim of the mug as she took the first sip.

Masked by the rich flavors of cinnamon and butter, the liquor slid down her throat with a soothing heat. Elizabeth closed her eyes in appreciation of the sensuous effect. When she opened them again, she found Jack gazing at her intently.

He moved closer, propped his heels on a stack of newspapers on the coffee table and stretched his arm behind her shoulders on the back of the sofa. She glanced around the room, then arched an eyebrow at him.

"Soft lights. Soft music. Alcohol. You wouldn't be trying to seduce me, would you?"

His eyes glinting with devilry, he lowered his hand to her shoulder. "Yup."

Chuckling at his blunt response, she took another sip from her mug. "Do you think it's going to work?"

"Yup."

He lowered his feet to the floor and set both of their mugs on the coffee table, then angled himself to face her. Her heart skipped a beat when he leaned closer, but she managed to return his steady regard.

"What makes you so sure, cowboy?"

He stroked one finger up and down the side of her neck. The caress played havoc with her nerve endings, making her shiver and feel hot at the same time. He raised her chin with his other hand, looking into her eyes as if he could read her thoughts.

"Chemistry," he murmured, stroking her neck again. "Don't you feel it?"

If she felt any more of it, she would melt into a boneless heap on the sofa cushion. "Chemistry can be dangerous."

"No problem. I'm a real careful guy."

And he was. In the beginning. Gathering her into his arms, he slowly lowered his head. Like a scientist working with highly combustible materials, he first kissed her as gently as a whisper. Elizabeth remained passive, enjoying the warmth of his mouth, the tickling brush of his mustache. She sighed with pleasure at the tentative stroke of his tongue across her lower lip.

His arms tightened around her; the pressure of his mouth increased. Raising her hands to his shoulders, she parted her lips. He accepted the invitation to deepen the kiss, and when she touched the tip of her tongue to his, the chemical reaction they had both anticipated took off in a flash of excitement.

One kiss led to another and another and another. Then a chain reaction of escalating needs began. A need to taste even more deeply. A need to touch with hands as well as lips. A need to be closer, to get more comfortable, to go beyond the limitations of clothing and touch warm, bare flesh.

She had never felt so desirable, so cherished, so...loved. The word *love* cleared away the sensual mists fogging her brain, allowing rational thought to return. This was happening so fast and it felt so wonderful, she was losing control of herself. Jack didn't love her. And she didn't love him. She was merely infatuated.

Pulling her hands from under the tail of his shirt—which she had feverishly yanked out of the waistband of his jeans—Elizabeth turned her head away from another soul-melting kiss and pushed against his shoulders. He groaned in protest. When she pushed again, he released her.

Chests heaving, they stared at each other. Though the fire crackled in the grate barely six feet away, Elizabeth shivered at the loss of Jack's body heat. He raised his hands as if he would reach for her, but she scooted back, fearing she would fling herself into his arms and forget all about caution and common sense if he touched her again.

"Whoa," he said, giving her a bemused grin. "Some chemistry, huh?"

"Definitely." Heavens, was that raspy voice hers?

"I've been thinkin' about doin' that since the minute I saw you standin' in the road, yellin' at ol' Buster."

"Oh, really? Why did you wait so long?"

"It wasn't safe."

"Safe?"

"Yeah." His grin turned wicked. "I didn't dare touch you before this, because I didn't know how long the storm would last."

Flipping her mussed hair over her shoulder, she turned sideways and crossed one leg over the other. "I'm afraid I don't understand."

"Come on, Beth, we've been flirtin' like crazy from day one. The only reason we haven't done anything about it is that we both know we could never be serious about each other. Since you're leavin' tomorrow, there's not enough time for either of us to get more involved than we should, so I figured it was finally safe to check out the chemistry."

"Oh, I see," she said, wanting to grab her mug and dump the remainder of her drink over his egotistical head. "You thought we could have a one-night stand."

"I didn't say that," he protested.

"You didn't need to, Mr. Zorn." Rising to her feet, she glared down at him. "Sorry to disappoint you, but this particular chemistry experiment is over."

Jack glared right back at her. "I never expected you to sleep with me. All I wanted was a few friendly kisses."

"Friendly? Just what do you think would have happened if I hadn't stopped you?"

Cursing under his breath, he grabbed her wrist and pulled her back down on the sofa beside him. "Look, I'm not some green kid who can't control himself, and I'm not a rapist. You've still got all your clothes on. Doncha think you might be overreactin' a little bit here?"

Yanking her arm out of his grasp, she scooted a foot away from him. Then the truth of what he'd said hit her. She certainly was overreacting, and she was angry about her own lack of control, not his. Humiliated beyond belief, she covered her face with both hands and groaned. "You're right. I'm sorry. Forget I said anything."

"You don't really expect me to do that, do ya?" he asked quietly. "Elizabeth? Come on, honey, talk to me."

She gulped at the lump in her throat, turning her head aside when he tried to lift her chin with his index finger. Finally she looked at him, inhaled a shaky breath, and asked, "What's wrong with me, Jack?"

"Not a damn thing. If I didn't think you were a pretty special lady, I wouldn't have wanted to kiss you."

"Then why is it automatically impossible for us to consider a serious relationship?"

He sighed, and from the corner of her eye, she saw him rub the back of his neck. "You know the answer to that. I'm a long way from rich, but I've still got my pride. I could never offer you half the things you're used to havin'."

Shaking her head, she uttered a bitter laugh. "That's what I thought. Lord, it's so ironic."

"What's ironic?"

"It always comes back to my money. I've spent most of my adult life avoiding men who were interested in me only because I have a lot of it. And now, I finally meet a man I find extremely attractive, a man I could honestly believe liked me for myself, and all he wants from me is recreational kissing, because I have too much of the wretched stuff."

"It's not just the money. I *do* like you, and I think you're a fascinating woman, but we don't have much in common."

Wrapping her arms around her waist, Elizabeth got up, walked over to the window and gazed out at the darkness. Then she looked at him over one shoulder. "Perhaps it's not *just* the money, Jack, but it's *mainly* the money. A lot of couples start relationships without having much in common."

Climbing to his feet, Jack crossed the room and stood close behind her. "That's true, but be realistic here, Beth. I didn't go to college. I've never traveled much of anywhere. I'm bound to this ranch, and you're a city girl right down to your pretty little toenails. In the long run, I don't think *you'd* be happy with *me*."

"And I have nothing to say about it? Who gave you the right to decide what will make me happy?"

"Aw, come on. Bein' out here's been a new experience for you, but think about it. You'd be bored with me in no time."

Elizabeth couldn't have disagreed more, but she didn't intend to beg him to change his mind. She had pride, too, after all. Sighing with resignation, she turned to face him.

"I never meant to hurt your feelings," he said.

"I know you didn't."

He shot her a skeptical look. "Hey, we're still friends, aren't we?"

"Of course, Jack." She smiled, hoping it looked more natural than it felt. "Please, don't concern yourself. It's probably a good thing that I'm leaving in the morning."

He leaned down and pecked her cheek, then muttered, "Aw, what the hell," and gave her a bear hug. "You go on and have a good time skiin' and forget all about me. This chemistry stuff's too damn dangerous for both of us."

After a long, sleepless night, Jack dragged himself out of bed before dawn. He took a shower and dressed, adding a layer of thermal underwear beneath his usual jeans and flannel shirt. Then he went down to the kitchen and started a pot of coffee.

Waiting for it to perk, he leaned back against the cupboards and found himself reliving for the hundredth time the last encounter he'd had with Elizabeth. She'd tried to hide it, but he knew she'd still been upset when they'd parted for the night.

Man, he should have listened to Uncle Billy and left well enough alone. He sure as hell never should have kissed her. Talk about playing with fire—his nerve endings still felt scorched. And while he wanted her to the point of pain, it wasn't just about sex.

Dammit, he really did like her. More than he should. All right, a lot more than he should. But no matter how hard he tried to rationalize it, the idea of somebody who'd barely escaped bankruptcy entertaining thoughts of getting serious about a woman with millions was just plain ridiculous.

She couldn't have meant what she'd said about being interested in him. Money issues aside, he wasn't so handsome women were beating down his door to jump his bones. But now that he'd kissed her, he didn't know if he'd ever be satisfied with anyone else. Go figure.

Well, she'd be gone in a few hours; he'd get back to work and life would go on. It was the best thing for both of them. Sooner or later he'd get his head on straight. But, damn, until that happened, he sure was gonna miss her.

His mother came downstairs and started cooking breakfast. Uncle Billy arrived from his trailer, and the kids scampered into the kitchen still wearing their pajamas with the feet attached. Elizabeth walked in ten minutes later wearing a bright purple ski sweater with a pair of black stirrup pants.

Jack grimaced at the sight of her lugging her suitcase. She obviously didn't plan to hang around a minute longer than necessary. Since she looked as if she hadn't slept any better than he had, he felt guilty as all get-out.

At breakfast she spoke little, ate less and hardly looked at him. Dammit, he wanted to talk to her alone and at least try to make her feel better, but he doubted she'd listen. Even if she would, he'd probably say the wrong thing. Though the roads had been plowed, the drive to Jackson was bound to be rough. He hated to think of her tackling it by herself, especially if he'd upset her even more.

No, his first instincts had been right. The best thing he could do for her was help her get on her way. Pushing back his chair, he got up, grabbed his coat and hat and picked up the car keys Elizabeth had left on the counter beside her purse. She didn't even notice.

He shrugged and went out the back door. After brushing the snow off her car, he fired up the engine, drove it to the fuel drum they used for ranch vehicles and filled her gas tank. Then he drove back to the house and left the engine running so the heater would start working before she came out.

Since he didn't particularly want to go back inside, he went to the garage and got out a snow shovel. This was as

good a time as any to clear off the back steps and cut a better path through the drifts between the house and the driveway. When he'd finished, he took the shovel back to the
garage and poked around, looking for the salt crystals from
last year.

There was a wicked patch of ice at the bottom of the
steps. They sure didn't need Uncle Billy to fall and break a
hip. He heard the back door open, followed by the sound of
his mother urging Elizabeth to drive carefully. Intending to
warn the women about the ice, he hurried toward the garage door. Hearing a startled shriek, he broke into a run,
making it outdoors just in time to see his mother hit the
ground at the bottom of the steps. Cursing under his breath,
he charged to the house. When he got there, Elizabeth was
already kneeling beside Hazel and calling to her.

"Hazel! Hazel, can you hear me?"

Jack knelt on the other side of his mother, took her hands
in his and rubbed them. "Mom! Mom, talk to me!"

To his intense relief, her eyelids fluttered, then slowly
opened. She groaned, shook her head as if to clear it, and
groaned again. "What? What happened?"

"You fell, Hazel," Elizabeth said. "Don't try to move."

"Where do you hurt, Mom?" Jack asked.

"I don't know. Everything feels kinda numb."

Exchanging a horrified look with Elizabeth, Jack shouted
for Uncle Billy. He appeared at the doorway with a child in
each arm, nearly dropping them when he saw what had
happened.

"Get some blankets," Jack said. "We've got to keep her
warm."

Billy set the children down and hurried away. Nathan and
Charlotte pressed their noses to the glass in the storm door.

"Nathan," Elizabeth called, "your grandma fell and hurt
herself. I need you to take care of Charlotte."

The little boy opened the door and stuck his head outside. "I will, Lizbeth. Will Grandma be okay?"

"We're doing our best to take care of her, honey."

Then Elizabeth looked back at Hazel and gasped. At Jack's questioning look, she nodded toward his mother's legs. Turning his head, he spotted a bloodstain low on the left leg of her jeans. He moved down to inspect it and nearly lost his breakfast when he saw the denim poking out in the middle of her shin. The only thing that would hold the cloth up was a broken bone, and the blood told him it must be sticking through her skin.

"We've got to get her to a hospital," Elizabeth said. "Should I call an ambulance?"

Jack shook his head. "I'll have to drive her to Pinedale."

"But if she's hurt her back, we shouldn't try to move her."

"We'd have to lift her off this frozen ground, anyway, and I can make it to the clinic in twenty-five minutes. If you call ahead, they'll have an ambulance waiting for her there."

Hazel groaned. "My leg's startin' to hurt, Jack."

"Yeah, I think it's broken, Mom. Hang on. Soon as Billy gets here with the blankets, I'll drive you to town."

"But who'll take care of the children?"

"I will, Hazel," Elizabeth said. "Don't worry about anything. I'll stay as long as you need me." Looking at Jack, she added, "Take my car. It's already warmed up."

"Thanks," he said, grateful for her clear thinking and her willingness to help.

Uncle Billy arrived then, carrying a stack of blankets. While the men wrapped Hazel up, Elizabeth dashed into the house and came back with a stack of newspapers and strips of cloth she'd cut from a dish towel. Giving them to Jack for a splint, she removed the kids' car seats from the back seat, then ran back into the house and packed a small suitcase for Hazel.

Though the men moved her as carefully as possible, Hazel cried out with pain when they lifted her. By the time they got her settled in the back seat, she'd passed out. Unsure whether that was a blessing in disguise or a sign of a dangerous head injury, Jack climbed in behind the wheel and headed for town, driving as fast as he dared.

Damn, he thought, shooting a worried glance at his mother in the rearview mirror. She'd need surgery to get that leg set. Thank God, he'd been able to pay their insurance premiums. And thank God, Elizabeth had agreed to take care of the kids.

Guilt pricked his conscience again. He should've shoveled those steps yesterday. And, while he wouldn't have wished an injury on his mother for anything, and it didn't make a lick of sense for his own peace of mind, he was damn glad Elizabeth was going to stay.

Chapter Four

Bone weary, Jack drove into the ranch yard twelve hours later, climbed out of the car and inhaled a deep breath of the cold night air. His mother had made it through the surgery in good shape. While she faced a long recovery, the surgeon had predicted she would be able to walk just fine. Sending up a silent prayer of thanks, Jack entered the back door.

Instead of the savory smells he usually encountered in his mother's kitchen, the stench of charred food greeted him. Uncle Billy and Elizabeth stood toe-to-toe by the stove, shouting so loudly at each other, neither of them looked up when he closed the door.

"If you're such a great cook, why didn't you do it yourself?" Elizabeth demanded.

"'Cause that's *woman's* work," Billy retorted. "If ya can't cook any better'n that, no wonder you're an old maid."

"Old maid!"

"Yeah. And don't think you're gonna get your hooks into my nephew. A rancher needs a woman who can pull her own weight. You couldn't do that if you only weighed five pounds."

"That's enough, Uncle Billy," Jack said. "You've got no call to talk to Elizabeth that way."

"No call!" Snorting in disgust, Billy stomped over to Jack and grabbed his coat and hat from their peg. "*You* try eatin' that slop. She can't even boil water without scorchin' it. I'm tellin' ya, city gals are like Christmas ornaments.

They're pretty to look at and fun to play with, but they're damn useless eleven months of the year.''

The old man shouldered his way past Jack and slammed the door behind him. Elizabeth turned to the stove, bracing her hands on the counter beside it. Jack hung up his coat and hat and pulled off his boots. Then he walked across the room and put his hands on her rigid shoulders, gently kneading the knotted muscles.

"I'm sorry about Billy. Don't pay any attention to him.''

Shaking her head, she turned to face him. Her cheeks were flushed, whether from anger or humiliation, he couldn't tell, but the pain in her eyes wrenched his heart.

"Why not?'' she asked. "He's right, you know. I grew up with servants, and I don't know how to do anything useful.''

"That's not true,'' Jack said. "You were a lot of help with Mom this morning, and you do a great job with the kids.''

She gave him a wobbly smile. "Thanks, but unless you're more capable in a kitchen than I am, we'll all starve before Hazel comes home. How is she?''

"Fine when I left. She's got a sister in Jackson who'll keep an eye on her.''

Charlotte ran into the kitchen and handed Elizabeth a sheet of paper covered with colorful squiggles. "I done, Wizabet. An' I hungwy.''

Jack picked up the toddler and nuzzled his cold nose against her warm little neck. She giggled and pushed him away.

"No, Unca Jack. Tickles.''

"Okay, squirt. You go color one of those pretty pictures for me, and we'll get supper ready. Whaddaya say?''

Charlotte nodded, and when he set her down, she ran back to the living room. Turning to Elizabeth, he found her eyeing him with a skeptical expression.

Gesturing toward an amazing array of pots and pans on the stove, all of which held blackened remains, she said, "And just what are we going to feed the children?''

"Pizza."

Her face brightened with hope. "There's a delivery place close by?"

"Nope." After checking the oven to make sure it was empty, Jack turned it on and took a box out of the refrigerator's freezer compartment. Then he opened it and started unwrapping the individual-size pizzas and placing them on a cookie sheet.

Elizabeth picked up the box and studied it. "Fred's?"

Jack grinned. "It's a company that sells frozen food. Salesman comes around with his truck every so often, and Mom stocks up on all kinds of stuff 'cause it's real easy. All you gotta do is read the directions on the box."

"Well, I hope you like eating it." Gesturing at the mess on the stove again, she sighed. "I'm obviously out of my depth with anything else. I'm sorry I ruined so much food."

Jack shoved the cookie sheet into the oven and pulled her into a hug. "Don't worry about it." Hearing her gulp, he held her far enough away to look into her face. Lord, he hadn't seen anyone look so dejected in years. "Aw, Beth, don't be so hard on yourself. You tried, and I appreciate it. I don't know what we'd have done this morning if you hadn't agreed to stay."

Her eyes misty, she gave him another wobbly smile. Then she sniffled and turned her head away. Unable to resist, Jack covered the side of her face with his palm, coaxed her into facing him again and leaned down to kiss her.

What started out as a simple gesture of comfort quickly escalated into a mutual passion that left him reeling. She was so warm and giving, and ever since last night he'd been so hungry to feel this way again, he shuddered with pleasure. She moaned softly and moved closer, wrapping her arms around his neck.

Needing to touch more of her, he slid his hands over the smooth line of her waist and hips, then cupped her sweet little behind with his palms and pulled her against his aching groin. He loved feeling the weight of her breasts pressing into his chest, hearing her sweet sighs, tasting her eager lips and tongue. With her in his arms, no man in his right mind would think about food.

When the stove's timer buzzed, Elizabeth jerked away as if she'd been goosed with a cattle prod. Raking his hand through his hair in frustration, Jack yanked a couple of pot holders out of a drawer and pulled the pizzas out of the oven.

"How long will your mother have to stay in Jackson?" Elizabeth asked, her voice husky.

"She'll be in the hospital for four more days. Then she'll go to Aunt Reggie's for at least another two weeks. She'll probably be home by the second of December." Jack looked at her, tried to smile and figured he'd failed miserably. "Why? Havin' second thoughts about stayin' here?"

"It might be easier for everyone if I took the children back to Connecticut. They could stay with me until Mary and Lawrence return from Europe."

Though he knew her idea had merit, Jack said, "I wish you wouldn't, Beth. We hardly ever get to see the kids and it'll break Mom's heart if they leave early. She already feels terrible about wrecking your vacation."

Chewing her lower lip, Elizabeth studied him for a moment. "The vacation was simply an excuse to escape an unpleasant situation with my parents. I could stay, but..."

"This chemistry thing has you worried."

"A bit. It does seem to be rather dangerous."

Jack chuckled. "I can understand how you might feel that way, but I can keep my hands to myself. Shoot, I'll treat you like I do Mary if that'll make you more comfortable."

"All right." She gave him a slow, sweet smile. "It might actually be fun. I've always wanted a brother."

With that, she left the kitchen. A moment later Jack heard her helping the kids get their hands washed. Scooping the pizzas onto plates, he told himself he'd made the right decision, but he didn't like it much. He just didn't feel like her brother. Keeping his hands off her for more than two weeks was going to be sheer torture. Dammit, he never should've kissed her.

For the next week Elizabeth lived from one domestic disaster to the next. How housewives maintained their sanity was a complete mystery to her. Determined to show Billy Zorn she was not as useless as a Christmas ornament, she did her best to keep the household running in some semblance of order. Unfortunately, it was an exercise in futility.

Though Jack had found his mother's cookbooks for her, they might as well have been written in Russian. Even if she understood the terms the books used, which, of course, she did not, Charlotte and Nathan demanded so much attention she rarely had time to cook much of anything. When Hazel came home, however, Elizabeth intended to ask her exactly how one went about folding an egg white.

She used the wrong soap in the dishwasher. The children had loved playing with the bubbles frothing out of the wretched machine, but she hadn't thought to turn it off until half the kitchen floor had been coated with sticky suds.

When they ran out of towels, Jack showed her how to work the washing machine and the dryer. Thinking that at long last she had found one household task she could master, Elizabeth gathered up all their dirty clothes. Ha! She'd shrunk two of her own sweaters and turned all of Jack's previously white underwear a putrid shade of green.

Intending to clean the bathrooms, she sorted through Hazel's collection of cleaners, reading every label until she'd practically memorized the directions for use. Armed with paper towels and a toilet bowl brush, she attacked the fixtures with more enthusiasm than skill. She was proud of the results, however, until she saw herself in the mirror and realized she'd made ghastly blotches all over her new cashmere sweater with the bleach in the cleanser she'd used on the bathtub and sink.

She refused even to think about what she'd done to the vacuum cleaner, but it truly was amazing how much damage one small, stray piece of color crayon could do.

While Jack was unfailingly kind and understanding, Billy taunted her with every mistake she made. She'd always thought she had a healthy supply of self-esteem, but it was dwindling rapidly. She'd always considered herself an optimist, too, but the only bright spot she could find in this whole humiliating ordeal was knowing Hazel would be coming home in twelve days.

Of course, she would still need Elizabeth's help, but at least there would be someone to ask questions of when the men were out working. And there would be another adult in the house to act as a buffer between herself and Jack. Which, in her opinion, they desperately needed.

As promised, he hadn't kissed her again or touched her with more than a casual, brotherly affection, but the sexual vibrations between them grew stronger every day. Each night at bedtime when they turned away from each other with strained smiles and went to their own rooms, she sank a little deeper into depression.

No matter how exhausted she felt, sleep would elude her for hours while she struggled to put Billy's indictment of her womanly skills into perspective. Dammit, she was *not* useless. She simply hadn't yet found her true mission in life.

Sighing, she would roll onto her side and clutch her pillow to her breasts. Who was she trying to kid? She could plan an elegant party or a charity function as well as her mother. She could manage an investment portfolio as well as her father. She could even play the piano as well as some concert pianists.

But when it came to the business of everyday living, Billy was right. For a man like Jack, she really *was* as useless as a Christmas ornament.

The day after Thanksgiving, Jack sat at the kitchen table, waiting for Elizabeth to finish scrubbing tomato soup off Charlotte's face and hands so he could continue arguing with her. If he hadn't seen for himself the messes Elizabeth had created during the days since his mother's fall, he never would have believed them. She took good care of the kids and Runt, and she had a lot of try in her when it came to cooking and housework, but the harder she struggled, the worse things got.

He'd helped her all he could, but the weather had turned nasty again, forcing him to spend longer hours taking care of the stock and keeping the equipment running. Besides, she seemed to resent his suggestions more than she appreciated them.

Uncle Billy had added to the problem by criticizing her constantly, which made her more nervous and, though it hardly seemed possible, more accident-prone. When Jack defended Elizabeth, Billy just got meaner. The old man would have to be blind to miss all the sexual sparks floating around in the air, and Jack figured he was scared to death his nephew was going to repeat his own worst mistake by falling in love with Elizabeth.

Jack had no intention of doing any such thing. He was, above all else, a practical man, and it was painfully obvious Elizabeth wasn't cut out to be a rancher's wife. Hell, she was probably counting the minutes until she could go home.

Funny thing was, despite all the hassles and tension, Jack still hated the thought of her leaving. She might be the most inept housekeeper in the world, but to his way of thinking, she was still one hell of woman.

He loved her soft, gentle spirit and her patience with the kids. He loved having someone around besides his mother and Billy to talk to, someone who read newspapers and knew the world didn't begin and end in Pinedale, Wyoming. He loved listening to her pull beautiful music out of the old piano every night after supper.

She'd get this sweet, kind of wistful expression on her face as she played song after song. For a little while, his worries would just sort of drift away and he'd feel things he couldn't begin to express in words. Having her around had added a new dimension to his life, and he knew he was going to miss her like hell when she was gone.

After letting Charlotte out of the high chair, Elizabeth turned to him, her jaw set and her eyes glinting with the light of battle. "Forget it. I'm really not interested."

"C'mon, Elizabeth, it'll be fun," Jack coaxed, trying to charm her with a smile. No such luck.

"I don't feel like going to a Christmas party." She gathered up a load of lunch dishes from the table and carried them to the sink. "And I don't have anything decent to wear."

"Nobody dresses up for this. We're just gonna help the Johnsons decorate their house. You need to get out and be around some other folks or you'll get cabin fever."

"I'm perfectly fine, Jack. Feel free to go without me."

Rubbing the back of his neck in frustration, Jack muttered a curse. Judging by the circles under her eyes and the dispirited droop to her shoulders, she was anything but fine. He hadn't been able to cheer her up, so when Ginny Johnson had called to invite them to her annual Christmas bash, he'd eagerly accepted. Not even Scrooge could resist the hilarity that always accompanied Ginny's parties.

Unfortunately Elizabeth was resisting the idea as stubbornly as Buster clung to his favorite spot in the road. Well, he couldn't whack her on the rump with a coiled rope, but he intended to win this fight.

Scooting his chair away from the table, he followed her to the sink and glared down at her. "I'm sick and tired of watchin' you mopin' around here and feelin' sorry for yourself."

"I'm not feeling sorry for myself," she protested, glaring right back at him.

"Oh, yeah? What would you call it, then?"

She blew out an exasperated huff that tickled him no end. It was more spirit than he'd seen out of her in two days.

"Look, Jack, I know my housekeeping abilities are not

up to your mother's standards, but I've been busy with the children.''

"I don't give a rip about your housekeeping. I care about you and the kids. They need to get out as much as we do, and there'll be a whole herd of other kids for them to play with. We're goin' to this party whether you want to or not.''

The little wretch saluted him. "Yes, *sir!*"

"Right," he said, biting the inside of his cheek to hold back a grin. "I'll be back by four. You three be ready."

With mutiny in her eyes, she saluted him again. Unable to resist, he leaned down and planted a quick, hard kiss on her lips.

"Why did you do that?" she whispered when he pulled back.

Lord, she looked so tired and vulnerable, he could hardly stand it. Maybe this wasn't such a good idea. Tucking a lock of her long black hair behind her ear, he said, "Because you've been workin' too hard and I hate to see you look so sad. You need to have a little fun, Beth. Ginny's a real character, and I know you'll enjoy the rest of the gang."

She gave him a crooked smile. "All right. We'll be ready when you get back."

It didn't take Elizabeth long to understand what Jack had meant when he'd called Ginny Johnson a character. Tall and blond, she greeted them at the door wearing a fuzzy red-and-white Santa hat, a tiny infant strapped to her chest in a corduroy carrier and a little girl about Charlotte's age propped on her hip.

"Come in, come in," she called, waving them inside.

When Jack had introduced Elizabeth and the children, Ginny stuck two fingers into her mouth and let out a piercing whistle. She introduced them to the group and commanded everyone to make the three strangers feel welcome. To Elizabeth's surprise, everyone did just that.

She met the Sinclairs, two families of Dawsons, Ginny's husband, Andy, and his parents and grandfather, the Bakers, the Jordans, and the list went on and on. As Jack had predicted, there was a whole herd of little kids, watched over by two older girls named Kim and Tina under the supervision of a delightful old lady everyone called Grandma D.

When it came to Christmas decorations, the word *restraint* apparently held no meaning for Ginny. Even the elk head mounted in the living room wore a string of tiny white lights wrapped around his antlers, a red ball on his nose and a pair of green sunglasses.

Elizabeth found herself swept up in the action and marveled at how much fun this relaxed, informal gathering was compared to one of her mother's parties. After a meal of chili, home-baked rolls and Christmas cookies, Hank Dawson sat back and grinned at Andy Johnson, who was the local sheriff.

"When're you gonna give in and turn Ginny loose with some outdoor decorations?"

The sheriff scooted his three-month-old son higher on his chest. "Don't give her any more ideas, Hank. She's got enough to do with Ellie and Little Bill."

Standing behind her husband, Ginny winked at Hank and mouthed "Next year" at him. Then she leaned over and pecked her husband's cheek. When she would have straightened up, he hooked one hand behind her neck and pulled her down for a kiss that practically steamed the kitchen windows.

"Knock it off, you two," Sam Dawson said with a chuckle. "You're gonna shock all of us."

Andy shot him a droll look. "The way this bunch has produced kids over the past couple of years, I doubt it, Sam."

Everyone laughed, but Elizabeth also noted more than one husband putting his arm around his wife and more than a few tender glances exchanged. Suddenly she felt lonely and out of place. The bond of friendship and affection in this crowd was something she had known only with Mary.

These people didn't compete with each other to display their wealth and status. They genuinely enjoyed each other's company and trusted each other enough to speak freely about their disappointments and worries as well as their hopes and dreams. It was as if the love each couple shared had overflowed their own family unit to encompass the rest of the group.

At that point, Ginny shooed everyone back to work. Elizabeth helped clear the tables, carefully dodging Hank and Emily Dawson's two-and-a-half-year-old twins, Bart and Jessica. Emily scooped the children up in her arms, carried them to the kitchen table and collapsed onto a chair. Becky Sinclair and Dani Dawson followed her, then motioned for Elizabeth to join them. Dani said, "Take a break, Elizabeth. We haven't had much chance to visit with you."

"Yeah, how are things goin' at the Bar Z?" Becky Sinclair said.

Elizabeth pulled out the last chair. "We're surviving."

Becky's eyes narrowed. "Is Billy givin' you a hard time?"

"How did you know?" Elizabeth asked with a surprised laugh.

"He's been soured on women for as long as I can remember. Grandma D says Hazel's bound to go to heaven after puttin' up with a brother-in-law like Billy all these years."

"You mean, it's not just me?"

"No way," Dani said, shaking her head as if in exasperation. "He didn't start speaking to me until I'd been married to Sam for almost two years."

"I thought he just hated me because I can't cook and I'm not a very good housekeeper."

"Do you need some help?" Emily asked.

Elizabeth grinned at the toddlers on Emily's lap. "I think you already have enough to do. Frankly, I don't know how you manage to look after children and accomplish anything else."

Becky rolled her eyes. "Who says we do? Keepin' up with the little varmints is a full-time job all by itself. But we're used to it and you're not. We'd be glad to give you a hand."

"If you wouldn't mind answering a few questions, that would help a great deal," Elizabeth said.

Dani said, "I live right up the road from the Bar Z. Why don't I drop by tomorrow morning and you can show me what you're having trouble with?"

Before Elizabeth could thank her, Hank strolled into the kitchen. Taking Bart into his arms, he said, "What is this, a hen party? Ginny says you're all supposed to come and sing Christmas carols."

When Elizabeth entered the living room with the others, Jack caught her eye and beckoned her to join him and the children on the floor. Charlotte climbed onto her lap, poked her thumb into her mouth and went to sleep. Nathan snuggled against Jack.

Hearing the traditional songs filled Elizabeth with longing for a home, a family of her own, and a circle of friends like this one. Her eyes met Jack's. His warm, intimate smile brought a lump to her throat. It was easy—too easy—to imagine the four of them as another family in this charmed group. Dammit, she wanted to be someone else. Someone normal and ordinary.

She couldn't, of course. Even if she gave her fortune to charity, she would still be Elizabeth Davies-Smythe inside. She had been raised from the cradle to be a rich man's wife. Her dismal performance as a housekeeper simply proved there was little point in rebelling any longer. Wouldn't her parents love to hear her admit that?

Stifling a resigned sigh, she turned away from Jack and found herself looking at Dani Dawson. The friendly little woman had seemed eager to help. Could she possibly turn a useless woman into one who could, as Billy had said, pull her own weight?

The thought stayed with Elizabeth for the rest of the evening. When they got home, Jack helped her carry the children inside and went out to check on Uncle Billy while she put them to bed. Hearing him come back in as she left the children's room, she went downstairs to thank him for taking her to the party.

He met her at the bottom of the stairs. "Want a nightcap?"

Detecting a mischievous glint in his eyes, she studied him for a moment. Since she couldn't figure out what he was up to, however, she nodded. "All right."

His arm around her shoulders, he escorted her toward the kitchen, halting in the doorway. She looked at him in query, chuckling when he pointed upward and she saw a sprig of mistletoe hanging overhead.

"I swiped it from Ginny," he said, turning her to face him.

"Isn't it dangerous to steal from the sheriff's wife?"

"She'll never miss it. This is what's dangerous."

Putting his hands on her waist, he pulled her closer, then lowered his head and kissed her. Yes, it *was* dangerous, she thought as tenderness heated quickly into passion. It was also unbearably sweet and exciting, and she wished she had never discouraged him from doing it.

She clasped the sides of his face, warming his cold ears with her hands, eagerly responding, sighing with disappointment when he abruptly released her. They gazed at each other for a breathless moment, the hunger they both felt as real and present as the pilfered mistletoe.

Shaking his head as if to clear it, Jack spoke in a low, rough voice. "I'm sorry, Beth. I know you didn't want me to do that again."

"Yes, I did." She glanced away so he wouldn't see how much she wanted him to kiss her again, kiss her and carry all that passion to its logical conclusion. "Being around all those happy couples . . ."

"Sort of makes you want to be part of one, doesn't it?" he said, finishing the thought for her. "I felt the same way."

She looked up at him. "Why haven't you ever married, Jack?"

He nudged her into the kitchen and mixed them each a hot buttered rum as he talked. "I've been married to this ranch. When I found out what a financial mess we were in after my dad died, I had to put havin' a wife and family on hold. There wasn't any money for dates, anyhow, and about all I could do was work and worry and work some more."

"The ranch is financially sound now, though, isn't it?"

He motioned for her to take a seat at the table. "Oh, yeah. We're even out of debt. But I'll never forget the nightmares and cold sweats I used to have whenever I thought about bankruptcy."

"You could get married now," she said, accepting the mug he held out to her.

"Aw, I don't know. I think love's kinda passed me by. The gals my age around here are already married, and what woman in her right mind would be willin' to put up with Uncle Billy and Mom underfoot all the time?"

"They're not so bad."

Grinning, he took the chair across from her. "Maybe not, but I'm probably gettin' too old and set in my ways to make much of a husband. What about you, Beth? I can't believe you haven't had plenty of chances to tie the knot."

"I told you before," she said. "Men tend to be more interested in my inheritance than they are in me."

He frowned thoughtfully. "What makes you so sure that's all they're interested in?"

She raised one shoulder in a half shrug. "That's the sort of social circle my parents enjoy. They're awfully frustrated with me at the moment."

"Why is that?"

"They want me to accept a proposal from one of my father's business associates. When I get home, they'll expect me to make a decision."

"I take it you don't love him."

"I suppose I could do worse. Warren's a nice man and we've known each other for years. But there's no... chemistry."

His eyes narrowed. His gaze focused on her mouth. Her breath caught in her throat and her lips tingled as the sexual hunger flared between them again. God, but she wanted him. And he wanted her. She could see it so clearly in his eyes. If he reached for her, she would reach right back and end this misery for both of them.

But he didn't reach. Instead he looked away. Then he finished his drink with one gulp, shoved back his chair and carried his mug to the sink. "Well, you'll probably find the right guy before long."

I already have.

The words hovered on the tip of Elizabeth's tongue. She managed to hold them back, but they were absolutely true. She'd known it for days, but hadn't allowed herself to admit it in so many words. What she felt for Jack was much, much more than a fierce physical attraction or an infatuation.

God help her, she was in love with him.

Chapter Five

After feeding the stock the next morning, Jack and Bill bundled up the children and drove to Jackson to visit Hazel. Elizabeth waved them off, then poured herself another cup of coffee, sipping it while she made a list of the questions she wanted to ask Dani Dawson. Studying it critically, she came to a startling realization.

Millions of women performed these tasks on a daily basis. She had allowed Uncle Billy's criticism to make her feel inadequate when she was simply inexperienced. Though she was hardly a genius, she had graduated with honors from Wellesley College. If all those other women could learn to cook and keep house, she certainly could, too. And she would, if only to prove to herself she wasn't useless.

By the time Dani arrived, Elizabeth was ready for a crash course. Dani cheerfully led her through job after job, explaining the intricacies of everything from sorting laundry according to labels and water temperatures to changing a vacuum cleaner bag. At noon, they returned to the kitchen. While Dani wrote out her favorite easy, no-fail recipes, Elizabeth opened a can of soup and made tuna sandwiches.

"May I ask you a question, Elizabeth?" Dani asked, pushing the recipe cards across the table.

"Of course." Elizabeth chuckled. "You've answered enough of mine today."

"Why are you so determined to learn all this stuff? Does it have something to do with Jack?"

Her cheeks suddenly warm, Elizabeth nodded.

"Are you falling in love with him?" Dani asked.

"Does it show that much?"

Dani gave her a sympathetic smile. "You don't seem very happy about it."

The need to confide was so great, Elizabeth poured out half the story before she realized what she was doing.

"I suppose it all sounds ridiculous," she said when Dani had coaxed the rest of it from her with encouraging nods and questions.

Dani shook her head, making her dark curls bounce around her face. "No, it doesn't. You're trying to show him you can adapt to his world. It's not a bad idea, at all, but..."

"But what?"

"But there's more to loving someone than cooking and cleaning. How you feel about each other and get along together is a lot more important."

"Oh, absolutely," Elizabeth agreed. "But Jack is such a practical sort of person, I doubt he'll allow himself even to think in terms of loving me unless I can, as Billy so kindly put it, pull my own weight."

"They put a pretty high value on that, all right," Dani said. "And you can learn to do this stuff, Elizabeth. There's no magic involved. If I were you, though, I wouldn't let Jack get too comfortable."

"What do you mean?"

"A man has other needs besides a full stomach and clean laundry."

Noting a wicked twinkle in Dani's dark eyes, Elizabeth said, "Are you talking about sex?"

"If you're serious about Jack, it might not hurt to show him what he's passing up. You wouldn't believe what I went through trying to seduce Sam."

Fascinated, Elizabeth leaned forward. "You seduced him?"

"I only had six months to convince him we were right for each other, and he was so darn bashful, I had to do *some-thing*."

"Six months?" Elizabeth wailed. "I only have three weeks before I have to take the children home. And I... Well...I couldn't seduce Jack."

"Why not? He's attracted to you. I saw that right away yesterday. Hasn't he tried *any*thing?"

"He's kissed me a few times, but...oh, forget it. I have more experience at discouraging men than I do at enticing them."

"Well, you don't have to be blatant about it. You could start by washing your stretch pants in hot water."

"But you said that would shrink them."

Dani chuckled. "Yes, it would. And you could put on a little perfume and offer to rub his shoulders when he comes in after a hard day outdoors. You'll find lots of opportunities to show him affection if you watch for them."

"You must have driven poor Sam crazy," Elizabeth said.

"He loved it."

Elizabeth laughed at Dani's smug grin, then sighed and shook her head. "I don't know if I have the nerve to do something like that. And it seems so...manipulative."

"Why is it manipulative for a woman to go after what she wants? If Jack was in a battle, do you think he'd ignore half his arsenal?"

"A battle?"

"Hey, these Wyoming ranchers are a hard-headed breed. If you want Jack, you're going to have to fight for him. You've got to shake him up or he'll just keep doing the same old thing. Believe me, I know what I'm talking about."

"I'll think about it," Elizabeth said. "But first, I need to prove I can cope with daily survival." She picked up the recipe cards and flipped through them. "Which of these is the easiest?"

By the first of December, Elizabeth felt like a new woman. Dani had phoned or dropped in every day, offering continued support. Becky Sinclair and Ginny Johnson were taking turns entertaining Charlotte and Nathan during the morning hours. Elizabeth was delighted to discover she could be quite efficient when the children weren't distracting her every five seconds.

She actually began to enjoy cooking simple, nutritious meals, and if the house was a bit untidy, well, no one died from it. She considered Dani's advice about seducing Jack, and decided she couldn't deliberately set out to torment him. But she *could* follow her natural instincts to show him affection.

If she wanted to put her hand on his shoulder when she refilled his coffee cup, she did. If she wanted to sit close beside him to watch TV, she did. If she wanted to smooth his hair down or rub his shoulders when he came in all cold and exhausted, she did that, too.

Jack didn't complain. In fact, she suspected he was looking for excuses to touch her, as well. Once she relaxed about her role in the household, he relaxed, too, freeing them to enjoy each other's company again.

In the evenings, after the children went to bed and Billy returned to his trailer, they sat by the fire and talked—about their families, their pasts, their disappointments and their dreams. It was a sweet, intimate kind of sharing that had nothing to do with sex and everything to do with emotions. She cherished those quiet hours with him.

It would have been awfully easy to bring sex into their relationship. The feelings and desires were certainly there on her part, and she often saw that special awareness in Jack's eyes. By some unspoken, mutual agreement, however, for the time being they focused on learning everything they could about each other.

It was a mysterious and wonderful revelation for Elizabeth. She had never been so close to anyone, man or woman. What she had thought was love only one short week ago paled in comparison to what she felt for Jack now. Whether or not he was ready to admit it, they were having a serious relationship.

When his mother called after breakfast on December second and postponed her homecoming until the following Monday, Jack had to bite his tongue to hold in a delighted whoop. He loved his mother, but being alone with Beth had been fantastic, and he wasn't ready for it to end. Smiling, he relayed the news to Uncle Billy and Elizabeth.

She smiled back at him, then leaned over to load the dishwasher. "Perhaps we could surprise her and decorate the house for Christmas this weekend."

"Sure thing," Jack said. "Bundle up the kids after lunch and we'll all go out and cut down a tree."

Watching her cute little behind move under her tight stretch pants, he exhaled a quiet sigh of admiration. He wasn't sure what had changed Elizabeth since the Johnsons' party, but whatever it was, he sure wasn't going to complain about it. She was cheerful and sexy and confident again, and she finally seemed to be getting the hang of cooking and keeping house. If she wasn't so damn rich....

"Are you gonna stand there daydreamin' all day, or are we gonna get that tractor fixed?" Billy demanded, startling Jack out of his reverie.

The old man slammed out the back door. Muttering, Jack put on his coat and hat and followed the old reprobate out to the machine shop. He picked up the wrench he'd been using on the tractor the day before and waved it at his uncle.

"What's the matter with you, Billy? Can't you even try to be pleasant? Elizabeth's doin' better now, and—"

"She's doin' better at gettin' her hooks into ya," Billy retorted. "And it's workin', too. You're fallin' for her like a green kid."

"It's none of your business if I do. And I've had a bellyful of your bein' so damn mean to her. She doesn't deserve it."

"Humph." Billy yanked the wrench out of Jack's hand and slammed it on the workbench. "All that happy little housewife stuff is just an act. She's doin' it now 'cause she's hot to get into your pants. But how long will she scrub toilets and wash clothes once the novelty wears off?"

Jack glared at the old man. "Shut up, Uncle Billy."

"No, I won't shut up. A woman like her will never be satisfied with a place like this. If you don't watch it, she's gonna have you wrapped around her little finger, and the next thing you know, she'll have you chasin' your own tail."

"Well, if she does, it'll be my problem, so butt out."

"I will if you'll think with your head instead of your privates. For God's sake, if you've gotta have a woman, at least find one who'll stick by ya."

"Where am I supposed to find her? In a bar somewhere? No thanks."

"You're gonna make a fool of yourself and get your heart broke," Billy insisted.

"Yeah, I might," Jack admitted. "But at least I'll know I'm alive instead of just lyin' in a damned rut."

"There's just no gettin' through to you. I'm goin' to town. Don't come crying to me when she leaves you flat."

The old man slammed out of the shop. Jack muttered, "Don't worry, I won't," and went back to the tractor.

Working with his hands usually soothed him, but not today. The tractor was as cantankerous as his uncle. While he told himself Billy had deserved everything he'd said to him, Jack still felt guilty about their argument. The old curmudgeon meant well, and he'd worked just as hard as Jack had to get the Bar Z back on solid financial ground.

But dammit, this past week had forced him to take a close look at his life, and he didn't much like what he'd seen. He was sick and tired of giving his whole life to the ranch. Sick and tired of doing what everyone else expected instead of what he wanted to do. Sick and tired of being alone.

Every day he spent with Elizabeth, he admired her more; for a spoiled heiress, she had a heck of a lot of grit. She obviously loved kids, and Nathan and Charlotte loved her right back. She loved animals, too. She'd hit it off with his friends' wives and got along great with his mother. And she'd been here quite a while now, and she didn't seem to be pining for the city at all.

Hank and Emily Dawson weren't any better matched in some ways than he and Elizabeth were, but they were happy as a couple of horses rolling in dirt after a long, hard ride. You could say the same thing about Ginny and Andy Johnson, Sam and Dani Dawson, and Becky and Pete Sinclair.

So why couldn't he fall in love with Elizabeth? It wasn't her fault she was richer than sin, and as long as he never touched a cent of her money, why should her fortune bother him or his ego? Maybe he should stop being so pessimistic and think about giving a serious relationship with her a shot.

Chapter Six

Whack. Whack. Whack.

With Charlotte propped on her hip and Nathan standing by her side, Elizabeth watched Jack work, admiring each smooth stroke of his ax. They had tromped through a wooded section of the Bar Z for more than an hour, looking for a Christmas tree, pulling the children on a toboggan Jack had found in the garage. In Elizabeth's opinion, the six-foot Douglas fir they had finally chosen was worth every bit of effort expended.

She would have made the trek for the scenery alone. Her initial impression of Wyoming as a cold, windswept, godforsaken place had changed dramatically over the past weeks. While it *was* cold and definitely windswept, she had never felt the presence of a higher power more deeply than she did here and now.

No human hand could have sculpted such majestic mountains, painted that wide blue sky to frame them or created this aura of serenity. It was a place that could inspire poetry and music, and make artists weep at the impossibility of capturing so much raw beauty on canvas. She was grateful to be here, and even more grateful to be able to share it with people she loved.

She would have been frightened to be out in this harsh country alone, but Jack's calm, assured presence banished her fears. Bundled up in snowsuits, boots and mittens, the children looked like fat little bears. Their rosy cheeks and shining eyes reflected their innocent joy in the outing, and their trust in the adults to protect them.

This was adventure. They had banded together, pitted themselves against the elements and gone in search of treasure. In doing so, they had kindled the spirit of a family. She felt loved and in love, connected to these people and the earth. She felt . . . happy.

"Timberr-rrr!"

Nathan's excited shout made Elizabeth laugh. Wiping his forehead with the back of his hand, Jack laughed, too. Her gaze met his, and for one unbearably sweet instant, she could hear his thoughts as clearly as her own. *Yes, this is special,* his eyes said. *This is one of life's rare, perfect moments, and I'm glad you're here with me.*

Pleasure unfolded inside her like a rosebud opening to a lush flower, filling the empty, lonely spaces in her heart. She smiled. He gave her a sexy wink.

The sad thing about perfect moments was that they were, after all, only moments. The wind kicked up while Jack tied the tree to the toboggan. Charlotte became crabby from missing her nap. Nathan didn't want to walk, but there was no room for him on the sled and neither adult could carry him.

By the time they arrived back at the house, they were all chilled and exhausted. Charlotte fell asleep before Elizabeth could peel her out of her snowsuit. When she came back downstairs after putting the toddler to bed, she found Jack and Nathan in the kitchen making cocoa. The little boy nodded off before he could finish his treat. Jack carried him to the sofa and covered him with an afghan.

Returning to his chair at the kitchen table, he stretched out his long legs, closed his eyes and said, "Do you hear that?"

Straightening from a weary slouch, she listened for a moment. "I don't hear anything."

Eyes still closed, he said, "Exactly. After all that whining, doesn't silence sound wonderful?"

"Well, now that you mention it . . ."

He opened one eye. "Think we were a little too ambitious in our search for the perfect tree?"

"Probably. I suppose parents learn their children's limitations with experience. The first part was fun, though."

"Yeah, it sure was."

They smiled at each other for what felt like a long time. Jack opened his mouth as if he intended to say something, hesitated, then shoved back his chair and pushed to his feet. "I'll put the tree in the stand and bring it in so it'll warm up before we decorate it. Then I'll have to check the stock."

Elizabeth silently watched him get ready to leave, wondering what he had really wanted to say. All afternoon, she had sensed a new warmth in his attitude toward her. Did she dare hope he was beginning to feel for her what she already felt for him?

She wanted to believe that. Oh, how she wanted to. Unfortunately, she had learned the hard way that when it came to matters of the heart, it didn't pay to let hope get in the way of caution. If one didn't wish for miracles, one was not disappointed when they didn't happen.

As the evening progressed, however, she found it increasingly difficult to remember those harsh lessons from the past. Uncle Billy stayed in his trailer. Without his dark, glowering presence, it seemed as if the house itself took on a lighter atmosphere.

Jack hauled box after box of decorations from the attic. Elizabeth had never bothered to buy a Christmas tree for her condo, and her mother had always hired a professional to do her holiday decorating. When Elizabeth admitted she had never actively participated in decorating a tree, Jack was appalled. To rectify the situation, he insisted on teaching her every step in the process.

She must have gone up and down the ladder a hundred times before she had the lights arranged to his satisfaction. Her mother's trees were works of art, involving a color scheme, a clever theme, or a carefully researched historical period. The only decorating tradition of which Elizabeth was aware was that every year's display had to be unique.

Jack's approach was exactly the opposite. For him, the boxes of ornaments and decorations contained a family history. A great-grandmother had brought the little silver bells from Ohio on a wagon train. His grandfather had carved and painted the toy soldiers when he was laid up with a broken ankle. Hazel had made the little pinecone reindeer when she was in the fourth grade.

Handcrafted heirloom or child's art project, he unwrapped each ornament from its protective layer of tissue as if it were an old and valued friend. It was difficult to find space for all of them, but they did. And then came the tinsel.

Elizabeth was a meticulous draper. Jack and Nathan were flingers. Charlotte was, too, but most of her tinsel wound up on the floor. When the magic moment of turning the colored lights back on arrived, Elizabeth surveyed their evening's work.

By her mother's standards, the tree was simply a hodgepodge of stuff, much of which was tacky. To Elizabeth, it was truly a case of the sum being greater than its parts. It represented all of the things she had always found lacking in her own family's celebration of the holidays. Whatever the future held, she would always remember this Christmas.

Jack stepped out from behind the tree, laughing to himself that some things never changed. Every year, his mother warned him not to set the tree so close to the wall that it would be hard to plug in the lights, and every year, he did it, anyway, because the tree always looked smaller when it was naked. The argument was as much a part of the Zorn family tradition as the tree itself.

The sight of Elizabeth's face halted him in midstride. She'd been fascinated with his stories about the ornaments, and so earnest about finding just the right spot to hang each one, he had to wonder what kind of weird perfectionists her parents were. He'd had to tease her like crazy to get her to loosen up and have some fun.

But it had been worth it. Her cheeks were flushed with excitement and her eyes glowed with the wonder of a child's as she watched the blinking lights. She looked over at him and smiled, and he felt about ten feet tall. God, she was beautiful.

And he loved her.

He wanted to wrap her in his arms and kiss the daylights out of her. He wanted to carry her upstairs to his bed and make love to her until they were both too weak to whimper. And then he wanted to ask her to marry him and have his babies and decorate Christmas trees with him every year for the rest of his life.

There. He'd admitted it. It scared him plenty. He couldn't dismiss Uncle Billy's warnings out of hand, and he had no idea how she really felt about him. Oh, she was attracted to him, all right. But did she love him? Enough to live in a run-down old ranch house way out in the middle of nowhere?

Maybe. She'd seemed happy enough today. Did he dare ask her? Just come right out and lay his cards on the table?

Not yet. He was, after all, a cautious and practical man. It was only the second of December, which gave him two weeks before she had to take the kids home. Plenty of time to convince her she couldn't live without him. He hoped.

Hazel came home on the fifth, praised Elizabeth's housekeeping efforts and laughingly confessed that she had once turned all of Jack's father's underwear pink. Billy continued to avoid the house. Jack couldn't seem to stay away from it or Elizabeth.

In fact, Jack was attentive and affectionate—even in front of his mother. He kissed Elizabeth every chance he got, stoking the passion between them, though he always stopped short of making love to her. There were times when she wanted to kill him for leaving her so frustrated, but she loved him too much to resist his advances.

Despite her fear of doing so, Elizabeth began to hope for a miracle. If only Jack would ask her to marry him, she would happily stay at the Bar Z forever. She suspected he was considering doing just that, and one afternoon his mother confirmed her suspicion.

Seated at the kitchen table with her broken leg propped on a chair while she frosted Christmas cookies, Hazel smiled at Elizabeth and asked, "Have you ever thought about givin' piano lessons?"

"No," Elizabeth said. "Why do you ask?"

"A talent like yours shouldn't go to waste, and you're so patient with kids, I think you'd be good at it. You could use it right here in Pinedale. Yesterday Donna Johnson told me our only piano teacher's movin' to Oregon."

Elizabeth set down the cookie cutter she was holding and turned to face the older woman. "What are you really trying to say, Hazel?"

"You know darn well what I'm sayin'. My boy's sweet on you, and I thought you should know you wouldn't have to give up all your own interests if he asked you to marry him."

"That's awfully nice of you, Hazel, but—"

"Yeah, yeah, I know. Mind my own business. But I just have to tell you, I think you've been awful good for Jack."

"He's been good for me, too." Elizabeth crossed the room and hugged Hazel. "You both have."

"Do you love him?"

"Yes. But I don't know if he's as serious about me as you think he is. We haven't talked about the future."

Hazel patted her hand. "Well, give it time, hon. The Zorn men are mighty careful about makin' commitments, but once they make one, you can count on 'em to keep it."

For the rest of the day, Elizabeth's hopes soared one moment, then plunged the next. Her time in Wyoming was running out. She would be back in Connecticut in only four more days.

Well, she refused to be discouraged. Jack was taking her to a party at Becky and Pete Sinclair's house tonight. Perhaps being around all those happy couples again would inspire him to declare his intentions. If not, she might have to follow Dani Dawson's example and seduce him.

"Tonight's the night," Jack muttered, cramming his razor and shaving cream into the bathroom cabinet.

He wished they didn't have to go to this party. He'd rather take Elizabeth out for a romantic dinner, but he hoped being around all those happy couples again would put her in a receptive frame of mind before he popped the big question.

God, but he was nervous. His hands were shaking so bad, it was a wonder he hadn't cut his own throat when he'd shaved. What if she laughed in his face? No, Elizabeth was too kind to do that. But she might say no.

If she did, he'd...well, he didn't know what he'd do, but he couldn't put it off any longer. If she said yes, they'd need a few days to make plans before she took the kids home. Telling himself to think positive, he hurriedly dressed and went downstairs to wait for her.

The evening started out pleasantly enough. Elizabeth wore he hair down, just the way he liked it. She wore his favorite sweater, too, the bright red one that hugged her breasts close enough to put a man's imagination into gear. And it was fun to drive off in the car without the kids along for a change.

She sat close beside him, her perfume filling his mind with all kinds of erotic images while she told him about Mary's latest phone call. Then she spotted a deer standing beside the road and rested her hand on his thigh while she turned to watch it. It was a sweet, unconsciously affectionate gesture that damn near made him drive off the road.

He felt more confident by the time they arrived at the party. Since everyone had left their kids at home and the Sinclairs had shipped their two out to Sam and Dani Dawson's house for the evening, it was easier to have an intelligent conversation than it had been at the Johnsons' party. Jack enjoyed himself a lot until they sat down to dinner.

Nobody made spaghetti like Becky Sinclair, and it tickled Jack no end when Elizabeth asked for the recipe. But when Pete started visiting with Elizabeth, Jack's amusement slowly turned to dismay.

Peter Sinclair was a damn good doctor and a friendly, down-to-earth kind of a guy. Everybody in town called him Doc and tended to forget he was from back east. He and Becky lived such a normal, low-key life-style, folks also tended to forget he'd inherited an enormous fortune from his grandfather.

Within minutes, Pete and Elizabeth were into a discussion of acquaintances they had in common, private schools, posh resorts and all kinds of other things Jack couldn't begin to relate to. They weren't at all rude about it; Jack could tell they were both trying to include him and Becky and the others in the conversation.

But they had their own kind of lingo that made it painfully clear Elizabeth was way out of Jack Zorn's league. He'd thought he could learn to cope with her wealth, but as the conversation continued, he realized he'd been naive. The money itself wasn't the problem. It was the range of experiences that went along with having a lot of money that killed his hopes.

Hell, he'd never heard a symphony orchestra play or seen a ballet performed except on TV—and he always zapped that kind of stuff with the remote control. He'd never been to Canada, much less Europe. And he wouldn't know a bear market from a bull market if the bear bit him on the butt and the bull trampled him.

Elizabeth might be the right woman for him, but he wasn't the right man for her. She deserved a rich, sophisticated guy like Pete, not some ignorant cowpoke with manure on his boots and rough, callused hands. He must have been nuts to think for one second she could ever fall in love with him.

Too bad he hadn't listened to Uncle Billy or figured it out for himself before he'd fallen in love with her. No way was he going to get out of this one without a broken heart. When she left, he'd be just another poor, damn sad cowboy they wrote all those country songs about.

Chapter Seven

Biting her lower lip to prevent herself from gnashing her teeth in frustration, Elizabeth climbed out of the car and hurried up the back steps in front of Jack. The Sinclairs' party had been lovely, but the way Jack had behaved all the way home, one might easily think he had attended his best friend's funeral. What on earth could have happened?

Kicking off her boots on the mat beside the kitchen door, she confronted him. "What's wrong, Jack?"

Starting as if he hadn't realized he'd been as silent as a fence post for the past twenty minutes, he glanced down at her, then hastily looked away. "Nothin'. I'm just tired."

"I don't believe that," Elizabeth said. "Did I embarrass you somehow tonight?"

"Of course not." He hung up his coat and hat.

"Then why are you suddenly treating me like a stranger?"

"I don't want to talk about it." He started to turn toward the living room. Elizabeth grabbed his arm.

"Well, we are going to talk about it. If I've done something to offend you, I want to know what it is."

He rubbed the back of his neck, then sighed with what sounded like resignation. "All right. Let's go in the living room and sit down."

Following him to the sofa, she sat at one end. She winced inwardly but didn't complain when he left a foot of space between them. He stared into the cold fireplace with a melancholy expression on his face. The silence stretched from seconds into minutes, each more excruciating than the last.

Unable to bear the tension any longer, she said, "I hate to see you so unhappy, Jack. Please, tell me what's wrong."

"Reality's wrong," he muttered without looking at her.

"I'm afraid I don't understand."

His laugh held no humor. "No, I don't suppose you do. I just realized at the party that I've been livin' in a dreamworld." Finally he turned his head and looked at her, his eyes filled with regret. "I'm really gonna miss you when you take the kids home on Friday."

Elizabeth shifted on the cushion, tucking one foot under herself. "You make it sound as if we'll never see each other again."

"We probably won't. By the time I ever get around to visitin' Mary, you'll be married and have five kids."

"I thought we were getting closer, Jack. That we were becoming ... more than friends. What if I wanted to come back to Wyoming?"

"Don't, Beth." His sad smile tore at her heart. The tender caress of his fingers against her cheek ripped a hole in it.

"Don't what?" she whispered.

"Don't start wantin' something we both know we can't have."

"Something we can't have? Or something you don't want?"

He uttered a soft, bitter laugh. "Oh, I want you, honey. I wouldn't deny that for a second. But I'm not the man you need."

"You don't know that. If I'm willing to take the risk—"

"No." He clasped her face between his hands and slowly shook his head. "I like and respect you too much to start something I know will only end up hurtin' you."

"You've already started it with your kisses and your flirting and ... I love you, Jack. Doesn't that mean anything to you?"

"Yeah." He swallowed, closed his eyes as if looking at her was painful to him, then lowered his hands to his lap. "Yeah, it means a lot."

"Then don't push me away. I realize we haven't known each other long, but—"

"That's not the problem, Beth. We could know each other for twenty years, but it wouldn't change who and what we are."

"I only want to be a part of your life," she argued. "I don't want to change you."

"I don't want to change you, either. But that's what would happen. I can't offer you the kind of life you deserve. Even if I had the money, I couldn't get away from the ranch long enough to take you on trips like you were talkin' about tonight, and—"

Livid, Elizabeth jumped up and glared down at him, propping her hands on her hips. "So it's money again. Dammit, Jack, didn't you learn anything from Becky and Peter tonight?"

"Yeah," he shot back, climbing to his feet. "I learned you're a Thoroughbred and I'm a plow horse. Nobody in his right mind would ever try to mix those breeds."

"The Sinclairs did. Peter's fortune is larger than mine, and he's as happy with Becky as any man I've ever met."

"It's different when it's the man who's got the bucks."

Elizabeth threw up her hands in outrage. "Of all the old-fashioned, chauvinistic ideas—"

"That's right," he interrupted. "And I've got plenty more where that one came from. Give it up, Beth. It won't work."

"It could if you would give it a chance. Loving someone isn't about money any more than Christmas is. It's about caring and sharing and a million other things money can't buy. Believe me, it can't buy happiness."

"Try livin' without any sometime and see how happy you are."

"Will it make any difference to you if I do?"

"What do you mean?"

"I can give away my fortune tomorrow with one phone call."

His mouth fell open and he stared as her as if she had suggested murdering the children. "No. Don't even think about doin' that on my account. I've got no right to ask—"

"You didn't ask. I offered. So tell me, Jack. Is my fortune what's really standing between us?"

He stared at her for a long, agonizing moment, then slowly shook his head.

"I see. The truth is, I'm not the woman you need." Elizabeth turned and walked to the foot of the stairs.

"Elizabeth, I'm sorry."

Pausing, she looked back at him. "Don't be. You never promised me anything. I appreciate your honesty more than you'll ever know."

Her head held high, she climbed the stairs. Her throat ached and her eyes burned, but she refused to allow so much as a single tear to fall. She felt humiliated enough without disgracing herself by weeping in front of him.

Nor did she cry when she reached the privacy of her room. Hugging herself, she crossed to the window, braced one elbow on the sill and gazed into the darkness beyond the glass.

She was disappointed, but not crushed. Hadn't she halfway expected things to turn out this way all along? It was time to grow up and face the truth about herself. For her, romantic love was only a fantasy, she simply wasn't woman enough to inspire any man to fall in love with her for herself alone.

If she couldn't have Jack, she might as well go home and marry Warren. Perhaps, over time, they would develop affection and respect for each other, and she would at least have children of her own to love and nurture. Did any man or woman ever get everything he or she wanted?

Of course not. She was not a spoiled princess who was incapable of making compromises when circumstances demanded them. She might never know the heights or depths of passion she believed Jack could have shown her, but her life could have meaning. And it would. Just as soon as she

could convince herself this pain in her heart was not goin
to kill her.

And she would die before she let him or anyone else se
how deeply he'd hurt her.

Jack's chest felt tight and the backs of his eyes stung as h
watched Elizabeth climb the stairs. He wanted to call he
back and wipe out everything he'd said, but he clamped hi
jaw shut and shoved his hands into his pockets. Though h
told himself he'd only hurt her pride, he didn't really be
lieve it. Elizabeth was good at hiding her emotions, but h
knew her well enough now to see past the brave front she pu
on whenever she felt vulnerable.

Damn. Had he just made the biggest mistake of his life'
What if Elizabeth was the only woman he could ever love?

The question haunted him for the next three days. Eliza
beth went about her business as if nothing had happene
between them. She took his mother Christmas shopping i
Pinedale, walking cast and all. Every time he heard then
laughing and gabbing up a storm in the kitchen, or saw he
playing with Runt or the kids, he doubted his judgment al
over again.

She seemed so content—as if she found great satisfactio
in her newly developed skills. He ached to hold her and kis
her. To have more of those long, quiet talks they'd share
in the evenings while his mother had been in Jackson. T
have her turn to him with a delighted smile when one of th
children did something funny or precocious, or share a pri
vate laugh of exasperation when Uncle Billy was acting up

But, of course, none of those things was ever going t
happen again. He'd pushed her away, hurt and embar
rassed her with his rejection. How could he blame her fo
using his mother and the children as a buffer between them'
Dammit all, he missed her and she wasn't even gone yet
She'd wormed her way into his heart, and he didn't know i
he'd ever be able to get her out again. He changed his min
a thousand times, but one thing kept him from telling her.

Elizabeth was right that loving someone had nothing to do with money. She was also right that loving someone was about caring and sharing. But it was also about wanting what was best for the person you loved.

No matter how hard he tried to justify it, he couldn't see how giving up everything she was used to having, to live with him would be best for her. Besides, he'd already botched their relationship so bad, she'd probably reject him if he told her how he felt.

By Thursday night, however, he was a desperate man. Elizabeth wore her bright red sweater at dinner, which aroused every one of his baser instincts. It hurt to watch her collect the children's toys and her personal belongings from the rooms downstairs and carry them upstairs to pack.

It hurt even more to realize she really was going to leave in the morning and he would never see her again. Dammit, he couldn't just let her go like this—not without some kind of a private goodbye. The evening dragged on and on and on.

Excited by the prospect of another plane ride and seeing their parents again, Nathan and Charlotte refused to settle down to go to sleep. Jack's mother parked herself in Elizabeth's room, talking as if she never expected to have female company again.

It was midnight before he finally found an opportunity to speak with Elizabeth alone. He felt like an idiot lurking outside the bathroom door while she brushed her teeth, but he did it. When she came out, she gazed up at him with a quizzical expression. "Did you want something, Jack?"

"Yeah. Would you come in here for a minute?" he asked, indicating the open door to his bedroom.

She preceded him into the room, raising an eyebrow when he shut the door behind himself. Jack cleared his throat; then raised his hands in a helpless gesture, because the words he'd rehearsed in his head all evening had deserted him. Finally he just blurted out the first thing that came to his mind.

"I don't want you to leave like this, Beth."

"Like what?"

"With us feelin' bad about each other. I never meant t◌ hurt you, but I know I did."

"I'm all right."

"Well, I'm not." He rubbed the back of his neck, the◌ swore under his breath. "And I don't know what to say t◌ make things right with you again."

"Do you care about me at all, Jack?"

"Yeah. You know I do."

"Then don't say anything." Stepping closer, she laid he◌ hands on his chest. "Just kiss me."

Her perfume filled his head. Blood rushed into his groin◌ His heart raced. "If I do, it won't stop with a kiss."

"I don't want it to." A sweet, womanly smile spread ove◌ her face. "If all I can have of you is a memory, let's make i◌ a special one."

No red-blooded man could have refused her request. Jac◌ didn't even try. His hands shaking with need, he pulled he◌ flush against him, lowered his head and kissed her.

Chapter Eight

Yes, Elizabeth thought as she surrendered to the magic of being in Jack's arms again. *This is what it's supposed to be like*. Deep, hungry kisses. Strong hands caressing her with a fierce, sweet urgency. Time suspended, excluding the past and the future from conscious thought, leaving only this moment and the joy of sharing herself with this man.

She needed to see and touch him everywhere, to be seen and touched by him everywhere. Without a word spoken, they cast aside clothing and inhibition. He lifted her onto the bed and they came together, exploring each other's bodies with greedy delight, as if they would cram a lifetime's worth of loving into one night.

Earthy and straightforward in his desires, he demanded equal honesty from her, freeing her to express her own desires in ways she had never done before. It was more than lust, more than sex, more than the physical pleasures they shared. With him, she felt beautiful and sexy, playful and passionate, and above all else, cherished.

How could a man kiss her so tenderly, touch her so gently, delay his own release so unselfishly for her sake, and not love her? How could he turn to her again and again with such desperate intensity, drive her to such dizzying heights of ecstasy, and believe they weren't meant to be together? How could he hold her so close and reach so deeply inside her, physically and emotionally, and be content to let her go?

She would never forget one second of this time with him. Never stop wanting him. Never stop loving him. No matter what regrets lay ahead for her tomorrow, she wouldn't have missed this night for anything.

Satiated to the point of exhaustion, she lay on her side facing him, memorizing his rugged features with her fingertips. When she stroked his mustache, he opened one sleepy blue eye, captured her finger between his teeth and growled deep in his throat. Laughing, she kissed the tip of his nose and ruffled his hair with her free hand.

He released her finger, then kissed her lips, pulling her so close she could feel their hearts beating as one. "I wish you didn't have to leave in the morning."

"Me, too." She gazed into his eyes, wanting to say more, but hesitating for fear of destroying this lovely mood. On the other hand, if there was any hope at all of convincing him they belonged together, she had to try, didn't she?

Her inner battle must have shown on her face. Brushing the backs of his knuckles across her cheek, he said, "What is it, Beth? I can practically hear the wheels turnin' in your head."

"I do have to take the children home," she said slowly, buying a little time to shore up her courage. "But I'll take the first flight back to Wyoming if you want me to, Jack."

His eyes took on a somber expression and he eased slightly away from her. That small but telling action hurt more than if he had hit her with one of his big fists. Clutching the sheet to her breasts, she sat up and reached for the robe she'd left draped over the foot of the bed. He grabbed her arm and pulled her back down beside him.

"Now, don't go flyin' off the handle," he said, propping himself up on one elbow. "I want you to come back. I really do, but—"

"But what?"

"But maybe not right away. You need to think this over carefully, Beth. Very carefully."

"What you really mean is that *you* need to think this over carefully," she said.

"We both do. I'm not talkin' about an affair, you know. I'm talkin' about marriage. And that isn't a decision we should make impulsively. We haven't even known each other two months."

Though her heart leapt with hope, she couldn't quite trust what she was hearing. "I know how I feel about you, Jack. Nothing is going to change that."

"Then it won't hurt to be apart for a while and think it over, will it?"

"Define *a while*."

"I don't know. Six months, maybe?"

"You don't want to have any contact for six *months?*"

His gaze darted away, as if looking at her made him uncomfortable. "I think we'll both have a better idea of how we feel if we don't."

Elizabeth's heart sank as the truth of what he was really trying to say pierced her bubble of happiness. "I see." Sliding from the bed, she picked up her nightgown.

He climbed out of bed and stood naked before her, hands on his hips as he scowled at her. "I didn't much like the way you said that. What is it you think you see?"

Unable to look at him and not ache to touch him, she jerked on her robe. "It's kind of you to let me down easily, but it's not necessary."

"I'm not lettin' you down, easily or otherwise. I'm just tryin' to be practical."

"I would have agreed with you if you had said two weeks. Or perhaps even a month. But six months?" She uttered a soft laugh and looked at the ceiling, fiercely blinking back tears. "That's not the kind of absence that makes the heart grow fonder. It's the kind that makes the heart forget."

His hands closed over her shoulders, turning her to face him. Determined to preserve what little was left of her dignity, she met his worried gaze without flinching.

"That's not true, Beth. I couldn't forget you if I tried."

"Oh, please, Jack. Be honest with yourself, if not with me. You don't want to marry me because you don't really love me."

"Yes, I do. But—"

Pulling out of his grasp, she held up her hands, palms out to ward him off when he reached for her again. "You don't have to explain."

"Elizabeth—"

"No!" Backing away from him, she wrapped her arms around herself, trying to contain the aching, cold sensation spreading from the pit of her stomach outward.

"I've waited a long time to find a man who could say 'I love you' to me without tacking on a but. I thought you were that man. Obviously, I was wrong. For me, no such man exists."

He scooped his pants off the floor, shook them out, then stepped into them and yanked them up over his long, muscular legs. "That's a bigger load of bull than Buster."

"No, it's the truth. The only people who will ever love me for myself are children like Nathan and Charlotte. So I'm going to go home and have some."

Zipping his jeans, he put his hands back on his hips and glared at her. "How are you gonna have kids without a man?"

"Finding a man who loves me is a problem. Finding one who wants to marry me is not. Warren Jameson will do as well as anyone."

"Are you tryin' to tell me you'd marry some guy you don't love?"

"Women like me have been doing it for centuries." She shrugged one shoulder, then laughed bitterly. "Oh, don't look so appalled, Jack. Warren wants a wife who is rich and ornamental. According to your Uncle Billy, I'm perfect for the position. Hey, if being a rich man's ornament was good enough for my mother, why wouldn't it be good enough for me?"

"Because you deserve better, dammit, and you love me."

"But you don't love *me,* Jack."

"I never said that, dammit!"

"You did when you said the word *but.*"

"If you'd just give it a little more time—"

She sighed, then sadly shook her head. "No. You still have too many doubts about me. I'm not willing to waste another six months of my life waiting for you to admit it. I've done everything possible to prove myself worthy—"

"Of course you're worthy, Elizabeth. Hell, if anybody's not worthy here, it's me. I could never fit into your world."

"I don't recall asking you to. I only wanted to be a part of yours. But you don't have enough courage to take the risk of loving me, and there's nothing I can do to change that."

"Are you callin' me a coward?"

"If the boot fits, cowboy. Your concern for my happiness is nothing more than a convenient excuse to deny your own feelings. You *do* love me, Jack. You're simply too frightened to put it to the test."

"I'm not afraid of anything."

"Fine. Let's forget it, shall we? I'll go back to my world and you stay here with your cows and we'll all live happily ever after."

"You're blowing this way out of proportion."

"Am I? Funny, I would have thought I was just being *practical.* What does it matter to you, anyway? Since I'm ready to go home and accept the inevitable, I'm not your problem."

Cursing under his breath, he rammed one hand through his hair, then grabbed his shirt and shoved his arms into the sleeves. "Nothing has to be inevitable, Elizabeth. And I don't mind tellin' you, I think you're actin' like a spoiled brat."

Elizabeth drew herself up as tall as she could and injected a haughty note into her voice. "Think whatever you choose. Now, if you will be so kind as to excuse me, I'll get ready to leave."

She marched out of his room and down the hallway to her own. Closing the door behind her, she stared at it until her muscles quivered from the strain of holding herself upright. Then she collapsed onto the side of the bed, hugging her waist and rocking back and forth, forcing the pain and loss she felt into a dark, hidden corner of her heart where no one else would ever see it.

If this was the price one had to pay for falling in love, perhaps she would be better off with a man like Warren. He would never thrill her the way Jack had, but he would never be able to wound her so deeply, either. At the moment, that thought held enormous appeal.

Hearing a soft knock on the door, she lunged off the bed and grabbed the first suitcase within reach. Pretending to rearrange the contents, she said, "Come in."

Jack poked his head inside. "Give it three months, Elizabeth. Then we'll talk again."

"You either love me, or you don't, Jack," she said without looking up. "Three months isn't going to change anything."

"We'll see. I'll call you at the end of March."

The door banged shut. Elizabeth shot it a glare, then closed the suitcase. Why, that egotistical jerk!. He could call whenever he wanted. She didn't intend to drag this misery out one second longer than necessary. With any luck at all, she would be married and pregnant in three months.

Chapter Nine

Fighting a grim sense of disbelief, Jack watched Elizabeth pack up her car the next morning. Surely, loving him the way she did, she wouldn't take off without a word of reconciliation. But she did.

During the next six days he told himself she would call any minute, wanting to make up. He believed that so strongly, he spent hours mentally rehearsing what he would say to her, planning his arguments to convince her he really did love her. But she didn't call. Not once.

Hazel went on with her preparations for Christmas. Uncle Billy did his chores and ate his meals at the house again, complaining about the weather, the price of beef and the government, just as he always had. Jack did his best to settle back into his own routine, promising himself that with time he would forget Elizabeth Davies-Smythe had ever set foot on the Bar Z. But he couldn't.

Whenever he went to town, at least one of his friends asked about her. Every time he fed Buster, put on his ugly green underwear, or saw the Christmas tree, he thought of her. No matter how hard he worked during the day, memories of the one night he'd spent with her haunted his dreams. And her accusations about his lack of courage bounced around inside his head like a bullet ricocheting off one impenetrable surface after another. Dammit, he wasn't an emotional coward. Was he?

Of course not.

Being cautious about making a commitment was not the same thing as cowardice. And all that business about her marrying some guy she didn't love had been nothing more than an attempt to blackmail him into doing what she wanted. She wouldn't really go through with it. Would she?

Of course not.

Elizabeth was too intelligent for that, and she had too much love to give to waste it on some dumb jerk her parents had picked out for her. After giving herself to him so completely, she wouldn't let another man into her bed, much less marry him. Would she?

Of course not!

If she hadn't called him by Christmas, well, he'd call her. They'd hash this mess out once and for all, and everything would work out just fine. All he had to do was stay calm and give her a little more time to cool off.

On the twenty-second of December, however, his little sister blew his one-sided plans to hell and gone. The phone rang as he was refilling everyone's coffee cups after supper. Jack set the percolator on the stove, grabbed the receiver with its extra-long cord and carried it back to the table with him.

"Hi, sis." His mother's and his uncle's eyes brightened with interest when they realized Mary was on the other end of the line. "Yeah, your packages got here yesterday. They all sound interesting. Well, of course, we've been shakin' 'em. How are Larry and the kids?"

All pretense of holiday cheer vanished from Mary's voice. "Fine, but I didn't call to talk about them, Jack."

"What's up?"

"There's something wrong with Elizabeth. I was hoping you could tell me—"

"Whaddaya mean, there's somethin' wrong with her?" he demanded. "Is she sick?"

"Not exactly," Mary said. "She's just acting . . . strange, you know?"

"No, I don't know." Unable to ignore his mother's and uncle's silent demands for information, Jack covered the receiver and whispered, "She's talkin' about Elizabeth."

Then he got up, carried the phone into the pantry closet and shut the door behind. The things a man had to do to get a little privacy in this house were unbelievable. "Whaddaya mean, *strange,* sis?"

"I don't know." Mary let out an impatient sigh. "I've just never seen her like this before."

"Like what?"

"It's like she's lost all her spunk or something."

"She's actin' depressed?" Jack asked.

"Well, she's cheerful enough, I guess, but I can't understand why she's suddenly kowtowing to her parents. I'll never believe she really wants to marry Warren Jameson."

"Whoa!" Jack shouted. "Did you say *'marry?'*"

"Yeah. They're announcing their engagement at her folks' Christmas Eve party. She's making a terrible mistake."

"What makes you so sure of that?"

"He's arrogant, he has no sense of humor, and the only thing he ever gets passionate about is his stock portfolio. Frankly, I was kind of hoping the two of you might get together while she was out there."

"We did."

"Oh, really?"

"Yeah, really. And dammit, she was supposed to give me three months."

"Tell me what happened," Mary commanded. "And don't leave out anything."

Though he resented his sister's bossy tone, Jack gave her a brief account of his relationship with Elizabeth.

"Did you tell her you love her, Jack?" Mary asked when he'd finished. "In so many words?"

"Well, yeah. I think so."

"You *think* so? Dammit, if you were that wishy-washy with Elizabeth, no wonder she didn't believe you. Of all the stupid, idiotic—"

"Now, hold on one damn minute. I was just tryin' to be practical. I mean, what the hell does a guy like me have to offer a woman like her?"

"The one thing she's never had, you big dope. Love."

"Her parents love her, don't they?"

"Jack, they're not like our family. To them, she's just another asset to bargain with. She's never really *been* loved, so she doesn't expect to *be* loved. She needs a lot of reassurance."

"Aw, come on. Her folks can't be that bad."

"They're not bad people, but they didn't marry for love, so they don't see any need for it. Elizabeth's fought their matchmaking tooth and toenail for years. And now, thanks to you, she's finally given up."

"Hey, it's not all my fault," Jack protested.

"Yes, it is," Mary shot back. "And what about you, Jack? You've been sitting on that ranch with Mom and Uncle Billy for so long, it's a wonder you haven't sprouted mold. When are you gonna have a life of your own? Or have you given up, too?"

"That's pretty damned easy for you to say, Mary. Nobody expected you to lift a finger to save this place. What was I supposed to do? Let Mom and Uncle Billy starve?"

"No, but you didn't have to make a martyr out of yourself. Larry and I offered to help—"

"Zorns don't take charity."

"You and your stiff-necked macho pride."

"When it's all you've got left, you hang on to it."

"And you're still hangin' on to it like that's all you've got. That's the real reason you're hesitating over Elizabeth, isn't it? Because she's rich?"

"So what if it is? You think it's fun being a male version of Cinderella?"

"You're not Cinderella! Your assets aren't very liquid, but the ranch has to be worth a couple of million bucks."

"Right. I'm cash poor and land rich. Give me two or three bad years, and I could still lose it all, sis."

Mary sputtered in outrage for a moment, then snorted in disgust. "Elizabeth's right about you. Not only are you an emotional coward, you're a damned snob in reverse."

"I am not."

"Are, too. And if you don't want to end up a sour, lonely old man like Uncle Billy, you'd better get your butt on a plane and get out here before Elizabeth does something irreversible."

"She won't marry that jerk."

"You don't think so? Her folks won't give her one second to change her mind. And there's something else you'd better remember, big brother. Elizabeth thinks you've rejected her and she's got just as much pride as you do. It's your turn to take some risks."

Jack winced at the loud crash in his ear. Then, cursing the female half of the species under his breath, he stomped out of the pantry closet and banged the receiver onto the hook.

"Well?" his mother demanded. "What's going on, Jack?"

Knowing he'd never hear the end of it otherwise, Jack quickly recounted the gist of his conversation with Mary. Hazel gave him a disapproving scowl that made him feel about ten years old. Uncle Billy sat back in his chair and proceeded to gloat.

"Whad I tell ya, Jack? I knew right from the beginning she wasn't the right woman for you. Didn't I?"

Jack stared at his uncle for a long moment, seeing him clearly for the first time in years. Dammit, Uncle Billy *was* a sour, lonely old man. The old son of a gun was actually enjoying this. Talk about misery loving company! Well, thanks, but no thanks, he decided

"That's what you said, Uncle Billy, but you're wrong," Jack replied. "Elizabeth's exactly the right woman for me."

Billy slammed one hand on the table. "Are you out of your ever-lovin' mind? That gal don't love you. It sure didn't take her long to find one of her own kind now, did it?"

"That's right, and it's all my fault." Bracing his hands on the other side of the table, Jack leaned down until he was nose-to-nose with his uncle. "She loves me, all right. And I'm done lettin' you poison me against her with all of your nasty remarks about women."

"Those remarks are based on hard experience. Why, my Ruth was just like her, only not as rich. If she couldn't stick it out here—"

"How do you know she couldn't? Did you ever really try to help her? Did you ever go after her and tell her you loved her? Find out what she needed that you weren't givin' her?"

"Hell, no." The old man drew himself up stiff and straight. "I wouldn't go beggin' after no woman, and if you have any pride at all, you won't, either."

"Well, I can sure see how happy your pride's made you all these years, Uncle Billy."

His face scarlet with rage, Billy pushed himself to his feet. "Don't you get smart with me, boy."

"I'm not a boy anymore," Jack said. "It's time I made my own decisions and my own mistakes."

"What's that supposed to mean?"

"It means I'm gonna go get Elizabeth, and I'm gonna marry her. Then I'm gonna bring her home and you're gonna treat her with respect, or you can get the hell off this ranch."

"Your daddy'd spin like a top in his grave if he could hear you talk to me that way."

"No, he wouldn't, Billy." Struggling to her feet, Hazel scowled at her brother-in-law. "He was so sick and tired of all your griping and moaning, he was plannin' to ask you to leave before that heart attack took him. The Bar Z was his operation from the beginning, and now it's Jack's. Not yours."

Billy stabbed the air with his index finger. "After all I've done for you—"

"Save it, Uncle Billy," Jack said. "We know you've put in a lot of hard work on this place, and we appreciate it.

We've also paid you fair wages for it. But you're miserable to live with, and I've had enough."

"That woman," Billy fumed, shaking his head. "That damned woman. This is all her fault."

"It's nobody's fault but your own," Hazel snapped. "And I guess maybe it's partly ours for letting you get away with actin' like a mangy old bear all these years."

Billy shot her a quelling glance, then turned his glare on Jack. "So you'd rather have that useless heiress around here than me, huh? That's just dandy. If I go, who's gonna feed the stock while you're galavantin' all over the country?"

"Sam's stepson is home from college for the holidays. I reckon he wouldn't mind earnin' some extra bucks." Sighing, Jack raked one hand through his hair. "Look, Uncle Billy, it doesn't have to be this way. You can stay on if you'll make an effort to be pleasant, especially to Elizabeth. But don't you ever call her useless again."

"She ain't even gonna want you now, kid."

"Maybe not," Jack admitted. "But I'm not gonna spend the rest of my life regrettin' I didn't even try to find out. If you'd done that yourself, you might still have a wife, and some kids of your own."

Billy marched to the back door, put on his coat and hat, then turned back for one last shot. "Mark my words, Jack. This is the worst mistake you could make. I'll be gone by mornin'."

"Don't forget the present Elizabeth left under the tree for you," Hazel said dryly.

With a disgruntled, "Humph," Billy slammed out of the house. Chuckling softly, Hazel turned to Jack.

"Don't look so worried," she said. "He'll go sulk in that rat-hole trailer of his for a while, but he's not goin' anywhere."

"Maybe I shouldn't, either," Jack said, casting a worried eye toward the window over the sink. "It's supposed to start snowin' again tonight and—"

Hazel thumped his chest with her knuckles. "Don't star
thinking that way, son. Get packed and drive on over t
Jackson before the roads close so you can take the first fligh
out in the morning."

"But what if—"

"Don't start that, either. Sam and Colin'll help me ou
until the rest of the family gets here. Go on. I'll call the air
port and see what I can do about getting you a reserva
tion."

"You really like her, don't you, Mom?"

Hazel smiled. "I sure do. And I promise, I'll never inter
fere in your marriage. Anytime you want me to move out
just say so. I can always go live with Reggie."

"We'll find a way to work it all out," Jack promised her

"I know we will." She gave him a none-too-gentle shove
toward the doorway. "Now, scoot. And don't forget the
present she left for you, either. Open it before you pack
'cause it's something you're gonna need. Oh, and bring
down my jewelry box. You can take Grandma Elsie's en
gagement and wedding ring set."

His heart pounding with hope, Jack grabbed Elizabeth's
package from under the tree and charged up the stairs to his
room. He didn't own a suitcase, so he made do with the
duffel bag his dad had used when he was in the service. Af
ter tossing in socks, underwear and jeans, he went to his
closet for shirts.

Damn, he thought, when he noticed his suit. A man
should get dressed up for his own wedding, but there was no
way he could pack that suit in a duffel bag without wad
ding it up. It was probably out of style by now, anyway
Well, he'd call Mary and ask her to buy him a new one. He
could pay her back later, and she'd know better than he
would what to get so he wouldn't stick out like a sore thumb.

Then he sat on the edge of the bed and picked up his
package. He usually ripped open a gift with about as much
finesse as a little kid, but this time, he hesitated. Elizabeth
had gone to a lot of trouble to make it look pretty, and for

all he knew, it might be the only present he'd ever get from her.

If Uncle Billy was right— No, dammit, he wouldn't think that way. He didn't dare, for fear of losing his nerve completely. Taking a deep breath, he tore off the wrapping paper and lifted the lid from the box. Then he threw back his head and laughed when he saw the neat stacks of spanking white underwear.

Picking up the note taped to the top undershirt, he read it aloud. "Dear Jack. Chartreuse simply isn't your color. Merry Christmas. Love always, Elizabeth."

He sure hoped she meant that "Love always" part. If she didn't, he was about to make a damn big fool of himself. Well, it wouldn't be the first time. And Mary was right. It was time he took a few risks.

Chapter Ten

Forty-eight hours later, Jack stumbled from the jetway at La Guardia Airport. He'd been rerouted so many times he'd lost count, and he figured God probably didn't even know where his duffel bag was. Served him right for taking off two days before Christmas without reservations beyond Salt Lake City.

"Jack! Over here, Jack!" a voice called.

Spotting his brother-in-law, Lawrence Stone IV, Jack heaved a gusty sigh of relief. Larry was some kind of big-shot, international financier. Jack didn't understand what the guy actually did to earn his money, but he'd been a good husband to Mary and a good father to Nathan and Charlotte.

"I thought you'd never get here," Larry said as they exchanged a brief handshake. "Come on. You're so late, I'm not certain we can get there in time, but we'll do our best. I'll send the car back for your luggage."

Jack accompanied him down a corridor teeming with people of every imaginable description. Then they climbed into a long, black limousine parked outside the nearest exit. The traffic was unbelievable, the freeways incomprehensible, and Jack figured the guy driving the limo had to have suicidal tendencies.

He wished he'd had time to shower and shave and change into the new duds Mary had bought for him. But after two solid days with little to do but think about what his life would be like without Elizabeth, none of that mattered. Nothing mattered now, but getting to her before she did something they would both regret for the rest of their lives.

* * *

"Don't do this, Elizabeth."

Stifling an impatient sigh, Elizabeth took another glass of champagne from a passing waiter, then smoothed down the long, red velvet skirt of her evening gown with her free hand. "Why? I'm not driving anywhere tonight."

"I'm not talking about your alcohol intake," Mary chided. "Don't let your father announce the engagement."

Forcing a nonchalant smile onto her face, Elizabeth turned to her friend. "I know you mean well, Mary, but nothing you can say will change my mind."

"Well, then, don't invite me to the wedding," Mary said. "When the minister asks if anyone can show just cause why you shouldn't be married, I'll jump up in the pew and tell everyone you deserve better than an odious toad like Warren Jameson."

Elizabeth giggled, whether from too much champagne or the mental picture created by Mary's threat, she couldn't have said. Not that it mattered. Now that she had given up on love for good, nothing seemed to matter very much.

She let her gaze roam across her parents' vast living room, noting the tasteful decorations and the elegantly dressed people chatting politely over the music played by the string quartet her mother had hired for the occasion. Compared to Wyoming, everything seemed so...subdued here. A vision of Ginny Johnson's Christmas party flashed through her mind.

What she wouldn't give to be back in that warm little house with its tacky decorations, where people talked and laughed as loudly as they pleased, stole food from each other's plates and sang Christmas carols—not in perfect harmony, but from the heart. Where children with sticky fingers and dirty faces romped among the adults who cared for them with love shining from their eyes. Where she had known and loved a special man named Jack.

Her throat contracted and her heart ached as if an invisible fist had closed around it and squeezed it viciously. This was neither the time nor the place for such thoughts, she scolded herself. Jack didn't want her. Warren did.

Despite Mary's opinion of him, Warren Jameson III wasn't really a bad sort. Though he didn't stir her senses, he was hardly repulsive. While he was a bit dull in the humor department, he wasn't crude or unkind. He was so obsessed with business, he might even be faithful to her.

A masculine arm slid around her waist, startling her. She looked up into the patrician face of the man she had agreed to marry, and felt that invisible hand squeeze her heart again.

"Ready, darling?" Warren asked, his smooth, cultured voice grating on her ears.

Ready? No! She would never be ready to smile and graciously accept toasts to their happiness, when this was more of a business merger than a marriage. Mary stepped into her line of vision, her big blue eyes—eyes so painfully similar to Jack's—begging Elizabeth to reconsider.

And suddenly Elizabeth knew she couldn't go through with this charade. She was acting out of pique—exactly like the spoiled brat Jack had called her. Marrying Warren wouldn't be fair to him, to herself, or to the children she wanted so desperately.

Inhaling a deep breath for courage, she shot Mary a reassuring smile, then turned to face Warren. Before she could open her mouth, however, the string quartet played a loud note. Her parents moved into the center of the room. Her father raised his arms to attract everyone's attention.

Desperate to stop him before he made this situation any more difficult than it already was, Elizabeth took two quick steps, halting at the sound of angry voices coming from the entryway. Roberts, the English butler who had faithfully served the Davies-Smythe family for as long as Elizabeth could remember, backed into the room, hands in front of him as if to ward off an attack.

"R-really, sir," Roberts sputtered. "This is most inappropriate. You can't come in here."

To Elizabeth's astonishment, a deep, achingly familiar voice said, "Like hell, I can't."

Then a large, work-roughened hand whipped through the doorway, grabbed the portly butler by the front of his pristine white shirt, lifted him into the air and set him off to one side as if he weighed no more than a rag doll. The room fell silent. All eyes turned toward the doorway.

When Jack stormed in a second later, a strange paralysis invaded Elizabeth's muscles, rendering her incapable of doing anything but standing there and staring at him. She heard Mary mutter, "It's about time," but she was so busy convincing herself she wasn't dreaming, the words hardly registered.

In a room full of tuxedos, Jack's jeans, boots, heavy coat and Stetson hat made him stand out like a zebra in a herd of white horses. The thunderous expression on his face, the fists swinging at his sides with each long, determined stride, and the aura of barely leashed fury radiating from him boded ill for anyone who got in his way. No one did.

Stopping not two feet from her father, he propped his hands on his hips and scanned the gathering. "Elizabeth," he said in a tone that made her grateful to be standing at the back of the room, "where the heck are you?"

A titter of nervous laughter followed his question, ending abruptly when Jack turned his head and glared in the direction from which it had come.

George Davies-Smythe stepped forward. "This is a private party. Who are you and what do you want with my daughter?"

The sight of her father and the man she loved squared off in a confrontational stance propelled Elizabeth into action. Ignoring Warren's demand to wait for him, she wormed her way through the clusters of guests as fast as her long skirt and high heels would allow. The room was huge, however, and so crowded it was like running a gauntlet the length of a football field.

"Name's Jack Zorn," she heard as she squeezed between two matronly women who were gaping at Jack as if he belonged in a zoo. "I've come to ask your daughter to marry me."

"That's impossible," George said.

"No, it isn't, Father," Elizabeth shouted.

Buzzing whispers traveled across the room at the speed of gossip. Larry Stone appeared at her side and began clearing a path for her. Clutching his coattail, she followed him into the small circle of space created by the tension and hostility vibrating between Jack and her parents. Then her gaze met Jack's.

Several days' growth of whiskers darkened the lower half of his face and lines of weariness bracketed his unsmiling mouth, but to her, he looked absolutely wonderful. His eyes were filled with the same emotions churning inside her. Desire. Tenderness. Love? Oh, yes, there was love shining there. For her.

"Elizabeth, do you know this person?" Marilyn Davies-Smythe asked.

Still gazing into the clear blue depths of Jack's eyes, Elizabeth nodded.

"Well?" her mother demanded. "Who is he?"

"He's Mary Stone's brother. I stayed at his ranch when I was in Wyoming."

"What is he doing here?" George demanded.

A slow, sinfully sexy smile spread across Jack's face. Without taking his gaze from Elizabeth's, he said, "I already told you that, mister. I've come to ask Beth to marry me."

"And I have told *you* that's impossible," George said, crossing the space to his daughter's right side.

"That's right," Warren said. Moving to Elizabeth's left, he put his arm around her waist in a possessive gesture that made her want to hit him. "We're announcing our engagement tonight. I'm afraid you're too late."

The look Jack gave him could have melted a frozen lake from fifty miles. Warren lowered his arm to his side. Jack gave him a grim smile, then turned his attention back to Elizabeth.

"Am I too late, Beth?"

Elizabeth had to clear her throat to make her voice work. "What changed your mind?"

"I missed you like hell, honey."

"And?"

"And I didn't want to end up like Uncle Billy. He let the love of his life get away from him for the sake of his pride. I'd like to think I'm smarter than that."

"This is absolutely the most preposterous thing I have ever heard," Marilyn huffed.

Ignoring her mother, Elizabeth stepped closer to Jack. "Are you saying you love me?"

"You're damn right. I love you. Period. No buts. Can you forgive me for acting like such a jerk?"

Elizabeth took another step forward. "If you can forgive me for acting like a spoiled brat."

Her father grabbed her hand and pulled her back beside him. "Use your head, Elizabeth. This man obviously has no prospects. The only thing he's in love with is your bank balance."

Yanking her hand away, she turned to face him. "Do you really think I'm so unlovable, Father?"

"Don't be absurd." George shot Jack a scathing look. "Ask him to sign a prenuptial agreement and you'll see how much he loves you."

Jack roared with laughter. "I'll sign any damn thing you want. As far as I'm concerned, Beth's fortune is more of a deterrent than an incentive, but I'll take her any way I can get her."

"How do you intend to provide for her?" Warren asked. "A woman like Elizabeth—"

"Needs to be loved like any other woman," Jack interrupted. "I may not be able to give her everything you can, bud, but I can give her everything that's really important."

"Such as?" George demanded.

"Such as a home, a family who loves her and the best friends and neighbors anyone could ever ask for."

"What kind of a home?" Marilyn asked.

"Well, ma'am," Jack drawled, glancing around the room as if noticing it for the first time. "It ain't as fancy as this one, that's for sure. But it's warm in the winter and cool in the summer, and it sits on five thousand acres of the prettiest land God ever made. We've got clean air and water, plenty of sunshine, and a fantastic view of the Wind River Mountains."

Elizabeth watched her mother's expression soften with every sentence Jack spoke. Then Marilyn said, "Do you really love her, Mr. Zorn?"

"I sure do. And I'll take good care of her, ma'am. You'd be welcome to visit us anytime."

Marilyn turned to Elizabeth. "Do you love him, dear?"

Before she could answer, George shouted, "She's agreed to marry Warren, and—"

"Well, she hasn't married him yet, George. Calm down before you have a stroke."

While her parents bickered, Jack took Elizabeth's hand and tugged her away from her father. "You never answered your mother's question. Do you love me, Beth? Enough to marry me?"

Meeting his worried gaze without hesitation, she smiled. "You're damn right I do, cowboy."

He threw back his head and laughed again, then leaned down, slid one hand behind her knees and lifted her high against his chest. Linking her arms around his neck for balance, she kissed him with all the passion she possessed. Awareness of time and place drifted away as he responded in kind, telling her without words how much he loved, wanted and needed her.

When the kiss finally ended, he raised his head and looked down at her, his eyes filled with a lusty promise she couldn't wait for him to keep. A smattering of applause turned into an ovation as he carried her from the room. Roberts hastened to open the front door for him.

"Thank you, Roberts," Elizabeth said over Jack's shoulder. "Please send for my car."

"Yes, Miss Elizabeth." The dignified butler surprised her with a broad grin and a wink. "I hope you'll be very happy."

"Oh, I will, Roberts. Believe me, I will."

Jack refused to put her down while they waited for the car to arrive. Utterly content to be held in his arms, Elizabeth rested her head on his shoulder and watched fat, sassy snowflakes fall from the inky sky. Then she tilted her head back and gazed into Jack's eyes. Her throat tightened and her eyes misted with happy tears.

"Thank you for the lovely gift," she whispered.

He frowned. "I didn't give you anything."

She reached up and covered the side of his face with her palm, smiling at the way his whiskers tickled her skin. "Yes, you did. And it's more precious to me than anything I've ever owned."

"What's that?"

"Your love."

"You'll always have it, sweetheart."

"I know. That's what makes it so precious."

He kissed her. Tenderly. Reverently. Passionately.

Church bells rang in the distance, carrying a message of hope, joy and reconciliation. No matter what problems lay in their future, Elizabeth would rather be Jack Zorn's wife than any other man's ornament. And she would always thank God for this big, gruff cowboy, who loved her without any buts.

* * * * *

A Recipe from Myrna Temte

I like to serve this for breakfast on Christmas morning.
You can bake it while the family is opening presents.

SAUSAGE OR TURKEY BAKE

1½ lbs sausage or 2 cups cooked turkey pieces
8 slices cubed bread
4 eggs
2¼ cups milk
¾ tsp dry mustard*
2 cups grated cheese
1 can cream of mushroom soup
½ cup milk

Brown sausage. Grease 9" X 13" pan. Put bread in
bottom of pan, then add sausage or turkey. Beat eggs,
2¼ cups of milk and mustard.* Pour over bread and
sausage. Sprinkle with cheese. Cover and store in the
refrigerator overnight. Next day, pour on mushroom
soup, mixed with ½ cup of milk. Bake at 350° F for
1 hour.

*If using turkey, use ½ to ¾ tsp of sage instead
of mustard.

The Forever Gift

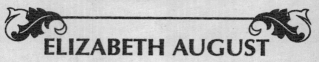

ELIZABETH AUGUST

A Note from Elizabeth August

Dear Reader,

As you may guess from "The Forever Gift," I love Christmas trees. My mother's family were farmers. During the summer, my grandfather would spot a tree in the woods he thought would be perfect for Christmas. When December came, he and my uncles would cut it and bring it home. There it would be set in the living room, and we would string popcorn and make paper chains for decorations.

My father's family had emigrated from Sicily and lived in the city. At Christmas, my grandfather would go out and buy the biggest tree the living room would hold. He had lights and beautiful glass ornaments for decorations. Then there was the tinsel. He would insist it be hung strand by strand until the tree was dressed in silver.

My parents' trees were a mixture of the two above.

My own is a real hodgepodge. I have a collection of angels that go on the upper branches. Then comes a variety of ornaments we've collected through the years. Some are of the traditional glass variety. Then there are crocheted and burlap ones I've made. Other ornaments we bought on vacations. But the most important to me are ones made by my sons and those given me by friends. All of the decorations hold memories for me, and as I hang them, I feel a unity with those friends and loved ones who mean so much to me. Perhaps that is why I cherish decorating my Christmas tree so much... it is a source of loving memories and a promise of future ones.

And to each of you I wish a joyous holiday season and may you, too, gather memories that will touch your heart and bring a smile to your face in the years to come.

Elizabeth August

Chapter One

"Doesn't that girl know how much trouble she can get into?" Abigail Jones muttered under her breath as she passed the young hitchhiker standing by the side of the road.

Her concern deepened. It was December and an even more immediate danger than an unscrupulous driver was the weather. Here, in the mountainous southwest corner of Idaho, winters were bitterly cold. At the moment, fresh snow was falling onto the two feet already on the ground. And the sun was setting, which meant the temperature would be dropping to even more frigid levels.

Abigail had spent the past few years working hard at not becoming involved in the lives of others. But her conscience wouldn't allow her to leave the girl standing by the side of the road on a night like this. Pumping the brake so she wouldn't skid, she came to a stop then backed up to within about six feet of the hitchhiker.

The girl approached and looked in through the window, then smiled with relief.

At least she was smart enough to take a look at who was offering her a ride before she got in, Abigail thought. Of course, I might be the foolish one, she added. She'd learned the hard way that a very unpleasant person could appear quite innocent at first glance. A rush of hurtful memories assailed her. Some people could even fool others for years. Abruptly she pushed the memories back to the far recesses of her mind.

"Thanks for stopping," the young girl said as she opened the door. Apology entered her voice. "You might want to put my suitcase and backpack in the trunk. They're kind of wet.''

"They'll be fine on the floor in the back," Abigail replied.

The girl nodded and clumsily shoved them inside. "I was so relieved when I saw you slow down," she said as she slid into the passenger seat, closed the door and pulled the seat belt around her. "Yours is the first car I've seen on this road in the past twenty minutes. I was beginning to think I was going to freeze, get covered with snow and, if any one did drive by, they'd mistake me for a clever snow sculpture of a hitchhiker."

Abigail saw the girl fumbling with the catch for the seat belt and realized her passenger's hands were so cold she couldn't work them properly. Reaching over she fastened the belt. Although she admired the girl's ability to jest in the face of adversity, she could not keep silent about the very real dangers. "This region is sparsely populated. You could very easily have frozen to death," she said. "On top of that, hitchhiking is not a safe way to travel, especially for a young girl."

"I know," her passenger admitted, "but I could only buy a ticket as far as Grasmere." She paused and frowned out the window, then added, "I figured I could walk the rest of the way but I hadn't counted on the weather being so cold."

As Abigail started to shift the car into gear a sudden thought struck her. "Are you sure you're headed in the right direction? There's nothing much down this road except for Blye's Stand."

"That's where I'm headed."

Abigail heard the uneasiness mingled with resolve in the girl's voice. She'd made it a practice not to pry into other people's lives. Still, she heard herself saying, "There's not much there."

"Yeah, I know," the girl replied. She laughed nervously. "My mom used to say that if you blinked you'd miss it."

"She's right," Abigail confirmed, pulling out onto the road again. She noticed that the girl's teeth were chattering slightly and her concern grew. "Where is your mother?" she asked, wondering if the girl's parents knew she was wandering around in the middle of nowhere in the dead of winter.

"She's dead," the girl replied stiffly. "So's my father."

Abigail heard the pain in her passenger's voice and a sister pain caused a knot in her stomach. "I'm sorry."

"Me, too," the girl replied. For a long moment a heavy silence fell over the car, then she said, "My name's Rose Courtland. Roses were my mother's favorite flower. I guess I'm lucky she didn't prefer azaleas or chrysanthemums."

The "Courtland" struck a bell. Abigail glanced toward her passenger. In spite of Rose's attempt at humor, she saw only anxiety on the girl's face. Returning her attention to the road, she said, "I'm Abigail Jones."

"Do you live in Blye's Stand?" her passenger asked.

"Yes." Out of the corner of her eye, Abigail saw Rose seem to stiffen and become sharply alert.

"What's it like? The town I mean."

Although her young passenger was attempting to sound casual, Abigail noted that the nervous edge in the girl's voice was even more pronounced. "There's not too much to tell. The population is currently calculated at one hundred seventy-nine. That includes a few outlying ranches and homesteads. The only businesses in town are Blye's General Store, a gas station and Kane Courtland's place."

Abigail glanced toward her companion when she mentioned Kane and saw Rose shift uneasily. Making an attempt to ease the atmosphere in the car, she continued conversationally, "We don't even rate a post office. There used to be one housed in the general store. The window and the boxes are still there but Lottie Blye runs it as a private concern now. She keeps stamps in stock and the townspeople bring in boxes to be weighed and stamped and picked up there. That way they can do their mailing at the same time

they do their shopping." Abigail wasn't comfortable trying
to make small talk and when she noticed the girl was only
half listening, she stopped talking.

A silence filled the interior of the car. For the next few
minutes Rose stared out at the road ahead, then abruptly she
asked, "Do you know Norval Courtland?"

Abigail again glanced at her passenger. The girl was
clearly eager to hear her reply. Abigail had never liked being the bearer of bad news but Rose was going to find out
the truth as soon as she reached town. "Norval Courtland
died several years ago," she said solicitously. "I'm not sure
when. It was before I arrived."

"I guess that just leaves Kane then," the girl murmured
under her breath.

The image of Kane Courtland came sharply into Abigail's mind. He was a big man, standing around six foot two
and strongly built. He wasn't what she'd term openly
friendly. She'd noticed that he'd watch people for a while
before he'd decide if they were worth his time. And judging
from his mostly solitary existence, he didn't find too many
who were.

"Do you know him...Kane Courtland, I mean?" Rose
asked.

Abigail noted that the attempt at casualness was gone
from her passenger's voice. In its place was an anxious interest. "I know who he is," she replied.

"What's he like?"

"I don't know him real well," Abigail replied honestly.
"From what I've heard, he's an honest, hardworking man."
This description had come from Lottie and Abigail had no
reason to dispute it. In addition to being Abigail's employer, Lottie was one of the founders of Blye's Stand. More
than half a century ago, she and her husband had settled on
the site of the town and she knew just about all there was to
know about the majority of the people who called the place
home. Lottie was fond of Kane and on several occasions had
assured Abigail the man had many good qualities. Abigail,

herself, had observed he did work hard and was always willing to lend a helping hand when anyone in the community needed aid.

Rose frowned at the road ahead. "He's my uncle."

Abigail hid her surprise. She'd thought Kane had been an only child. "I'm sure he'll be glad to see you," she said, more because she had the feeling the girl needed to hear this than with any real conviction it was so.

"I'm not so sure about that," Rose returned, confirming Abigail's suspicions. As if she couldn't hold it in any longer, the girl continued nervously, "My mother ran away from home when she was seventeen. My father, John Kreck, was a rodeo rider who'd stopped by to pick up a saddle my grandfather had custom-made for him. He got killed before he got around to marrying my mother. Then she discovered she was pregnant. She told me she didn't come back because she couldn't stand the thought of being trapped in a one-horse town again. But I think the real reason was she was too embarrassed and not too sure my grandfather would take her back. Anyway, we did all right on our own. She was a terrific waitress and got good tips."

Rose paused for a breath, then hurried on, "A little over two years ago, she got killed in a car accident. I was thirteen then and determined to stand on my own two feet. Besides, I figured if my grandfather wouldn't want his daughter back he sure wouldn't want an illegitimate grandchild. So I told the social services people I was an orphan."

Rose frowned darkly and her jaw tensed. "That was a big mistake. They put me in the foster care system. Some of the families were great but some weren't and I never knew from one day to the next if I was going to stay where I was or be moved. Then they moved me in with this family where the father—" her voice faltered and she turned to stare out the window again "—the father started making advances toward me."

A chill ran through Abigail as the girl's words stirred old memories. "Did you report him?"

"Sure but he claimed I was the one who came on to him. The social worker sided with him and put on my record that I was a troublemaker. Incorrigible, I think was how she labeled me. And she left me in that house. The father, he started pawing me even more because he felt safe. I figured nothing could be worse than putting up with him so I decided to run away and come find my grandfather and my uncle."

A protectiveness toward Rose swept through Abigail. "You did the right thing."

"I don't know if my uncle will think so," Rose replied, repeating her doubts. Then she smiled lopsidedly. "But I figure if he's got any decency he won't throw me out until after Christmas. That'll give me a couple of weeks to prove to him I can be useful to have around. I can cook and clean."

Abigail caught the note of desperation in the girl's voice. Deep inside she felt a bond with this child. "If he does throw you out, you can bunk with me," she heard herself saying. "I live in an apartment over Blye's General Store. You can't miss the place. My entrance is up a flight of stairs in the rear." Even as she spoke, Abigail was shocked at herself. Hard-learned lessons had caused her to vow to keep at a distance from others and here she was inviting this girl to live with her. It'll just be for a short while, she assured herself.

Relief mingled with gratitude on Rose's face. "Thanks."

Ahead of them, Abigail saw the lights of town. Kane's place was just across the street from Lottie's store. It was a single-story rambling affair. His workshop, where, depending on his mood and his current customer orders, he made finely crafted saddles and bridles as well as belts and custom-fit Western boots, was attached to one side. Pulling up in front of the entrance to the private portion of the house, she set the car in park but left the engine running. "I'll wait," she said, watching Rose obviously working up her courage to get out of the car and face her uncle. "If he in-

ites you in, just wave. If he doesn't, come on back and I'll
ut you up.''

Rose gave her a shaky smile. ''Wish me luck,'' she said,
pening the door.

While Rose got her things out of the back seat, Abigail's
attention shifted to the house beyond. From her window
he'd seen Lottie and Kane sitting on the wide roofed front
porch on summer nights talking. But, although Lottie had
often urged her to join them, Abigail never had. Unable to
ace having those she considered friends turn their backs on
er yet again, she'd chosen not to encourage any real
riendship, even with Lottie. And, as far as Kane Court-
and was concerned, she was sure he would not have wel-
omed her company.

Abruptly the door of the house opened and Kane's strong
orm was silhouetted against the light from inside. Her
ervousness for Rose increased and she shifted her atten-
ion back to the girl. There was a look of apprehension on
Rose's face.

''The bigger they are the harder they fall,'' the girl said in
a conspiratorial whisper. Again a nervous smile played at the
orner of her mouth. ''Maybe he'll turn out to be just a big
eddy bear.''

''Maybe,'' Abigail replied encouragingly. ''Teddy bear''
vas not a term she would have ever chosen to describe Kane
Courtland. But she didn't want to discourage Rose.

With a final impish grin, Rose closed the car door, turned
o the house and walked to the porch.

In the light from the porch lamp, Abigail could see Kane
ind Rose talking but she was too far away to be able to dis-
ern the expression on either's face. However, after only a
ouple of minutes, Rose turned and waved, then followed
er uncle inside.

Abigail silently wished the girl luck as she pulled away.

Chapter Two

A little over half an hour later, Abigail stood looking at the Christmas tree tied to the luggage rack on the roof of her car. She'd left it to be unloaded last. Now the decorations for the tree and the gifts to go under it were in her apartment and it was time for the tree to join them. It looked even larger than when she'd purchased it. But she wanted a big tree. Her apartment was spacious enough. It had once been home to the Blyes until they'd built the separate two-story residence on the other side of the store.

She felt like a kid at her first Christmas. In a lot of ways this was a first Christmas for her. Her mind went back eleven years to the last Christmas she'd shared with her mother. The following summer her mother had died. That had been the beginning of what she labeled the dark years of her life. She willed herself to put the memories of those times in the far recesses of her mind. She could not change them, nor could she erase the fear that Martin Gelespe would show up and destroy the safe haven she'd made for herself here. But she also couldn't bear the cold, barren existence she was living, either. It was time to start building good memories again to fill her life with some sense of warmth.

"I saw the tree on top of your car. Thought you might need some help getting it up those stairs to your apartment."

Abigail jerked around at the sound of the male voice. Kane Courtland was standing a couple of feet behind her. "Thanks, but I can manage," she replied.

He frowned impatiently. "There's nothing wrong with accepting a helping hand once in a while. You can consider it my way of thanking you for giving my niece a lift."

The cold wind whipped around Abigail. She turned to look at the narrow outside stairs leading to her second-floor apartment. "You don't need to go out of your way to thank me," she said stiffly. "But you're right. I could probably use some help."

"That was real hard for you to admit, wasn't it?"

She met his gaze levelly. "Yes."

A hint of a smile tilted one side of his mouth. "At least you're honest." Then the smile vanished and he turned his attention to unfastening the ropes holding the tree in place.

He was a handsome man in a rugged sort of way, she conceded. And she had noticed him more than she wanted to admit. She found herself recalling when, a couple of weeks after she'd arrived in town, he'd come by the store and asked her for a date. She'd been pretty sure Lottie had put him up to it. The woman was an incurable match-maker. But Abigail hadn't wanted to be matched with any-one. All she'd wanted was to be left alone. She'd turned him down and he'd never asked again. Which was just as well, she told herself sharply, bringing her mind back to the present. She didn't need any complications in her life, es-pecially in the form of Kane Courtland. All she wanted was peace and quiet and a safe haven.

She focused her attention on the tree he was freeing.

Several minutes later as they entered her apartment bear-ing the six-foot evergreen, she said sincerely, "I really do appreciate your help. Getting this tree up those stairs on my own would have been difficult."

But Kane wasn't paying her much attention. Instead his gaze was traveling around the sparsely furnished room. "Where's the stand?"

"I haven't gotten it out yet," she replied, releasing her end of the tree so that it came to rest gently on the floor.

His gaze leveled on her. "This is the first time you've set up a real tree, isn't it?"

A rush of memories flooded over her. Hot tears suddenly burned at the back of her eyes. "No." The word came out stiffly. Determinedly she forced a nonchalance into her tone. "But it has been a long time."

For a moment Kane studied her and she saw the curiosity in his eyes. Then, to her relief, it vanished as if he'd decided that being curious about her was a waste of his time. His manner became businesslike. "You'll need help putting it in the stand. And the bottom should be sawed off a bit so you have fresh wood that'll allow the tree to absorb water. I'll be back."

"Really, I'm sure I can..." she began, only to find herself talking to empty space as he released his half of the tree and strode out.

Deciding that protesting would not only be futile but foolish, she tossed her coat on a chair, found the stand and read the instructions for setting it up. After all, she reasoned, he posed no threat to her and she could use the help. By the time Kane returned, she had the stand assembled.

It took him only a few minutes to saw off the necessary portion of the base and a couple of the lowest branches so there would be enough trunk space to fit into the stand. Then he hoisted the tree up and into the stand while she lay on the floor and guided it into place.

A knock on the door interrupted as she began setting the screws that would hold the tree steady.

"Come in," Abigail called from her prone position on the floor.

The door opened and Rose entered. "Thought I'd better come see if there was a problem." Relief spread over her face when she saw them wrestling with the tree. "I was afraid Uncle Kane might have been giving you a hard time for bringing me here," she said straightforwardly. Her gaze shifted to him. "I know you said I was welcome in your home and that you just wanted to come and thank Abigail

or bringing me here, but when you were gone so long, I got
o worrying that maybe you were just being polite to me and
night be angry with her.''

"You'll find that I generally speak my mind plainly,''
Kane replied.

"Good, because so do I,'' Rose returned, facing him
quarely.

Watching them, it occurred to Abigail that Kane could
have his hands full with his niece. Although Rose was look-
ng for a home, she obviously had a strong streak of inde-
pendence that wouldn't allow her to beg or cower.

"You came along at a good time,'' Kane said. "We could
use another hand. Either you or Miss Jones can determine
f the tree is standing straight while the other tightens the
crews.''

"I'll do the screws since I'm already down here,'' Abigail replied.

Another knock on the door interrupted before Rose could
begin her task. "I'll get it,'' the girl said, dashing across the
room, clearly trying to be as helpful as possible.

This time it was Lottie Blye who entered. "I saw the pa-
rade coming over here and I hate to miss a party.'' As she
spoke, her gaze traveled between Kane and Abigail and she
grinned. She was a lean woman and for the most part looked
all of her seventy-plus years. Except for her eyes. They had
a youthful glimmer and could hold a truly mischievous
sparkle when something struck her as peculiar or interest-
ng. And right now that sparkle was there.

"I thought I'd put up a tree this year,'' Abigail said feel-
ng the need to explain why Kane was in her apartment before Lottie jumped to the wrong conclusion. "And Mr.
Courtland offered to help me get it in the stand.''

"I figured it was the neighborly thing to do,'' Kane added
coolly, his tone warning Lottie not to get any romantic no-
tions.

Mentally Abigail patted herself on the back. She'd been
sure Kane wasn't really attracted to her. Now she had even

more proof. And I'm pleased, she told herself, again de-
claring that all she wanted was a safe haven with no emotional complications. And I'd also like to get out from under
this tree, she added silently.

"I'm helping, too," Rose interjected.

Lottie looked mildly piqued by Kane and Abigail's attitude. Then with a smile of friendly interest she turned her
attention to the young girl standing beside her. "And
who..." she began to ask. The rest of the question died in
her throat as amazement showed on her face.

"This is Rose Courtland, my sister Janice's daughter,"
Kane said. "She arrived just tonight."

Abigail was startled by the gentleness with which Kane
had pronounced his sister's name. She did not doubt that he
had cared for Janice Courtland. A surge of sympathy for
him swept through her.

"Good heavens!" Lottie gasped. "She's the spitting image of Janice at that age. Pretty as a picture."

Rose flushed under Lottie's scrutiny.

The older woman smiled a warm, welcoming smile.
"What a wonderful Christmas surprise. Where's your
mother?" Her gaze traveled around the room as if she expected to see Janice there.

"Mom died in an accident," Rose replied.

Lottie's smile was replaced with an expression of sympathy. "I'm sorry to hear that. But at least you're here. It's
about time Kane had family to share that big house with."
She gave Rose a tight hug. "Welcome to Blye's Stand."

"Rose, meet Lottie Blye," Kane said as his niece was being released.

Rose eyed the white-haired woman with interest. "The
town is named after your family?"

"It's named after my dear departed Joe," Lottie replied.
"He bought this place and had it declared a town just to
impress me so's I'd marry him. I was just seventeen at the
time and he was twenty-eight."

Rose's eyes gleamed. "How romantic!"

"He was that." Lottie frowned regretfully. "Too romantic for his own good. He died falling off a cliff just because he thought I wanted a stupid flower growing near the edge." Tears flooded her eyes.

Abigail knew from experience this could lead into the telling of several stories about Joe Blye's antics. The man seemed to have a knack for doing the unusual. Normally she didn't mind listening to Lottie's reminiscences but she was growing weary of her current position. "I'm beginning to feel like the floor of a forest," she said, as another needle dropped into her hair.

"Oh!" Rose's attention jerked back to her assigned task.

With Lottie helping her, both Kane's and Abigail's patience was tried before the two spotters were satisfied the tree was as straight as it could be. But finally, with Kane glowering at them threateningly and Abigail protesting that she was getting claustrophobic, they finally gave their permission for the tree to be secured in the stand.

"Now where do you want it?" Kane asked as Abigail squirmed out from under the branches and rose to her feet.

"By that window," she replied, hurrying to shift a table out of the way as Kane carefully maneuvered the tree to the designated spot.

"You'll need to fill the stand with water and make sure it stays filled," he instructed as he released the pine tree and stepped back. "It should drink a lot of water over the next few days."

Abigail nodded. "That part I remember." Old memories again washed over her as she stared at the tree and hot tears burned at the back of her eyes. She scowled at herself. It had been a long time since she'd cried and she wouldn't now. Tears, she reminded herself, were a useless waste of energy. "I had just forgotten how much of a group effort it takes to put up a real tree."

She stiffened at the sound of her own voice. This had been meant as a private thought. Instead it had been spoken aloud with a wistfulness that revealed some of the emotion she was feeling. Exposing herself like that made her feel vulnerable and she didn't like feeling vulnerable. Immediately a polite but cool mask descended over her features as her gaze shifted to Kane, Rose and Lottie. "Thanks for the help."

For a moment Kane studied her as if trying to see beyond the cool facade now in place. Impatience flickered in the dark depths of his eyes. Then, as if losing interest, a matching cool politeness spread over his features. "You're welcome," he replied, picking up his saw and heading for the door.

But instead of following, Rose cast Abigail an encouraging smile. "Maybe Abbie would like some help trimming her tree?"

The use of the nickname gave Abigail a jolt. Her family had called her that. But she hadn't allowed anyone to refer to her as Abbie in years. It felt too personal. Usually when someone used it she informed them politely but firmly that she preferred to be called Abigail. But as she turned to Rose to do just that, the plea in the girl's eyes caused the words to stick in her throat.

"You'd like some help wouldn't you," Rose coaxed.

"Sure," Abigail heard herself saying. "Sure, why not."

Rose smiled brightly. "It'll be fun," she declared, shifting her attention to her uncle. "We'll have a tree-trimming party. Mom and I used to have them. We'd invite the neighbors over and she'd serve cookies and popcorn and drinks, and we'd decorate the tree."

Abigail was still finding it difficult to believe she was encouraging this gathering. Yet even as she cautioned herself that this was not wise, she heard herself saying, "I do have some soda in the refrigerator and I could make some popcorn."

Kane will refuse to stay, she told herself assuredly, certain he would save her from the momentary insanity that had caused her to accede to Rose's wishes. But when she looked at him, instead of the protest she expected to see on his face, there was an expression of polite indulgence.

"If Miss Jones wants some help, then we can stay," he said.

Abigail groaned mentally. I hope I don't live to regret this, she thought frantically. Then remembering that she'd given herself permission to begin gathering good memories again, she reasoned that this little party couldn't do any harm. Letting people help her trim her tree shouldn't be a threat to the protective shield she was determined to keep around her emotions.

"I can supply the cookies and more soda from downstairs," Lottie volunteered. She grinned at Rose. "Why don't you come help me pick out the snacks. We'll leave Kane and Abigail to make the popcorn."

"I've never been any good at making popcorn," Kane said before Lottie could capture Rose by the arm and drag the girl along with her. "I'll help bring things up from downstairs. Rose can help Miss Jones."

His determination to make it clear to everyone present that he had no desire to spend time alone with her, grated on Abigail's nerves. Disconcerted by this reaction, she reminded herself that she didn't want to spend time alone with him and he was saving them both from any further matchmaking Lottie might have been considering. Smiling, she added her vote to his side. "That's a terrific idea."

Again Lottie looked disappointed. Then the mischievous gleam returned to her eyes. "Okay, but when Kane and I return, he's going to start calling Abigail by her first name instead of Miss Jones and Abigail will stop calling him Mr. Courtland and address him as Kane. And . . ." She glanced at Kane pointedly. "We will all remove our coats so we don't look as if we're going to bolt for the door at any moment."

Abigail had noticed that, although both Rose and Lottie had tossed their coats on the chair with hers, Kane had kept his coat on . . . another sign he hadn't planned to stay any longer than necessary in her apartment.

"Fine," Kane agreed, though he looked like a man trapped in a situation he didn't want to be in but was uncertain of how to extricate himself.

Abigail tried to think of a polite way to insist that she and Kane retain their formal manner toward each other. She felt more comfortable that way and knew he did, too. But before she could think of anything to say, Lottie had shrugged into her coat and both she and Kane were on their way out of the apartment.

"Is there some kind of feud between you and my uncle?" Rose asked as soon as she and Abigail were alone.

Abigail saw the worried look in the girl's eyes. Clearly Rose was fearful she had done something that was going to turn Kane against her or at the very least upset him. "No, not at all," Abby assured her. "We're just not interested in being a pair and don't want to encourage Lottie. She's a very persistent matchmaker when she sets her mind to it."

Rose nodded her understanding, then frowned at the door. "He's a very grim man."

Abigail's concern for the girl again blossomed. "Is there a problem between the two of you?" Then again she heard herself saying, "If you'd rather stay here with me, you're welcome to." *Encouraging a friendship is only going to bring you disappointment and hurt,* her inner voice cautioned. Remembering the painful lessons that had taught her this, she knew she should heed the warning. Still, she felt too strong an empathy for this child not to offer aid.

Rose smiled gratefully. "Thanks again for the offer, but there really isn't a problem . . . exactly." Her smile faded. "It's just that I can tell he's uneasy around me but he's being real nice. He had me put my things in my mother's old room and he said he'd bring her things down from the attic if I wanted to make the room more feminine looking. And he said he was glad I came here. But I'm just not sure if I should really believe him or if he's just doing what he feels he's obligated to do because I'm family."

Having been told many times by Lottie how strongly Kane felt about family ties, Abigail had to admit that Rose's assessment of his actions could be correct. However, she didn't want to discourage the girl. "It sounds to me as if the two of you just need a little time to adjust to each other. You've got to have been a shock to him, and he has been a bachelor all of his life. He's not used to having a teenager under his roof."

Rose looked somewhat relieved. "You're probably right. My mother used to say both he and her father were quiet sort of men." Her manner became apologetic. "I hope you don't mind my inviting us to help you decorate your tree. It just suddenly occurred to me that my first evening with him might go more smoothly if there were a few other people around to help break the ice."

Abigail could understand the girl's reasoning. Kane Courtland was an intimidating man. Of course, he didn't intimidate her, she added quickly to herself. Aloud, she said, "No, I don't mind. I thought it was a good idea," she added, hoping to help Rose feel more relaxed.

But as they popped the corn and Rose reminisced about Christmases she'd spent with her mother, Abigail began to regret her decision. The girl stirred up memories Abigail only rarely allowed herself and she never dwelled on them too long. They made her want more in her life than she felt safe to seek.

Kane and Lottie's return eased her mood. Kane's presence was a sharp deterrent to the rekindling of those gentler, softer emotions Rose's reminiscences had begun to uncover. His manner toward her, although polite, was cool and distant, letting her know he was only there because this was his niece's wish.

And that suits me just fine, she told herself as she hung a blue glass ball on the tree. Turning, she stifled a gasp of surprise. Kane was standing directly behind her barely a foot away and she'd nearly collided with him. The broad expanse of his flannel-shirted chest sent an unexpected current of excitement racing through her. That's an idiotic reaction, she chided herself. There had never been anything but a chill between her and Kane Courtland and there never would be.

"I didn't mean to startle you," he said.

She looked up into his face to find him studying her speculatively. "I thought you might like to put this one on the tree yourself." As he spoke, he extended a clear crystal hand-blown ornament toward her. "The price tag was still on it. Seems you paid quite a bit. I figured it was special."

Abigail gently cradled the fragile, elongated bubble in her hands. All of the other ornaments she'd bought for the tree were inexpensive, purchased at the discount store. For this one, however, she'd paid an exorbitant amount. She'd caught a glimpse of it out of the corner of her eye as she passed the window of a gift shop in Mountain Home. She'd come to such an abrupt halt that a shopper walking behind her had nearly collided with her. But the ornament was almost exactly like one her mother had cherished and seeing it had been a shock.

After staring at it for a long moment, she'd ordered herself to walk on. But instead, she'd remained frozen in front of the window while recalling the many times she'd watched her mother hang that one particular ornament on the tree. "This was given to me by my mother the first Christmas after I married your father," her mother would say. "It had been given to her the first Christmas after she'd married and it will pass on to you the first Christmas after you're married."

Standing there in the cold afternoon air looking in that window, Abigail's stomach had twisted at the memory of her last sight of her mother's heirloom. It was shattered shards of glass on the floor. Her stepfather had claimed to have accidentally knocked it off the tree but she was certain he'd broken the ornament on purpose. On the surface, he'd been a charmer with an easy smile. Beneath, he'd been a jealous, possessive man who didn't like being reminded that her mother had once loved someone else.

The remembered image of the broken ornament had caused a rush of anger mingled with deep sadness. Again she'd ordered herself to walk away from the window. But instead she'd gone inside and purchased the crystal ball.

"I thought it was especially pretty," she said, Kane's gaze causing her to feel the need to give some explanation for this extravagant purchase. "I guess you could say it caught my fancy and I couldn't resist the impulse to buy it."

"I suppose it's only natural to be attracted to something pretty," he replied.

Abigail saw a heat flare in his eyes and her breath locked in her lungs. She hadn't had much practice in reading men but she knew without a doubt that he was referring to an attraction he felt for her. Pleasure mingled with fear. This was definitely treading on dangerous ground, her inner voice warned.

His jaw tensed and a coolness descended over his features. "But acting on that impulse can sometimes lead to trouble," he finished.

As he turned away and strode to the table to pick up another ornament, she frowned at his departing back. His admission of finding her attractive had shaken her. But even more disconcerting was the way his rejection of this attraction stung. I'm not looking for any ties, she reminded herself curtly. I should be relieved he's chosen to keep his distance.

"Don't be silly. Buying something a little extravagant once in a while can't cause any harm," Lottie admonished, jerking Abigail's attention away from Kane as she came over to take a look at the ornament. "And it is lovely." Rose joined her and both voiced their approval.

Ordering herself to put Kane out of her mind, Abigail hung the ornament on the tree. But as she adjusted it so that the light would catch it, she felt a prickling on the back of her neck. Turning, she discovered Kane studying her once again.

"I'd never have thought of you as the collecting kind," he said, his gaze traveling around the room as he spoke.

The furnishings did give proof this observation was valid. Other than the purchases she'd made that day centering around the Christmas tree, there was nothing there, no piece of furniture nor ornamentation, that didn't belong to Lottie. Sharply she recalled a time when she'd had a room filled with knickknacks and memorabilia. But that had been a long time ago and she'd been a different person then. "You're right. I'm not," she replied.

The expression of a man mentally patting himself on the back for having judged correctly showed on his face. "A true wanderer. You like to keep your possessions at a minimum so when you get ready to leave there's nothing to slow you down. You can throw everything you own into the trunk of your car and take off."

He had described her present existence perfectly, she admitted. She'd also caught the underlying disapproval of this kind of life-style in his voice. Well, if she'd had a choice, she wouldn't have chosen this path for herself but she'd had no choice, she rebutted silently. Aloud, she said with schooled indifference, "Correct again," then returned her full attention to decorating the tree.

"Maybe if all of us made her feel really welcome here in Blye's Stand, she'd stay," Lottie interjected, casting Kane a sharp glance. "After all, Abigail has stayed put here for nearly two years now."

An impatience in Lottie's voice gave Abigail the distinct impression Kane and her employer had had this discussion before.

"Looks to me like she's not showing any inclination to nest," he returned dryly, his gaze again surveying the room.

"Well, she's at least going to stay until after Christmas," Rose blurted. "Unless you and Lottie arguing about her upsets her and makes her want to leave."

Abigail saw the sudden anxious concern in Kane's eyes as he glanced at his niece. Clearly he had not wanted to upset Rose. "Sorry," he apologized. "I don't want to chase anyone off."

Abigail had to admit the honesty in his voice rang true. But she was also certain his real concern was only for Rose. *If I packed up and left before dawn, he wouldn't grieve,* she thought wryly.

Relief showed on Rose's face. "It's Abbie you should be apologizing to," she instructed her uncle in calmer tones.

Kane turned back to Abigail. "Sorry," he said. "Whatever life-style you choose is your business, not mine."

He sounded contrite and she knew he meant the apology. She also knew he was telling her that while he found her attractive, he wasn't interested in a woman who so obviously didn't want any roots. Well, she wasn't interested in seeking his attention, she assured herself. Aloud, she said nonchalantly, "No problem."

He nodded as if to say he'd already been certain she didn't care what he thought, then he turned his full attention to Rose.

Chapter Three

Abigail lay on her couch looking at the decorated Christmas tree. It was nearly midnight. The others had left ages ago. After they'd gone, she'd taken a warm shower, dressed in a pair of heavy flannel pajamas and started to climb into her bed. Then she'd changed her mind. She'd pulled on her robe, grabbed up a blanket and gone into the living room. There, she'd plugged in the lights of the Christmas tree, then moved the couch so she had a full view of the decorated evergreen and curled up under the blanket.

Immediately images of past Christmases had flooded her mind. The happy ones came first. But now the bad ones had forced themselves to the surface. Quickly she blocked them out.

Her jaw firmed with resolve. It was time to start building new memories to replace those she wanted to forget, she ordered herself. And this tree was going to be the first, she added, a determined expression spreading over her face. Concentrating only on the beauty as the lights gave a sparkle to the ornaments, she felt herself relaxing. She was almost asleep when a knock on her door caused her to jerk awake.

Who would be calling on her at this time of night? she wondered groggily. Shifting into a sitting position, she frowned at the door dubiously. Maybe she'd just dreamed the knocking.

But even as this possibility occurred to her, again there were a couple of sharp raps on the wooden barrier.

The thought that Rose and Kane had quarreled already and the girl had come to take Abigail up on her offer, crossed her mind. Tossing off the blanket, she went to answer the door.

But it wasn't Rose standing outside, it was Kane.

"I saw the lights of your tree come on a little while ago and thought I'd take a chance that you were still awake," he said.

Abigail shivered as the cold wind whipped through the open door. For a moment she stared at him dumbfounded. He was the last person she'd expected to find at her door. Then recovering her voice, she asked stiffly, "Did you forget something?"

"I thought I owed you more of an apology than the one I gave," he replied. "Do you mind if I come in?"

There was an uneasiness in his manner that made her certain he didn't want to be there. But there was also a look of purpose on his face that told her he wasn't going to leave until he'd done what he'd come to do. It had begun to snow again and the wet flakes were turning to small droplets of water where they landed on the floor. "I suppose you'd better before I have to get out the mop," she said, stepping back to give him room. The uneasiness she'd seen on his face in the light from the porch lamp seemed even more pronounced as she switched on her living room light. She hoped he'd say whatever he'd come to say and leave quickly.

Kane paced to the middle of the room, then stopped abruptly and turned to face her. "I didn't mean to sound judgmental about your choice of life-styles," he said gruffly. "I really meant it when I said however you want to live your life is your business."

"Thanks, I think," she replied, noting that he sounded more edgy than apologetic this time. But what truly bothered her was her awareness of him as a man. To her shock, she found herself wondering how the texture of his jaw would feel if she ran her finger along it, and the urge to comb back his snow-dampened hair with her fingers was strong. This is crazy! she admonished herself. She was just feeling safe enough to consider leading a less insular life. She wasn't ready to begin feeling the kind of emotions his presence was eliciting. And she especially didn't want to feel them toward him. He'd been very open about his disapproval of her. She motioned toward the door. "Now that you've said your piece, you can go."

Self-directed anger showed on his face. "I didn't say my piece too well, did I?"

Abigail studied him. Clearly there was something else other than an apology on his mind. "Are you ready to tell me the real reason you're here?" she asked bluntly. As a possibility dawned on her, her shoulders squared with pride. "Are you here to order me to stay away from Rose?"

"I'm not real smart about dealing with teenagers but I know that would be a mistake. Besides, the girl is as headstrong as her mother. If she wants to be your friend, she's going to be your friend."

"You seem to have spent some time thinking that out," she remarked dryly. The physical attraction she'd been trying to ignore since he entered turned to a cold chill.

He shifted uneasily. "You're right, I did." His jaw tensed and his voice took on a low growl. "I'm not good at subtleties or lying. But I didn't come here to confront you. I needed someone to talk to and I figured you'd be the one most able to give me the answers I'm looking for."

Abigail stared at him in shocked surprise. "You came to me for advice?"

"Not advice. An explanation." His expression grew even grimmer. "I don't understand how a person can turn away from their family...just leave and disappear forever. Not even let the people who care about them know if they're doing well so those left behind won't spend restless nights wondering if the person who left is ill or in need."

The accusation in his voice caused her back to stiffen with pride. "You're talking about your sister, not me."

He frowned impatiently at her denial. "When I learned about John Kreck's death, I went looking for Janice. But she hadn't told anyone from the rodeo where she was going or if she did, they'd promised not to tell me. I couldn't come up with a clue as to her whereabouts. All these years, she's been at the back of my mind. I've woken up in cold sweats from nightmares in which I knew she needed my help and I couldn't get to her. Doesn't your conscience bother you just a little to think of those you left behind worrying about you?''

She'd seen the shadow of pain in his eyes when he spoke of his sister. But that didn't excuse the accusations he was throwing at her. ''My situation isn't the same as your sister's,'' she said curtly. ''I don't have any family. I don't have anyone who is going to wake up in the middle of the night worrying about my well-being. If I did, I would get word to them.''

He looked taken aback. ''Lottie said you told her you didn't have any family but I figured you'd simply said that so she wouldn't ask questions about people you wanted to forget.''

''I have never lied to Lottie,'' she said firmly.

''I'm sorry.'' He grimaced self-consciously. ''I seem to be saying that a lot tonight.''

''You've certainly said it enough,'' she replied. His judgmental attitude toward her had made it easy for her to maintain a comfortable barrier between him and her. But now she understood why he'd been so disapproving of her and couldn't make herself fault him for it. In fact, she was having the strongest desire to try to comfort him. Feelings like that are only going to lead to you getting hurt, her inner voice warned. If he ever finds out about the past you are running away from, he'll probably be first in line to condemn you, she warned herself. ''I'm tired and I think it's time for you to go home,'' she said quietly.

But instead of heading to the door, he remained with his feet firmly planted. ''There's something else I need to know first.''

Kane Courtland could certainly be trying on a person's nerves, Abigail thought, watching him standing there like an immovable mountain. "What is that?"

His gaze narrowed on her face. "I want to know if Rose said anything to you to indicate that she's uncomfortable around me. I want her to feel at home in my house. I don't want her running away like her mother did. But I have the feeling she suggested the party because I make her nervous."

The concern in his eyes touched a chord deep within Abigail and she found herself wishing someone would care that much about her. *I don't need anyone but myself,* she snapped back at this dangerous weakness. To Kane she said levelly, "Rose wants to be accepted by you but she's afraid you won't like her and won't want her to stay."

He began to pace tensely around the room. "My father made some mistakes with my sister. I know that. My mother died when I was twelve and Janice was fourteen. My father was overly protective and overly strict with my sister. When she fell in love with John Kreck, he should have been more understanding. Instead he treated her like an adolescent ... forbidding her to see the man ... threatening to lock her in her room if she disobeyed."

Kane came to a halt in front of Abigail. "I can understand her running away. What I can't understand is why she never came back or wrote or did anything to let us know she was even still alive."

Abigail saw the hurt lacing his anger and frustration. She didn't doubt that he honestly wanted Rose to feel welcome, and it occurred to her that if he understood why his sister behaved as she did, he might not make the same mistakes his father had. "I didn't know your sister so I can't be certain of her motives. However, according to Rose, her mother told her she didn't want to be stuck in a one-horse town. But Rose really thinks her mother didn't come back to Blye's Stand or contact you or your father because she was embarrassed by her unwed motherhood and she wasn't sure your father would take her back.''

Kane scowled darkly. ''Pride. It was her Courtland pride that made her determined to make it on her own. I thought that might have been at least part of the reason.''

''Rose has a lot of her mother's pride,'' Abigail heard herself warning.

Kane nodded. ''I know.'' A smile of admiration abruptly tilted one corner of his mouth. ''She's already informed me she has no intention of being a burden to me or staying if I don't want her here. The girl's got spunk.''

Abigail recalled the cold wet teenager she'd picked up on the road. ''But she still needs family. She needs someone who cares for her and will give her a helping hand when it's necessary.'' Almost immediately she regretted this outburst as Kane's gaze narrowed on her.

''That's a surprising attitude for someone who's so determined to live her life strictly on her own,'' he remarked.

The admission to herself of just how lonely her life felt at this moment caused her stomach to knot, but her pride would not allow Kane to see her pain. A mask of nonchalance descended over her features. ''I'm an adult not a child.''

He continued to study her. ''Everyone can use a friend.''

''The problem is knowing the difference between a real one and a fair-weather one.'' Inwardly Abigail cringed when she realized how open she'd been.

''You're never going to find out if you never allow anyone to be a friend.''

She was tempted to tell him she knew from experience there were storms so severe that when they'd finally passed not even the staunchest ally still remained. Instead she merely shrugged and said, ''I prefer not to be disappointed.''

''That's one heck of a cynical attitude you have, lady.'' A lock of her short black hair had formed a curl in the middle of her forehead. He combed it back with his finger as he spoke.

His touch sent an unexpected current of heat racing through her. You'd only be asking for trouble if you encourage a friendship with him, she warned herself. A coldness descended over her features. "I think it's time for you to leave, Mr. Courtland."

"So we're back to a more formal relationship again," he observed. He smiled wryly as he took a step back. "That's probably for the best. You look real cute dressed in that old robe and those flannel pajamas. I was beginning to think you might be a woman I should consider getting to know. But that ice in those green eyes of yours is enough to convince me I'd be wasting my time if I tried. I've never known anyone as determined as you to keep people at a distance. Good night, Miss Jones."

Abigail stood stiffly watching him leave. For several minutes after he was gone, she continued to stare at the closed door. The remembered feel of his touch as he combed the lock of hair from her forehead haunted her. The loneliness of her life enveloped her and she found herself wondering what being held by him would have felt like.

Her hands balled into fists. "Thoughts like that are only going to lead to trouble and hurt," she warned herself sternly, then added firmly, "I may be a little lonely at times but I'm comfortable and I'm safe."

Curling back up on the couch, she assured herself that her life suited her just fine.

"No more late nights for me," she grumbled the next morning as she pulled on her jeans. And she should have slept in her bed, she added, rubbing a cramp in her neck. Instead she'd slept on the couch, letting her Christmas tree be the last thing she saw before she dozed.

It's not smart to get too sentimental about anything, she reminded herself.

From below she heard the clink of metal and knew Lottie was stoking the small ancient potbellied stove at the rear of the store. The stove not only helped heat the downstairs but there was a grouping of chairs around it for customers who wanted to sit and warm themselves. Some of the older townsfolk gathered there on a fairly regular basis to exchange gossip. Just like out of a Norman Rockwell painting, she'd thought when she'd first seen it.

Glancing at the clock, she ordered herself to finish dressing and get to work. After all, it was the holiday season and business in the store was brisker than usual. Of course, most of that was due to Lottie's mailing business. People were coming in to drop off packages and buy stamps for cards, and while they were there they usually picked up a few extra staples.

She was stocking shelves a little later when a familiar young voice said, "Hi."

Glancing over her shoulder, she saw Rose coming down the aisle. It didn't take any searching to see the nervousness behind the girl's smile. "Morning," Abigail returned in friendly tones.

"Uncle Kane sent me over to mail some packages. They were boots and belts customers wanted before Christmas." A look of admiration showed in the girl's eyes. "He's working on a saddle and bridle now. He really makes great-looking stuff."

"Yes, he does," Abigail agreed. She'd seen some of Kane's work and had to admit the man was a fine craftsman. And she knew from Lottie that he was well-known in the rodeo circuit as one of the best boot and saddle makers available. Even some of the most exclusive stores in Texas ordered his work for their special holiday catalogs.

"He says when the holiday rush is over, he's going to make me a pair of boots." Hopefulness showed on the girl's face. "That does sound as if he's planning on letting me stay, doesn't it?"

Abigail gave her an encouraging smile. "Yes, it does."

Rose drew a relieved breath. Then her jaw tensed. "I don't want him to think I came here to freeload off him. I want to prove I can be useful. I know how to clean a house pretty good but I don't know how to cook much. Mom wasn't very good in a kitchen. She didn't have to be. She could bring food home from the restaurants where she worked." A plea entered Rose's eyes as she finished asking in a rush, "I was wondering if you knew how to cook and if you'd teach me."

Abigail warned herself she was in danger of becoming too involved in Rose's life. But she felt an empathy for the girl and wanted life to turn out better for Rose than it had for her. "I'm not a gourmet cook but I'm fairly good at the basics. Sure, I'll teach you."

Rose beamed. "Basics is great!"

"Always glad to hear a happy customer," Lottie said coming down the aisle from the other direction.

"Abigail's going to teach me to cook," Rose informed her, still grinning broadly. "I want to prove to Uncle Kane I can be useful."

Lottie nodded. "I've always felt a person should pull their own weight." A gleam entered her eyes. "And as long as you're doing this cooking for your uncle, you might as well make his favorite dishes. I happen to know he's real fond of pot roast cooked with onions, carrots and potatoes. You look in his freezer. I do his ordering and I know it's well stocked. Get out one of the packages labeled chuck roast."

Rose's smile faded. "But will it have time to defrost?"

"No need to defrost it," Lottie replied and launched into instructions on how to start with a frozen piece of meat.

Abigail, still worried about getting too involved in Rose's life, saw an escape. "Why don't you teach Rose how to cook?" she suggested.

Lottie held up her hands and shook her head. "I'm plenty busy for a woman my age."

"I'll go find that roast and set it out so's it'll have a little time to thaw," Rose said, making a quick retreat as if afraid Abigail might renege on her promise to help.

As the girl hurried away, Lottie's gaze leveled on Abigail. "It's not going to hurt for you to prove to Kane Courtland that you can cook. I'm still a firm believer in the way to a man's heart being at least partially through his stomach. And, I should add he likes corn bread and apple pie, too."

Abigail frowned at her. "I'm not interested in finding a way to Kane Courtland's heart."

"Well, maybe you should be. He'd be a good catch for any woman. He's thirty-one now and it's time he was settling down. And you're nearly thirty. It's about time you were settling down, too."

"I'm twenty-seven," Abigail corrected. Then heard herself adding, "And I'm as settled as I'm ever going to be."

Lottie frowned at her obstinacy. "Marriage can be real good with the right man." Her voice took on a motherly tone. "I've never really pried into your personal life."

Abigail nodded in agreement. She'd always felt lucky about that. She'd been traveling, looking for an out-of-the-way place to begin a new life when she'd happened into Blye's Stand. Pulling up in front of Blye's General Store to buy a soda, she'd seen the HELP WANTED sign. Figuring it couldn't hurt to ask, she'd gone inside and applied. It had been her policy not to lie when asked a direct question. Because of that, she hadn't found a job for a while and her funds were getting low. People, she had learned, were nervous about hiring a woman with a prison record.

The interview had begun just as Abigail had suspected it would. Lottie had asked for references.

Abigail had none with her. And, because she didn't want to make it easy for anyone from her past to find her, she had no intention of divulging any names or addresses of past employers for Lottie to contact. So she'd simply said, "I don't have any."

Immediately she'd sensed Lottie's hesitation. But she wa
beginning to feel desperate. Besides, this small town in th
middle of nowhere seemed like the perfect place to begi
again. She'd decided to try a direct approach. "I can assur
you I'm not wanted by the law. I'm honest and hardwork
ing. And I really need a job."

She'd expected Lottie to politely but firmly send her o
her way. Instead the elderly woman had said, "Let me se
your hands."

Abigail did as requested. Lottie had studied the palms fo
a long minute. "Looks like you're no stranger to har
work," she'd observed. Her mouth formed a thoughtfu
pout. "Interesting fate line, too." Releasing the hands, she'
looked Abigail in the eyes. "You're hired on a trial basis. I
you do a good job, don't cause me any trouble and don'
steal from me, you can stay."

From that day to this Lottie had only once asked Abigai
about where she was from and if she'd left family behind
Abigail had answered honestly, saying she was from Nev
Jersey and had no family.

"I've always just assumed you had a bad experience witl
a man," Lottie was saying, bringing Abigail's mind back t
their present conversation. "But you shouldn't judge al
men by the faults of one. There are a lot of good ones ou
there. And Kane Courtland is one of the best."

"I'm not judging anyone," Abigail replied firmly. "I'n
simply not interested in getting married."

Lottie frowned abruptly as if a thought had just strucl
her. "Are you already married? Is it an abusive husban
you're running away from?"

Abigail was almost tempted to lie and say yes. That woul
at least put a stop to Lottie's attempts at matchmaking. Bu
being honest was too important to her. "No."

Lottie shook her head. "Well, someone must have hur
you real bad."

"I simply prefer not to set myself up for any disappointments," Abigail replied, and pointedly returned her attention to the shelves she was stocking.

"This is going to be so terrific!" Rose beamed as she set the table in the huge country kitchen that served as both cooking and dining area in Kane's home.

Abigail frowned when she saw the girl arranging a third place at the table. "Just set two places. I think you and your uncle should enjoy this dinner alone."

"But you've worked hard on this meal, too," Rose argued. "You came over on your lunch hour and helped me get the roast started and you can't leave before the corn bread and apple crisp are finished because I don't feel confident about how to tell if they're done. I'll probably burn them."

"I'll stay until they're done, but I'm not staying for dinner," Abigail replied firmly. "You and your uncle need time to get to know each other."

"I suppose you're right," Rose conceded. Concern for Abigail suddenly showed on her face. "But if you don't eat with us, you'll have to go home and cook another meal."

To Abigail's shock, instead of viewing her departure from Kane's house as a blessing, she experienced a rush of loneliness at the thought of going back to her empty apartment. That apartment is your haven, your sanctuary, she chided herself. Aloud, she said with forced cheerfulness, "I really don't mind."

Rose suddenly brightened. "You can take a plate of dinner home and some corn bread and some dessert."

"That's really not necessary," Abigail protested. The truth was, she realized, she didn't want to take anything back with her that would remind her of this kitchen.

Kane's house had possessed a much more comfortable, homey atmosphere than she'd expected. Now, with the smell of good food permeating the big country kitchen, she felt the cold shield she kept around her more tender emotions threatened.

"Did your mother teach you to cook?"

Abigail's attention jerked back to Rose. "Yes, she did." Suddenly the images she'd been trying hard to suppress flooded over her. A wistful smile played at the corners of her mouth. "She was what some people would call an innovative cook. She'd get bored with regular recipes and add something a little different. Usually her combinations worked out fine but there were a few times..." Abigail grimaced playfully.

Rose laughed. "Your mom's creative combinations sound like my mom's normal cooking." A sudden sadness entered her eyes. "But we used to make some great Christmas cookies."

Abigail's wistful smile returned. "Cookies were my mom's favorite experimenting medium. Her peanut butter-chocolate chip were spectacular. I used to joke that my friends only hung around with me because of her cookies."

The bile suddenly rose in Abigail's throat. In a way that accusation had proven to be true. Even those she'd considered her closest friends had turned away when she'd needed them the most.

"Abbie!"

Rose's panicked voice snapped Abigail's mind back to the present. "What's wrong?"

"You looked so pale there for a moment, I thought you were going to faint," Rose replied, watching her anxiously.

Abigail forced a smile. "I never faint. I'm fine." And I'll stay fine as long as I don't ever start counting on anyone but myself, she added silently. A prickling on the side of her neck caused her to glance toward the door. Kane was there.

"All this talk about cookies is making me hungry," he said, letting her know he'd heard at least part of her exchange with Rose.

"I hope so because Abbie has been teaching me to cook and we've got a great dinner prepared." Nervousness edged Rose's voice. "I hope you like it."

"I'm sure I will," Kane replied, continuing into the kitchen. "It smells delicious."

Abigail was aware that, from behind his easy smile, he was studying her covertly and his scrutiny made her nervous. The smells and homey feel of this kitchen had caused her to again momentarily lower the shield she kept around herself. She promised herself she would be more careful in the future. The timer on the stove sounded and she breathed a mental sigh of relief.

"Are they done?" Rose asked as both she and Abigail peered in at the corn bread and the apple crisp.

"What do you think?" Abigail asked, returning to her role as teacher.

"The corn bread looks golden." Rose inserted a toothpick in the center of the bread, then pulled it out. "Nothing stuck to the toothpick," she observed. "I think it's done."

"I agree," Abigail confirmed.

A quick discussion about the dessert determined that it, too, was ready to be removed.

And now I'm free to go, Abigail thought with relief. She'd tried to ignore Kane. But even with her back to him, she hadn't been successful. Reminding herself that his only real interest was in Rose had helped some. Still, he made her uneasy and she wanted out of there as quickly as possible. "I'll just be running along now and let the two of you enjoy your dinner," she said as Rose set the dessert on the top of the stove then turned off the oven.

Kane stepped in front of the doorway, blocking Abigail's exit. "Surely after working so hard on this meal, you're not going to leave without enjoying it with us," he said.

Abigail read the challenge in the blue depths of his eyes. It was as if he guessed he made her uneasy and was taunting her for this cowardliness.

"I asked her to stay but she refused." Rose looked beseechingly at her uncle. "Maybe if you ask her, too, so she knows she really is welcome, she'll change her mind."

The challenge in Kane's eyes grew stronger. "We would both very much like for you to stay for dinner. Besides, my father used to warn me to be cautious if a cook refused to eat her own cooking."

Abigail paled. "I would never purposely do anything to harm anyone."

Kane frowned in surprise at her response. "I was only joking."

"I'm sorry. I guess I'm more touchy about my cooking than I should be," Abigail said quickly, furious with herself for overreacting. But it wasn't his jab at her culinary skill that had truly bothered her. Any hint that she would willfully harm another person opened a deep wound. However, normally she would have hidden it better.

Rose cast her uncle a "you're no help" glance, then turned to Abigail. "Really he was only teasing. My mother used to tell me he ragged her all of the time."

Kane's attention abruptly shifted to the child. "Your mother actually talked about me?"

Abigail saw the sudden anxiousness on his face and knew he was worried about the picture his sister had painted of him.

Rose grinned mischievously. "Don't worry. She said you were a typical kid brother. You could be a real pest. You never thought any of her boyfriends were good enough for her and you even tried to scare some of them off. But she also said that down deep you had a good heart. That was one of the things that gave me enough courage to come here."

Kane visually relaxed. Then he returned his attention to Abigail. The challenge was gone from his manner. In its place was a gentle coaxing. "Will you please stay for dinner?"

The blue of his eyes reminded her of a clear summer sky and for a moment she felt wrapped in warmth. He's merely attempting to placate his niece, she reminded herself curtly, annoyed by these strong reactions she was having to the man. Again she started to issue a polite yet firm refusal. But before she could speak, Rose interrupted.

"You might as well give in," the girl said with authority. "We're not going to stop trying to persuade you and the longer it takes to convince you to stay, the colder the food will get."

Abigail looked from the man to the young girl, then breathed a sigh of resignation. "I know when I'm fighting a losing battle."

Rose grinned brightly. "I'll get out another place setting."

Abigail felt herself grinning back. The child's enthusiasm was catching. But as she began removing the roast from the pan, she cautioned herself to keep in mind that her welcome in this house was merely temporary. Kane only wanted her there to please Rose, and Rose was looking to make friends here in Blye's Stand so she would feel more at home. Abigail did not doubt for one moment that if Kane and Rose learned about her past, they, too, would believe the lies just like everyone else had. And that would put an end to any further invitations. Prepared to fend off any personal questions, she seated herself.

To her relief the dinner conversation centered around Rose's mother. Kane told tales of his and Janice's youthful exploits and Rose talked about her life with her mother. A couple of times, Kane subtly steered the conversation toward Abigail but each time she managed to quickly steer it back to Janice.

Still, she began to feel a strain as the meal wore on. The caring she saw in Kane's eyes when he talked about his sister and the protectiveness she saw when he looked at Rose caused a longing within her. She was forced to admit she missed having someone to care about and having someone who cared about her.

As Kane finished telling about how Janice had made him climb a tree to rescue a stray cat his dog had frightened, Abigail could stand no more. She'd been sure she'd learned to live with her loneliness, to even become comfortable with it. Now she felt all knotted inside. They'd finished their desserts. She reasoned, it wouldn't be improper for her to suggest they straighten up so she could go home. And even if it was a little impolite, she didn't care. She had to get out of there. "I apologize if I seem to be rushing you," she said, pushing her chair back and forcing a smile. "But I'm a working girl and I have to get up early tomorrow morning. Would you mind if we cleaned up now?"

"This meal was the best I've eaten since I don't know when," Kane said, also pushing his chair back and rising. "I insist on doing the dishes."

"I'll help," Rose chirped, her face filled with pleasure. She smiled gratefully at Abigail. "You can sit and relax and keep us company. You've already done your part."

Abigail continued to stand. "I'll help," she said, wanting only to get the job done so she could go home.

"No, really, you relax," Rose insisted.

Seeing that she wasn't going to win this argument, either, Abigail decided on a different tack. "I really am exhausted. If you don't need my help, I think I'll just go on home."

Rose looked sympathetic. "You do look tired." Abruptly she rushed to Abigail and gave her a hug. "Thank you so much. Now go ahead and run along. Uncle Kane and I will clean this up."

"We'll clean it up as soon as I get back from seeing Abigail to her door," Kane said, already heading out of the kitchen.

The brisk, businesslike edge in his voice made Abigail feel like a nuisance. He's carrying this politeness thing too far, she grumbled to herself as she followed. "It's really not necessary for you to see me home. I only live across the street,'' she protested as he retrieved their coats from the closet.

Rose had followed them to the foyer. "You could slip and fall."

Abigail saw the gleam of a matchmaker in the young girl's eyes. "I'm sure I can cross the street just fine on my own. There's no reason for your uncle to go out into the cold," she said firmly.

Kane was holding her coat. "Rose is right. You could slip. Besides, my reputation as a gentleman is at stake."

Abigail was about to launch into another protest when his hand brushed against her shoulder as she slipped into her coat. A current of heat so strong she had to close her mouth to stop a gasp rushed through her. "Fine, if you insist," she managed, quickly finishing getting into her coat then taking a step away from him.

"I rarely bite," he said a couple of minutes later as they crossed the street.

She glanced over at him to discover him studying her from behind a shuttered mask. So he had noticed her movement away from him in the hall. She'd hoped she'd been nonchalant enough he'd have missed it. "A girl can't be too careful these days," she tossed back flippantly.

He cocked an eyebrow. "Are you flirting with me, Miss Jones?"

To her surprise, Abigail was sure she heard a note of encouragement in his voice. Her heart suddenly began beating faster. You're inviting trouble if you continue with this, she warned herself. "No," she replied firmly.

For a long moment he studied her, then said, "Guess that's just as well. I admit, I get lonely at times and you are an attractive woman, but we seem to be cut from different cloths. I'm a man who believes in roots and you appear to be working real hard at not laying down any."

Abigail frowned at the snow-covered road in front of her. This time instead of his alluding to her apparent wander-

lust style of life as if he considered it fact, there had been the
hint of a question in his voice as if he was looking for a denial or confirmation that his assessment was true. And she
had to confess that if she was looking for roots she'd be very
tempted to consider planting them with him. But we'd both
live to regret that decision, she reminded herself. "You're
right," she replied.

He nodded and fell silent.

I made the right choice, she assured herself as she walked
beside him. Whatever he felt for her couldn't be very potent. That was the second time in less than twenty-four
hours he'd admitted to being attracted to her, then dis-
missed the notion without acting on it. And I should be relieved he doesn't feel strongly enough to try to change my
mind, she added. But deep inside she experienced a sharp
pang of regret.

As they climbed the stairs to her door, he broke the silence between them. "I want to thank you for being so nice
to Rose. I get the feeling she's still a little intimidated by me
and I want her to feel comfortable here. And the dinner was
delicious."

"Thanks." They had reached the door and Abigail turned
away as she unlocked it. Being near him made her uneasy.
Looking at him made her even more uncomfortable. She
was beginning to like the cut of his jaw too much. But for
Rose's sake, she forced herself to meet his gaze one last time.
"Your niece is a very nice girl. You should feel lucky to have
her in your life."

"I do," he replied. Then issuing a polite good-night, he
left.

Inside her apartment, Abigail noticed her hands were
shaking as she unfastened her coat. She found herself wondering what would have happened if she'd let herself flirt
with Kane Courtland. "Thoughts like that are definitely
going to lead to trouble so stop it!" she ordered herself.

Resolutely she pushed him from her mind and hung up
her coat.

Chapter Four

"Morning," a familiar male voice said.

Abigail had been kneeling, dusting and restocking a lower shelf. Now as her eyes traveled up a pair of very sturdy, very masculine, jean encased legs, a heat stirred within her. She'd managed to avoid Kane Courtland for the past couple of days and she'd spent the better part of this morning trying not to think of him. Now, here he was, igniting feelings she didn't want to have. "Morning," she said, hiding the effect he was having on her behind a cool mask.

The matching coolness in his expression helped dampen the fires her first view of him had kindled. "Was there something you were looking for you couldn't find?" she asked in her best helpful-salesperson voice.

"Have you asked her?" a young voice yelled from the other end of the store.

Looking past Kane, Abigail saw his niece with Lottie by the package window.

"I was just getting ready to," Kane called back but Abigail saw the hesitation in his eyes and knew he was having second thoughts.

"Maybe it'd be better if you didn't ask," she suggested, keeping her voice low enough that only he could hear her.

"Maybe," he conceded. Also keeping his voice low, he continued, "When Lottie hired you without knowing anything about you, I thought it was bad judgment on her part. I figured you'd move on pretty quick and probably take a few of her belongings with you. I was wrong. You've stayed longer than I expected, you've been a hard worker and you've been honest. But you're hiding something and, whatever it is, it's made you pricklier than a cactus. My common sense tells me you're a woman I'd be better off avoiding. But my niece likes you and I want to make this Christmas as happy for her as possible."

"I appreciate your bluntness," Abigail said truthfully, honestly grateful for his open disapproval. It was certain to put an end to the unexpected and unwanted moments of attraction she'd been feeling toward him.

His manner became stiffly polite. "We'd like to have you join us for dinner and help us trim our tree afterward. Rose is inviting Lottie, too. She wants to make a party of it."

"I think I'll just stay home and wash my hair," she returned, assuring herself it was a relief to be taking herself out of Rose's life.

Kane drew a frustrated breath. "Rose will be real disappointed if you don't come."

"I'm sure you and Lottie will find a way to overcome her disappointment," Abigail replied, surprised he'd even made the effort to try to change her mind.

Kane nodded. "Yeah, maybe that would be for the best."

Abigail regarded him dryly. "You're beginning to sound redundant."

A crooked smile tilted one corner of his mouth. "Guess I am."

Abigail's heart lurched at the unexpected embarrassment in his expression. Fervently she wished she'd never taken such a close look at Kane Courtland. She was finding him much more appealing than she ever dreamed she would and that appeal seemed to be growing in spite of her efforts to stop it.

"We're going to have such a great time!" Rose's voice was filled with laughter and excitement as she strode down the aisle.

"I don't think I'm going to be able to make it," Abigail said apologetically as the girl reached them.

Rose's elation plummeted. "But you have to. Uncle Kane is going to teach me how to make his famous chili." Her gaze shifted to Kane. "Please, help me convince her to come."

Kane reminded Abigail of a man caught between a rock and a hard place. "I do make a terrific chili," he said.

"And Lottie's going to bring some chocolate chip cookie dough all ready to be cooked so we can bake the cookies while we trim the tree and eat them while they're hot. Please, please, please come," Rose coaxed.

Kane's gaze leveled on Abigail. "I'd appreciate it if you'd come."

"Of course she'll come," Lottie said, joining the group at that moment. "Truth is, the arthritis in my hands has been bothering me more than usual lately. I'm counting on Abigail to make the cookie dough and help with the baking."

"Great!" Rose cast Lottie a grateful smile. Then, grabbing the sleeve of Kane's coat, she began pulling him down the aisle. "Come on, we've got work to do."

Watching Kane being practically dragged out of the store, Abigail frowned. Rose's ploy was obvious. She was getting herself and her uncle out of there before Abigail could flatly refuse their invitation. But it wasn't going to work. Abigail turned to Lottie. "I will mix your cookie dough but Rose can help with the baking. I'm not going. Kane doesn't want me in his house."

"I'll admit, the two of you seem to mix like oil and water," Lottie replied. "But we need to think about Rose. That girl's been through a lot and I'd like to see her have a real nice Christmas. Now, I don't want to hear any more protests from you." Without giving Abigail a chance to respond, she walked away.

Abigail scowled at Lottie's departing back. In spite of the woman's dictate, she considered another protest but knew it would fall on deaf ears. "I might as well give in to the inevitable," she muttered under her breath, returning to dusting the shelves and restocking them. She'd ignore Kane and think of Rose. Lottie was right, the girl had been through a lot.

Still, as she and Lottie mounted the steps to Kane's front porch that evening, Abigail felt a rebellion brewing inside. She didn't like being where she wasn't wanted.

She was about to plead a headache when Rose flung the door open. "They're here," she yelled over her shoulder in the direction of the kitchen.

Abigail saw the look of excitement on the girl's face and knew she couldn't disappoint her. "You'd better put the cookie dough in the refrigerator until we're ready to cook it," she suggested, handing the bowl of batter to Rose.

"Right," Rose said, taking it. Kane had joined them and Rose's grin broadened. "Just wait until you taste Uncle Kane's chili. It's wonderful." In the next breath, she was on her way to the kitchen with the cookie dough.

Kane helped Lottie out of her coat while Abigail shed hers on her own. She had hung it in the closet and was starting to follow Lottie who was now heading to the kitchen when Kane caught her by the arm. Again a startling surge of heat traveled through her.

Stopping abruptly, she turned to him. The quickness with which he released her let her know he had not wanted to touch her. Her back stiffened and she prepared to blurt out the headache excuse and get out of there.

But before she could speak, he said, "I want to thank you for coming. This means a lot to Rose."

She could not deny the honesty in his voice but she was also aware of the guardedness in his eyes. He wanted her there but only for his niece's sake. *And that's the only reason I would have come anyway,* she reminded herself. "I do want Rose to have a nice Christmas," she returned.

He nodded to indicate they were in accord. Then with a flick of his wrist, he motioned for her to precede him into the kitchen.

As they began to eat, Lottie said, "I think I should do my part in these cooking lessons, too. Come Christmas Day, I'll bake a turkey with Rose's help and I'll expect you—" she glanced at Abigail "—to join Kane and us and help us eat it."

Abigail smiled noncommittally while silently promising herself she'd plead illness when the day came.

"My mom tried baking a turkey for Christmas once. Usually she just brought home something from the restaurant where she was working, but that year she decided we'd do something special," Rose said, wrinkling her nose at the memory. "She never had much patience. She got it started late so she figured she'd just cook it twice as fast by setting the oven at a higher temperature. It turned out burnt on the outside and raw on the inside. We ended up eating peanut butter and jelly sandwiches." A wistful smile played at the corners of her mouth. "But we ate them on our best china and she put garnishes of parsley on top. She used to say anything could taste like a gourmet meal if it just looked the part."

Abigail tensed as she saw Rose's chin tremble. Remembering how she'd felt when she'd lost her own mother, she knew the pain the girl was feeling. Then Rose began to cry. Abigail glanced at Kane to find him watching his niece with an expression of distress mingled with helplessness.

"I'm so sorry," Rose blubbered, pushing her chair back from the table. "I just miss her so much." In the next moment she was running from the room.

Without thinking, Abigail raced after her. Reaching the door of Rose's bedroom, she saw the girl fling herself on the bed and bury her face in the pillow in an attempt to muffle her sobs. Approaching the bed, Abigail looked down at the crying child and her heart bled for her. "I thought maybe you could use a friend right about now," she said. Her words startled her. It had been a long time since she'd allowed herself to even consider letting anyone get close enough to her for her to consider them a friend. You're treading on dangerous ground, she again warned herself. But she couldn't turn away.

Rose lifted her head from the pillow. "I ruined dinner," she sobbed.

"No, you didn't ruin dinner." Seating herself on the bed, Abigail gently combed the tear-wetted strands of hair back from Rose's face. "You simply added a dramatic flair."

Rose smiled crookedly through her tears. Then the smile vanished to be replaced by fear and anxiousness. "I've tried so hard to be cheerful and happy so Uncle Kane will like having me around. I can't believe I broke down like that in the middle of a special dinner he and I prepared together. He's probably wishing I'd never knocked on his door."

"Considering everything I know about Kane Courtland, I'd say you're wrong," Abigail said reassuringly. "In fact I know he wants you to stay."

"I want that very much," Kane's voice sounded from behind them.

Abigail jerked around to see him standing in the doorway with Lottie peering around his shoulder. His words had been spoken with tenderness and there was a protectiveness in his expression that promised a lifetime of security.

A sob caught in Rose's throat. Shifting into a sitting position, she faced her uncle. "Do you really, even after I cried into your chili?"

"It could have used a little more salt anyway," he replied, with a lopsided grin.

The sensation of being in the presence of a warm and caring family flowed through Abigail, and with it came a twist of pain for what she could never have. As Kane approached the bed, she rose and let him take her place.

"I've got a sort of early Christmas present for both of us," he said as he seated himself. "I would have told you sooner but I wanted to give you time to learn to like it here. I've hired a lawyer who is already working on getting me appointed as your legal guardian. And I've got a friend who's a judge and he's promised to provide a temporary custody order for me."

"Oh, thank you, Uncle Kane." Rose threw her arms around him and hugged him.

As he hugged his niece back, Abigail found herself wondering how it would feel if she was the one being hugged by Kane. A curl of heat swirled through her. Curtly she pushed the thought from her mind.

"How about if we finish dinner," Kane coaxed, gently releasing Rose. "We need our energy for the tree trimming."

"Right," she returned, smiling happily. Drying the remaining wetness from her cheeks with the sleeve of her sweater, she scooted off the bed.

Starting down the hall, Kane placed his arm around Rose's shoulder. "Tomorrow we'll also see about getting you enrolled in school so you can begin classes as soon as the holidays are over."

Rose rewarded him with a mock grimace. "I knew there was going to be a catch to this."

He grinned back and ruffled her hair.

Abigail felt relieved and happy for the girl. It was clear the bond between uncle and niece was already strong and growing stronger with each passing moment.

As she followed them down the hall, her gaze came to rest on Kane's strong arm and she found herself visualizing that arm wrapped around her shoulders. A sense of security like being snuggled in a warm blanket on a cold winter night spread through her. Quickly she shoved the image from her mind. There was no security for her anywhere and especially not in the person of Kane Courtland.

She drew a steadying breath as she again seated herself at the table. Determinedly she returned her attention to eating her dinner. But as hard as she tried, she could not make herself entirely ignore Kane. She found herself noticing the long craggy dimple that appeared on the left side of his face when he smiled. And he had the nicest laugh.

You've got to get a grip on yourself and stop thinking so much about him, she ordered herself a little later as she carried in a freshly baked batch of cookies to the tree trimmers.

Rose was suddenly in her path. "I'll take those," the girl said with a giggle, taking the platter.

Abigail noticed the girl's cheeks were flushed with mischievous excitement. She glanced toward Lottie and saw the woman watching her with an expression that reminded Abigail of the cat who'd swallowed the canary.

Rose took a step back, then blurted, "You're under the mistletoe."

Abigail looked up to see a bundle of greenery tied with a red bow suspended from the ceiling. Quickly she took a step away. "And now I'm not."

"It's bad luck not to get a kiss under the mistletoe if there's an eligible bachelor anywhere nearby to bestow it," Lottie insisted.

For one brief second Abigail found herself wanting to be kissed by Kane. You are asking for trouble! her inner voice screamed and sanity returned. She frowned impatiently at Lottie. "I've never thought of you as being superstitious."

Lottie stepped forward blocking Abigail from continuing into the living room. "I won't be responsible for anyone having bad luck. Now you just trot yourself back under that bough and get yourself kissed."

Abigail glanced at Kane. He was watching the exchange with a shuttered expression. He'd probably rather kiss a toad, she thought dryly. Aloud she said, "I'm sure Kane is not the least bit interested in participating in this bit of holiday folklore and I, most certainly, am not."

Rose's mouth formed into a pout of disappointment. "Uncle Kane, it's a tradition! You don't want to be responsible for Abigail having a whole year of bad luck."

Abigail saw him hesitate, then suddenly he was moving toward her. "Nope, wouldn't want that on my conscience," he said as he reached her. Looking down at her, he added gruffly, "They're never going to give us any peace until we do what they want so we might as well get it over with."

I can handle this, she assured herself. Then Kane cupped her face. His fingers weaving into her hair sent rivers of fire trailing through her and the feel of his strong callused hands on her cheeks caused her breath to lock in her lungs. She was acutely aware of the light scent of his after-shave and her skin tingled where his warm breath brushed against it. She felt as nervous as a teenager being kissed for the first time.

Don't buckle, she ordered her legs when they threatened to weaken. This will be over in a moment.

Then his lips found hers. She'd expected a quick, cool cursory kiss. Instead the contact was warm and soft and his mouth lingered on hers for several seconds. Deep within the embers of desire ignited. Then she was being freed.

As his hands released her and he lifted his head, she felt a sharp sense of regret that the kiss was ending. Unable to stop herself, she looked up into his face. A fire that matched the one within her showed in the blue depths of his eyes.

He's an upstanding, respected citizen, she reminded herself, fighting desperately to keep a practical perspective. She forced herself to recall the sea of disapproving faces she'd faced in her lifetime. If she did encourage a relationship with him and then the truth came out, at the very least, she would be an embarrassment to him. Considering past experience, she also knew it was inevitable that he would join those disapproving masses. A deep sadness spread through her but it was quickly overshadowed by the icy chill of reality.

Impatience showed on his face as he saw her retreat back behind her cold shield. Then, as if to say 'if that's your choice, it's fine with me,' his expression became one of indifference.

He turned to Rose. "Have I earned one of those cookies now?"

"Yeah, sure," she replied, disappointment evident on her face.

Abigail glanced toward Lottie to see her give Rose a we-tried glance.

Hopefully this will put an end to any further escapades they might have been considering, she thought as they returned to trimming the tree. But as she returned to the kitchen to check on the next batch of cookies, she couldn't make herself forget the look of passion she'd seen in Kane's eyes. She told herself it was most likely nothing more than lust. But the thought that maybe he could fall in love with her taunted her. When she returned to the living room to help with the tree trimming, she found herself covertly watching him. You've got to stop thinking about him, she ordered herself but just seeing him was causing a curl of pleasure to spread through her.

By the time the last decoration was hung on the tree, her nerves were worn thin. "It's late," she announced, yawning to give evidence of her tiredness. "Time to say good night."

"Abigail's right," Lottie conceded, regretfully turning away from admiring the tree to smile at Rose and then Kane. "It's been a wonderful evening. But these old bones need their rest."

Without giving them any argument, Kane headed for the hall closet to get their coats. "I'll see the two of you home."

Abigail was about to politely but firmly say she would see Lottie home and then find her own way herself. But Lottie spoke up first.

"On an icy night, I'm always grateful for a strong masculine arm to lean on," the older woman said. Then with a coquettish grin, she added, "In fact, I always enjoy a strong male to hold on to on any occasion."

Abigail had faced many a losing battle in her day and knew one when she saw it. Keeping her protest to herself, she pulled on her coat, bid Rose a warm good-night and stepped out onto the porch.

The sky was clear. A crescent moon was a sliver of silver amid an array of twinkling stars. As she had been on many occasions since coming here, Abigail was awed by the beauty of this wilderness.

"Nice night."

She'd been so absorbed in her admiration, she jumped slightly at the sound of Kane's voice behind her. "Yes, it is," she replied honestly.

"It's a lot prettier than any you'd find in a city with all that pollution and noise," Lottie said, holding on to Kane's arm for support as they descended the steps. Starting across the street, she added, "And we don't have to fight traffic."

"Of course, some people would eventually find all this quiet and solitude boring," Kane returned. "What about you, Miss Jones? Have you found yourself getting bored here yet?"

Abigail, having determined that Kane was providing Lottie with all the aid she needed, was walking on the other side of the elderly woman, a little apart from her companions. Looking around Lottie, she found him studying her. "I'm sure nearly everyone gets bored once in a while, no matter where they live," she replied factually, then heard herself adding, "But I like it here. The quiet and solitude suit me just fine."

Surprise mingled with skepticism on Kane's face as he continued to study her until he was forced to turn his attention to helping Lottie up the curb.

His scrutiny and her own openness had caused Abigail's nerves to tense further. They were now on the sidewalk, halfway between the store and Lottie's house. As Kane and Lottie turned toward her elderly employer's home, she stopped. Lottie didn't need her help and she didn't want Kane feeling he had to walk her to her door. "I'll say good night here," she said, seeing this as the perfect opportunity to separate from her companions. Before either could speak, she added another quick thank-you to Kane for inviting her to his home, then hurried off in the opposite direction.

Kane's image continued to plague her as she entered her apartment and hung up her coat. Life had been a lot more comfortable when she'd been able to picture him as the grim, self-righteous, arrogant, judgmental type.

Plugging in her Christmas tree, she slouched on the couch and stared at it. A wistfulness entered her eyes as she considered how her life might have been if she'd been allowed to follow a different path. Again Kane's image formed in her mind. "Go to bed and forget about that man," she ordered herself.

But, as she started to obey, a knock sounded on her door. Answering it, she found Kane there.

"Mind if I come in? It's cold out here," he said when she simply stood mutely looking at him.

"Yeah, sure," she replied, thinking he looked even more appealing than he had just a few minutes earlier. His looks couldn't have improved that fast, she scolded herself.

"I wanted to thank you for being so kind to Rose tonight," he said, continuing to watch her as he closed the door.

"I told you I think she's a nice kid," she replied, wishing she hadn't allowed him in. No man had ever threatened the shield she kept around herself the way he did.

He was studying her even more closely now. "Until tonight I was convinced you'd built a wall around yourself no one could penetrate. But that was no ice maiden who comforted my niece."

"It was only a temporary lapse," she assured him. The problem was she hadn't yet rebuilt her barriers and the urge to reach out and trace the line of his jaw with her fingertips was close to overwhelming.

"I'm sorry to hear that."

The honest regret she saw in Kane's eyes caused her heart to race. The desire to let her guard down grew stronger. She forced herself to think of the consequences. Eventually she'd have to tell him about her past. She'd never feel comfortable until she did. Then what? her inner voice demanded cynically. Even those who had originally believed her side of the story had been led to question their faith in her by those who believed the worst of her. She couldn't face that kind of rejection again. "It's late. Rose will be wondering what happened to you," she said with dismissal.

For a long moment he regarded her in a tense silence, then said, "Sorry. I'm obviously wasting my time and yours. I won't be bothering you again. Have a good night."

Abigail felt a sharp jab of pain as he turned to leave. The words to ask him to stay formed on the tip of her tongue. You'll regret it, her inner voice warned.

Suddenly he turned back and cupped her face in his gloved hands. "If you ever change your mind and decide to let the ice maiden melt for good, you know where to find me."

She stood dumbly as he kissed her lightly then left.

The warmth of his lips lingered on hers. Going to her window, she watched him cross the street. She was filled with regret so intense it brought hot tears to her eyes.

Chapter Five

Later that night, sitting alone in her darkened living room, she could still feel the imprint of Kane's lips on hers. She groaned aloud as she was forced to face the truth. In spite of all her efforts not to, she was falling in love with Kane Courtland.

"Maybe it's just a passing thing...an infatuation," she reasoned. After all, she hadn't had much experience with romantic entanglements.

Rising, she walked over to the window and looked out at his home across the street. The lights were on in his workshop and she guessed he was finishing Christmas orders.

She pictured him seated at his workbench, intent on the job at hand. Her fingers came up to touch the glass pane in front of her as she visualized herself brushing back the lock of hair that seemed to always be falling on his forehead.

She trembled with frustration and forced herself away from the window.

The next morning Abigail awoke with a monster of a headache. All night she'd been tormented by nightmares. Most of them had involved people yelling accusations at her or turning away from her as if she carried the plague.

"And that pretty much sums up my life since I was seventeen," she muttered into her morning coffee. Walking over to the window she'd looked out the night before, she saw Kane come out onto his front porch to gather up an armload of wood.

The urge to go over to his place and fix him breakfast and sit in front of the fireplace beside him was so strong it was a physical pain. As if he sensed her presence, he looked up. He didn't wave, but she knew he saw her. For a moment he simply stood gazing in her direction, then he turned abruptly and went back inside.

Well, she had made it clear she didn't want him in her life, she reminded herself. And staying away from him would be the smart thing to do. But the pain she'd been feeling had intensified when he turned away from her just now.

Her chin trembled. It wasn't fair for her to have to live out her life alone. "I could take a chance. I could tell him the truth." Fear pervaded her. She'd have to include the lies that had been spread about her, too. And there was a big chance he might believe those lies.

Besides, just because she was falling in love with him didn't mean he would fall in love with her. Her head throbbed even more in spite of the aspirin she'd just taken.

"A person has to take a risk once in a while," she murmured to herself, using the sound of her voice to give herself courage. She'd left her apartment intending to go directly to work. Instead she'd crossed the street and was now standing poised to knock on Kane's door. She'd been standing there building up her nerve for the past two or three minutes.

Abruptly the door opened. "I saw you crossing the street," Kane said, regarding her from behind a shuttered mask. "Did you want something, Abigail?"

Again fear threatened her resolve. She took a step back. "Maybe this wasn't such a good idea."

"While you debate that with yourself, you might as well come in." Before she could escape, his hand closed around her arm and he pulled her inside.

As nervous as she was, the strength of his grip sent a current of excitement racing through her, and even through her heavy coat she was aware of the warmth of his hand. You're going to be tormented by thoughts of what might have been if you back out now, she warned herself as he released her and regret at the loss of his touch filled her. "I was wondering if we could talk...privately. I could fix dinner for the two of us tonight."

He smiled with satisfaction. "I'll be there."

As appealing as his smile was, it only made her more tense. "Good," she managed to choke out, wondering if he'd still be able to smile at her after he heard what she had to say. "See you at six," she added over her shoulder, making a quick exit.

"I'll probably live to regret this," she muttered under her breath as she crossed the street. But he was worth taking the risk.

By the time Kane knocked on her door at six sharp, Abigail's nerves felt as if they were ready to snap. She'd decided on steaks, baked potatoes and salad for dinner. This was an easy meal and one she'd have to work at to ruin. Of course, in her present state, she probably couldn't even make an acceptable peanut butter and jelly sandwich, she admitted.

"Whatever you've invited me over here to tell me can't be that bad," Kane said as she opened the door and he saw her face.

She'd ordered herself to appear casual. Clearly she'd failed. Pretense had never been her strong point, she reminded herself. Aloud, she said, "Yes, it can."

The smile on his face dimmed. Entering, he studied her with concern as he handed her the prettily wrapped package he was carrying. "I brought you something for your tree."

"Thank you." To her chagrin, her hands shook as she accepted the gift. Avoiding looking at him, she concentrated on unwrapping the package without dropping it. Inside was an ornament with her name painted on it along with the date. Ribbon and sequins had been glued to it to give added flair.

"I couldn't think of what to bring you. Then Rose mentioned that her mother used to give personally decorated ornaments to friends at Christmas. She volunteered to make this one. I hope you like it," Kane said.

"It's lovely," she replied, tears burning at the back of her eyes. It had been a very long time since anyone had given her something made just for her. Going over to the tree, she hung it near the crystal ball, then she turned back to Kane.

"I'm glad you like it," he said as he removed his coat and hung it in the closet.

Embarrassment swept through her. "I should have taken your coat. I seem to be a little short on manners tonight."

He frowned. "I'd like to think we're on friendly enough terms that you don't feel you have to wait on me like I was a stranger coming into your home."

For a long time now, she'd worked hard at not allowing what others thought to hurt her. But she knew that if he turned against her the pain was going to be difficult to bear. "You might wish you'd never met me once I've told you about myself," she blurted.

Surprise registered on Kane's face. "Appears to me like we'd better talk this out right now."

"I've spent time in prison for killing a man. It was an accident but I couldn't prove it," she said bluntly.

Kane studied her thoughtfully. "Why don't you start at the beginning and tell me what happened?" he suggested.

Abigail's stomach knotted. There was no turning back now. "Tom Gelespe was my stepfather. We'd always gotten along just fine. He was a real charmer. Everyone liked him. It was my seventeenth birthday. My mother had died just over two months earlier. He'd offered to have a party for me but I wasn't sure I could make it through an entire evening of putting on a happy face, and I didn't want to break down in front of my friends."

"That's understandable," Kane said encouragingly when she hesitated.

Fighting back the fear of his rejection, she continued grimly, "With just family I would have felt more comfortable. But I was an only child and both my mother and real father had been only children. And my grandparents on both sides had passed away. So I didn't have any close blood relatives left. Tom, however, did have a brother... Martin Gelespe. Claire, Martin's wife, had always been kind to me and offered to have a dinner at their home with just her, Martin, their three children, Tom and me. But Tom said her kids got on his nerves and I decided I wasn't in the mood for any kind of party. So he suggested that he take me out someplace nice for dinner. I agreed. He chose one of the most expensive restaurants in town. The meal was very pleasant and he was at his most charming."

A bitter smile played across Abigail's features. "I remember thinking how lucky I was to have such a caring stepfather."

"Go on," Kane prodded when she hesitated once again.

Abigail had expended a great deal of energy trying not to recall the details of that night. Now as the events again played vividly through her mind, she trembled. "Soon after we got home, I went upstairs to my room to shower and go to bed. I was drying my hair when Tom came into my room. He started talking about how now that I was seventeen I'd probably start going out on more dates. At first, I was confused. I didn't understand what had caused him to want to come into my room and talk to me about that. Then he said something to the effect that he didn't want any stranger taking away my virginity."

Bile rose in Abigail's throat. She swallowed it back. "Tom's talking about my virginity made me uncomfortable. I told him he didn't have to concern himself because I was planning to follow my mother's wishes and abstain until I was married. Then he said something about the best laid plans. I remember he used the word 'laid' because he suddenly laughed as if this was some sort of joke. I told him I was really tired and wanted to go to bed."

A tremor shook her. "He said going to bed was what he had in mind, too. Then he started toward me. I thought maybe he was just going to give me a fatherly good-night kiss. Instead he said a seventeen-year-old girl should have something special to remember her birthday by. He said he wanted to be the first to introduce me to the joys of sex . . . that waiting until my marriage night was old-fashioned. The next thing I knew, he was grabbing me and forcing me down on my bed."

Abigail's hands balled into fists so tight her nails bit into the palms of her hands. "I fought him. I'd turned the hair-dryer off when he'd come in but it was still lying on the bed. I managed to grab it and hit him with it. That hurt him enough that he released his hold and I ran. I managed to get down the stairs before he caught up with me. He was in a rage. He started half dragging, half carrying me into the living room. I was struggling frantically. He had to release his hold a little to get me turned around when we reached the couch. I used the opportunity to push against him. He lost his balance and we both fell. That was when his head hit the coffee table and he died."

Kane reached out and stroked her jaw. "You had the right to defend yourself," he said sharply. "You did nothing wrong."

She saw the protectiveness in his eyes and wished she could end her story there. But she knew she couldn't. A cynical expression came over her face. "I thought that, too. I felt horrible that he was dead. But I'd been struggling for my life. It had been an accident. However, Tom's brother, Martin, didn't see it that way. And, neither did the press, the police nor the judge."

A cold chill raced along her spine. Now came the really hard part. Now she had to tell him about the lies that were said about her. "My mother had bequeathed to me what remained of the money my father had left her along with her inheritances from her parents. And I had a trust left me by my father's parents. All totaled, it wasn't a fortune but it was large enough to see me through college and provide me with a nest egg to begin life on my own. Tom was the executor. Martin idolized his brother. He refused to believe Tom would behave in the manner I'd described. He got it into his head that I'd killed Tom because Tom wouldn't let me have free access to my money. He went to the police with this theory and they bought it.''

She saw Kane frown. Now that he knew about the money, he was probably already beginning to doubt her, she thought cynically. She wanted to stop but knew she couldn't. Unable to watch him turn against her, she walked to the window and stood looking out with her back to him.

"The press had a field day," she continued in a monotone. "They found a boy I'd dated once and refused to go out with again because he'd been a bore and made uncomfortably lewd advances on our first date. Out of spite, he told them I was spoiled and self-centered. He even claimed that we'd never gone out again because I'd insisted on going to the most expensive places and he couldn't afford to date me. The waiter at the restaurant who had remarked several times during the meal about how nice it was to see a father and daughter enjoying an evening together now swore I'd flirted outrageously with Tom during the meal while my stepfather looked embarrassed by my blatant behavior."

Rage at the injustice done to her swept through her. "They even twisted what I'd said to a friend at my mother's funeral." A ragged edge entered her voice as she fought back angry tears. "My mom had died of cancer, and during the last year of her life she'd suffered greatly. The last two weeks had been the worst. I'd been by her bedside night and day and knew how much pain she'd been in. Still, her death was devastating to me. I felt so alone. I completely broke down at the viewing. A friend of mine consoled me, pointing out how much my mother had suffered and I'd agreed that for her sake death was probably a blessed relief."

Again the bile rose in Abigail's throat. "The reporters talked to this friend and she told them what had happened. But they put their own spin on the story. They pointed out that my mother had been the executor of my inheritance from my real father's parents. Then they quoted me as saying I considered her death a blessing and a relief. The implication was that I'd thought I'd get free access to my money now that she was dead."

"Surely someone spoke up for you," Kane said.

She turned to discover him studying her narrowly. "A few did but they were treated as if they were naive fools whom I had duped." Her shoulders straightened with dignity. "The police built a case against me. I requested a lie-detector test and passed it but the DA said that only proved I didn't have a conscience. Even though their evidence was only circumstantial and I was just seventeen, he had me declared an adult and then threatened to try me for first-degree murder. But he was willing to plea-bargain. In the end, my attorney convinced me I would be safest to plead guilty to a lesser charge of manslaughter. The judge obviously believed the lies. He gave me the maximum sentence."

Abigail stood, her chin firm as she continued to meet his gaze with defiance. "Now, I wish I'd taken my chances with a jury. But I was young and scared. Even so, I almost balked and pleaded innocent when the moment came for me to voice my plea in front of the judge. He must have sensed it because he advised me to listen to my lawyer, so I did."

Her back stiffened more as she braced herself for Kane's rejection. "Now you know my side of the story. But I don't have any proof that what I've just told you is true."

Kane regarded her in silence, his expression noncommittal as if he was still mulling over what she'd said. Disappointment filled her. You didn't honestly think he'd believe you, she chided herself cynically.

Then abruptly he broke his silence. "No." He pronounced the word with firm conviction. "I will never believe you would kill anyone on purpose and certainly not for money. You've worked hard to keep yourself apart from the people here but when help was needed you've been there. Last winter when Mable O'Riley had twins you voluntarily cleaned her house weekly for three months. And when she insisted on paying you, I happen to know you used that money to buy clothes for the twins and her other children. That's not the act of a woman who'd kill for money. And when that stray dog got hit by the truck last spring, you wouldn't let Doc Howard immediately put it to sleep. You took responsibility for its medical bills and insisted he try to save it. That's the act of a woman who sanctions life."

His faith in her caused a surge of hope. But she'd learned the hard way that faith could be easily destroyed. "You say that now but Martin Gelespe hasn't shown up yet."

"And you're expecting him to?" Kane prodded when her pause threatened to lengthen into a silence.

"Maybe, eventually," she replied. "He's found me before."

Kane nodded as if she'd just supplied the last piece to a jigsaw puzzle he'd been trying to put together. "I've always suspected you were hiding from something or someone." He continued to study her thoughtfully. "What do you expect to happen when and if he does arrive?"

She faced him grimly. "I know what will happen. Martin has made it his purpose in life to make my life a living hell. He went to every parole hearing I had and fought against me getting out of prison. But, in spite of him, I was finally paroled. There wasn't much of my inheritance left. My legal fees had eaten most of it up. There was no money for college and not enough to live on for long. I'd gotten a high school equivalency diploma while I was in prison but I wasn't trained for anything. And a lot of people aren't real enthusiastic about hiring ex-cons. Mostly I washed dishes or did janitorial work."

She met his gaze forthrightly. "I'm not complaining. I've never minded hard work. I was just glad to be out of prison. Sometimes, I worked at two jobs, sometimes three when I couldn't find full-time employment. I was determined to build a decent life for myself. But no matter where I was working, Martin would show up and try to get me fired. Eventually I'd become 'bad for business' and he could chalk up one more victory. Finally I completed my parole. I told myself I was truly a free woman.''

She wrapped her arms around herself attempting to ward off the chill that was spreading through her. ''I left New Jersey and headed west. I found a job in St. Louis and settled into an apartment. I made friends with my neighbors. The girl next door, her name was Paula, was divorced with two small children. She worked as an operating room nurse and had to sometimes be on call at night and on weekends. When the hospital would summon her in on those odd hours, she'd call me and I'd go over and stay with her kids. I'd been in St. Louis for about a year when Martin showed up. He stood outside the door of the apartment building telling everyone they had a cold-blooded murderess living in their midst. As proof he handed out packets of photocopies of the newspaper articles dealing with his brother's death and my plea of guilty.''

Remembered disillusionment brought back the hurt she'd worked so hard to bury. ''All those people who I'd thought were my friends suddenly began avoiding me. Paula didn't want me around her children any longer.'' Her expression became stoic. ''And so I packed my belongings and left. I just kept moving, never staying in one place long enough to make friends or for Martin to find me. Finally I ended up here. For the first time in a long time, I felt as if I'd found a real sanctuary. It's pretty here and peaceful and I figured it was out of the way enough there was a possibility he wouldn't ever find me, so I took a chance and stayed.''

Kane tucked a finger under her chin and tilted her face gently upward. ''If Martin Gelespe ever does come to town, he'll have to answer to me. It's not right to torment another person the way he has you.''

Abigail had not believed she would ever again feel as safe as she felt at that moment. "Thank you for believing in me."

He winked and kissed her lightly on the tip of her nose. "Now how about that dinner you promised?" he coaxed gently.

His kiss and the wink had so disconcerted her, for a moment his words didn't register. Then abruptly she blushed. "Dinner! Oh, yes." Remembering the potatoes baking in the oven, she made a dash for the kitchen. To her relief they were done but not overcooked.

Kane had followed her and insisted on helping. For the next several minutes they concentrated on cooking the meat and preparing the salad. But as they sat down to eat, he again turned his attention to her.

"What do you think you would have done with your life if Tom Gelespe had been a decent man?" he asked.

There had been moments when Abigail had wondered this same thing herself. "I don't honestly know," she replied. "I suppose I'd have gone to college but I'm not sure what I would have majored in. Business, maybe. I've always liked math and I enjoy keeping the records for Lottie." She'd meant to stop there but heard herself admitting, "And I'd like to have had a home and children."

"Seems to me that it's time for you to forget about Martin Gelespe and get started on really living your life," he suggested.

"I'd like to," she replied, the thought that Kane would be the perfect way to begin playing through her mind.

"Tell me about your childhood," he requested as he cut a bite of steak. "The good times," he specified.

It had been a long time since she'd talked about herself. Once she got started reminiscing about the happy times, she couldn't seem to stop. When she did, Kane would coax her into telling more. "I feel as if I've been talking nonstop," she said with embarrassment as they finished their desserts and coffee.

"I've enjoyed listening," he assured her, then glanced at his watch. "But it's late and I'd better be getting home."

His sudden desire to leave surprised her. I've been boring him and he's merely stayed this long to be polite, she wailed silently. Well, she hadn't had much practice with dating, she defended herself. Still, his wish to escape her company hurt. "Thanks for coming," she said stiffly, rising and getting his coat from the closet.

"I'll see you tomorrow," he said as he pulled it on.

"Sure, see you tomorrow," she replied, guessing he wouldn't come looking for her.

As he reached for the door, he abruptly stopped and turned back. Approaching her in one long stride, he dropped a light kiss on her lips. "Thanks for dinner," he added then immediately completed his departure.

"Maybe I didn't bore him as much as I thought," she murmured hopefully, a smile spreading over her face as the warm feel of his mouth continued to linger on hers.

But as she began clearing the dishes, Martin's image came back to haunt her. The thought of him showing up in Blye's Stand caused a cold sweat to break out on her brow.

A sharp knock on her door made her jump. Half expecting to see Martin there, her hands shook as she answered it.

But it was Kane who stood there.

The sight of him brought a rush of pleasure. Then she saw the stern look on his face and an uneasiness spread through her. "Did you forget something?" she asked.

"I've been telling myself all evening to go slow," he said, his gaze boring into her. "But I'm finding that real difficult. I'm attracted to you, real attracted. And I got the feeling the other night under the mistletoe that you're not totally indifferent to me. You said you wanted a husband and children. You also said you like it here and feel safe here. I'm going to need help raising Rose and, as Lottie has pointed out numerous times, I should be marrying and starting a family of my own. So I'm asking you to marry me."

Abigail stared at him in stunned silence. Maybe I've fallen so hard for this guy, I'm having fantasies, she thought frantically.

Kane frowned self-consciously. "I know this is a little abrupt. But once I've made up my mind to something, I like to act on it."

Abigail's heart was now pounding wildly. This was no fantasy. He was really asking her to marry him. More than anything she'd ever wanted in this world she wanted to say yes, but Martin's image was still strong in her mind. "My marrying you wouldn't be fair to you or Rose," she forced herself to say. "If Martin does show up, the least I'll be is an embarrassment to the two of you. It's possible you could even find yourselves ostracized because of me."

"I'll decide what's fair for me and Rose," he returned. "You think about my offer and we'll talk again tomorrow evening."

Before she could respond, his mouth found hers. This time the contact was forceful yet at the same time coaxing, encouraging her to participate. Fire raged through her and she was swept up into a world of sensation.

Then slowly he lightened the kiss. As he began to lift his head away, he paused and gazed into her passion darkened eyes. A smile of satisfaction showed on his face. His lips returned to hers for one final small taste, then he released her and stepped back. "Looks to me like there's enough attraction on both sides to make this marriage work," he said in a low growl. "It's time you stopped running. I'm offering you a place to call home, Abigail."

Too shaken to speak, she stood mutely as he strode out, closing the door behind him. She was still finding it difficult to believe he'd actually proposed. Of course he hadn't mentioned love. What he had admitted to was a feeling of lust for her, the desire to have a family and the need for a mother figure for Rose. This was not the romantic proposal she'd hoped a man would make to her one day. Still, she found herself wanting desperately to accept. She'd learned to care for him. He could learn to care for her, she reasoned.

But that night while she slept, Martin haunted her dreams. Awakening the next morning she was more exhausted than when she'd gone to bed. She also knew she couldn't accept Kane's proposal. Eventually he'd regret marrying her. Either Martin would show up and Kane and Rose would find themselves tainted by their association with her or Kane's lust would eventually fade and he'd feel trapped in a marriage he no longer wanted.

"I'll tell him I'm leaving as soon as the holidays are over," she stated with resolve as she dressed for work.

But as she started to enter the store the next morning, Rose yelled a greeting and hurried across the street to join her. "I've got a note for you," the girl said handing Abigail an envelope.

Inside was a letter from Kane. In it, he explained that an unexpected business trip had come up and asked her to look after Rose for him until he returned.

"I won't be any trouble," Rose promised.

"You're never any trouble," Abigail replied, giving the girl a friendly smile. A sadness swept through her as she admitted to herself how very fond she'd grown of Rose. Leaving here was going to be much more difficult than she'd imagined.

Chapter Six

Abigail stood at the door of the store staring across at Kane's home. It was the morning of the third day since he'd left. Telling herself that after the holidays, he would be out of her life for good, she ordered herself to use this opportunity to get used to his absence. But instead, she missed him horribly.

Adding to her strain was the living arrangements she'd been forced to accept. Because she had no guest room for Rose, she was spending the nights in Kane's home. The constant reminders of him she found there were only making her decision to leave more painful. "It's the right thing to do," she muttered under her breath. Still, that didn't ease the regret she was feeling.

The sound of a car approaching caught her attention. She looked down the road and her blood began to race. It was Kane. He saw her when he parked. Climbing out of his car, he waved but didn't head in her direction. Instead he walked around to the back of his car and pulled his suitcase out of the trunk.

She noticed a tiredness about his movements and wondered if his trip had gone badly. The urge to race across the street and comfort him was strong. Instead she forced herself to simply wave back.

He acknowledged her greeting with a nod, then mounted his porch steps and went inside.

A jab of pain pierced her and she realized she'd been hoping he'd missed her so much he would forget about unpacking and immediately come to see her. Now that was a really stupid romantic notion, she chided herself. Besides, it was better he felt no strong emotional attachment to her. She was going to have to leave. This way, she didn't have to worry about causing him any distress.

"I've definitely made the right decision," she assured herself, turning away from the door and going back to work.

A few minutes later, she was stacking cans on shelves when he entered the store. He greeted Lottie with a friendly wave and smile. But the smile, Abigail thought, looked forced and as he reached her it faded until his expression was polite but shuttered.

"I was wondering if we could talk in private," he said.

"Sure," she replied, certain something was wrong and wondering what it could be.

Following her into the back room, Kane closed the door, then turned to face her. "I didn't go on a business trip," he said. "I went to New Jersey to look up Martin Gelespe."

Abigail's back stiffened. She felt as if a knife had been thrust into her and twisted. "I guess after you'd had some time to think, you decided it would be wise if you checked on my story," she said coolly. "Is this where you tell me to be packed and out of town by sundown?"

He scowled impatiently. "I didn't go there to hear his side of the story. I went there to tell him to leave you alone or I'd have the law after him for harassment."

"I doubt very much he cares about threats," she replied. As a reason for Kane's uneasiness occurred to her, she glanced nervously toward the door. "Should I expect him soon?"

For the first time since his arrival back in Blye's Stand, Kane smiled at her. It was a warm, reassuring smile. "He's not looking for you any longer. He hasn't been looking for you since you left St. Louis. You are truly a free woman."

Abigail stared at him in disbelief. "What? Why?"

Kane's smile disappeared and in businesslike tones, he said, "It was his wife, Claire, who put a stop to his activities. Apparently, soon after Claire and Martin were married, Tom attempted to molest her. The two of them were in the kitchen and Tom was just beginning to be forceful when Martin came in the front door. Tom immediately stopped and went out to greet his brother. Claire knew how much Martin idolized Tom. Afraid Tom might be able to make Martin believe the whole incident had been her fault, or she'd overreacted to a little brotherly playfulness, she straightened herself up and never told Martin about Tom's behavior. She did, however, always manage never to be alone with Tom again unless she had something she could use as a weapon in her hand. He took the hint and kept his distance.''

Anger swelled within Abigail. ''Why didn't she come forward when I was arrested? She could have supported my story.''

''She did. At first, she remained silent because she knew how devastated Martin was by his brother's death and she did love her husband. She didn't want to cause him any more grief. And she was sure the police didn't really have a case. But when you were arrested, she went to see your attorney without Martin's knowledge. He put her through the kind of grilling she would be put through on the witness stand. By the time he was finished, he'd made it sound as if she'd been the one to make a play for Tom and that she'd come forward out of spite because he'd rejected her. She told me he convinced her that you were safer to plead guilty to a lesser charge than, with her as your only defense witness, to stand trial for first-degree murder and most likely end up with life imprisonment.''

''I suppose he was right,'' Abigail admitted grudgingly. ''Public sentiment seemed to be running pretty strong against me.''

Kane scowled with contempt at what had happened to her. ''It's not fair but, yes, he was probably right,'' he agreed, then continued, ''so Claire went home and kept quiet. She did, however, make it clear to Martin that she didn't believe in vindictiveness. Because he knew she would disapprove, he made certain she didn't find out about the times he spoke to the parole board and about his getting you fired from various jobs. It wasn't until after he'd been to St. Louis that she discovered the stack of photocopied articles, began suspecting he'd been harassing you and confronted him. When she found out what he'd done, she broke down and told him the truth about his brother.''

Kane extended a letter toward Abigail. ''She sent this.''

Taking it, Abigail opened it to find a guilt-ridden apology from Claire with the promise that Abigail would never be bothered again.

''And so,'' Kane said as she put the letter back into the envelope, ''you are truly a free woman.''

''I am a free woman,'' she repeated, needing to say the words herself. A sense of relief so strong it caused her to want to laugh and cry both at the same time swept through her.

Kane looked suddenly very tired. ''And now I'm going home to get some rest. We'll talk more later.''

Before she could say anything, he'd strode out of the room and down the aisle. Abigail stared at his departing back. He hadn't sounded particularly enthusiastic about talking later and a suspicion began to form in the back of her mind.

As the day progressed her suspicion grew. In spite of the good news he'd brought her, she forced herself to recall that he'd smiled only once and there had been an aloofness about him, as if he was working to keep a distance between them.

It was midafternoon when Rose came into the store. ''Uncle Kane asked me to pack your things and bring them over to you to save you the trouble of collecting them,'' the girl said, setting Abigail's overnight bag on the counter.

Abigail had learned to read Rose well. The girl's smile was too wide and her cheerfulness sounded forced. ''What's wrong?'' she asked bluntly.

Rose's pretence of good humor faded. ''Ever since Uncle Kane came back, he's been edgy. I've been trying to convince myself he's just worried because he has so much work to do. But he's not working. He was but he hit his thumb with a hammer and now he's just pacing around his workroom like a caged animal.''

Tears began to roll down the girl's cheeks. "I think he's decided he doesn't like having me here. I think he feels like I'm a nuisance. I told him I'd be fine on my own when he went on his business trip, but he insisted he couldn't leave without having someone to look after me. I think that made him feel trapped.''

Abigail was furious with Kane. She agreed that he felt trapped but it wasn't by his niece. Giving the teenager a reassuring hug, she said, "I'm certain he's not getting tired of you.''

"What's going on here?" Lottie asked with concern as she hurriedly joined them.

"Just a little misunderstanding," Abigail replied. "Rose, you stay here with Lottie," she ordered, then added over her shoulder as she headed for the door, "I know what Kane's problem is and I'm going to take care of it right now.''

Before Lottie or Rose could question her, she'd left the store. Reaching Kane's front door, she pounded on it.

Answering her summons, he regarded her with polite coolness. "I asked Rose to return your things to you. I guess she forgot.''

"She didn't forget," Abigail replied, brushing past him, then shoving the door closed behind her. "She returned them in tears. She thinks you're tired of her being here and want her to leave.''

"That's not true," he said gruffly.

"I know that," she shot back curtly. "And I told him so." She glared at him. "It's that marriage proposal you made to me that has you so uneasy, isn't it?''

The way his jaw tautened and his lack of response let her know she'd guessed correctly. Deep inside she'd been harboring the hope that even if he didn't want to marry her right now, he might fall in love with her once they'd had time to get to know each other. Now, seeing the guardedness in his eyes, even that hope vanished. Clearly he wasn't interested in getting to know her better.

"Well, you don't have to worry any longer," she continued dryly. "I understand the situation fully. You proposed in a moment of chivalry mingled with some lust. And I suppose a dash of fear at the thought of raising a child on your own added a little more incentive. But now you regret your rash proposal and you're afraid I'm going to take you up on your offer." Pride glistened in her eyes. "Well, I'm not. So you can rest easy."

Abigail was furious with herself for the hurt she was feeling. She told herself she should be glad she'd found out the truth so quickly. At least she wouldn't be embarrassing both him and her by trying to further a relationship he didn't want. Her head held high, she turned to go but as she reached for the doorknob, Kane's hand closed like a vise on her arm.

He jerked her around to face him. "There was nothing noble about my asking you to marry me," he growled. "And I'm not afraid of raising Rose on my own. She's practically grown as it is." The blue of his eyes darkened in frustration. "I wanted you for my wife and I was afraid Martin might actually show up and you would run before I had a chance to court you."

Abigail stared at him in confusion. "You're not making any sense. If what you just said is so, why have you been sulking around this house all day?"

Releasing her, he shoved his hands into the pockets of his jeans, then squared his shoulders and straightened into a defensive stance. "I didn't want to make a fool of myself."

The hope that had vanished reappeared. "Kane Courtland, you're the last man I'd ever suspect of making a fool of himself over a woman."

"Me, too," he admitted. "My sister's leaving caused me to be real cautious of women. I vowed I'd stay at least ten paces from any female who even looked like she might be the leaving kind. And from the first day you arrived, you sure as heck looked like you were. But I still couldn't stop myself from asking you out. When I did and you made it plain you weren't interested, I told myself to walk away and never look back."

A heat showed in his eyes and Abigail felt her body warm under his gaze. "I'd have been smart to have heeded my own advice and I did for nearly two years," he continued huskily. "It wasn't easy, either. I'd never felt so strong an attraction before. I'd see you walking to work with that cute little swing to your hips and I'd want to go over to Lottie's store and strike up a conversation."

He grinned dryly at himself. "Instead I'd settle for a one-sided conversation with myself about you. I'd tell myself you were bound to bring me nothing but trouble. I figured you were running or hiding from something or someone. And I figured that any day you'd get bored here and pack up and leave. The way you kept everyone at a distance, even Lottie and the people you helped like Mable, made me certain you weren't a woman looking for ties that bind."

Abigail couldn't fault his reasoning. She had behaved exactly as he'd described.

Kane frowned derisively. "I still kept an eye on you, though. I told myself I was merely looking out for Lottie to make sure she didn't get caught in the middle of whatever you might be running from. But the truth was you were the one I was thinking about protecting if some brutish husband or ex-boyfriend turned up."

Abigail studied the taut line of his jaw guardedly. She wanted to believe every word he said but she was afraid. She'd suffered too many disappointments in her life. "I knew you were watching me," she confessed. "I'd get this prickling sensation on the side or back of my neck and glance toward your place and see you on the porch or at your workshop window. I thought you disapproved of Lottie hiring me and were keeping an eye on me to make certain I didn't rob her."

Stiffly Kane cupped her face in his hands. "I was the one I was worried about. The night you brought Rose here, I couldn't stay away from you any longer. I'd seen the Christmas tree on top of your car and told myself that the only gentlemanly thing to do would be to offer to help you get it up to your apartment. Besides, I figured I owed you a debt of gratitude for bringing Rose to me. I promised myself that I'd simply help with the tree, thank you for rescuing my niece and leave. Then Rose showed up and Lottie showed up and I found myself trapped into staying."

Tenderly he stroked her cheek and rivers of fire spread through her. "I was sure I could still walk away from you," he continued gruffly. "And I was doing real well at keeping my feelings under control until I saw that wistful look in your eyes when you were holding that crystal ornament. Even after that, I continued to work at convincing myself you weren't the woman for me. But every time I had myself believing that you'd do something or say something and I'd want to take you in my arms."

His touch was igniting a blaze within her and he was saying all the right things. Still her fear lingered. "If what you're telling me is the truth, why have you been avoiding me?" she demanded in frustration.

He frowned at her obtuseness. "Because, like you said this morning, you're a free woman now. You can live where you please without the worry of Martin hunting you down and trying to destroy the life you've built for yourself."

Releasing her, he stepped back. An expression of self-mockery played across his features. "I know you don't want to marry me. I saw the shock on your face when I asked you to and you were real quick coming up with Martin as an excuse for refusing me. I'm not totally thickheaded. It's pretty obvious you don't feel any strong emotional ties to me. As for your claim that you like the solitude here, I don't really believe you honestly want to get stuck in this wilderness for the rest of your life. It's my bet you simply convinced yourself you were happy here because you thought it was a good hiding place. Now that you don't need to hide any longer, I figure you might stay just long enough for the holidays but come January second, you'll want to be packed and gone. But I knew if I didn't stay away from you, I'd try to change your mind and that would only embarrass both of us."

He kissed her lightly. "Have a good life, Abigail Jones," he said, then turning away from her, he started down the hall.

The warmth of his mouth lingered on hers as he walked away. She'd seen the pain in his eyes and knew he'd been telling her the truth. "So far, you've done all the talking. Now I have a couple of things I'd like to say," she called out to his departing back.

As he came to a stop, she continued tersely, "The first is that I could have hidden out in a crowded city as easily as I've hidden out here. But I do like it here and have no plans to leave. The second is that I was under the impression it was up to me, not you, to decide whether or not I would marry you, Kane Courtland."

He'd turned to face her. But he didn't approach her. Instead he stood studying her as if afraid she might not say what he wanted to hear.

"Yes, I was shocked when you proposed," she admitted. "But I refused you for the reasons I stated not because of how I feel about you or about living here in Blye's Stand."

"And just how do you feel about me?" he demanded, suddenly striding toward her.

A jumble of words filled her mind. "You're a good, honest, hardworking man," she began, wanting to tell him fully how much he meant to her.

Impatience caused the blue of his eyes to darken warningly. "That's not what I want to hear," he growled as he reached her.

Unable to resist the impulse that had plagued her for days, she lifted her hand and, with her fingers, combed back the wayward lock of hair that had again fallen on his forehead. "However," she continued, allowing the anguish she'd suffered this day to show, "you can be extremely frustrating at times especially when you start making predictions about my plans without consulting me." Her expression softened. "But I've fallen in love with you so I guess I'll have to overlook that."

Relief showed on his face and he drew her into his embrace. "I ruined a belt and a boot today forcing myself to stay away from you," he said gruffly. "And I swear I've worn a groove in my workroom floor pacing it."

Nothing could feel so secure or so exciting as his body pressed against hers, Abigail thought. Except maybe his lips on hers, she amended. "Am I going to have to go stand under the mistletoe before you kiss me, Kane Courtland?" she demanded impatiently.

A heat that warmed her all the way to her toes showed in his eyes, then his mouth found hers.

Abigail awoke Christmas morning and smiled softly as she snuggled more firmly into the crook of the muscular arm wrapped around her. She lifted her left hand just enough to see the gold band around her third finger.

"Merry Christmas," a husky male voice murmured in her ear.

Turning to the speaker, her smile broadened as she looked up into Kane's face. "A very Merry Christmas to you, too."

He grinned. "This certainly has been one of the most surprising. I went from being a bachelor to an uncle with an orphaned niece to a married man."

"I hope that's not a complaint," she teased.

"Never. I love having Rose here. But I have to admit you're the nicest Christmas present I've ever received," he said, kissing her on the tip of her nose. Suddenly a mischievousness sparked in his eyes. "Of course, there was that sled I got when I was five."

She ran her hand playfully over his hair-roughened chest as her mouth formed a mock pout. "I'd hate to think I was less fun than that sled."

Laughing, he pulled her more securely against him. "Nothing could be more fun than you," he assured her. Abruptly a seriousness descended over his features. His gaze bore into her. "But if you ever start getting bored here, I'd like some advance warning."

"I doubt very much I'll get bored," she replied, then smiled softly. "However, if I did, I'm sure you could quickly remedy the situation."

"I'd definitely try," he assured her.

Trailing kisses over his neck and shoulders, she said against his skin, "Rose and I agreed that we'd wait until seven before everyone bounded out of bed to attack the presents under the tree. That gives you an hour to give me some idea of what persuasive measures you might use."

"That," he replied, his hand moving caressingly over her back, "would be my pleasure."

A sense of well-being and joy spread through Abigail as his mouth sought hers. And a Merry Christmas to all, she wished silently. Then the rest of the world was forgotten as his touch ignited desire.

* * * * *

A Recipe from Elizabeth August

This is a delicious Christmas treat while you're drinking coffee and watching the kids open gifts. Enjoy it!

QUICK-AND-EASY COFFEE CAKE

Cake
1½ cups all-purpose flour
¼ tsp salt
2 tsp double-acting baking powder
⅓ cup sugar
¼ cup butter
1 egg
⅔ cup milk

Preheat oven to 375° F. Grease 9"x 9" pan or a 9" cake pan.

Sift together flour, salt, baking powder, then set aside.

Cream together sugar and butter until light, then beat in egg and milk.

Add sifted ingredients to butter mixture. Beat until batter is smooth. Place in greased pan.

Topping
2 tbsp all-purpose flour
2 tbsp butter
5 tbsp sugar
½ tsp cinnamon
2-3 tbsp melted butter

Combine the flour, the 2 tbsp of butter and the sugar, and blend these ingredients until they crumble. Add cinnamon.

Spread the cake batter with 2-3 tbsp of melted butter.

Sprinkle topping over the cake and bake for approximately 25 minutes.

The authors of Jingle Bells, Wedding Bells *cordially invite you to join them for more great love stories....*

Throughout 1995, look for four exciting books by these bestselling authors...

NORA ROBERTS
THE RETURN OF RAFE MACKADE (*Heartbreakers*)
Silhouette Intimate Moments in April
One of the infamous *MacKade Brothers.*

After ten long years, reckless Rafe MacKade was back—and lovely Regan Bishop's life would never be the same!

BARBARA BOSWELL
THE ENGAGEMENT PARTY
Silhouette Desire in June
Book #1 in Silhouette's cross-line continuity series,
Always A Bridesmaid.

When Hanna Farley attended her friends' engagement party, she had no idea she would be the next one with a ring on her finger.

The authors of
Jingle Bells, Wedding Bells
cordially invite you to join them
for more great love stories...

ELIZABETH AUGUST
IDEAL DAD (*Fabulous Fathers*)
Silhouette Romance in January

Though Murdock Purnell was the perfect dad for her son, Irene Galvin wasn't so sure this sexy loner was the ideal husband for her.

They're all coming your way, only from ❤️ *Silhouette*®
TM

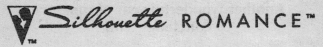

Silhouette ROMANCE™

'Tis the season for romantic bliss.
It all begins with just one kiss—

UNDER THE MISTLETOE

Celebrate the joy of the season and the thrill of romance with this special collection:

Available in December, from Silhouette Romance.

SRXMAS

MONTANA
Mavericks

Stories that capture living and loving
beneath the Big Sky, where legends live
on...and mystery lingers.

This December, explore more MONTANA MAVERICKS with

THE RANCHER TAKES A WIFE
by Jackie Merritt

He'd made up his mind. He'd loved her almost a lifetime
and now he was going to have her, come hell or high
water.

And don't miss a minute of the loving as the passion con-
tinues with:

OUTLAW LOVERS
by Pat Warren (January)

WAY OF THE WOLF
by Rebecca Daniels (February)

THE LAW IS NO LADY
by Helen R. Myers (March)
and many more!

Only from ▼ *Silhouette*® where passion lives.

The Loop™

Is the future what it's cracked up to be?

This November, discover the bright lights of the big city with Becky in

GETTING PERSONAL: BECKY
by Janet Quin-Harkin

A small-town girl, she came to the big city seeking fame and fortune…and ended up taking personal ads over the phone for the local "alternative" paper. Life seemed pretty boring until she started following a cute mystery man named Michael. What made a guy like him desperate enough to take out a personal ad? Bursting with curiosity, she waited and watched—until *he* caught *her*.

The ups and downs of life as you know it continue with

GETTING ATTACHED: CJ
by Wendy Corsi Staub (December)

GETTING A LIFE: MARISSA
by Kathryn Jensen (January)

Get smart. Get into "The Loop"!

This November, share the passion with *New York Times* Bestselling Author

(previously published under the pseudonym Erin St. Claire)

in

THE DEVIL'S OWN

Kerry Bishop was a good samaritan with a wild plan. Linc O'Neal was a photojournalist with a big heart.

Their scheme to save nine orphans from a hazardos land was foolhardy at best—deadly at the worst.

But together they would battle the odds—and the burning hungers—that made the steamy days and sultry nights doubly dangerous.

Reach for the brightest star in women's fiction with

MIRA™

MSBDO-R